BEQUEST

BEQUEST

A.K. SHEVCHENKO

headline

First published in 2010 by HEADLINE PUBLISHING GROUP

2

Cataloguing in Publication Data is available from the British Library

ISBN 978 07553 5635 5 (Hardback)
ISBN 978 07553 5636 2 (Trade paperback)

Typeset in Garamond by Ellipsis Books Limited, Glasgow

Printed and bound in Great Britain by Clays Ltd, St Ives plc

Headline's policy is to use papers that are natural, renewable
and recyclable products and made from wood grown in sustainable forests.
The logging and manufacturing processes are expected to conform to
the environmental regulations of the country of origin.

HEADLINE PUBLISHING GROUP
An Hachette UK Company
338 Euston Road
London NW1 3BH

www.headline.co.uk
www.hachette.co.uk

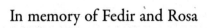

In memory of Fedir and Rosa

PROLOGUE

Cambridge, 1 April 2001

'It is the lighting,' she reassures herself. 'This eerie lighting is the reason.' The tiles below the fluorescent tube glisten. The artificial blue sheen fills the room and turns his face pale and washed clear of freckles. She is standing over the trolley, unsure what to do with her hands.

She has a sudden urge to adjust the sheet, to iron out two inconspicuous creases under his shoulder. Her fingers touch the trolley and she quickly pulls them away, feeling the cold of the steel creeping through her fingertips, up her arm, to her shoulders, seeping into her chest. It is freezing here. Well, she thinks, why shouldn't it be? That is the nature of the place.

They have left the door half-open, and she can see a man in a long, oilskin apron hosing down another steel trolley. The water is pink and frothy, a mixture of blood and detergent. He works with determined meticulousness, washing away the remains of another life. He directs the tight jet into the corner and she remembers she has heard this sound before. Rain hitting the tin roof – last week, when they were hiding.

There is another sound, closer to her. Click-clack. Black shoes with navy shoelaces. The sound is restless, impatient. It seems to have a slight stammer, like the echoing second hand of their office clock, like the owner of the black shoes, when he pronounces her name again: 'K-K-Kate . . .' She tries to remember why she is here, glances at him for a prompt. He looks like a college tutor – dishevelled, quietly intelligent – but then, most policemen probably do here, in this university city.

Kate had a laugh with him this morning on the phone, when he wrestled with her unusual last name, all clusters of consonants, with some robust vowels thrown in for good measure: 'If it's a name you can't pronounce, that will be me,' she told him. It is nice to share a bit of humour with a stranger first thing on a Monday morning.

But this was in the previous life, before he broke The News.

She confirmed the time and address, left the office, took a train then a taxi. She has read about this protection mechanism: in a state of shock, people often continue to move, talk, act for a while as if nothing has happened. The brain shuts the feelings down. Bangs a heavy lid on top of them and waits.

It seems strange that they have asked Kate to do it. She is neither a relative nor a friend, and she does not represent the Embassy. Just a sort of Anybody, who might identify His body.

In the chill room, she suddenly realises that she has taken too much time for a mere acquaintance, and she nods hastily. 'Yes, it's him.' The Detective Inspector gives her a puzzled look. Her words have not come out. She tries to push her voice to the surface again. 'Yes, this is him.' She pronounces his rolling, unEnglish name and runs out of breath.

'Thank you, Miss L-L-L . . .' He struggles with her name again. 'Th-th-thank you, Kate.'

They walk out, and upstairs into the grey afternoon corridor, and she stumbles over the medical waste-bin with its bright daffodil-coloured bag. Why did they choose yellow? Such an incongruous colour for this place! She is irritated and glad at the same time. Glad to be out of the bleak icy room, out of the basement, glad to experience her first emotion.

The DI runs his fingers through his hair, making it even more unkempt. He bombards her with questions, repeats them again and again until she answers.

'How well did you know the deceased?'

Better than myself, she thinks, and answers aloud: 'Not well at all.'

'He put you as his next-of-kin in this country – can you explain why?'

She shrugs her shoulders, trying to look natural. 'No idea. Maybe because I am a lawyer – somebody who could settle his affairs in case—'

'In c-c-c-case of what?' His stammering is more prominent now, when he rushes to interrupt.

'Just in case.' She cannot concentrate on the answers any more.

'Are you in possession of any items that belonged to the deceased?'

Kate shakes her head. A little too vigorously, perhaps.

'When did you last s-see the deceased?'

Why is he saying 'the deceased' all the time, avoiding the name? Is it some technique they use, to try to take you out of the situation, so that you answer the questions calmly before you are overcome with grief?

The policeman almost pushes her to the exit, signs the book and lets her out. But she knows that he is locking her away when he says, 'W-we will contact you soon. P-p-please do not leave the country.' Despite the stammer, his 'please' is the firmest one she has ever heard.

The outside world surrounds her with colours and textures, but she is not a participant any more.

A spectator of the 3-D blockbuster called 'Ordinary Life'.

An ambulance whizzes past her and screeches to the Accident and Emergency entrance on the left. Kate remembers that this is a hospital after all, a place designed to save the living.

A red-haired boy is talking to a Japanese girl in a shiny nylon jacket by the door of the research laboratory. His hands speak for him. He clenches his fists, brings them to his chest, then thrusts the palms open, like a magician in training. His spell seems to work because the girl smiles and nods, smiles and nods, like an oversized porcelain doll.

Next to them a girl too young to be a doctor tries to park her bright Mini under the sign 'Authorised University staff only'. The car objects with noisy bursts. Rust has stained its white stripes, but is still invisible on the green bonnet.

Kate drifts past the magician, the doll and the Mini, and suddenly doubles up. The punch in the stomach is so violent that she has to crouch right here, behind a police car. A hot wave rises to her throat, burning through her body.

God, she is not ready. For his death, for this agony. And for this new, unknown feeling of danger.

'If you f-f-find you have any items that belonged to the deceased . . .' the policeman had said to her.

Yes, he left her three items. No, he left her to deal with those three items, all on her own. Something from his dream. Something

4

that will save his nation. She is in this world without him, but with his secret.

'Are you OK?' The DI is standing over her. He looks concerned. Even his stammer seems to have disappeared. 'Let me give you a lift to the station, it is only four minutes' drive.'

'I'll walk,' she manages, but he is already opening the car door for her.

In the car the policeman's questions are still echoing in her ears, breaking through the white noise of pain:

'Where were you yesterday between seven and eleven p.m.?'

She turns to him. 'You said it was an accident. You don't suspect me, do you?'

The DI winces and looks away, as if he can see something invisible to Kate through the car window. 'With the toxicology report inconclusive . . . It could be suicide, of course.' He stops. He is obviously annoyed with himself; he has said too much. They continue their journey in silence. 'D-d-do give us a c-call if you remember anything,' he says, instead of 'Goodbye'.

She needs to move to survive. On the platform she negotiates every step, carefully placing her feet on the soiled tarmac. She wanders in the direction of Nowhere. Her steps are getting heavier, her heart is beating faster. Faster, heavier. Heavier, faster, in a particular rhythm: 'a-train-of-pain-is-carr-y-ing-me-a-way . . .'

When is the next train to King's Cross? She needs to get into the carriage, to escape from here, from the fluorescent room, from the man in that room who is . . . who *was* the love of her life. She can see him very clearly on the platform now: he is walking away from her, sweeping his fringe off his high forehead with his long, aristocratic fingers. She calls out for him, but when he turns, his face is one blurred blob, as if he is an undercover witness in a police video.

'Why can't I see your face?' She panics. 'What else is there I cannot see?' She recalls the policeman's embarrassed mumbling: 'With the toxicology report inconclusive . . .'

'Were you taking drugs? What else I did not know about you? Different name? Another love? Another life?'

The train is approaching the platform: 'Do-it-for-him, do-it-with-him, do-it, do-it . . .' Suddenly it hits her. She knows what to do with his secrets, where to find out the truth. It means an urgent flight abroad, some cancellations and lies . . .

'Listen,' she even uses his favourite phrase to convince him, 'I have no choice, it is a zero option for me. I have to go. To find the rest of your soul. Even if it destroys me.'

PART I

The Search

'It's a poor sort of memory that only works backwards.'
White Queen, *Through the Looking Glass*
Lewis Carroll (1832–1898)

Chapter 1

TARAS

Moscow, February 2001

'It is the lighting,' he reassures himself. 'This eerie lighting is the reason.' The tiles below the fluorescent tube glisten. The artificial blue sheen fills the room and turns his face in the mirror pale and washed clear of freckles. Taras is standing over the sink, unsure what to do with his hands.

The room is criss-crossed with the shadows of the giant neon remains of . . . *lfa Bank* on the roof of the building across the road.

There is no one else in the washroom, so Taras has plenty of time to examine his reflection while scrubbing and rubbing his hands: cadaverous skin tone, black tinge on the lower lip. The top lip is hidden under the thin strip of wheat-coloured growth. Does he really, as his landlady told him, look older with a moustache? And what did she mean by 'older'? Mature and distinguished – or drawn and haggard?

Taras scrutinises his face for the evidence of today's discovery – a spark, a hidden smile? – but all he sees is this pale mask with lacklustre eyes. He cannot be *that* tired, surely? 'It's definitely the lighting,' he decides. Now, the hands. 'It is only the fifth wash

9

today – quite an improvement from yesterday,' he registers impartially, like a coach talking to a not very accomplished pupil.

He stretches out his palms and looks at them indecisively. 'What now? Dry them with a paper towel, or walk along the corridor, flapping like an excited cockerel?'

'Dignity, Lieutenant Petrenko,' frowns the coach.

Taras goes out of the washroom, pushing the door open with his shoulder, and heads for the cosy glow of the security guard's booth at the end of the corridor. It is so inappropriate here. A plywood casket at the entrance to the edifice where every column is a monument to Power. The guard looks incongruous, too. The stern, stone-faced sergeant is gone for good. Inside the booth a retired Colonel is sipping herbal tea from a chipped cup with a red flower pattern and a gilded rim. A mellow scent of dry strawberry leaves, a familiar childhood smell, fills the booth.

The guard looks up from his copy of *Izvestia*.

'Working late, Lieutenant Petrenko? Not celebrating Army Day?' He does not show his surprise. Old training. Or just none of his business. His time of X-raying other people's minds is over – he is simply topping up his pension.

What is he going to buy with the extra cash? wonders Taras, signing himself off. An American spray to relieve his angina? A Barbie doll for his granddaughter?

It must be hard for a former KGB Colonel to cope with this new availability of everything and anything. Soviet shortages and empty shelves were his advantage, his key to power: 'We have it, they don't. We have the access, the channels, the influence, they don't.' Now 'they' and 'we' is about numbers. Freedom and choice, as long as you have the money to buy.

Taras needs to talk, to offload his emotions. He is about to return to an empty flat, and his own mirror reflection is not the most exciting conversationalist.

'It looks like you cannot celebrate either,' he starts. 'After all, the Army Day is your day, too.'

'Not any more.' The colonel shrugs his shoulders, looking at Taras above the rim of his glasses. 'Besides, even though they renamed it "The Day of the Defender of the Motherland" almost a decade ago, I still cannot get used to it.'

'This scent – is it raspberry tea you are drinking?' Taras decides to change the subject.

'Oh no.' The Colonel lights up.' 'It is made from wild strawberry leaves. I have plenty of those at my *dacha*. "No waste production" we are talking here, Lieutenant Petrenko. Everything is used: my granddaughter picks the berries, Valentina Nikolayevna, my other half, collects and dries the leaves. This tea has a magic formula, I tell you. You know, I have been drinking it ever since we planted wild strawberries, and I have discovered that it cures more ailments than they describe in the reference books. The secret is to collect the leaves at the end of May, when they are still full of freshness and young juices . . .' And before Taras knows it, he is stuck, nodding from time to time, reduced again to a listener's role.

'And, of course, one should not forget the beneficial properties of the drink for a certain male problem . . .' The Colonel pauses.

He is not that old, actually, thinks Taras. Retirement in their organisation does not mean old age. He uses the pause to halt the Colonel's flow. 'Fascinating – but I'd better go. The metro closes soon.' His steps echo in the vast lobby, as if there, in the darkness high above, a giant is following his every move.

The brass handle warns Taras about the temperature outside. Opening the door, he breathes in the Moscow winter night, then briskly crosses the deserted Square, not checking for cars – it is too late and cold for the rush hour, anyway. A blizzard is dancing around him. Three more minutes of squinting against the wind, of icy numbness on the tip of his nose, and he dives into the wave of warm air. He loves the Moscow metro. The grey marble dignity of Mayakovskaya station; the patriotic red granite of Paveletskaya; the nostalgic uplifting frescoes of happy Ukrainian farmers at Kievskaya . . . Every time he puts a coin into a slot, steps on the escalator, gets on a train, he feels that somebody is taking control of his life. Dictating his direction. Carrying him, caring for him. Only here, during these journeys, does he admit to himself that everything in his life now is *ersatz* – a cheap replacement. Like the chicory brown liquid, sold as decaffeinated coffee in their canteen. No kick, not much taste, same disappointment. And to think that he is two years older than Jesus was when He died!

Taras works for the FSB – the Federal Security Service – but is stuck in the archives, instead of the Counter-Intelligence Unit he dreamed of.

Focused, determined, good strategist was written in his Academy graduation appraisal. But there was one more thing written there – one word that crossed out every single one of his dreams. Nationality – *Ukrainian.*

Who would have thought that by the time he graduated from the Moscow FSB Academy on Michurinsky Prospect, Ukraine would have become an enemy?

Much to the envy of his university friends, he lives in the capital but spends most of his meagre salary on the rent of a dingy studio in Chertanovo, a dormitory suburb of identical tower blocks on the edge of Moscow, near the Ring Road.

True, he looks much younger than his age – his biceps are still making his shirt-sleeves tight, and pretty girls throw quick glances at him in the streets – but where would he bring a girlfriend, if he had one? Back to a sofa-bed with broken springs?

A proper girlfriend, of course. Lusya, a salesgirl from a vegetable stand around the corner, does not count. They started chatting over a pineapple, moved to a discussion about overpriced tangerines, and then to other, forbidden fruit.

Four years of occasional quick thrusts, fuelled by cheap plonk. She often questioned him, drunkenly, about his plans for the future, about making a home together. He sighs occasionally, remembering her nipples, the playfulness in her eyes every time she handed him a bag of apples, pretending he was just another shopper . . .

It is quite a relief though, not to spend another evening guessing whether, depending on the vegetable-stand deliveries schedule, Lusya's hands would smell of bananas or rotten cabbage as she puts her arms around him.

Since she left, Taras is reduced to watching the *plechevyje* 'shoulder girls' on his way to the tower block from the tube station. These teenagers are always hanging around by the Ring Road, pulling their synthetic jackets over their miniskirts, waiting for a truck to stop. They are driven from city to city in the illusory safety of a Kamaz truck in return for a fast service, throwing their skinny legs across the trucker's shoulders somewhere on the dark side of a road. He pulled one last year. Well, almost. Even that exercise was doomed.

One of the girls had looked at him from under her fringe when he was passing her. She had the moist, hazel eyes of a sick puppy. He never spoke to her – there was merely a mouthed, 'Come on,' with a nod. And yet she smiled (was it timidly or triumphantly – he could not tell in the dusk of an early winter evening) and trotted after him along the narrow path beaten in the snow, shoulders up, eyes following his every move, sniffing loudly. Suddenly it occurred to him that she must be under age, whatever she pretended, and that if he took her back to his flat, she might remember where he lived, might even come back again, try to blackmail him.

'Great career move, Taras,' he congratulated himself. 'Come on, go for it – why not lose your future for a fleeting urge!' So he turned and simply waved her away. She stopped, keeping his gaze, unsure what to do, shifting from one foot to the other. He waved her off again. Only now did she understand, and burst into a husky torrent of swearwords, kicking at the snow with the toe of her scuffed boot. Taras watched her shuffling back to the Ring Road. They were quite similar in a way, he and she: the same anxious yearning for another life, the same provincial aloneness in a big city.

There was one major difference, however: she had given up early on, whereas he had chosen to engage in battle, all thanks to his Academy training.

Know Your Enemy was a five-lecture course at the Academy, which he still finds pretty effective.

Step one. Identify your enemy first. Understand the objective and the weaponry, work out the tactics.

Step one was easy. The enemy: Megametropolis. Objective: dispassionate devouring of provincial victims. Weaponry: isolation, provision of a hated job, past memories. Tactics: slow suffocation of dreams and ambitions.

Step two. To fight the enemy, you have to focus on the tasks, not on your anger or resentment. Self-discipline is the key.

He wages war with this city, moving from day to day, from task to task, supported by a cushion of steam as he takes another breath in an open swimming pool on frosty Sunday mornings, and comforted by subtitled American films, taken from a local video rental two evenings a week.

Most of the time, Taras manages quite well . . . except for the memories. Memories are the worst. They are much harder to fight. They are invisible, can ambush him when he least expects it: strike with a melody, float in on a scent, brush past him in a crowd.

But Taras has found a way to resist them. Three evenings a week, after a forty-minute crammed bus journey, he enters the club, puts on his boxing gloves and concentrates on his left hook, his right uppercut. All he needs to think about then is where the next blow is coming from.

Living in this city for him is his preparation for action. He has developed a habit of observing its life, analysing its moves and mistakes, its victims. He can do a quick exercise now, actually. The metro train is gaining speed. Eyes half-closed, Taras scans the passengers – a habit acquired in the Academy. A couple in the corner – he is whispering something into her ear, leaning over a little too much. Overweight, balding, obnoxious. The girl's frostbitten hands are nervously crumpling the white mohair hat on her lap. She is laughing, throwing her head back slightly. It is obvious where she will end up tonight.

The carriage jolts, and the boy opposite, in a black leather jacket too thin for a February night, slides off his seat. He pulls himself back with one jerky movement. His glazed eyes stare intently through Taras, into the black hole of a tunnel. He rocks forward in a syncopated rhythm. Not an addict yet, just a beginner, decides Taras.

Next to him, a man in a deerskin hat buries his head in a

newspaper. His hat and sheepskin coat are expensive, but old-fashioned. He leans his elbow on a patent black briefcase with battered corners. A chief engineer or even a director of a plant – something military, guesses Taras. Used to have a black Volga with a personal driver. Now the orders have dwindled away and he is travelling by metro, hiding his face, embarrassed. The newspaper he pretends to read is *Argumenty i fakty*.

Arguments and Facts. That is Taras's job now. To study the facts and to provide the arguments.

Seven years ago, when the FSB announced its new 'policy of transparency', the internal memos suggested that, as a preventive measure, it would be only reasonable to do some 'careful screening' of the files that were open for public access. What if a nosy journalist, not realising the consequences, tried to fish out some facts for an instant of scandalous glory? Somebody remembered that Lieutenant Petrenko, who joined the Service from the Academy in June, had a History degree, and Taras was sent to the archives to sift through the files of NKVD, the sinister predecessor of the KGB. Witness to the time of Stalin's paranoia and the sinister Troika Trials, of a country's elation and a nation's terror.

He hadn't learned about the tragedy of Stalin's rule until university. Nothing was ever mentioned during his school history lessons, but then he had not had much chance to learn anything there at all. The school in his remote mountain village had been just one big room in a shabby thatched *hata*, an old Ukrainian house, where a dozen children of all ages were taught a little of everything by one pensioner teacher, who relied more on his failing memory than on the ragged textbooks.

The first day of school in September always welcomed pupils with the fresh, nauseating smell of the cheap black paint used to cover the graffiti on the desktops. The whitewashed walls of the village school were bare, decorated only with a portrait of Lenin over the blackboard and two faded botanical posters that hid the peeling plaster on the wall opposite the window. Taras hated school. He examined every detail of the botanical posters, counted the rusty drawing pins that secured the oilcloth over the windowsills, and waited for the bell to declare his freedom, his chance to rush through the sleepy village street. Past the vast puddle that never dried out; past the dilapidated single-storey building of the farmers' cooperative union, flying a faded flag; past the permanently padlocked village shop; past the black and tan hens, romping in the dust with snotty toddlers. And then on the path that led to the damp, mushroomy freshness of the woods, to the lopsided thatched hut, to his secret place at the end of the vegetable patch, behind the rows of corn and sunflowers. There he would lie on his back and watch the limitless sky above, dream of the time when he became a hero, when he would travel far away from here, just following those clouds, following his dreams, and . . .

This free spirit is still there, deep inside him. During his archive hours he often raises tired eyes from the spidery writing of the files, from the hastily typed verdicts, looks at the detested green wall, smells familiar cheap paint, and feels convicted, like the people whose destinies are piled in front of him. There is a doomed infinity in these files. Instead of diminishing, they are breeding, multiplying, cloning the same phrases: *10 years without the right of correspondence . . . Sentenced to be shot . . . 15 years of corrective labour in a colony of strict regime . . . Children of the enemies of the people to be sent to an orphanage . . .*

And he can hear them, too. Not always, not every day. But when he is overworked, when the Archive corridors are quiet, there is a distant echo. Whimpering pleas for mercy, muffled confessions, faltering betrayals. He is drained by all these emotions, as if he is caring for the terminally ill. Except that with the terminally ill there is, eventually, an end.

The file that he pulled off the shelf this morning, case N1247, looked identical to the others – thick, yellow-paged, with a tidy frayed cotton ribbon bow. The title, written in the top left corner, promised the thrill of adventure – exactly the story the journalists would be hungry for. It had not excited Taras, though. All these files start off as whodunits but in fact, most of them turn out to contain nothing but chilling interrogation reports of innocent people, often arrested as the result of a letter from some anonymous 'well-wisher'.

Case N1247 seemed no exception. The first two documents, with the smudged two-headed-eagle stamp of the Russian Secret Police, were stitched to the piece of thick cardboard with white waxed thread. He checked the dates: *March 1749 . . . July 1749 . . .* The words, strung together like oddly shaped beads, with knots of letters, are long gone from the language. Taras quickly scanned the contents. The file contained reports spanning across three centuries, all connected by the same family name. Two hundred and fifty years of supervision, he thought. It must have been really something, this case, worth all the legwork and the paperwork!

Then followed the usual reports, exposing the members of the same family as enemies of the people and English spies, all sentenced to hard labour camps for their betrayal of the motherland.

December 1923: Arrest of the 'People's traitor', the Ukrainian Ambassador to Vienna.

November 1937: Report on the arrest and interrogation of Anatoly Polubotko, a Professor of Applied Mathematics from Kiev University.

The last report in the file was dated March 1962. Taras reached for a *Classified* stamp, as for other cases still not closed – then stopped, his hand mid-air. He looked at the signature under the report – one too familiar to miss. Was it . . . Could it really be . . . He made a quick calculation. Yes, it could. His boss would have been around twenty-four then, so it was probably one of his first cases.

Taras opened the file again. He noticed that the waxed thread keeping the documents together was slack. Had some pages been pulled out? He turned to the last page of the cover, to the list of people who had worked on the file before him, with titles, dates, times. Archivists tend to be precise, especially the NKVD archivists. There were seventeen names on the register – surprisingly few, considering the case had not been closed and all this was still going on. Next, Taras scrupulously checked each document in the file against the List of Contents on the inside front cover. It took him two hours to find that three documents were not in the file. He looked at the brief description of the documents at the back of the file.

Three key, mind-blowing, history-changing documents were missing.

As new evidence was diligently added to the file, nobody noticed the disappearance of some of the earlier documents; nobody checked the whole file. Until now. If somebody had stolen these documents for later use . . . He made a quick calculation. The time for 'later use' started ten years ago.

Taras read the name of the archivist against the date 17 November 1942, then leaned back in his chair, balancing it with his feet against the wall. He crossed his hands behind his head, shut his eyes and with his broadest grin welcomed Lady Luck, bringing his big break. In his mind he was building a staircase, leading up to his new career, to the exciting assignments, to his escape from this place.

It is the chance of a lifetime, and he will not lose it. Not now. Not with this signature under the report of March 1962. Not with this name against the date 17 November 1942. He knows where to find the missing pieces of the jigsaw. Or at least where to start looking.

His 'archive mole' status now has a totally new meaning: he has been digging away quietly, waiting for his time to come. If these seven missing pages were found and thrown on the scales of today's politics, they would be weightier by far than the arguments of parliamentarians and the spreadsheets of the economists. They would tip the political balance in Europe, change history – and he, Taras, would be a key player.

Taras swaps the warmth of the metro for the wintry street, where the dry snow squeaks under his feet during the brisk, ten-minute walk to the stinking darkness of his apartment block. The rubbish shaft is overflowing. Somebody has pinched the bulb from the porch again. He takes the lift to the seventh floor, wondering how they manage to scratch the graffiti so deeply into the plastic. Reaching his flat at last, he opens the door and marches straight into the bathroom. He doesn't even notice this hand-wash – too late for self-control.

He follows his nightly routine: kettle on, butter and cheese out of the fridge, bread out of a plastic bag. Then he sits at the kitchen table, tightly squeezed between the wall and a windowsill, rests his chin in his wet palms and looks out of the window, waiting for the water to boil. The screams from the flat below become louder, there is the sound of broken glass, doors slamming, a child trying to say something – no, to cry something out. 'They forgot to feed Vasya again, those drunkards, and he is asking for food,' guesses Taras.

What an Army Day celebration he has had – having a cup of tea in a tiny kitchen, listening to his neighbours' fighting. Perhaps he should have joined his mates from the Academy – today is their annual gathering. But they will be talking about children and recent trips abroad, about promotions – this is the professional jargon he does not yet understand.

Soon, maybe in six months even, he'll be coming back from special assignments, working on some challenging tasks. Maybe, to a loyal girlfriend? She will be kind, patient, and quietly, unobtrusively pretty. A doctor? No, then she will be on shifts or out, visiting the sick. He needs her at home, waiting for him.

A journalist? Dangerous, since she will talk. A teacher would be ideal. They will live in this flat for a while, until he can afford something bigger and better, and she will nod understandingly when he says to her, 'I am off again. Don't know when I'll be back – maybe tonight, maybe next week.'

And when he returns home, looking up from the path at the third window on the seventh floor, she'll be there, at the kitchen table, marking essays. And all those people from the apartment block opposite will watch her and think, Her man is away but she is there, waiting for him – what a lucky fellow!

A cheap Indian tea bag, two white sugar cubes in – another routine. Taras takes a sip of his tea, looking out of the window. Nobody bothers to pull the curtains, even though the buildings are too close for comfort. The house lives its daily soap opera, preparing for the night. Taras knows the participants and their roles only too well. Fourth floor, three windows to the left – a man in a vest and tracksuit trousers is lying on the sofa, waving two schoolgirls away from a TV screen. It is too late for them to be up, but their father is never interested. The mother is a shuttle trader, probably, like many other mothers in Moscow now: travelling to Turkey, bringing heavy holdalls full of clothes to one of the markets, shuttling back. Providing for the family, hardly ever seeing the kids.

Sixth floor, the window opposite: she never draws the curtains when she sits in her bra, facing the mirror at the windowsill. An aging, lonely woman, taking her make-up off with well-practised, mechanical, circular movements.

Fifth floor, two windows to the right – they are fighting again. Or rather, he is beating her up again. Taras cannot see the look on her face, but he imagines a look of subservience, twisted in pain as the heavy fist reaches her jaw. Why can't she leave him? There are no children, as far as Taras can see, and judging by the bare walls and the man's swollen red face most of the money is spent on vodka. She is caught on the treadmill of so many Russian women, oiled by the popular wisdom: 'If he beats me he loves me', 'Better a bad husband than none at all'. Doesn't she realise that she has a choice?

Taras thinks of today's file. Arguments and facts. He knows the facts, now he has to provide the arguments. His choice is harder than that of the woman opposite. He considers his options – actually, there are not that many.

He can tell. He can sell. Or he can keep this to himself.

The first two options would change the lives of millions. The third is just between him and his conscience. He decides to follow the advice of Colonel Surikov, his tutor at the Academy: 'If you cannot see the whole picture of the operation, start small and worry in chronological order.'

So, he will start with one line from the file N1247, with that name of an archivist against the date 17 November 1942. It means a visit back to his youth, to his university town. Just one phone call before he goes, to make sure she is still alive. He could visit her next Saturday. A quiet weekend, student memories. And nobody needs to know. Yet.

Chapter 2

Lviv, Western Ukraine, March 2001

Her electric doorbell plays the familiar tune. The same it used to when he was at university. She is not opening the door. By now the sound has no beginning and no end, just the same pattern of tones, over and over again. A melancholic waltz, something very familiar. A few years ago, the ringing of this bell was quite a novelty. Taras remembers it well. Every note brings an instant wave of other sounds: student banter, laughter, her persistent hospitality, interrupted only by her even more persistent cough. They used to call her flat 'an extension of the History Department'. After all, her family's past was an integral part of the history – evacuation, Stalin's camps, *samizdat* dissident leaflets.

Another nickname for her flat was 'Sara's soup kitchen'. It is still a mystery to Taras, how she always managed to feed their hungry crowd on her meagre pension. Maybe the rumours about her receiving dollars from Radio Free Europe in recognition of her husband's dissident glory were true, after all. What was her husband's first name, by the way? Vasyl . . . yes, Vasyl Ivanovych. Taras must remember to express his condolences. He read the man's obituary several months ago, a quarter of a page in the national newspaper.

Taras keeps pressing the button until she opens the door at last.

'Sara Samoylovna, *zdravstvuyte*!' he greets her in Russian. She grew up in Moscow and still feels more comfortable speaking Russian, rather than Ukrainian.

'Tarasyk!' She recognises him straight away. 'Were you ringing for long? When I am in the kitchen, I can't always hear the door-bell. It was my daughter's present for our Golden Wedding anniversary. Now, with my husband gone, my life gone, I often ignore its jingling.'

'International Women's Day is next week, so . . .' He thrusts flowers at her. He does not remember the last time he bought flowers for a woman.

She seems genuinely pleased with the flowers. She *is* genuinely pleased to see him. She is the most sincere person he has ever met, in anger and in kindness. He has seen both. A smile covers her delicate features with a fine cobweb of wrinkles. She is petite, smaller than he remembers her, wispy-haired, bird-eyed. Even dressed in a shapeless flannelette gown, she still has the beauty and fragility of a late October rose: faded petals, lone radiance.

She is fussing around him, trying to take his coat, offering worn felt slippers that had once been green, and Taras understands that she is giving herself time to catch her breath. She has obviously slowed down. For her to get to open the door has probably meant serious negotiating with her body.

He follows her into the study. While she shuffles ahead of him, he takes a moment to glance into the hall mirror. His cotton sweatshirt is casual, but not cheap. His glasses frame is German, well-made, thin metallic silver – he hopes she will notice. He would like her to admire him at last. To say: 'Oh Tarasyk, you look so well! Gone are the times when I used to call you "our poor relation"!'

The apartment looks as if she is ready to move – carpets rolled to the walls, empty shelves, books, books everywhere: dusty piles on the chairs, leather-bound volumes on the old-fashioned red sofa. Through the open bedroom door he can see another pile on the floor, next to the fifties-style bed with aluminium cones on the bedframe. Reading his thoughts, Sara Samoylovna apologises: 'Please ignore the mess. You probably know, my husband passed away this year and we are trying to sort out his library. We are giving a lot of books to the university.' Her 'we' sounds conspiratorial, as if she is discussing every title with her deceased husband. 'All this sorting, it takes most of my time nowadays.'

She breathes out sadness with physical effort, moving the pile from the sofa, clearing space for Taras to sit, before he reaches to help her. She chuckles: 'Tarasyk, you take a seat and I'll stand next to you. I've had enough sitting in my life.' He has heard this joke so many times before. After the war, arrested as the wife of the people's enemy, she spent seven years in prison, and was only rehabilitated after Stalin's death. Her persistent cough is the legacy of a damp cell. She has shrunk even more since he last saw her, and now, when he sits down and she leans on the table, they are at the same level and she does not have to talk to the *Just Do It* sign on his Nike sweater. Another one of her age-defying little tricks.

What a woman! Taras is so carried away by her ingenuity, that he nearly misses her question: 'How is your research going? You are so lucky to work in Moscow, Tarasyk.'

Nobody here knows about his course at the FSB Academy on the outskirts of Moscow, even though he spent twenty-two long months there. Nobody knows about the FSB Archives either. Sara

Samoylovna asks him about his position as a researcher at the Institute for History and Archives, the famous azure building near Red Square. That is where he is supposed to work, according to his cover.

He has expected this question, and he has an answer ready – but she keeps talking avidly, as if she has been starved of words. She is short of breath, and between wheezy gasps she attacks Taras with short bursts:

'So, tell me, have you got a proper girlfriend? You are probably too busy for that, working hard as always. Besides, the girls in Moscow are not the easiest ones to please. Once they start going out with you, they will take all your time – believe you me, I know what I am talking about! I wish I could go back to Moscow with you, to my childhood. The city must have changed enormously. I probably wouldn't recognise my streets. I remember everything: poplars, ponds . . . My memory is still sharp, you know, too sharp sometimes. There are so many things in my past I am trying to forget. God, the times have changed! If fifteen – no, even ten years ago – somebody had told me that the Declaration of Ukrainian Independence would happen peacefully – no blood-bath, no street arrests – I would have laughed, Tarasyk. I would have told them to – well, you know. I don't remember many swearing expressions from my prison days, but I still remember August 1968, the Soviet tanks in Prague. By the way, you recall those articles about the Cossacks, the ones my husband was arrested for, after the war? The ones that were labelled "Nationalistic"? I showed them to you once, remember? Well, here is a final twist in this story. I had a call from the editor of a serious national magazine, asking for my permission to publish them as a part of this year's tenth Anniversary of Independence celebration! And to organise the public readings, as well! Who could ever think of the chance of *that* happening?'

Her dry body shakes from another bout of coughing. Taras watches her with concern. She purses her lips into a neat O, and a cracking sound is followed by another wheezy gasp as she takes the air in. The cough stops as unexpectedly as it started, and Sara Samoylovna smiles at Taras. 'Talking of memories, when you called, you mentioned something about the museum at the Institute, didn't you?'

Taras beams at her. 'Indeed I did. The Institute has decided to honour its best students, and I am in charge of creating a special memorial room. Your husband was a student there in the thirties. We are planning to have a separate stand, commemorating his work. The Institute has a collection of his publications starting from 1947, but unfortunately, we do not know anything about his life and research during the war. Perhaps you've got some documents, books or letters which could help?'

He sounds enthusiastic and confident. He has chosen the right approach. Her husband's memory is her only possession, and she is a generous soul. She would love to share it with the world. Sara Samoylovna turns on her heels with an agility extraordinary for her age and pulls out a desk drawer. She takes out two faded yellow triangles, a thin clothbound book printed on coarse, cheap, grey paper and a notebook under a black oilskin cover. She hands everything to Taras: 'Have a look and see if that might be of interest. I'll make you coffee while you are reading – strong, Turkish-style, the way you like it.' *God, she even remembers that!* He turns to thank her, but Sara Samoylovna has already disappeared into the kitchen. It is too poignant for her, he guesses. Nobody has ever seen her crying, and she would not let it happen today.

Taras starts with the triangles. Unfolds one carefully – it is so frayed, he worries that it will disintegrate under his fingers, turn into yellow dust. He recognises the handwriting he saw at the back of the file 1247.

A letter from the front. Three lines, three lifelines – to let her know that he is still there:

How are you, my dearest? I am all right.
Missing you and thinking of you both.
We will throw the Nazis out very soon and I will be
with you again.

Could she read the truth between those lines? About freezing trenches, deafening explosions, his fear before the attack? It takes Taras a couple of minutes to fold the letter back. He does not bother to open the second triangle – the words will be the same. It is not what he is looking for.

Taras turns to the paperback book. There is a black outline drawing of a girl on the cover – a kneeling, mourning figure. A date at the bottom: 1942. A red faded title *Tristan and Iseult* .

He opens the first page. There is a dedication in blue ink, in a chain of tiny, spiky letters.

Sara, my dearest! Today is your twentieth birthday. I wish
I could give you a better present in these hard times. At
least this book is about love. I hope that it can become
our guiding star in this unhappy world. I cannot give you
diamonds or gold today, but I know that our love is priceless.

What did she look like in those days? wonders Taras. He has never seen any young photographs of her. He must ask her to show him some. But not today. Another time, if there will ever be one.

He picks up the thick notebook and opens the oilskin cover. The handwriting resembles a thin wire, entangled in the pale blue squares of a maths exercise book. Practice in the archives has taught him how to decipher the most illegible scribbles, and in a couple of minutes he can read this diary easily, revisiting an odd word now and then:

18 September 1941

Congratulations – I am a married man! Never did I imagine it would happen like this. As our town was so close to the western border, it was important to evacuate the archives fast – hence all the panic with packing and travelling. It was decided that Central Asia would be not only safe, but also warm in winter. We were going to Tashkent, capital of Uzbekistan. The train crawled, sometimes waiting for hours, letting through heavy military echelons, heading west. There were forty of us in a goods wagon, all my colleagues from the Archives. We travelled for a week, when our train stopped not far from a station, amid the Steppes. To escape from the smell of stale straw we slid the door open, straight into the rustle of crickets and the huge red disk of the evening sun, straight into the pre-war world. How could I resist a walk?

Sara followed me, deep into the cornfield, narrowing her eyes at the sunset. She came to the Archives to work during her summer holidays, a month before evacuation. She has dreamy hazel eyes and tightly plaited black braids. There is something fragile about her, something from another age and another world, the world of Chekhov and Turgenev, where girls in long white dresses are strolling in the gardens under lacy umbrellas . . .

I have just reread my notes. I cannot imagine myself, the Head of NKVD Archives, thinking and writing like this even three months ago! Am I really in love?

I still cannot explain to myself how everything happened. I have read about people making love at the funerals of their relatives, during the epidemics of cholera. When the future scares you and you are exhausted by constant unhappiness and desperation, when neither your body nor your soul can take any more pain, passion acts as a strong and powerful drug, giving a short oblivion. I can understand it now.

I remember every touch, every kiss, but cannot remember falling asleep. When we woke up at dawn, the train was gone, and so were all our belongings and documents.

It took me and Sara six hours to get to the station – and I thought we were half a kilometre away! I had my NKVD ID card in my pocket. I had never used it to get anything before, but it does work wonders, as I discovered.

The harassed, unshaven stationmaster gave us some bread and green tea and managed to squeeze us on the next evacuees' train to Krasnodar. From there we boarded another train to the Uzbek capital.

When we registered with Narkomat at Tashkent, I was told that our suitcases and personal documents had disappeared, but that the Archive files had been looked after by my colleagues and were all safe. Major Alexandrov was very helpful. He managed to get me a room and some temporary papers.

Sara was like a scared nestling blackbird. She is still a child, relies on me totally, especially now. I could not possibly leave her. What would she do without passport, clothes or money, thousands of kilometres from home? So, when Major Alexandrov asked me: 'And who is she?' I had to answer, 'This is my wife.' There was no surprise in her eyes, only tears. Tears of happiness or despair? I don't know. I'll never dare to ask. She was given new papers with her married name (my name!) on them. Poor Sara –hardly any courtship, no marriage proposal, no flowers and no ceremony!

24 October 1941

Today is my birthday. Will my next twenty-seven years fly by as quickly?

So here I am, aged twenty-seven, in the most incredible circumstances: married to an eighteen-year-old Jewish girl, living in the glass veranda of a small house in Tashkent, with five other families occupying four other rooms, and still trying to be sane! But never mind, the war will be over soon, things will get back to normal, I'll continue my research dissertation and have a real family life.

Sometimes I think about Vera. How am I going to explain everything to her after the war?

31 December 1941

Today is New Year's Eve, but life is so hard that it is impossible to get into a festive mood. We were given two sausage sandwiches at a New Year's Eve party at the Archives. Quite a celebration, as we haven't eaten sausage or butter since we left Moscow.

Winter this year in Tashkent is the coldest the old people can remember. With minus 40 Celsius outside, our summer veranda, even with a steel stove, is not much fun! Nobody expected the war would last till winter, and poor Sara does not have anything to wear. She is determined to continue her studies here and attends the lectures at Leningrad University, evacuated to Tashkent.

When I watch her tramping through the snow in my socks, sandals and pyjama trousers, our landlady's old rabbit jacket covering her thin shoulders, my throat tightens with despair and tenderness.

21 January 1942

Not only am I a married man, now I am going to be a father!

What do I know about bringing up children? Only what I learned from bringing up Sara in the last six months. She tries hard, but sometimes her naïve stubbornness shines through. Today at the market I swapped my bread ration cards for an excellent, useful book – *The Formation of Character* by Robert Owen. My child's future education is definitely worth a day with an empty stomach.

Shall I write to Vera about the news?

12 June 1942

Haven't written anything for a long time. Today *Pravda* has published a Treaty between the Soviet Union and Britain about the joint actions during the war and about the Allies' joint actions when the war finishes. The Treaty is valid for twenty years. It means that my son or daughter will have a peaceful childhood and youth, unlike my generation: we always expected a war. Who knows, in twenty years' time all wars could become history. Why couldn't this have happened twenty-three years earlier?

5 July 1942

It's a girl! I took Sara to hospital last night, though we both thought it might be too early. This morning, when I came to see her, the nurse told me that my daughter was born at 6.30! Both mother and baby are fine.

Sara has written me a quick note, describing what she has been through. She normally has beautiful handwriting, but now, when she is so weak and exhausted, it is barely legible. She has asked for a boiled egg, that's all she wants. I searched the market, but could not find any eggs. I was even prepared to trade my shoes for an egg, but . . . nothing! What a world was my (yet nameless) daughter born into! If she survives now, she will live to be a hundred, I know.

I am so glad that I have a daughter! Girls are more sensitive and delicate creatures than boys, and to have additional love and tenderness around you during these hard times is a particular luxury.

5 August 1942

Today is a month since my daughter's birth. Natasha has grown noticeably; her eyes have changed colour, and have become clearer. She is so thin; her shoulder-blades are sticking out like two folded angel's wings.

Her mother was reading *War and Peace* before going to hospital, and decided to call our daughter after Tolstoy's heroine. I did not object – she looks like her mother, and Sara is still as spontaneous and guileless as Natasha Rostova was. She is now at our canteen, having lunch (or to be more precise, bland barley soup), and the baby is with me. Natasha sleeps on two chairs, moved together, on archive files covered with my old, holey cardigan instead of a mattress. As they say, a girl *v pohode y v bede* – 'on the march and in calamity'.

So far, educating my daughter is all about tolerating hardships as well as her parents try to. Forgive me, Robert Owen!

Tiny Natasha already feeds us; her dependant's ration card brings more bread into the family. Amazing.

1 September 1942
Today is the first day of the university lectures. Natasha has a fever, so Sara could not take her to the nursery and cried all morning. She is only nineteen, and a year of family life, a year of war, has not brought her much happiness so far. I am supposed to give her strength and faith, but it is not easy. For the last two months, all you can hear from the radio information bulletins is: 'No changes at the fronts . . .'

I am ashamed of myself for this, but at the moment, my hopes for a better future for us centre on a time when we will be able to eat our fill!

Kostya, my old university friend, was in Tashkent for a week and came to visit us. His family is in Kazakhstan, living in a cowshed near the small station of Chelkar. The only food they can get is some dried camel meat and rice. In winter, the walls of the shed are frozen through. I should help them move here – hopefully, this winter will be warmer. We talked about our friends. Misha and Valentin were killed at the fronts, both within three months of joining. The war gets closer every day. Kostya has heard nothing about Vera, and I still haven't written to her about *my* news.

An aroma of coffee wafts into the room. Sara Samoylovna follows, carrying a white ceramic cup, covered in amorphous brown splashes. She places the cup on the desk, sliding it away from the edge. The cup leaves a wet trace on the polished surface. It is only half-full, but Sara Samoylovna is happy with her efforts.

'Who is Vera?' His question sounds too curt.

Sara Samoylovna blushes and instant colour fills the faded petals. There is a hint of coquetry in her smile. 'Vera was a girl my husband was going to marry before the war. They studied together, and then my husband was sent to work in the Archives while she remained in Moscow. Amazingly, after the war we became great friends, and—'

But Taras is not listening. He is reading the last page of the diary:

17 November 1942

I have just found out that there is a plan to centralise all the regional archives after the war and to move them to Moscow. I had to make a decision fast. What I am doing now may seem wrong, but only if you look at it in the short term. I have to do it not for myself, but for the generation of my children or even grandchildren, for the time when my motherland becomes free and independent.

Sara Samoylovna leans over his shoulder.

'That was my husband's last entry in the diary, two days before he went to the front. You see, he was so sad to leave his baby daughter. It was hard for me to remain in Tashkent, but it was so much harder for him to leave us.'

'This is *so* interesting, Sara Samoylovna!' Taras coughs, masking his excitement. He wonders what her reaction would be if he said instead: 'Oh no, Sara Samoylovna! This diary entry has nothing to do with you and Natasha. This is about the documents your husband removed from the NKVD file N1247 in November 1942. I saw his signature in the file – he worked on it during the war . . .'

But Taras doesn't. He needs to ask her now if there were other papers with the diary. He will tease it out gently. No pressure: general information first, then repeat the question, adding more detail.

'How did you manage to save the diary through all these years?' he begins cautiously.

'Oh, my husband squirrelled it away.' She is not one to accept an undeserved tribute. 'We only found the diary after his death. We were sorting out the books for the university library and the diary was tucked behind the volumes of *The History of Ukrainian Towns* on the second shelf, together with some papers. I have made several copies of the diary, it is such an exciting read, so if you would like one for the memorial room . . .'

'That would be fantastic!' says Taras. The copy of the diary would be useful – it will give him proof. Not as useful though, as the documents, stolen in 1942. Seven pages – this is all he needs. Four would be handwritten; three would be typed on the old-fashioned typewriter, with vowels 'a' and 'o' jumping slightly above the line. Seven pages which, if made public, will bring a country crashing down.

Seven pages, which one country will never forgive and another country will never forget.

Your husband was a very brave man, Sara Samoylovna, thinks Taras. It takes a lot of courage to live with such a secret.

His eyes fall on the photograph of her grandson on the shelf – familiar smile, familiar freckles. Sarah follows his look. 'He studies abroad now, you know. We are so proud of him!'

Taras takes a deep breath to ask Sara about the 'papers' she found with the diary when she tells him the answer herself.

He frowns for a nanosecond and turns away, stares out of the window at the scaffolding on the house across the street. The builders' cradle swings in the wind like a pendulum, like his feelings after what he has heard. He does not look up at her, does not comment. Sara Samoylovna carries on – delighted, excited, proud – until he cannot take it any longer.

Taras rises quickly and whispers hoarsely, loudly, into her thinning grey crown. About his flight at six and other friends he needs to see. About her excellent coffee and a great contribution to the memorial room. He manages a farewell smile and leaves, clutching the photocopy of the diary in his hand so tightly that his knuckles whiten. He can still see her leaning on the doorframe, trying to cover her disappointment with her luminous, young smile. She was rather hoping he could stay longer. She had cooked his favourite borshch with mushrooms and garlic, no meat, and . . .

It probably took her all morning, thinks Taras. Never mind. She should get used to seeing people off by now.

The snowy alleys of Stryisky Park are five minutes away from the cobbled street where she lives. He almost jogs to the top of the hill, leaving breathless herds of tourists at the gates below. The day is ringing with frost and sun, and he can see the old town from here. Gone is the aristocratic presence he remembers: the medieval square with the Armenian corner café, Turkish coffee, cooked on hot sand, artists in the courtyards, residences with fruity stucco mouldings near Lychakivske Cemetery. Trams burrow through dark, swarming crowds, and there are eyesores of plywood kiosks on every corner. He is alone here, above the hustle.

Taras leans over and arranges his thoughts and the snow into three neat piles.

Pile one. At least he knows that the documents were found with the diary. His analysis was correct – he knew he should have started here. He has discovered their present location and it makes his search more focused, more personal.

Pile two. He needs to go to England. Urgently. Now. Not easy, but not impossible either.

Pile three. He has to inform his boss and seek his help. Karpov has amazing contacts, he can arrange all the permits. Taras has more than enough arguments, just needs to pick up the right ones. Carefully.

In a way, it was helpful: Sara Samoylovna has confirmed his suspicions, has helped him to narrow the options. And yet he can't forgive her for what she has told him. For what he has to do now. For what it will do to her.

Chapter 3

Moscow, March 2001

The silence is becoming awkward. Taras needs to break the ice fast, while it is still a thin layer of the first ground frost. He knows that one careless word or wrong move will ruin everything. He rehearsed this conversation in his head a dozen times, practised the right facial expression in the mirror during one of his washes, timed himself (*If you cannot explain your case in seven minutes it is not a case any more* – another quote from Surikov, his Academy tutor). He chose the place with care. The canteen in the basement has the feel of a monastery vault. The hum of small talk, the chink of plates, are always thicker here: his boss can hear him above the chattering and clinking, but this corner is quiet enough to avoid unnecessary attention.

Taras emphasised every word, as if he were reading the bullet points of a presentation. He mentioned the need to go to Britain casually, almost in passing, among other necessary steps of the operation. The Head of the Archive Department listened, not raising his eyes from his plate once during those seven minutes.

He has not commented, has not asked a single question. They sit in silence. Taras watches his boss eat. The threads on his rosacea-touched cheeks move in a slow chewing rhythm. How does he manage to stay in the Service, when people ten years younger than him are pushed into retirement? wonders Taras. Whom does he drink with, and how often?

Karpov crunches through the vitamin C in the oily cabbage salad, meticulously munches the tasteless cutlet. He scowls, as if his brain is connected to his stomach, and the food is giving him a headache. But Taras knows his boss well. He ponders, considers, and weighs the pros and cons. By the time he swallows the last piece of cutlet, punctiliously collects up the fried breadcrumbs, balancing them on his fork, he has made his decision.

'I would not tell anybody else about this, Taras. It will mean lengthy reports and at least three months of waiting for the clearance. Besides, these reports can be easily copied and passed to my former drinking pals, our rivals from other National Security Services. People would do anything for money these days. When I joined the KGB forty years ago, I didn't do it for money, you know. For power and privileges, maybe, but even they were not that important. It was such a busy and interesting time! Every day the tasks were different. We censored the newspaper articles, checked the songs of the restaurant musicians, hunted the under-ground dissident magazines, stopped the emigrating Jews from smuggling secrets to the West . . .'

Taras is used to Karpov's lengthy reminiscences. Usually, the Good Old Days song is followed by the intention to leave the Service: 'It's all changed, Taras – methods, approaches, people jumping sides. I promise you, I will retire tomorrow. I will plant an English lawn instead of my wife's vegetable garden at our *dacha* in Malakhovka, and I will have the time at last to read some historic memoirs. I'll start with Marshal Jukov's book – I am so lucky to have the first edition of 1969!' Sometimes priority is given to the pleasures and dangers of under-ice fishing. Occasionally there is a lecture on the poor quality of history teaching in Karpov's grandson's school.

Taras waits.

His boss starts on his bowl of lemon jelly. Taras wonders how long it will take him to swallow the first morsel. The remaining, bigger piece wobbles, and Karpov winces. Either because his taste buds have finally responded to the jelly, or because the wobbling movement is against Karpov's character – everything in him is accurate and measured. He unfolds the paper napkin, wipes his lips and clears his throat. Dislodged mucus produces a quacking sound.

'It makes quite an interesting read, this case N1247,' he says finally. 'Especially the report on the trip of that *devitsa*, Sofia. It must have been quite a thing to travel across Europe on her own more than two and a half centuries ago. How high must the stakes have been, for her to dare to do it? Notice, by the way, that the word *devitsa* meant *virgin* and *young girl* at the same time. As purity disappeared from our society, the word changed meaning, and is now used to label girls of a certain kind. Interesting metamorphosis, isn't it?'

Karpov stops examining the jelly and fixes his watery blue eyes on Taras. 'Have you read the file attentively, Lieutenant?'

'I have, Nikolay Petrovych,' replies Taras. He should really address his boss as 'Colonel', but his name and patronymic is what the man prefers; it is closer, warmer, almost familial. Does he know, wonders Taras, that his nickname around the Archives is 'Papa'?

'Well, you are a historian, Taras, so do give me your professional assessment,' continues Karpov, eyeing with suspicion the brown liquid and pieces of dry fruit floating in his drink.

Taras understands the question. Or rather, what's behind it. He needs to tread carefully here.

'I find it amazing, really,' he starts, 'that after two hundred and fifty years of scrupulous following, the investigation ended so abruptly, and nothing has been added to the file since 1962. The case is not closed, as you know, and any new investigation, if started now, could be potentially damaging.'

'It could be fatal, my boy, *fatal*!' Karpov stresses the last word, raising his eyes from the glass and looking straight at Taras. No clarification needed at this stage. They have understood each other.

'You know,' Karpov goes on, 'when I joined the Service, it didn't matter whether my colleagues were Georgians, Uzbeks or Ukrainians. We all worked together, we were a team. I know sometimes they used to say that *pytaya grafa*, Question five on nationality in all the official forms was more than just a number. It was a verdict: not much chance of a good university education, and a cross on your career if the answer to question number five was not right. But it mattered mostly if you were Jewish, to be honest. Who would have thought that your nationality, your own *pyataya grafa* would block you from promotion today!'

Though Karpov keeps inspecting his glass and does not look at Taras as he says this, the young man is absolutely sure that the 'you' in Karpov's speech is highly personal and addressed only to him.

'We could try to repair the damage, Taras.' Karpov carefully fishes a shrivelled apple slice out of his drink and places it on his plate, next to the unfinished lemon jelly.

When he says 'we', does he mean 'me and him' or 'him and his invisible, powerful drinking pals'? wonders Taras.

'International Women's Day is in three days' time,' Karpov says next. 'It is much harder to buy presents for my spouse now, thirty-seven years into marriage. She'll be thrilled when I tell her that the present will be brought from England. She'll have to wait for a bit though, as it will take a week for me to arrange your passport and visa. How is your English, by the way?'

'It's OK, Nikolay Petrovych,' nods Taras, coughing to hide his excitement. His trip is approved.

Karpov does not need to know about his battle with English words during his language classes at the Academy. How the phrases he tried to learn, falling asleep over the Muller's English Dictionary, were miraculously deleted from his memory next morning. He spent hours scribbling words on white stickers and left them everywhere – above the sink, near his bed, on his desk. He sat in the language lab, listening to the intonation drills again and again, and then dreamed of a small, neat grey-haired lady in a bow-tied blouse. She would greet Taras from the textbook cover, she would stretch her lips in a rubber smile, she would repeat the same phrase: *'Would you like a cup of tea, Mr Priestley?'* with icy politeness. She was never happy with his pronunciation, with his heavy r's and hard s's, this Mrs Priestley. Taras shudders, shaking off a nightmare.

On the way home he remembers his first language assignment in the Academy, his practical test. Hotel Ukraina, a room on the ground floor. Hotel security had called him for assistance in questioning a street money-changer and a farmer from Hertfordshire. The former, a cocky loudmouth, had vigorously denied involvement in illegal money-changing, well aware that a bundle of banknotes passed to security later would change matters in his favour.

The farmer was panicked into surrender. He did not know that street money-changing was illegal; several people in his tourist group had done it and got a much better rate than the hotel was offering. Taras was pleased and surprised: he could understand the farmer very well – but then, the poor old boy was quite repetitive. 'There was this man . . . He came to me on the street . . . He asked me if I wanted to change money . . .'

'If only all Brits spoke like that, I would have got a higher grade at the English comprehension test,' sighs Taras, scanning the people on the escalator.

He could not tell Karpov about his routine of watching American videos twice a week, in English with Russian subtitles. Knowing his boss, it would have caused more suspicion than approval, and besides, Karpov would not find the phrases Taras learned through subtitles ('We're gonna have fun, baby . . . I tell ya, you're a mess, buddy!') particularly inspiring. Taras decides to pick up a couple of tapes tonight and to start buying the *Moscow Times* in English.

That night, the evening routine takes place as usual: handwash, kitchen, kettle on, butter and cheese out of the fridge, bread out of the plastic bag. He looks out of the window.

Fifth floor, two windows to the right: the light of the reading lamp should be stronger, then the old man would not hunch over the books so much. This pensioner always reads late, makes notes, the permanent white shape of a teacup on the table next to him. At his age, the imaginary world is the only escape from the sweeping changes in the country.

Taras needs to do some reading as well. He clicks open his brown briefcase – real leather, not oilskin, the first thing he bought when he started this job – and takes the notes out. He has spent four hours today hand-copying some of the case documents. He pulls out the first one:

Report on the interrogation of Oksana Polubotko, born 23.03.1943

Kiev, 18 March 1962

Conclusions and resolutions

To be kept under supervision.
Isolation recommended.
Provide survival, in case the identity needs to be used in the future.

Chapter 4

Kiev, March 1962

The monotonous drone is getting under her skin. She opens her eyes. The bulky fan is humming on the interrogator's desk, but the windowless room is fogged with cigarette smoke. The light, turned on to her face, is dazzling her. She cannot see him. She imagines him as a gigantic fish. Glassy, expressionless eyes. Slippery scales. Deformed, gasping mouth.

He has amazing stamina, this KGB interrogator. She does not know how long she has been here; she does not know what he wants of her.

'Your name.'

'Oksana Polubotko.'

'Date of birth?'

'Twenty-third of March 1943.'

'Your occupation?'

'Student.'

'In detail.'

'I am a second-year student in the History Department of Kiev University.'

'Are you related to Anatoly Polubotko?'

'Yes, he was my grandfather.'

'What do you know about him?'

'Only that he died in 1937. He was shot as a traitor to the nation.'

'Are you related to Oleg Polubotko?'

'Yes, he was my father.'

'Do you remember him?'

'Yes, I remember him well. I was ten when he was arrested, a month before Stalin's death. He was not released for another year, and died from tuberculosis on his way home from Magadan in 1954.'

'Were you aware of his research into his ancestry?'

'Yes, he was always proud of our Cossack roots.'

'What did he tell you about his research?'

'Only that our family name might change the destiny of our country.'

'Did he send a letter to London?'

'Yes. In 1953, just before his arrest. He said he was doing it to rehabilitate the name of my grandfather.'

'Did he receive a reply?'

She is getting tired of this. 'You know perfectly well he did not. He was arrested a month later.'

'Did you send a letter to London?'

'Yes. I sent one three months ago.'

'Why did you decide to do it now?'

'Well, I thought that times had changed, since there were so many publications about the truth of Stalin's rule last year. I just wanted to prove that my grandfather was not an English spy, and that my father did not try to falsify any documents. What is wrong with trying to clear their names? Their rehabilitation is important for the sake of my mother, for the sake of my future children.'

'Are you in possession of any documents concerning the case?'

'No.'

'Have you ever received any letters or documents from London?'

'No.'

Pause. The smoke thickens, it is difficult to breathe. How long are they going to keep her in this place?

'Your name.'

'Oksana Polubotko.'

'Your date of birth?'

She closes her eyes. She needs air, and water, and sleep. They will let her go soon, and she will forget this fume-filled hell like somebody else's nightmare. Only her smoke-impregnated dress will remind her that this night was real.

Will they allow her to leave the building through the turnstile, like an ordinary overworked secretary or will they push her into that bread van again and drop her off somewhere in town?

It had happened so quickly. She was walking home after the university poetry evening. She left after midnight, with half the audience still there.

The evening was a revelation. Young Moscow poets were reciting in a manner so different from the optimistic rhythm of Soviet poetry: the tidal wave of intonation was bringing rich, decadent vowels, unknown yearnings, forbidden thoughts. She imagined herself in a high-ceilinged apartment overlooking the Seine, not in this university hall, packed with boys in fashionable nylon shirts and narrow ties, girls in bell-shaped skirts and matching hairbands. She was wearing her green dress – the one her mother had made from her grandmother's silk fabric. Oksana only wonders how Granny managed to stash it away, save it during all the moves, arrests and confiscations. The dress is the exact copy of the one she saw in a French magazine brought to lectures by her friend: soft lines, open neck, flowing skirt. It has a tight bodice – so tight, in fact, that it has to be worn with care; the fabric was so old, her mother warned her, that the thread could disintegrate. So, when she wears this silk wonder, she has to move slowly and gracefully, sit with a straight back and lift her hand in a small, smooth movement. Nobody would guess that her grace and bearing – so like those of a Hollywood icon – are caused by a set of seams ready to burst.

After leaving the university, she walked past the recently rebuilt drama theatre and took a short cut, steep steps up the hill. The building on the left was catching up with her. What a dark, grotesque place. They called it 'The House with Chimeras', but she had nicknamed it 'The House of Nightmares'. The statues, grey and motionless in the daylight, were alive at night: elephants lifting their rain-gutter trunks, mermaids sobbing, huge frogs leaping from the roof, a giant octopus sliding slowly towards her down the wall. She reached the top of the steps and paused to catch her breath.

The night air was frosty. Winter was surrendering slowly to spring this year, but despite the cold, everybody was talking about a new spring – 'a political thaw', they named it in the papers. Several professors allowed their students to question some text-book paragraphs; art exhibitions challenged the Soviet posters; vinyl disks, bought on the black market, asked the girls in perfect English whether they were 'lonesome tonight'. Black-market Elvis recordings were often bartered for another treasure – a copy of

Inostrannaya Literatura, the monthly magazine, with translations of Remarque and Hemingway.

Oksana had a spring in her step, too. Sasha, her fiancé, was due to return from Moscow on Friday. She could not wait – and not only because she missed him. She had such a special surprise for him: the American pianist Van Clibern was in town and she had managed to exchange a bottle of her mother's Latvian perfume for three concert tickets: for Sasha, herself and her mother. She would have to slip the truth about the cost to her mother somehow. Maybe mention it airily after the concert, when they would be walking home and she would be wrapped in music and joy, so rare in her life.

Oksana had unbuttoned her old coat, not that anybody could see her dress now, as the street was deserted – apart from a lone bread van being unloaded at the bakery. She hardly had time to think that it was too early for the fresh buns, when they threw her into the van. Strong hands, one quick move: covered crate out, the girl in the green dress in. There was no bread inside – just a pungent, stale, sweaty smell. She had no time to get scared even, as the drive took no more than three minutes. She had lived in this area all her life, no medals for guessing where they took her to. She always quickened her pace when she had to pass the grated windows of the KGB Headquarters. Her grandfather was brought here when they arrested him, then her father. She should never have allowed her neighbour to do that Tarot reading: a card pulled out, a quick concerned look, then a reshuffle and the same card pulled out again. 'A curse over your family,' she had murmured not looking at Oksana.

There is this voice again. Controlling her through smoke and light and noise.

'Let us continue. Have you ever received any correspondence from London?'

'No.'

'Are you in possession of any documents, concerning the case?'

'No.'

The sudden silence is more deafening than the interrogator's voice. The Fish is scribbling some notes. She wants to ask him when she can go home, but the smoke fills her lungs, her eyes tingle disloyally. She is afraid that if she opens her mouth again, her voice will rise to a shriek and the tears will pour. She has had enough . . .

. . . and so has Taras. He folds the lined sheets, puts them back into his brown briefcase.

Thank you, Oksana, he thinks. It was your star performance this morning that persuaded Karpov. I am going to London and I am taking you with me – with some other files, of course. I cannot wait to meet you in person – and I will, I promise, as soon as I return from Britain.

Taras leans on the table, looks out of the window. The tower block opposite is gaping with black, sleepy holes, though several TV screens still glow. He counts the insomniac windows, drums on the table with his knuckles, echoes the rhythm of the dripping kitchen tap. Finally he gets up to rinse the cup, carefully wipes every single breadcrumb from his oilskin-covered table. In the bathroom he covers his hands in thick lather, leaves them under the intermittent, feeble stream, examines his face in the mirror. ('Careful,' his coach warns him. 'It should not become another routine.') This time the feeling shows – in the rapid flaring of his nostrils, the enlarged pupils, the hidden smile under the gingery moustache. It is deeper than excitement. He has never been on a hunt, but he is sure this is a hunter's thrill – when the prey is close, rustling through the bushes, unaware of imminent death.

He turns the radio on. It is the *Weather on the Planet* time. An enthusiastic girl's voice is teasing the sleepless and the dreamers with remote places and exotic temperatures:

'Los Angeles, eighteen degrees, sunny. Cairo, twenty-three degrees, storms expected. Oslo, two degrees Celsius.'

And finally: 'It is raining in London. The temperature is seven degrees Celsius.'

Taras stands in the middle of the bathroom, listening, drying his left hand, wiping carefully between each finger. Should he go straight to Cambridge or spend a couple of days in London first? There's no rush. He has two weeks to decide. He will carry on with his job, he will rummage around in the archives. He will open the files, and read, make notes and classify. He has waited for his chance for years, he can wait for fourteen more days. He will worry in chronological order.

Chapter 5

Cambridge–London, March 2001

Taras has planned the trip following the Rule of Three Questions. He remembers Colonel Surikov putting them on the blackboard every week, all through the year of the 'Tactics and Operations' course in the Academy. *Where? When? How?* Then he would always add, tapping the blackboard, crumbling and grinding the chalk with unnecessary force: 'Remember, there is no question *Why?* Somebody has already answered it before the beginning of the operation. At your level, you only have to decide on three things: *Where, When* and *How.*'

Taras has no choice over the first question. *Where* has to be Cambridge.

Taras does not use a map as he gets off the bus: he learned the route. No need to get lost, wander, ask for directions, to attract unnecessary attention.

He stops by the sign 'Private. Masters Lodge' for a moment and smiles, remembering Surikov's comment at the Academy. 'Remember, "private" is not just a military rank. Private is a capitalist notion, alien to our communal mentality, to our way of living – no wonder there is no direct equivalent Russian translation for the word "privacy"!'

At last, the college building just as he imagined – castle-like tower with three black cockerels on the crest over the gates. A portly man in a bowler hat stands in the gateway. He does not say anything to Taras, but then he does not need to. It is obvious that Taras is not a welcome visitor here. He is just somebody who has chosen a longer route to his small hotel in Chesterton Road as an excuse to have a glimpse of another world. Stopping at the college gates under the sign 'No bicycles and no dogs' he is caught in a flow of students. The majority wear a paradoxical combination of short-sleeved T-shirts and college scarves.

'Few things look sadder than an Englishman shuffling in his thin-soled gentleman's shoes through January snow in Moscow. Warm him up, give him a drink, and he is all yours' – yet another of Surikov's pearls of wisdom. Taras can certainly see his tutor's point as he notices the goose-bumps on the bare arms of a boy in a blue T-shirt, crossing the road in front of him.

He wonders how many in this crowd would join 'the magnificent five'. How many already have? Would they end up like Kim Philby, in a woolly old cardigan in a Moscow flat? These are not the questions that Taras needs to answer now, with his *When* and *How* still unresolved.

There is a fair in full swing on Midsummer Common, just before the bridge. Here the sounds of laughter and music are loud, with the flashing lights to match. Taras crosses and stops by the board with the printed poster: *Crystal Ball readings. Princess Anne's destiny read.* Below, in ballpoint pen, there is an addition in block letters: *SUCCESSFULLY.*

An older version of Sara Samoylovna is sitting next to the poster, knitting an endless scarf. She raises her eyes for a moment: 'Would you like to know your future, young man? Five pounds only.' Taras wonders how he would justify these five pounds on his expenses claim ('investment in the future?') and walks past with a firm, 'No, thank you.' A creaking voice reaches him: 'You know the ropes, young man, you know the ropes. Just be very careful with them.'

What on earth does she mean? It must be some sort of an idiom, thinks Taras. He'll have to look it up in the dictionary. The green space across the road beckons – dozens of students are enjoying the first spring grass. He remembers the name on the map: Jesus Green. If he takes the path that slashes it diagonally, he can follow the river path to the left and cross back to Chesterton Road. He reaches the dark wooden bridge and stops in the middle, letting a couple of students pass.

'Darren, stop this very moment!'

Taras turns his head towards the scream. A toddler runs across the bridge. An harassed, overweight young mother tries to catch him. She is slowed down by dragging after her an empty pushchair and her broken leadership skills. The boy understands his mother's scream as the command, 'Go!' and starts to climb the latticed railings.

'Look, Mum! Flower shwim-min!' He is balancing on the balustrade, bending over the water. Taras calmly steps behind the boy and gently, as if picking up a kitten, slides his hands under the tiny armpits. He lifts the light body into the air and puts Darren firmly on the bridge, to face the consequences and his mother.

'Oh, thanks!' She puffs out with obvious relief. 'It's such a dangerous place! A kid died here last year.'

'How did he die?' asks Taras.

'Fell into the water. It's quite shallow here, but he hit the lock and broke his neck. See those lilies? His mother brings a bouquet here every week. It floats down the river when they open the lock for the barges.'

Taras can just see white petals among the debris of twigs, cigarette butts, scraps of wrappers by the lock wall.

The girl's voice changes into another high-pitched scream: 'Darren, stop! Wait! Don't cross the road, there's a car coming! Darren, *do as you are told*!' She waves at Taras hastily and continues the daily race, chasing her escaping child.

Lucky boy, thinks Taras. Gliding through his carefree existence, unaware of the dangers awaiting him at every corner . . .

Holding back the desire to skip, he walks to the hotel a touch faster than usual – to plan, to prepare. The girl has just given him an idea . . .

The next day, he calls Karpov from his hotel room. An international call to his boss's country *dacha* takes an eternity to come through. After the necessary jokes about the weather, the conversation moves to the list of presents: fishing tackle for Karpov, a new Lego set for his grandson.

'So,' echoes the receiver, 'do you think B is the right size?' Taras knows that his boss is not talking about the lingerie for his wife. He is referring to plan B of the operation.

'Yes,' says Taras firmly, 'B should be just right, I think. Thank you, Cambridge is lovely. Too quiet for me though. I might go to London tomorrow.' He replaces the receiver and looks out of the window, watching a fat, puffy-faced woman pulling a shopping trolley crammed with Co-op groceries. He rises decisively.

He is not going to sit here procrastinating, dragging his days like a supermarket trolley. London tomorrow, then back – for reconnaissance and preparation.

The midday train is cutting through the fields, taking only a handful of cheap day return passengers to the capital. Taras has four comfortable seats and a table to himself. In fact, he has the whole carriage to himself, apart from a snoring pensioner in one corner and a snogging school-skiving couple in another.

He opens his brown briefcase and takes out the file.

May 1748. Top secret. To His Excellency General Pustovitov, the Head of Secret Police, St Petersburg. From the agent Khristoforov Zakhar. On devitsa *Sofia Polubotko, granddaughter of the late Cossack Colonel Pavlo Polubotko.* Doneseniye.

Currently travelling through France. Further surveillance recommended. We kindly request your permission to inform our Ambassador in London, Count Saltykov, about her trip.

What an interesting word is this old-fashioned *doneseniye*, thinks Taras. It means both 'a secret report with accusations' and 'something carried to the end'. Is that because every *doneseniye* carries the burden of lies and betrayal?

'Take the report on the trip of that *devitsa*, Sofia,' Colonel Karpov had said to him at lunch. 'It must have been quite a thing to travel across Europe on her own more than two centuries ago. How high must the stakes have been for her to dare to do *that*?'

Chapter 6

Champagne, France, May 1748

She has lost all sense of time. By now the creak of the worn-out wheel-springs has no beginning and no end, just the same pattern of tones, over and over again.

The sleeping coach, which at the beginning of her journey seemed so luxurious compared to *polukartok* – the light open carriage her father used for trips to the fairs – is now all corners and angles, her elbows and back marking every pothole of the poor French roads. And she had thought that long horseback rides in the steppes and tough winters at the *hutir*, their lonely farm, had prepared her for the journey!

'Sofia should have been born a boy,' is the most frequent comment in her household. As a child, while the *hutir* girls were playing with straw dolls, Sofia, if she was not up a cherry tree in the orchard or riding through the pastures, could be found in a shady corner trying to read the leather-bound books from her grandfather's *skrynya*. This heavy oak chest, her grandfather's portrait and two silver candelabra were the only pieces salvaged from their previous house. Her mother had once shown her an engraving of a five-window mansion in Chernihiv. The family had abandoned it hastily, tipped off by a well-wisher about the search warrant from the notorious Russian Secret Police. 'We used to be very rich, Sofia.' Olena's words had stuck in her throat.

But Sofia does not feel so destitute now. Her parents have ten pairs of helping hands at the *hutir*, they own a mill, twenty beehives, three hundred grey cows of the famous breed so sought-after at the fairs, and they can hunt in the woods of the *Sotnyk*, the richest local landowner. Sofia is quite contented with her life. In fact, she has only been seen crying once, when she was fifteen, when Father sold her favourite stallion together with forty other horses to a merchant from Breslau. When Sofia heard about that, she did not scream, did not wail, as the *hutir* women would do. She just walked out of the courtyard, hollow-eyed. Her gait, her shoulders cried for her with every step – hurting, hating, bitter, beaten, betrayed.

Late that night, the torches of the search-party were frantically zigzagging the courtyard, ready to spill out into the woods: 'The poor girl could meet anybody out there, and the humans might be more dangerous than wolves these days!'

Sofia came back at dawn, walked across the room to kiss the *obrazok* and curled up on the bench, her face to the wall, the metallic taste of silver still on her lips. She was breathing in the smell of damp clay, mixed with the scent of wormwood and peppermint, drying on the oak beam above her. Slowly, carefully, she was breathing out her pain . . .

On the day of her sixteenth birthday, walking with her father from the stables, Sofia announced, her voice trembling, what she had rehearsed a hundred times in her mind. 'I have been thinking about the Kiev Academy, *Tato*. I want to study there.'

'That is impossible.' For once, Yakiv Polubotko was relieved that this time, things could not go the way his daughter wanted. 'Only the sons from noble families can be accepted at the Academy.'

'But I am from a noble family,' Sofia protested.

'Yes, but you seem to forget that you are a girl.' Yakiv tried to be patient.

'*Tato*, but the Academy was founded by a woman! And our Panas has a place there already, but you know he is more interested in sabres and pistols, and he doesn't want to go. I am determined to study, *Tato*, whatever it takes. I have to see the world. Look what happened to Olexiy.'

The story of Olexiy Rozum, the innkeeper's son, was a village legend. When he was not wandering dreamily with the family flock of sheep, he had sung in the choir of a little village church, which stood on the post-road to Chernihiv. 'You might as well sing – you are no good as a shepherd,' his father had grumbled.

Olexiy's fate had a double chin and smelled of expensive tobacco. An imperial courier, sent by the Russian Empress Yelizaveta to get some rare Tokay wine from Hungary, had stopped at the inn to change horses and rest on the way back to St Petersburg. He was opening his silver snuffbox when he heard Olexiy's voice. It was pure, angelic, totally out of place in the sooty darkness of the inn.

When the courier took Olexiy Rozum with him to seek his fortune in the capital, he was twenty-two, ignorant and talented. A few years later, now called Alexey Razumovsky, he had become one of the chief choristers in the Court Chapel, then a Count, then a Field Marshal. There was even a rumour that the Empress was charmed not only by his voice . . .

Yakiv looked at his daughter. He knew that if he said no, Sofia would walk out that very minute. Not run away, but walk out with dignity, never looking back.

'Think again, girl,' mumbled Yakiv. 'Remember, your name means "wisdom" in Greek.'

That autumn, Panas Polubotko was admitted to Sodales Minoris Congregationis and given a tiny room at the *boursa*, a student's house on the embankment, not far from the Academy. There were two fraternities – the Sodales Majoris for philosophers and theologians, and the Sodales Minoris for younger students. Though the full course lasted thirteen years, many students would come from Latin schools in the middle of the course, stay for two years and then leave the Academy to continue their education at the universities of Bologna, Strasbourg, Berlin or Konigsberg. Some of them left to do their military service, whilst others went to work as Chancellery officials.

So far, nobody had suspected that Panas was, indeed, Sofia. Life at the *hutir* had made her strong and fit, and the tender smoothness of her cheeks did not surprise anybody; some students were much younger than her. In a dark-blue loose coat, her cropped hair resembling an upturned pot, she plunged into the world of lectures, dramas and disputes with the naïve audacity of a novice. She marched under the congregational banner to the Monastery of Lavra for the monthly open disputes. She sang Psalms in the streets to earn some money – and then, with a coin in her hand, she would hurry to the Cabinet de Lecture, a bookshop full of treasures, or to the art shop, run by a merchant from Lombardy. Her coins could not buy her much, but she would spend hours dreaming of what she would buy if she saved enough.

Sofia's academic year was highlighted by a remarkable event – the first official visit of Yelizaveta, the Empress of All Russias, to the city. Kiev was at the very frontier of her Empire, and Peter the Great's daughter had travelled slowly, visiting innumerable shrines and monasteries on the way. She was rumoured to be in a bad mood, fatigued by the journey, infuriated by the recent conspiracy against her. The Kievites, in fear that Her Majesty might find their city less than inspiring, spared no cost or effort in the preparations for the solemn entry of the Royal procession.

The procession drove into the city through the Golden Gates, where an actor, dressed as Kiy, the founder of Kiev, approached the first carriage on a chariot with two winged Pegasuses and offered the Empress the keys to the obedient city. She was greeted by the students of the Academy, dressed as Greek gods and heroes. Sofia, dressed as Apollo, could not take her eyes off Yelizaveta. But who was the man in the Field Marshal's uniform next to her in the carriage? Could it be Olexiy, their singing shepherd? Sofia looked at him and thought: He will not be the only one from our village to go far. One day I'll be the talk of the village too! *Tato* will be proud of me, I know he will be. Maybe even Olexiy will be proud of me . . .

Her chance came three months later. She was poring over *De Istituzione Grammatica*, fighting with the conjugations, when the door burst open. She had forgotten how big her father was; her tiny, tidy, dark room suddenly became cluttered, claustrophobic.

'Oh, *Tato*! I have so much to—' She rushed to Yakiv, and only now noticed his concerned frown. 'Is everything all right at home?' She could hardly hear herself whisper.

Yakiv sat on her bed, looking out of the window.

'Your mother and sisters send their regards. Panas says he misses you.' He turned to her. He looked so sorrowful that Sofia's stomach churned and she almost missed the meaning of what he was saying: 'Sofia, I am glad that you are happy here. I love you more than life, you know, and I trust you more than myself. But I need your help, Sofia, I really do. This is bigger than my love for you, more important than your studies. I received a letter from France. You need to go to London. Come home with me, I'll explain everything.'

At first, Sofia opened her mouth to protest. She wanted to say that she was not ready, that one year was not enough – all right, it was more than enough for Latin, but not for Rhetoric and Philosophy – that she could not possibly do what was asked of her. She was sinking in the sea of new discoveries, fears, questions so quickly, that to save herself from drowning, she blurted out: 'Of course, Father. When do I have to leave?'

She has been travelling for a month now, dressed as a student going to the German University to continue his studies. There is nothing unusual in such a journey. Yakiv first suggested that she should travel by sea: south, to Sych, the Cossack state, and then on board a trading vessel across the Black Sea. But her mother protested. 'Sometimes,' she whispered to Sofia, echoing the wayfarers' winter evenings stories, 'noble widows travelling to holy places fall into the Tartar traps in the steppes and,' she lowered her voice, as if the robbers could hear her, 'their possessions are stolen and the poor women sold at the Kafa slave market in Crimea.' Yakiv hid a smile in his jet-black moustache, but Olena's mask of sorrow, resolutely worn for the next three days, made him consider the alternatives.

Sofia could have taken the river route. Local flax and hemp,

Yakiv told her, were transported by barges, then by road through Russian territory to the Baltic port of Riga and thence shipped to England. But Sofia rebelled at that. Heavy, 30-ton barges, creeping along the Desna River, always reminded her of the fat snails that lived in the overgrown corner of their kitchen garden: slothful and drowsy, dark moist sides, heavy carcasses on top. She would much rather travel with a caravan of *chumaki*, the Cossack traders whose carts, loaded with salt, grain, linen and leather, rumbled across Europe.

'*Tato*,' she turned to her father, 'their routes are well-trodden and safe; nobody has a better knowledge of when to travel and where to stop.' Besides, several *chumaki* families lived in the nearest village, and her dearest parents would have been much happier if she were looked after by the neighbours during her journey, wouldn't they?

Her mother turned away, muttering prayers into the far corner of the room, where the fragile light of an incense candle flickered under the tarnished silver of the *obrazok*, her dowry icon. But Yakiv nodded approvingly. He was quietly proud of his daughter's curious mind and avid desire to travel. 'The real Cossack spirit,' as he would say.

The *chumaki* caravan followed the Westward Trail to Poland and Prussia, which ran almost all the way on *hostinets* – the broad, dusty road, alongside wild meadows, where the grass would reach the bellies of the free-roaming horses, past the clean and orderly villages with small whitewashed, thatched houses.

The traders shared with her the ancient, unwritten code of the road. She learned how to convert the caravan into a small fortress for the night, with carts blocking all the corners. She loved their plain food and simple jokes, but most of all she enjoyed the fireside stories about the old times and the real Cossacks, called 'the new knights of Europe' a hundred years ago. She learned about the *charakterniki*, the indestructible Cossacks, who would not burn in fire, could live underwater, could turn into animals and throw red-hot canon balls with their bare hands; about the Cossacks' fearless warfare. 'War to them, Sofia, was water to fish. To die in the battle was all they dreamed about.'

There was only one story she did not like – about the golden rule of the Cossack state not to have women around, under the threat of the death penalty: neither sisters, nor lovers, nor mothers.

'Why did they have this rule?' she asked an old *chumak*.

'They were soldiers, Sofia, with strict military discipline. How could they waste their time on love and marriage?' he replied, winking at her. Sofia frowned and bit her lip, but did not ask any more questions.

After Warsaw, the girl was left on her own to go through Poland to Bohemia, then to Nurnburg and then through Nancy, the residence of the Dukes, to Lorraine. Not entirely on her own, though. Vasil, their family servant, came as a coachman. The war in Europe was over, but the roads still swarmed with robbers. Sofia's carriage was stopped once on the road to Olys. She was already clasping her father's heavy Turkish pistol, ready to defend herself. But the brigands decided not to bother with a poor scholar. Little did they know that the iron rims of the carriage were stuffed with golden coins, carefully hammered in by Yakiv.

'We are here, Sofia!' shouts Vasil at last.

Sofia looks out of the window. They are passing a small sandstone church. The spike of the lead dome looks like the beak of a thirsty bird, desperate for a drop of rain. The carriage crosses a bridge with carved, sad-faced sea-monsters, and stops. Sofia steps out and stretches, getting used to her legs again.

There is a gate at the end of the bridge, with crisscrossed swords on the emblem, and a poplar alley leading to a building that looks like a château. She walks unsteadily to the fast-moving shallow river, washes her face, letting the water run through her fingers. The water changes her reflection into hundreds of sparkling ripples: an exhausted student in a dusty, crumpled blue coat. 'Time to be yourself, Sofia,' she smiles and hobbles to the château, delighted that this part of her journey is finally over.

'We are approaching London King's Cross. Please make sure that you take all your belongings with you.'

Taras is grateful for the reminder. Sofia still has a fair amount of travelling to do before she reaches London, but Taras has already arrived there. Placing the folder about Sofia's journey into the briefcase again, on top of Oksana's file, he pats the plastic almost tenderly. He has to look after these two girls, divided by centuries, united by the same name, holding the same secret.

Not for long now, not for long.

Chapter 7

London, March 2001

'There's a visitor in Reception for you, Miss Fletcher,' chirrups Amy. 'No, he can't make an appointment for tomorrow. He says it's urgent, and he's only in the country for one day. He's already been waiting for an hour. No, Kate can't see him. She's not here. You're the only one left in the office.

'Miss Fletcher will see you now, Mr Voy . . . Vysh . . . Vyshnevsky,' she continues cheerfully, turning to the visitor. 'It's a shame Kate is not in the office at the moment. Not only because her name is also str—' she almost says 'strange', but quickly corrects herself, 'because she's got a name like yours, but you would find her much easier to deal with. She is our expert on Eastern Europe.' There is more to her smile than professional training, since Mr Vyshnevsky is an attractive young man, dressed in an expensive, understated Savile Row suit.

Taras smiles back. He is quite pleased with himself: he managed to find out the girl's name (Amy), discover the origin of her accent (Essex) and is about to see a senior partner at the prestigious law firm – all with his conversational experience of one three-hour interrogation session in the Hotel Ukraina. If only he had had more chance to practise before this trip! How does the proverb go? 'Practice does perfect?' Or 'Practice makes perfection?'

His inner lesson is interrupted by a rustle. 'Mr Vyshnevsky, sorry to have kept you waiting. How can I help you?'

Taras has no time to consider the grammatical construction he has just heard. He turns in the direction of the monotonous female voice, saying, 'Baron Vyshnevsky, actually – the Polish government was kind enough to return the title to our family. I am sorry that I came without an appointment, but I am only in London for a couple of days. I just need to speak to somebody about a family matter. It is extremely confidential . . . Your firm is renowned for its discreet and straightforward approach. I am sure I can count on that, Miss Fletcher?' He pauses, waiting for confirmation.

'Fine. We can talk in Reception, there is nobody here.' She gestures over at the cream armchair he has left a minute ago.

Miss Fletcher is not exactly a picture of grace. A picture of greyness, more like: the suit colour, the hair shade, even the skin tone. He should find out from Amy the last name of that other solicitor – Kate, wasn't it? – for his next visit. If he ever needs the next visit . . .

Miss Fletcher is looking at something above his head, not at Taras. 'This blue and white print next to the clock – is it new? I have never noticed it before.' She turns to Amy. 'Who chose it? It's absolutely ghastly. Not at all the professional image we are trying to project.' She marches to the far corner, not giving Amy a chance to respond. Taras gives the print a closer look as he passes it: very Impressionist, a blurred image created by a myriad white and blue dots. Obviously, it is not precise enough for Miss Fletcher. Clarity is her weapon.

They settle in the corner, Miss Fletcher facing the window, Taras facing her and the picture. He picks up where she interrupted him. 'As I have said, this is a very delicate and confidential matter. My great-grandfather escaped from Poland at the beginning of the twentieth century. It was a troubled time for my country, but he managed to sell his breweries and deposit the money in London. The title was returned to the family, but as for the breweries, we still have to buy them out from the state. The family has decided to use the money deposited in London. We need to know how we can claim the inheritance and how soon we could get the money.'

'It is not that simple, Mr Volishy . . .' Miss Fletcher gives up. 'It is not that simple, Baron.' It seems simple enough to her though. Taras does not need to ask any more questions. Miss Fletcher is sailing in familiar waters: the legal world is her reality. They don't teach communication skills there however; an hour later, Taras manages to escape with all the facts he needs, but without providing any additional information or leaving his contact details.

He leaves Lincoln's Inn and strolls down to the Embankment, airing his information overload. He absorbs the sights and sounds of the busy river, oblivious to the other stream of heavily polluted, enraged, congested traffic on his left.

The clouds, tired of fighting for a place over London, have retreated for a short break, giving the sunshine a chance to linger for a while. What a chameleon of a city, thinks Taras:

the buildings, which change colour from grey to yellow under the rare rays of sun, with the green, dappled lizard spots of squares and parks thrown in. The rhythm changes too: slow-paced around the clubs and galleries of St James, accelerating into the regular, stern-faced beat of the City, pulsating in a frenzied techno-spin around the Soho nightclubs.

Taras's impersonation routine fits the mood of this changing capital. He enjoyed the invented name, the Baron's clothes. He had to rehearse his Polish accent for hours. He acted strictly according to the operational manual: located the place, found out the timescale – all without revealing the operational goals.

He came well prepared: Karpov supplied him with a list of legal firms working in Eastern Europe. Taras studied a map of central London for hours, looked at the detailed description of the firms until he chose this one. Well known, but not too pompous. Middle of the road – quite literally, with offices in the middle of the row.

Taras considers the information Miss Fletcher armed him with. If it takes more than a year for a Polish Baron to claim his inheritance, then for a country on the verge of economic collapse, with the sums involved, it would take much longer. The stakes are so high, though. It could be this country's lottery ticket, its only chance of survival.

Analytical mind, good ability to understand a bigger picture was written in his graduation appraisal. He fully understands what dangerous consequences this game could lead to, what conflicts could erupt. At the moment he is the only one who could stop the process. What was the slogan on that T-shirt his former academy mate Adamov gave him last year: *Destined for greatness, but pacing myself.*

In the hotel bathroom he washes his hands for longer than usual, practising his open, shy smile in the mirror. He is ready for the next step.

Chapter 8

KATE

London, March 2001

'It was the lighting,' she reassures herself. 'That eerie lighting was the reason.' She is standing over the sink, her eyes closed, unsure what to do with her hands. She tries to remember the nightclub: a stuffy room with a small dance floor, criss-crossed with throbbing shadows. The artificial blue sheen filled the room, making the faces pale, almost cadaverous. Or was it the blaring techno music? It was not the drink, that's for certain. She only had one glass of champagne, and another glass of acidic white wine, and then Philip introduced her to Mojitos. They were very light, he said, mostly lime juice and mint leaves, so she only had a couple – maybe . . . or was it more?

A steel band is squeezing her temples tighter and tighter, swirling her into a spiral of pain. Kate lifts heavy eyelids and slowly turns her fragile head to the alarm clock on the windowsill. No surprises there. She is already late. She needs to move now, if she wants to get to the conference. It would be easier to attend and pretend than to explain to Carol Fletcher that she could not make it because she had been clubbing until dawn. Kate has to admit, her boss is an exceptional and zealous

79

lawyer, but her relationship with legal papers is much stronger than with people.

The part of her brain that is awake assesses the situation. Philip has already left for the office, so he can't help. Well, she probably couldn't talk to him anyway. Her mouth is parchment-dry, her palate like sandpaper to her tongue.

Kate stretches her left hand out, fumbles through the box on the bathroom shelf, as if she is playing a Touch and Guess game in the children's activity centre. She guesses the washed cotton softness of Philip's crumpled handkerchief, the twisted plastic of a hairclip she thought she had lost. The cool foil smoothness of the pack of painkillers is not there. She will have to venture downstairs. Her bag normally has so many exciting, unexpected things in it, she never knows what she may find. But she will have to track down the bag first.

What time did they get back home this morning? She tries to remember the celebrations in the exclusive Members Only club: the stylish bar crowd, languidly eyeing each other, on the watch for celebrities. A triumphant look on Philip's face when the waiter asked a relaxed group at the corner sofa to leave because his, Philip's, party had arrived. To her relief, talking over that resounding music was almost impossible – they don't have much to say to each other these days. Maybe Philip's secondment to the New York office is not such a bad thing after all.

'Kate will join me every other weekend, it will be great,' he was saying to Mark and Alex yesterday. He was patting Kate's knee absent-mindedly as he was talking – a gesture long forgotten. Or maybe it was just a result of all the cocktails he had drunk?

In an ultimate attempt to shake off her headache, she staggers into the shower and, after some hesitation, turns the lever to blue.

Icy water helps a little, and her thoughts jump to something she has tried to avoid for the last three months – her relationship with Philip. When did they start to build the wall between them? They add little glass bricks every day, cementing them with silences and misunderstandings. They can still see each other, still manage to shout across sometimes, honing their building skills in pointless arguments.

Recently, waiting at a supermarket delicatessen counter, she read the descriptions of the cheeses in the display cabinet. In an attempt to educate her taste buds, the supermarket experts were suggesting the choice of five strengths – 'full-bodied, very strong, mature, mellow, very mild'.

That's what their relationship had been like at the beginning – 'full-bodied and very strong'. Kate had bumped into Philip during the Freshers' Week at the overcrowded Buttery bar. She was literally pushed into meeting him. The excitement of instant friendships and accessible alcohol was spilling into erratic gestures, and somebody's elbow just shoved her into Philip's back. She felt his shoulder blades through thick cotton, breathed in cigarette smoke mixed with lavender. A waft of familiar detergent suddenly made her homesick. She stood there, lost and vulnerable, for a moment, then he turned. They ended up in her room that night. By then they were both quite drunk and it was a hasty, greedy passion. They taught each other tenderness later.

They became inseparable. Once, for a Rag Week challenge, they even walked around the campus all day with their elbows and ankles tied together, dragging each other to lectures, trying to imagine how Siamese twins must feel. And they giggled, and chuckled and laughed. Philip was reading Maths, Kate was reading History.

For Philip her course was a permanent source of jokes. 'Seriously, Kate how can you study this: "Protests in Plantagenet England"?' he would ask, laughing. 'What use will you ever find for that?'

'You just don't get it, do you?' Kate tried to be patient. 'You know Macpherson, our tutor – the one always wearing hand-knitted pullovers – look what he has written: *'Hi-story has to be greeted personally. As if you are saying: "Hi, story!" You look at the stories of real people, examine lives ruined by decisions of the politicians, analyse power games led by individuals, look how they influence the lives of millions.'*

'I grew up with this sort of history, Philip. My *babusya* – my Ukrainian nan, Dad's mother, you know – well, she used to tell me all these stories about the Cossacks when I was little, and I imagined a brave boy in a light *chaika* boat, or a drunken Colonel on a horse. Stop it, Phil, or I'll start mocking your formulas – they're dry and lifeless, like stick insects! And if you ask me what practical use there is in reading history, then let me explain: it gives you a perspective, gives you the whole list of "transferable skills", and it will definitely help when I do a Law conversion course.'

Their university was considered prestigious, and at the milk round, where the companies selected their new workforce, Philip got a job in a big City auditing firm. Kate stayed behind to do the Law course.

During that year they did not see much of each other, and their phone calls were from different planets: he was full of his new job and the thrills of London, while she was drowning in belated attempts to achieve academic perfection. The First remained a dream, but Kate still managed to get a job in a small, well-respected London law firm.

When they moved in together, Kate discovered that she was now living with a different Philip – white-shirted, pin-striped, with a polite smirk instead of the disarming smile she adored. They rented a house in the right part of town – the one which counted with his workmates; they ate at the right places and met the right people. Philip travelled a lot, entertaining clients, working late, coming home too tired to talk. Most nights she shared her takeaway with a nagging anguish, the fear of a child trapped in a dark room. Afraid to run, afraid to stay, afraid to scream.

When the relationship taste changes to 'mild', thinks Kate, you realise the true sense of be-long-ing: you are longing for little things, that make love real. A glance, a touch, a quick note . . .

She pulls the curtains and presses her nose and forehead against the cold glass. It brings temporary relief and gives her an idea of the weather outside. She turns to the mirror doors of the wardrobe, trying not to look at herself. Her tousled brown hair could be classified as the grave error of a trainee stylist. She needs to do some careful painting in a minute, to cover the blue circles under her eyes and to change her pallid face tone to a healthy apricot. Art was never her favourite subject at school, but today she has no option.

She tries to think about the conference. She did not want to go in the first place, since she finds these things a waste of time, but Carol said, 'Such events are a must for networking, especially for a young, aspiring lawyer.' She can always find an argument to which it is impossible to respond. 'Aspiring to what? To become like you?' Kate nearly asked, but looked at Carol's tightly zipped lips and decided against it. Any advice from Carol sounded like a verdict. Kate has been sentenced to four hours in the company of a hundred complete strangers, who were pretending to listen to a dozen well-phrased common opinions. Well, by the time she gets to the conference, she might be lucky – her punishment might be reduced to an hour.

She knows why she was invited, since the conference is about changes in Eastern Europe, about 'the new political agenda'. She is supposed to be – no, she *is* – quite interested in the events in Ukraine. In fact, it was her unpronounceable Ukrainian last name that had secured her the job in the first place.

When the Iron Curtain lifted, many Ukrainians who had come to Britain after the Second World War for different reasons, through various routes, developed acute bouts of nostalgia and started looking for relatives. They would visit the villages and towns where they had grown up, find their long-lost relations, however distant, even try to leave them some inheritance. Perhaps, by doing that, they were hoping to return home after death. In fact, many did, leaving money for burial in their birthplaces.

One of the senior partners in the law firm where Kate now worked had a Ukrainian neighbour and spotted the market niche quickly. He knew that old Ukrainians were a tight bunch. They tended to live in clans of their own, strictly adhering to all their traditions and religious holidays, remaining suspicious of 'foreigners' even after many years of living abroad. So, for writing their Wills and dealing with other legal matters, they would rather turn to a young lawyer with a Ukrainian name, than to an experienced Smith or Jones.

The bouts of nostalgia were contagious. Kate chanted a mantra, 'It is unprofessional to get personally involved,' many times, and yet found herself listening to more and more life stories, arranging flights and funerals, searching for the relatives of her clients, instead of working full-time on Wills and Grants of Probate.

She did not speak Ukrainian, but loved the melody of the language and could pick up some words she recognised from her grandmother's prayers. *Babusya* came to England from Germany after the war. She never talked about her past. Only once had Kate heard from her a story about a teenage girl, who was forced by Nazi soldiers into a train together with other Ukrainian girls. She was sent to hard labour camps, then worked for a German farmer. The farmer's family was kind to her, and even gave her some cups as a farewell present. Kate did not ask *Babusya* the name of the girl, but from that day on, every time she was visiting her grandmother's house, she would peep into a cupboard. There, on the top shelf, behind brightly coloured wooden *pysanky*, Easter eggs, was the old lady's pride and joy. A Meissen china service. Twelve cups and saucers with a dainty flower design. The blue petals were like veins, showing through aristocratic skin. *Babusya*'s house was full of other peculiar, impractical, magical things. Cushions, embroidered in red and black; plastic flowers so richly purple, they seemed even more artificial than they were; an icon in an ornate silver framework; books in an unknown alphabet.

It was a world of make-believe, of touch-pretend, of playing to oblivion, interrupted only by her grandmother's gentle but firm calls for dinner.

One day Kate was playing at being a princess who went to tea with her royal grandmother. She tried to pick up a china cup with appropriate delicacy, but the brittle treasure slipped through her fingers, and with more a sigh than a crack, fell to the floor, shattering into tiny fragments.

Time stopped. The almond-eyed Madonna pulled her grown-up Jesus closer, looking at Kate reproachfully from the wall. Eleven beauties on the shelf were mourning the death of the twelfth.

Kate's fantasy world turned hostile. From now on she was a menace, an intruder, a wicked witch. Kate was still in shock an hour later. She was sitting on the sofa, her palms squeezed between her knees, rocking herself backwards and forwards. Her grandmother's attempts to distract, to cuddle, to talk were met with a jarring change of the nervous rhythm. *Babusya* had to do something fast. She opened the cupboard decisively, and reached for her cherished cups. She smashed them one at a time, looking straight into Kate's eyes, repeating: 'See? You matter to me much, much more than those pieces of porcelain!' It was a quiet, harmonious dance – the ringing sound of the cups striking the floor, the graceful wave of *Babusya*'s hand – one-two-three-four, one-two-three . . . Kate stopped rocking and watched, mesmerised.

When the sixth cup turned into white pieces, she jumped up, clung to *Babusya*'s warm thigh and started chanting a Ukrainian prayer. She had heard *Babusya* whispering it so many times before, that the words she remembered but could not understand, rolled out of her mouth like glistening marbles, as if she were practising the notes of a melody she had known for a long time but had never dared to sing aloud. It was her first step into reality, her first lesson of the complex subject 'coping with loss'. Her imaginary world had let her go. *Babusya*'s prayer became a ritual, a reminder of her strength.

Another ritual was *Babusya*'s Christmas soup. Every year on 6 January the family would gather around *Babusya*'s table for the Holy supper, the Ukrainian Christmas Eve – according to the Gregorian calendar and the Orthodox tradition. Kate loved the celebration. She was the only one at school to have two Christmases and, more importantly, two lots of gifts from *Babusya*.

The table for the Holy Night, the annual masterpiece, was a

Lenten fare of twelve dishes, but Kate could hardly eat anything. She was waiting for *kutya*, a 'liquid Christmas pudding', as she once explained it to her schoolfriends, made from steamed poppy seeds, wheat, raisins, honey and nuts. Her heart would beat faster in anticipation of the moment when relaxed, replete conversation at the table would stop and her grandmother would solemnly bring in a big soup tureen. It was the time when everybody was united by taste, that rare time when her mother would smile at her father, when her toddler brother would sit still. Kate was always served first. She was the main participant in the Ceremony of the First Spoon. *Babusya* would ask anxiously, 'How is it?' And Kate would reply, weighing every word, a real connoisseur, giving an official opinion.

'Not bad, *Babusya*. Can I have some more?' To eat *kutya* on any other day of the year would have taken the magic away, and Kate always looked forward to the next big day, to her exclusive right of approval.

But apart from the second Christmas and the melody of childhood prayers, Ukrainian roots had never been an important part of Kate's life. They were an echo from the past, something unusual to tell or not tell her new boyfriends, to justify her last name, in which vowels tumbled over clusters of consonants.

Kate's name is always misspelled and now she can see yet another version of it on a card, gleaming at her from the far end of the conference room. To reach her seat she has to walk (or run, or crawl – the choice is yours, she thinks ruefully) directly in front of the speaker. On another day she would rather die of shame on the spot or prefer a softer option and stand near the door waiting for the conference to end. But today, with her senses numbed by headache and tiredness, she does not really care.

While she is pondering whether to hunker down along the wall and then make a final quick move to her chair or duck to her seat across the room, the Chairman announces the final speaker, the Ukrainian Minister of Finance. There is a stir of genuine interest, and not only because he is speaking last. He is young and energetic, and his English is surprisingly good. Kate decides that his address is her last chance to get to her seat and braces herself for action.

'What do you know about my country?' he starts. 'Maybe that it has the richest black soil in Europe, poisoned by Chernobyl radiation . . .' He pauses.

Kate moves forward, her eyes firmly on her seat, but does not make it in time. She freezes in the middle of the room, under disapproving stares, as the Minister carries on, 'Or maybe you know Ukraine as a country of good footballers and pretty girls?'

The audience laughs as Kate darts to her seat. She feels herself blushing, as if the audience is laughing at her. She pulls the chair away and finally sits down, just as the Minister turns to more serious subjects.

'Ukraine is not a country well known in the West, and yet it is the second largest country in Europe in territory, the fifth in population, and . . .'

Kate finally relaxes and lets her mind wander. She glances at the programme and the list of participants, handed to her at the door: representatives of companies with interests in emerging markets, City analysts, a couple of students of politics, several journalists. They have already spent two hours in listening mode, practising the expression of sophisticated engrossment. She notices a young man sitting across from her at the table. He is probably not that young, but his fringe and freckled face give him a boyish expression. He is one of those 'permanent boy' types, who never seem to grow old, decides Kate. The Boy, as she has nicknamed him already, is listening, not raising his head, examining the floor. She is not sure whether it is an effect of the speaker's words or whether he is a fellow-sufferer. Another late clubber.

Kate turns her attention to the Minister. His broad shoulders are bursting out of the Armani suit every time he touches his heavy footballer's jaw or drops his heavy palm on the podium to emphasise his point. Kate reminds herself that 'attend and pretend' tactics will only work if she can report to Carol something more substantial than her admiration for the Minister's looks.

Her reminder comes just in time, before his final remark: 'But there are many other hidden treasures in my country. Find them, work with us, and those treasures will work for you.' His last words are met by a jumble of sounds – approving laughter, a wave of relieved applause, shuffling of chairs. 'Good ending to the conference, time for a well-deserved lunch.' A man in a yellow tie next to Kate addresses his remark to a dark-suited City type whose hair is slicked back to perfection. Both are ignoring her. Fair enough – they are united by the first three hours of doldrums.

Kate looks at the unfamiliar faces around her, sighs and heads towards the door. She is pushing her way through the feast of skilful networking: nibbles of gossip in the matter-of-fact conversations, bites of possible useful contacts. A moment later she is stuck. She moves, but does not advance. At first she does not understand why. Then she feels a firm, steel grip – somebody has grasped the sleeve of her jacket.

Kate turns, annoyed, to see who is delaying her. It is The Boy from her table. He is quite tall, looming above her, still holding her jacket sleeve.

'I am sorry, I did not know how to stop you from leaving so quickly. I really want to talk to you.' His accent is hard to place – German or Eastern European, perhaps. The tone of his voice is so apologetic, and the smile hovering over her is so disarming, that Kate surrenders. She finds herself smiling back.

'I don't think we have met before?' she says.

'No, but I saw your name on the place card – it is Ukrainian, isn't it?'

Kate nods reluctantly.

'I have noticed from the list of participants that you are a solicitor,' continues The Boy, 'and I think you might be the right person to help me.'

Kate gives him a closer look. The metal frame of his glasses does not hide the sunny freckles running across his nose. His green eyes, turning down at the corners, make him look like a children's clown. A sad one – either his performance was cancelled or his young audience did not laugh. He stoops slightly, as if to hide his height, and every time he speaks he is nervously brushing his boyish fringe off his forehead with long, thin fingers.

They are the fingers of a surgeon, or a pianist, Kate thinks, then shakes her head, as if to stop her mind from wandering. He is too young to require a Will, but might be of the right age for an inheritance. This conversation could replace her networking session – she would have something to tell Carol about. Kate glances at her watch. She has an hour before her boss will want to see her in the office, so there is still time for a quick espresso at a five-seater Italian sandwich bar near the tube station.

'Would you like a coffee, Mr . . .?' Kate asks in what she considers to be a professionally inviting voice. She is with a client now, and can put both her and his coffee down as 'client entertainment expenses', even if only to annoy Carol.

'Andriy,' he smiles again.

On the way to the bar he tells Kate that he is a researcher, specialising in political changes in society, that he was incredibly lucky to win a research grant to Cambridge. His tutor, a youngish Cambridge Fellow, visited Eastern Europe several times, and Andriy spends hours debating with him the real reasons for the recent rapid changes on the political map. His English is plain and accented, with heavy r's and hard s's, but quite accurate – not many mistakes so far. For some reason yet unknown to Kate, his fringe brushing gets more and more twitchy, and he avoids looking at her. By the time they are perched on the bar stools, she already regrets inviting him for coffee. She puts her elbows on the wiped plastic surface of the counter and gives him an impatient look.

At last Andriy fires an unexpected question at her. 'What did you think about the Minister's speech?'

Great. He was watching her at the conference, caught her expression – 'total absence of presence', as her English teacher used to say. Kate's disappointment is creeping up the scale, changing into irritation.

'He seemed quite . . . quite believable from what I heard. And he made a joke about the treasures – a change from the stern, unsmiling bankers. Why do you ask?'

'I want you to look at this. The documents, as you can see, are not in English, so I have added my translation of the originals. I have spent a long time with the dictionaries, trying to get the exact meaning of every word.'

At that point, Andriy turns from a sad clown into a confident wizard, producing a transparent plastic folder out of thin air.

Kate looks at the neat handwriting with all the t's crossed and the i's carefully dotted. The handwriting of a teacher – somebody keen to inspire. But inspiration is the last thing Kate is feeling at the moment. She is late for the office meeting, and weary, and the steel band is back – not squeezing her head yet, but already resting heavily on her temples. She pushes the folder gently back towards Andriy.

'Could we meet some other time, perhaps? I would love to read it. I really must go now, I am running late, so if you leave me your number . . .' She is already sliding off the stool.

'No, please, just look at this!' He seizes her sleeve again.

Is the sleeve-gripping practice common in his country, or is it just his impulsive manner? wonders Kate. She opens the file reluctantly, to gain a minute or two, to get herself some thinking time for a good escape plan, but is soon engrossed in reading, realising that the thin plastic folder in front of her is holding more than the pages copied in neat teacher's handwriting. The story is fascinating. And big. Enormous even – if it is true, of course.

'There is a spelling mistake,' she comments absent-mindedly. As a solicitor, she has got into the habit of checking every word. 'It says "hetman" here – shouldn't it be with an "i" – a "hitman"?'

Andriy's laughter is so contagious, that Kate lifts her head and smiles, even though she cannot understand why a passing remark about the spelling mistake has led to such a reaction.

'The spelling is absolutely correct,' explains Andriy. 'This is a historical term, and has nothing to do with the gangster world. "Hetman" is certainly not a "hitman", quite the opposite. It is the title for the Cossack Army Commander in the sixteenth century, later becoming the title of the leader of the Cossack state.'

'Oh, I know about the Cossacks,' interrupts Kate. 'My grandmother often called me a Cossack when I was small. I was a real tomboy, loved climbing fences, playing football, and she would say when I grazed a knee: "There, be brave like a Cossack, don't cry!" She is Ukrainian, my nan, by the way. I grew up with her Cossack stories . . .'

Andriy listens avidly, leaning forward, watching her face intently. Kate stops, embarrassed. Why on earth is she telling him the stories of her childhood? A man she has just met, a foreign researcher – and, above all, a potential client.

'Well, if you know so much about the Cossacks, it should make you even more interested in this case,' comments Andriy, as if reading her thoughts. 'What would you say to earning . . .' He conjures up another item, this time a ballpoint pen, and scrawls a figure on the corner of a coffee-stained napkin. Now the handwriting does not inspire at all, but the number does. He shoves the folder back to Kate.

She looks at the number on the napkin: 'Is that what it's worth today?'

'No, that is what you could get if you help me.' Andriy is much calmer now; the fringe has been on his forehead for some time. She prefers it when he sweeps it off; he has quite a high forehead. He adds an equals sign, and three letters – N, O, W and another number.

Kate feels the blood rushing to her cheeks. She shakes her head. 'It is impossible, it is . . .' she glances at the front page of an abandoned copy of the *Financial Times* on the counter '. . . it is more than the Netherlands' GDP!' She tries to sound firm. 'It looks like skulduggery to me.' That is Carol's favourite word. She listens to the sound of it. *Skul-duggery*. Kate imagines it dig into the skull and snap there.

Andriy looks at her earnestly. His knowledge of English does not extend to Carol's vocabulary.

'It is not that difficult to check, is it?' he says coolly. 'And what if it is true?'

'Well, then, it may be . . .' Kate stumbles, looking for the right word '. . . it may be tempting. By the way, where did you get these documents?'

'It would take a long time to explain everything. If you really find it interesting, we can meet again and I will tell you all about it.' He says 'yoooo', dragging it out slightly. His fringe is resting on his forehead; he is far less agitated now.

'Kate . . .' He hesitates. 'Can I ask you to swear that you will not tell anybody about this?'

She thinks of the report she has to produce for her colourless spinster of a boss about today's conference and looks at Andriy. He is either extremely naïve or a brilliant actor. In fact, his face is so solemn that she tries not to giggle. She puts her hand on her heart, says, 'I swear,' and thinks, All we need here is a tree-house and a torch for a real sense of adventure. She takes his number, waves at him, walks to the station. She is pacing herself, trying not to skip the flights of stairs in front of the potential client.

As she rushes into the office, already half an hour late for her meeting with Carol, she wonders which 'no-arguments' phrase is awaiting her today. The new blue and white print in reception slows her down. Nerves and tiredness make Kate an owl with perfect night vision: she observes the world in small detail. The small detail in this painting means a myriad of dots. *Pointillisme.*

When Kate was twelve, her mother took her to the Impressionists exhibition. One of the paintings was a bright chaos of brush-strokes. She did not like it, wandered to another side of the gallery, but some force (well, her mother, actually) asked her to look again. Kate could not believe it. A bright, blooming spring cherry tree was beckoning her from across the room.

Kate steps back, trying to choose the right corner from which to look at the painting. Somebody has done it before her. The best view of the calm, foggy landscape is from the visitors' sofa. That is art therapy: simple, soothing, effective. Wait and enjoy. Maybe that is what her boss is doing at the moment – enjoying her waiting . . .

In the lift Kate wonders which colours she would choose to paint Carol with; which brush-strokes she would use. By the time she reaches Miss Fletcher's office, she decides that geometry would be more appropriate. Defined, precise lines made with a ruler and sharp graphite.

To Kate's surprise, Carol's 'no-arguments' phrase today means just that. She is too busy to have an argument. She raises her head to ask: 'How was the conference?' and sails back into her paper world, where solicitors who are thirty-five minutes late for meetings simply miss the boat. Kate looks at her almost lovingly. Perhaps, with a little retouching, a little colour – red lipstick there, brown eye-shadow here, she could be painted after all.

Something is scratching her elbow. Andriy's plastic folder. They must use a scented disinfectant to wipe the surfaces in that coffee shop, because the plastic folder smells of tangerines. It is too big for her bag, and half of it is sticking out.

Probably, the half she has not read yet. Well, as the meeting with Carol is not meant to be, she might as well do it now. She sits at the desk and pulls out a lined sheet with Andriy's translation of the first document:

A.K. Shevchenko

13 February 1922
Vienna
URGENT. TOP SECRET.

To the People's Commissar of Foreign Affairs from the Ambassador
of the Soviet Socialist Republic of Ukraine to Austria.
   Tovarishch Sveshnikov!
   The extraordinary circumstances demand that I inform you imme-
diately about the meeting I have had today. I have every reason to
believe that this meeting could be of the utmost importance for the
future of our independent socialist state . . .

Chapter 9

Vienna, February 1922

He must have lost all sense of time thinking about his past glory and his present position. By now the chimes are more impatient, the sound has no beginning and no end, reminding him that it's six o'clock. Time to wrap up for the day.

Februaries in Vienna are damp, with grey slush under the feet and the winds getting to your bones. The Ambassador has just spent three hours enjoying this weather at the launch of a new apartment block on the corner of Johannesgasse: flats for workers, with a machine-equipped laundry, public tubs and showers, a Kindergarten, and a large communal courtyard. They are so keen on the lack of privacy, these Social Democrats!

They were very keen to listen to his socialist ideas too. After all, he is representing a new, independent socialist state in the heart of Europe. A state that will grow and prosper, fed by socialist ideas, while the whole of Europe is crawling out of the economic crisis. After two hours of standing and freezing, the Ambassador was invited to make a speech. He told them about the signifi-cance of building homes, not houses; about the importance of participation in *Arbeiterkultur*, the network of athletic competitions and music clubs . . .

The Ambassador didn't mention that socialism was not about playgrounds and paddling pools. It was necessary to create the right symbols, of course, like these housing blocks, to show the future role of the proletariat. To design big posters with vivid, memorable slogans, to replace the icons and the Tsar's portraits. But that was not what socialism was about either. It was about control. It was so much easier to rule a society where everybody was equal. Not equally happy, but equal in the belief in future happiness.

He was tidying the papers on his table, his fingers still red and uncoordinated, looking forward to an early night, but they would never let him, would they? His weasel of an assistant scurried through the door – nose first, sniffing the air for moods and favours.

'There is somebody waiting to see you, *tovarysh Posol*.'

Even though the secretary was pronouncing 'Comrade' in the softer, Ukrainian way, it still sounded harsh, unexpected. Only five years ago he was called 'Master', not 'Comrade Ambassador', and nobody would have dared to interrupt him during his afternoon sleep in the mansion! He had been shrewd enough to back the right horse though: after the revolution, the governments and states were proclaimed like hot race results. His horse had won the race driven by rage and blood. A good mix for mutinies, not enough for running the country. They are giants on ceramic feet, this mob of a government, like those figurines so popular in Vienna now: bizarre, useless, with neither the beauty of the real sculpture nor the functionality of the crafted clay. No skills, no craftsmanship can add value to the cheap, primitive material. These Red bandits would not even know how to manage the family estate that they had taken away from him! Thank God (or whoever these atheists thank now), at least they comprehend that knowledgeable, firm, educated people like him are a rare asset for any government.

His post was regarded as politically important, as the Embassy was one of the first foreign representations of independent Ukraine; he was living in the centre of a recovering Vienna, in a spacious aristocratic flat with fashionable, streamlined furniture, designed by the Wiener Werkstätte, enjoying the exhibitions at the Museum für Kunst und Industrie. He had to face the eternal trade-off of pleasure for power; bartering luxurious textures for solid, inflexible substances. The gold and velvet of the Opera balls for the steel in his voice, the champagne crystal for vodka glasses, the welcoming redbrick of his mansion for the grey concrete of the Red Viennese housing programme.

'*Tovarysh* Ambassador,' his secretary is still standing, fussing, at the door, 'the name of the visitor is Grygor Polubotko. He is the owner of a Ukrainian shop in Northern Argentina. He keeps repeating that it is a matter of state importance. Shall I tell him not to wait?'

The Ambassador has heard about the Ukrainian settlements in Latin America. Farmers, lulled with promises of acres of free land, would move halfway across the world only to discover that the plots were down south, 1,000 kilometres away from Buenos Aires, in the jungle; that red soil was unsuitable for growing wheat; that ants and snakes were in abundance. And yet they persevered, built whitewashed Ukrainian *hatas* with wells in the gardens, ploughed the fields and prayed. The Ambassador is curious, and flattered. 'All right, let him in.' This shopkeeper must have done a bit of travelling to see him in Vienna.

The visitor settles in the corner, obviously uncomfortable in the Ambassador's plush office. He is heavily built, as if cut out of a solid piece of wood. An artisan marionette with awkward, predictable movements: the twitch of a bull's neck, fingers scratching the embroidered stand-up shirt collar, buttoning and unbuttoning the old-fashioned jacket. His broad, sun-tanned face bears an expression of eagerness and uncertainty familiar to the Ambassador. The farmers on his estate looked like that when they were coming to see him with a request.

He wants to return, guesses the Ambassador. Has heard about the social equality and collective farms and wants to join the builders of socialism, misses his Motherland – we've heard it all before. It's strong boots like his I've needed today, not these leaking lace-ups. My feet would have felt so much better now. Warmer. And drier.

After half a minute of constrained silence, the Ambassador is beginning to get annoyed. He knows only too well that successful negotiations are dependent on the timing of a pause. Make it too short, and you lose control. Make it too long, and it becomes hostile.

He waves at the visitor to come closer to his desk. Hopefully, from here this immigrant will not see his drenched feet and soaked trousers. The visitor reads the gesture as an invitation to speak.

'*Pane* Ambassador,' he begins – 'Master Ambassador' – instantly scoring points. 'My name is Grygor Polubotko. I run the Ukrainiana shop in Apóstoles, in the Argentinian province of Misiones. We started with six families in 1897, and now it is a big Ukrainian town with almost ten thousand people. We have a church with thirty-two icons brought from Ukraine, and our children attend the Ukrainian school in the village.

'I run the shop, but I also work on the land. We cultivate yerba maté – Argentinian tea – corn and cotton.' His voice swells with pride in what they have achieved. He uses many obsolete words of the Western Ukrainian dialect and heavily accentuates the end of each phrase, as in Spanish. Wriggling his numb toes, the Ambassador is waiting for the 'but'. It does not come.

'In March last year I received some newspapers from Buenos Aires, and cried with joy,' continues Grygor. The Ambassador scrutinises the wrinkles, cut deeply around the man's eyes, like cracks into the soil during the drought and imagines the salty liquid disappearing into them before reaching the cheeks.

'On the twenty-first of March 1921 the President of Argentina was the first in Latin America to officially recognise Ukraine as an independent state. We are all waiting for the first Ambassador of Ukraine to arrive in Buenos Aires,' continues the shopkeeper.

'You will have to wait for some time, you ignorant idiot, as Argentina has recognised the wrong state. Not the Ukrainian Socialist Republic, but the government of the Ukrainian People's Republic, which is now illegal and in exile. Is that what you crossed the ocean for?' the Ambassador is about to say, but decides in favour of saving his sore throat. He nods to Grygor, and barks, mixing his words with a cough: 'I will inform our government about the success of Ukrainians in Argentina. I am sure that it would help to strengthen the relations between the two countries in future.'

'Thank you. I think there is something I could do to help the independent Ukraine,' says the visitor. 'The matter is of state importance and quite urgent, so I have decided not to wait, but to speak to you.'

Here it comes, thinks the Ambassador. Bet he wants to come back. I was right, as usual.

'As I have mentioned already, my family came to Argentina in 1897,' continues Polubotko, 'I was still a boy, but I remember the journey well – first to France, then a long, difficult ocean crossing. We were promised land, you see, but nobody told us what to expect in Patagonia, nobody gave us any idea of the distances. I remember, even ten years ago, to travel across the country to Buenos Aires I had to use a horse and a cart, and it was such a slow journey! Luckily we have the railway in Posadas now. Anyway, I have returned to see somebody in the Ukrainian Catholic Church, to talk about our youth. You see, they grow up, and move into big cities, and forget their language and their roots . . .'

The Ambassador is losing patience. This shopkeeper has all the time in the world in his jungle, but he, the Ambassador, is a very busy man. And a tired one, too.

'Can you keep to the point, *tovarysh* Polubotko.' He shows his authority, deliberately calling the visitor 'comrade'.

Grygor starts speaking faster, stringing together Ukrainian and Spanish words. Understanding him becomes a challenge even for such an accomplished linguist as the Ambassador.

He rises. 'I am sorry, Comrade Polubotko, I have another meeting.'

The farmer's face changes expression from pleading to demanding. 'As I have told you, the matter is of state importance. I am in possession of a document which could bring the Independent Ukraine the sum of . . .'

Three hours in the freezing cold have affected my hearing, thinks the Ambassador, and asks Grygor to repeat the figure.

The shopkeeper's hand moves stiffly from the jacket button to the pocket. He produces a piece of paper, folded in four, and hands it to the Ambassador. He backs away from the table, but this time decides to give his button a rest and puts his hands in his pockets.

The Ambassador notices that Grygor has carefully rolled his palms into fists before sinking them into the lining. Preserving his working tools in cloth, he jokes to himself as he unfolds the sheet, covered in scribbles. He reads then rereads it several times, his expression changing: surprise, concentration, appreciation. Eyebrows up. Lips in a tight circle. As if he were an actor, trying on the Greek masks before the performance.

By now the pause is totally controlled by the visitor. His tone is measured; he has the confidence of a survivor reliant only on his own mind, hands and intuition. 'Like I said, to get to Argentina we travelled through France first. The document was given to my father by a French family; they were the keepers for over one hundred and fifty years. I have brought you a copy. The original is at home, in Apóstoles. I didn't want to drag it across the continents until time dictates its presentation. As you can see, *pane* Ambassador, the conditions of the Will make it possible now to claim the money for the first time in two hundred years.'

'But why don't *you* do it? Just you, without sharing it with anybody, you dullard?' the Ambassador is about to shout, but after inhaling deeply, he breathes out only the first part of the question.

The shop owner-cum-farmer shakes his head, scratching his neck against the collar: 'I cannot claim the money myself. According to the second condition, the descendant has to live in Ukraine. I cannot move back – my life is in Argentina now. However, if the claiming descendant lives outside Ukraine, according to the Will, he can still claim, giving ninety-five per cent of the sum to the Ukrainian government for the development of the new state and keeping five per cent. I was planning to travel to Kiev to talk to the government about this document, but my friends in Buenos Aires warned me that Kiev is now a very dangerous place. It has changed hands twelve times in the last four years, apparently, with various factions fighting for it, so I decided that the safest bet would be to travel to see you in Austria. All I will ask for is five per cent. We need to do so much in Apóstoles. I want to open the repair works for tractors, and another shop, and . . .'

The Ambassador ceases to listen. He is holding in his hand a key to power, not a piece of paper with semi-literate scrawls. With this money, the state could build lots of housing blocks, Red Vienna-style. He would manage the process, and become a national hero. The crowds would worship him and these Red gangsters could not stop him then.

He turns to the farmer. 'We would be eternally grateful to you, *tovarysh* Polubotko. I need to write the report to my government. How long are you going to be in Europe?'

'I have to leave this week.' The sun-tanned face is shadowed by concern. 'The rains are getting heavy, they might wash away the crops.'

He thinks of rain, though soon with his five per cent he could be one of the richest landowners in Argentina! thinks the Ambassador, but says aloud, 'Tell me how to find you. We will contact you within a month.'

The secretary is puzzled that the Argentinian shopkeeper had spent so much time with the Ambassador. He was not invited to take notes at the meeting, nor could he hear the conversation through the heavy door of the Ambassador's office. He is even more intrigued when, after the meeting, the Ambassador does not go straight home, as he had intended. Instead, he spends two hours writing an urgent and confidential report to the Ministry. He pours hot, sticky sealing wax on the back of the envelope and asks the secretary to send it to the *Narkomat* of Foreign Affairs by courier as soon as possible.

So the secretary has to use his imagination. In the report to his controller at the NKVD Foreign Department he describes the secret meeting of the Ambassador with the Head of the Argentinian mission of Ukrainian immigrants – it is a bit of an exaggeration maybe, but had some elements of truth. He suggests that the Ambassador might be playing a double game, especially taking into consideration his bourgeois past. He recommends that the Ambassador's letter be checked before it goes to the secretary of Foreign Affairs. He attaches the Ambassador's letter to his report and sends the package by courier the same evening. Not to the *Narkomat* of Foreign Affairs, but to his boss at NKVD. On the way home he treats himself to a big slice of Sachertorte. Licking the chocolate sauce off his lips, indulging in the smooth richness of an almond sponge, he celebrates his little victory over his snooty, smug, fat-headed bastard of a boss.

Chapter 10

London, March 2001

The silence is becoming awkward. Kate needs to break the ice fast, while it is still a thin layer of the first ground frost. She knows that one careless word or wrong move will ruin everything.

'I should have spotted it straight away,' she repeats, just to say something. Her eyes are firmly fixed on the coffee stain on the table. 'Your first document claims that the Will was deposited with the Bank of England, yet the second document suggests that the Will is in Argentina.'

Andriy offers no comment.

'It does not mean that both documents are forgeries, simply that there is a contradiction. There should be only one original of the Will.'

'Probably,' says Andriy at last.

'Probably what?' Kate finds a one-way conversation exceedingly strenuous.

'The first document states: "*probably* deposited with the Bank of England", as far as I remember.' He sounds unconcerned. 'If you cannot help me any more, I will have to find somebody else.' His eyes are now the colour of a winter sea before the storm.

Kate sighs. 'All right, let me run a couple of checks. I'll give you a call next week.' She regrets it as soon as she says it. The prospect of financial rewards is quite remote; the stakes are too high. When will she master the art of saying 'No'? When will she stop getting involved in the fantasies of others? Besides, she has thousands of niggling bits and pieces to do, as usual, by yesterday.

Getting angry with herself does not help, so she turns to Andriy. He is too outspoken, almost rude. But then, he comes from the world where everyday conversations are as abrupt as socialist slogans. He exudes nervous energy, but softens it with his open smile. She finds him as controversial and intriguing as the documents he pushed across the bar table towards her. His file still has the tangerine smells of that cleaning liquid.

It is curious how direct the link between sense and memory can be: now, when she passes the fruit street-traders or juice bars, when she watches a TV chef slicing the colourful flesh to garnish a new concoction, it always brings the memory of Andriy. Bright, fresh, thin-skinned. A tangy smile. Acid humour. Sweet and sour.

Only when Andriy leaves does she realise what she has committed herself to. *Babusya* has tried to teach her to knit many times, without any success – Kate never had the patience to find the end of the thread in the tangled wool. Andriy's thread is much more elusive. The Wills Kate deals with are all based on the Inheritance Law of 1858. She knows nothing about the Will practice 300 years ago.

Consoling herself that it will at least be educational, Kate slips past Carol to the Law Society Library. Shame she cannot ask her boss for advice after that daft Girl Guide promise to keep a secret.

She steps into another century in the dark, oak-panelled hall in Chancery Lane. The only reminder of the modern age is a young librarian with a spiky haircut wearing a bright lilac shirt. He is staring out of the window, oblivious to the visitor, absent-mindedly pulling at the earring in his left ear. Kate's, 'Excuse me, where can I find something about early eighteenth-century Wills?' sounds like an intrusion.

The Lilac Librarian is very knowledgeable. 'Well, the good news is that we have a lot of information on the subject. We have the indexes of the British Record Society and the Society of Genealogists. We also have Probate Act books and Will Registration books.'

'What is the bad news then?' Kate tries not to sound disheartened.

The librarian is getting his revenge for being disturbed. 'All the documents, written by court clerks up to 1733, were in Latin, as well as the probate comments appended to the bottom of the Wills. The original Wills are usually in Latin or in English. How is your Latin, Miss . . . ?'

'Kate, please.' She quickly saves him from struggling with her last name and attempts a shortcut: 'Would you happen to have any guide to Will writing or inheritance laws around that time? In English, rather than in Latin, please.' For the first time she regrets that in trying to protect her brain from what she considered useless information, she more often than not skived off her Latin and History of Law classes.

The librarian disappears into the dusty universe. He emerges three minutes later with a heavy volume.

'This could be of interest to you.' His own interest in Kate is already fading away. 'You can read it over there.' He points in the direction of a green lamp on a massive carved desk and goes back to his busy world of window gazing.

Kate looks at the title. *A Treatise on Last Wills and Testaments. Published 1734.* The russet leather of the binding smells of dried mushrooms. The embossed lion on the royal coat-of-arms looks relieved to be separated from a ferocious unicorn by a shield. He seems to be leering at Kate, inviting her to test her Latin. The paper must have suffered chicken pox or some other form of contagious rash, as brown oily spots appear almost on every page.

Stains from hot candle wax? guesses Kate. Appreciating the luxury of electricity, she pulls the green lamp closer and reads the first paragraph:

> *Suffice it therefore for these pupils of Latin, that those marginal notes especially proper to their studies are left in Latin. The rest, because it belongeth to all, meet it is that it be written in such a language as may be understood of all.*

Thank you, distinguished scholar, for caring about us ignorant souls, thinks Kate. But am I up to your *language as may be understood of all*?

Ten minutes, seven pages later she remembers what drew her to become a solicitor in the first place. The curtain of ornately woven phrases, with peculiar endings, half-crossed f's instead of s's, rises gradually, reluctantly. The treatise is teasing her, inviting her into a world full of passion, ambition, greed. A comedy of manners that Molière would have enjoyed.

Mr Smith was unwilling to bequeath his son all the leaves ('woods', assumes Kate) unless he was educated appropriately. Either his son was not into forestry or was just plain stupid, but he did not go to university and contented himself with the fields. He probably had enough land anyway.

The Jacobs family agreed to accept as a witness a pregnant servant, who was standing behind the screen while the Will was being dictated. A pretty girl, sobbing into the lacy *engageant* of her sleeve. He would have married her, he had promised her the earth. He was the eldest son, after all, would have inherited everything. He got the earth instead, but left her and their future child an annual pension for life.

'When the sun rise at Easter'; 'if the King of Spain die this year' – what were the motives of these people who added such conditions to their Wills?

Kate nearly skips a paragraph about soldiers' Wills, when the word 'Alien' leaps at her from the page. She reads the lines several times in disbelief, as though this were a prize letter, confirming that she has won a million.

An Alien Soldier may make a Will if he be an Alien Friend, and not an Alien Enemy. He hath the same Military Privileges which respect the form and substance of the Testament:

First, whereas no other person can die with Two Testaments, yet a Soldier may; and both Testaments shall be deemed good.

So, there *can* be two wills, after all. Supposing there is one in the Bank of England and another in Argentina – if they are both originals, if they match, and the Argentinian descendant can prove his ancestry, then . . . she tries not to get too excited. Well, then there might be a case after all.

Kate calls the Bank of England next morning. She listens to Vivaldi's 'Four Seasons' for five minutes before being connected, at last, to the Archive Department. A tired woman's voice explains to her that, yes, she could come and look at the bank documents. The archive is open by appointment from ten o'clock until half past four. Most records over thirty years old are accessible to the general public. Which period, which aspect of the research would she be interested in?

'The eighteenth-century ledgers.' Kate tries her luck.

'We have an extensive collection of ledgers – over eight thousand volumes,' continues the tired voice. However, due to lack of space the ledgers of that period have been moved to another building, so Kate would need to fill in a special requisition form. Then she would have to wait for five days before the ledger became available. She could only look at it in the Archive search room. No photocopies, no cameras. Pencils only. The tone of her voice reminds Kate of the rustle of tyres on the wet November tarmac. 'She is a Tyre Woman, not a tired woman.' Kate is surprised at her own wickedness. She preferred the melancholy of Vivaldi's violins, but the ledger beckons. 'Could I have an appointment as soon as possible, please?' she asks.

Tyre Woman's voice is suddenly warmed by emotion. This is her daily moment of glory, and she sounds triumphant as she says: 'The Archive is a very busy place at the moment. The researchers book months in advance. When would you like to come?'

Kate realises that the word 'tomorrow' would be meaningless in this conversation, but tries it anyway. Surprisingly, Tyre Woman declares that there is a cancellation at nine-fifteen next morning. 'Ask and you shall be given' indeed.

After the morning rush, she enjoys the quiet gravity of the entrance hall – black marble columns, mosaic floors – and loves the colour of the guards' uniforms, which are pinkish, almost flirty. 'Houblon' pink they call it, don't they? Named after the Governor who introduced it. She does not know anything about Mr Houblon's financial acumen, but he would definitely have made it as a textile designer.

Her fashion observations are interrupted by a tall, shy man with an unexpectedly bushy sailor's beard on his young face. He introduces himself as Roger, Assistant Archivist. He is glad to see Kate. Or perhaps he is just glad to see any human being who is prepared to swap the spacious grand hall and the airy courtyard for the windowless room of an Archive Department.

Jolly Roger proves to be even more crudite than the Lilac Librarian. His speech is monotonous, and delivered as if he has learned the text by heart and is giving Kate a guided tour.

'During the period that interests you, the Bank was still at the rented premises at Grocers' Hall. We are lucky to have some interesting documents – staff records, diaries, papers. It was a time of great scandal, when one of the Bank Directors, Humphry Morice, discounted fictitious bills to an amount of almost £30,000, an enormous sum in those days. We could show you his private business journals and correspondence, as well as—'

This time, Kate comes with a well-prepared defence: 'It is fascinating, but I just need to see the records of the deposited funds, please. Could be deposited as gold.'

Jolly Roger nods, but does not surrender: 'Of course. Under its Charter the Bank could trade in gold and silver from as early as February 1695, and since 1700 the Bank of England stored any imported gold or silver, for which the Bills of lading were deposited. The repository of bullion was called "the Warehouse", and the first bullion broker was appointed in . . .'

Kate wonders how many more young men with encyclopaedic

knowledge of the eighteenth century she will encounter during her search, and resolutely interrupts, 'Just the ledger, please.'

Roger sighs and rounds up his tour: 'Please fill in the form. The code for the Drawing Office ledgers is C98. You can come back in five days' time.' This disgruntled sailor with a ballast of unclaimed knowledge is hardly a Popeye prototype.

For the next five days the ledger is constantly at the back of Kate's mind. Or even at the front of her mind, because it has created some frownlines on her forehead, noticed by both Philip and Carol. Luckily, Carol attributed it to Kate's workload, and Philip to his imminent departure to New York. 'It's only for three months, darling,' he told her. 'So don't go getting all upset. You'll see me in two weeks' time anyway – I have already booked you a ticket. Just think of all the holidays we'll take when I get the promotion . . .'

When she comes back, Tyre Woman is waiting for her in the hall. She nods to Kate and marches ahead of her, measuring the corridor, throwing her legs forward like a pair of compasses.

Poor Roger! No wonder he was so keen to converse with Kate – it is not all plain sailing for him here. Intimidated by his boss's presence, he barely acknowledges Kate as he puts the heavy ledger in front of her.

She reads it even more intently than the treatise on Wills. Overwhelmed by the familiar distinguished names, puzzled by some of their instructions – . . . *and deliver some pens, as the bank has better pens than my household,* watching the words *received, removed, delivered* multiply on every page. Two hours later, she turns the last page a little too hastily, passing all her frustration into the ledger. She has found nothing.

Somebody coughs politely at her left ear. Kate raises her head and finds Jolly Roger looming above her. He places two heavy volumes on the table and pushes them towards Kate.

'As I said,' he starts, then repeats, 'As I said,' then stops, embarrassed.

Kate suddenly feels sorry for him and pulls the heavy volumes closer. 'Thank you, Roger.'

'As I said, we have very few records for that period that would be of relevance to your research,' he finally manages. Then, encouraged, he goes on: 'You mentioned that the deposit was made in gold, so I've brought you one of the early bullion books we hold and another stock ledger for the period you were interested in. Even though,' he confides, 'the register for the Wills is now held at the Society of Genealogists, some abstracts can be found at the back of this stock ledger, dated 1710 to 1736. These sources are invaluable for researchers, as all social classes can be found here – merchants, servants, foreigners. It is important to mention that the value of the stocks held is often quite low. Or extraordinarily high. If you look at page five, for example—'

'Thank you, Roger, I'll definitely look at page five,' interrupts Kate. She has never felt so rude in her life, but there is no other way to escape from the lecture. She opens page five reluctantly, if only to pacify the over-excited archivist, and gasps, as if she has received a letter with a lottery-winning cheque, though she had never, actually, bought a ticket in the first place.

Half of the page is covered by the heavy curls of the word *Memorand*, with a smaller underlined *Foreign Gold deposit* underneath. Kate praises the calligraphic skills of the person who wrote the most important words she has seen in this case to date:

Anno 1723

Memorand. That Colonel Pavlo Polubotko of Chernihiv, Cossack Army Treasurer, po . . . (what is the next word? Professed? Oh, possessed! Possessed by what? Disease? Demons?) *possessed of . . . thirty thousand six hundreds one pounds eighteen shillings and three pence in the capital of eight barrels of gold, deposited in the Foreign Warehouse. Erected by an Act of Parliament of the fourth year of His Majesty King George and attended with annuities of four p: Centum.*

. . . by his Last Will and Testament dated in Chernihiv the twenty-fourth day of January one thousand seven hundred twenty-three Colonel Polubotko . . . nominates his son Yakiv Polubotko and his successors as legatees . . . having a particular bequest in the above-mentioned stock in his said will . . .

Registered this midday of July anno 1723.

Below, somebody has copied the abstract from the Will with the same calligraphic skill and ardour:

My Will is that none of my said legatees shall claim or have any interest money for the legacy or legacies in this Will, given until such time that Ukraine becomes independent. Also my Will is that then it shall be in the power of my executors and survivors or survivor of them to receive in all such sum. But for more surety's sake it is the best to have the opinion of the Banks Council thereon for the executors disposal of the principal funds.

Kate reads the extract again and looks at Roger with such admiration that he blushes underneath the bushy growth on his face.

'Thank you, Roger! Most interesting.' She tries to hide her excitement. 'I should probably look through this stock ledger now.' She opens the second volume, and with the confidence of a seasoned researcher, finds the records for *July, Anno 1723* within minutes.

There are records of Spanish and Russian coins, French gold 20-franc coins 'delivered to the cashiers'; 'foreign bar gold received from the Foreign warehouse'. Some of the records have signatures against them, the others – intertwined initials.

When she finally finds what she has been looking for, she chuckles, as if the record had informed her that from this moment, her lottery prize money had doubled.

Deposited with Mr Clark the Treasurer are 8 barrels of gold till further notice. And this shall be your warrant.

The signature is neat and completely illegible. Different alphabet, another thing she could have learned, but never did. She copies the note and carefully draws the hooks and loops of the signature.

She cannot wait to share her findings with Andriy, cannot wait to meet him at the Italian sandwich bar by the tube station. She notes, surprised, that she already refers to it as 'our *usual* meeting place' when she speaks to Andriy, even though they have only met there twice before.

She is taken aback by his reaction. Because there is no reaction at all. As if he has known it all along, has seen it before. As if Kate has spent the whole morning breathing the archive dust for her own enjoyment.

He confirms the signature and asks eagerly: 'So, when can the money be claimed?'

Kate is so annoyed that for a moment she turns into Carol –

is abrupt, efficient, and speaks in official tones. She will smother him with her knowledge, entangle him in legal terminology. He will not understand, he will ask her to clarify. He will beg, and she will condescend. Perhaps.

'Claiming the inheritance is not that easy', she begins, crossly. 'According to English law, the Will must name one or more executors or trustees in order to carry out its provisions. The executors of this Will are deceased, as we know. The death certificate of the testator has to be presented and the identity of the claimant checked. There was a famous case at the end of the nineteenth century when one Australian descendant had trouble proving his identity and the inheritance money was not released by the bank.'

Pause. She looks at Andriy defiantly. He nods.

'Once the Will has been presented and the identity of the claimant proven, the lawyers will be instructed to prove the Will, or, in other words, to prepare the legal document to one or more people, authorising them to carry out the duties as personal representatives of the deceased. Sometimes the insurance companies or the building societies may release the money to the next-of-kin without a Grant of Probate, if the amount held is small and there are no complications. As we both know, due to the enormous sum to be claimed, this would not be possible in our case.'

Andriy reclines on the back of the chair. He listens attentively, but looks relaxed, even tranquil. As if he is the one doing the counselling, while Kate pours out her problems. She has another one for him to cherish.

'Of course, there is one more important issue to consider. In the case of an International Will, a solicitor or notary public, authorised for the purposes of International Wills, must issue a special certificate which makes the Will formally valid. When the testator's permanent home is abroad, the laws of the country of domicile will determine whether a Will was effective.'

Pause. Nod.

Fringe brushed away.

Kate looks at Andriy's high forehead, as if she can read the message written there. 'It is also essential to check the Will against fraud or mistake, or whether any undue influence was used in the execution of the Will, as that could constitute good grounds to invalidate it.'

'How long would all these procedures take?' asks Andriy softly, ignoring her stare.

'Well, if everything is checked properly and swiftly, it could take anything from several months to a year.' She is worn out. And not winning either.

'I have also sent a letter to the Archives in France,' she goes on. 'When I was reading your notes, there was another thing I found odd. According to the Polubotko family legend, the Will was kept in France by the French Count Orly, and then passed to Grygor Polubotko's great-great – whatever – grandfather at the end of the eighteenth century, when he stopped in France before emigrating to Latin America. Why was the Will kept in France, I wonder? Why was a French Count, of all people, chosen to safe-guard it?'

'But while we wait for the letter of explanation to arrive from France, we can continue our research, no?' Andriy is his abrupt self again. And he hasn't answered her question either.

Kate resorts to her last argument. 'By the way, I've never asked you – how much do you intend to get out of this?'

He takes off his glasses. Closes his sad spaniel eyes, rubs the bridge of his nose with his long index finger. Massages in everything he has just heard. For an instant he looks exposed and vulnerable and Kate is shocked by how much she wants to hug him now. Or maybe even kiss his cheek. But Andriy already puts the thin-rimmed defence on again and says earnestly, in his plain English: 'I just want to do it for my country.' She has heard this phrase before, in the American films with a 'patriotic message' and always found it bluntly theatrical. But Andriy sounds so genuine, that Kate is puzzled. Astonished at how keen she is to help him. Even more surprised that she wants to do it, not just for the sake of his country. And not for that ephemeral, over-the-horizon fee, either.

So, when Andriy asks her, 'What should be the next step?' she finds herself saying, 'Well, I think we need some favourable winds.' He looks at her bewildered. She laughs. 'I thought you spoke Spanish. I mean, it looks as if we have to go to Buenos Aires. The Easter holidays are not until mid-April this year, so we might be lucky with the tickets.'

She watches Andriy's smile disintegrate. First the corners of his lips are wiped out, then the sparkle in his eyes is extinguished. 'I cannot go, Kate,' he says. He is inspecting the chaos of her desk, as if searching for the reasons there. As if he really wants to go, but is not allowed to.

She wonders whose permission he needs to ask.

When he admits, 'I do not have a visa or money for this trip,' Kate feels a familiar executive buzz. She loves arranging flights, passports, visas. Should be running a travel agency. 'No logic whatsoever, but good at logistics,' as Carol once said about her to one of the partners. Sandra, their Department Secretary, overheard, bless her. Kate knows now where this girl's loyalties lie.

She turns to Andriy. 'Leave it with me. Just give me your passport details. Don't worry, it will all be added to our legal expenses,' she says hastily. She hasn't got the time to think how she is going to explain to Philip the significant sum borrowed from their joint account; nor the fact that she will spend the long-awaited New York weekend in Buenos Aires instead, with another man. She is bouncing with energy, as if she has just drunk a freshly squeezed orange juice. She is ready for action.

Chapter 11

Buenos Aires, March 2001

The monotonous drone is getting under her skin. She opens her eyes. The plane is turning, the warm orange glow is flooding the cabin. She presses her nose against the transparent circle, trying not to mist it over. She has always dreamed of watching the sunrise above the clouds.

The panel is already lit, and the friendly metallic voice informs her that the thirteen-and-a-half-hour flight will soon be over. They have talked for a good ten hours out of the thirteen. It started with a forced, confined togetherness – the proximity of a long journey. She hasn't noticed when and how they moved to the game of Patience, placing the cards of their lives in order.

The Knave of Diamonds. Happy-go-lucky. Long blond hair, worn in a pony tail. Antony, Kate's younger brother, in his second year at university. 'I think he chose Medicine so that he could remain a student for seven years. He is too careless to become a doctor – it worries me. We are so close that sometimes I feel jealous of his friends.'

The Queen of Hearts. Rose in her hand, an elusive smile. Carmen, Andriy's Cuban ex-girlfriend. 'We were at university together. She taught me a bit of Spanish. Not Castellano, but Cuban pronunciation. They glide through sounds, you know.'

'What happened?' asks Kate, instantly regretting it. Too nosy, too unprofessional.

'She wanted to return to her country, and I didn't want to leave mine,' says Andriy.

Kate opens her mouth to ask: 'Is anybody waiting for you at home now?' but doesn't. Maybe because she is scared that he might ask her the same question.

The King of Clubs. Grey beard, black cross. The death of Andriy's grandfather. 'He had a phenomenal, encyclopaedic knowledge of history. He refused to polish historical facts to please politicians, so they accused him of Nationalism, stopped publishing his books and articles. They crushed him – he lived in fear till the day he died. Not for himself, for us. I will never forgive them for what happened to him. "Be careful with history, Andriy," he used to say. Every time I tried to talk to him, he would shield himself with a Chinese proverb: "The more you know, the less you understand." I just couldn't reach him. As if he was afraid that his knowledge would harm me. He left me his secrets in the end.'

The Ace of Spades. Black arrow straight into the heart. The divorce of Kate's parents. 'They were too busy sorting their own lives out, expected me to be "grown up" about it. The trouble was, I *was* almost grown up. I yelled, I hated them both because I love them both. They saw a teenage rebellion, while it was sheer terror of becoming an adult without their support. That's why I have been too protective with Antony. My mother is constantly travelling, trying to save the world – she is working for an international charity. My father has remarried, so every time I stay with him, I feel like a guest. Very welcome, but still a guest. I was very lucky that my father's mother lived near my boarding school – I used to escape to her for the weekends. We are very close: she gives and gives – generous, unconditional love. She speaks Ukrainian. It would be fun for you to meet her. What do you call your grandmother, by the way? *Babusya*? Me too . . .'

Often after a long flight of shared self-searching, the night confidants would be barely nodding farewells to each other, hiding their faces behind their bags. How many times have you seen fellow passengers progress into friends? Or at least pen pals? Too much exposure, too much soul stripping. That is why you pay for counselling – come in, cry it out, leave the pieces on somebody's floor.

Kate does not feel embarrassed at having told Andriy everything. Well, almost everything. Somehow she has not mentioned her problems with Philip. Surprisingly, she has not talked about Philip at all. Not that I avoided the subject, she thinks. We simply had many other topics of conversation.

In fact, she has not even thought about the reasons she must give Philip when she comes back from Argentina, about the long-distance hasty call she had to make to him: 'I am so sorry, Philip, I have to change the ticket because I'm not coming next weekend . . . Of course I want to see you, don't be silly, but something has come up . . . Yes, it is urgent and important enough to . . . will explain later.' And then, barely audible, 'Love you too.'

She turns to Andriy. He has been sleeping for the last two hours. The sun has reached the tip of his turned-up nose, and now surreptitiously crawls towards his trembling eyelids, checking every freckle on the way. Kate wishes she could do the same. Just stroke him gently – from the temple, down the cheekbone to the corner of his mouth, slide the finger along the upper lip . . . Andriy stirs, and she quickly looks away, opens the phrasebook obediently waiting on her lap. What an appropriate page.

El negocio	Business
Tengo una cita con . . .	I have an appointment with . . .
Aqui tiene mi tarjeta	Here is my card
Encantado de conocerle	Pleased to meet you

She is here purely for . . . what's the word? *El negocio.* The fact that she is about to land in Buenos Aires with somebody she likes (she forces herself to accept that it is only that and no more) is secondary. Tertiary. Irrelevant. The bump of the undercarriage touching the runway and Andriy's, 'Morning, Kate,' come at the same time. Welcome to Latin America. Welcome to reality.

They walk out of the plane straight into a steam bath, into the clammy Argentinian summer. The humidity is squeezing into the air-conditioned tunnel. It lingers inside the airport, seeps into the black, yellow-roofed taxi. It fuses with post-sleepless flight tiredness, makes Kate desperate for one breath of unheated air. Or, even better, for a gust of November wind from the Thames.

Andriy chats to the driver in Spanish. 'He says the hotel is very close to Plaza San Martin tube station – that's line C. We are nearly there, but we are crawling through the *circulacion* – the traffic.' He sounds sympathetic, consoling – does she look that tired?

'You must have been very close.' Kate is not talking about the distance to the main square, but about Andriy and his Cuban girlfriend. 'Your Spanish is quite fluent.'

He frowns. 'We were.' End of conversation – terse as usual.

One more reason for Kate to be relieved when the drive to the uniformed, marbled Hotel Marriott, with its lobby oasis of artificially cold air, is over. Two hours until the meeting. Shower – go horizontal, eyes closed, no dreams. Back to the lift, to the plastic politeness of the concierge. The hotel is far grander than she expected. Carol is right in one thing. Kate is certainly good at logistics, to get *this* for the money she booked it for!

She recognises him instantly, although they have only spoken on the phone – or have tried to speak on the phone, as his English was at the stage of a frozen embryo. The faxes were in Spanish, written and translated by their Department Secretary, Sandra, thanks to the perfect timing of some evening classes. She would go far, that girl.

Pablo Petryshyn, the Head of the Union of Ukrainians in Argentina, is measuring the lobby with the precise steps of a retired General. His thinning grey hair is combed over in a futile attempt to cover his baldness, and the moustache is groomed to the same bushiness as his brows. Despite the heat, he is wearing a navy blazer with shiny brass buttons. He smiles at Kate, showing the yellow teeth of a smoker, and gestures towards the disfigured leather of the lobby armchairs. 'It is more comfortable and cooler than my office,' explains Pablo. His name, he tells Kate, is the Argentinian version of the Ukrainian 'Pavlo'. They have to communicate through Andriy, who discovers the hard way that Pablo-Pavlo's Ukrainian is not easy to understand either.

'Kateryno,' Petryshyn addresses her in the Ukrainian manner, 'what you asked me to do was not easy. Not easy at all. But since we, Ukrainians abroad, should help each other . . .' He pauses, looking at Kate, waiting for appreciation. She smiles gratefully, without reminding him how much his help is costing her.

'Of course, our Ukrainian diaspora is not as big as it is in the States, with its two million, or Canada with its one million Ukrainians. But this also means that we don't have the same support, the same funding as the diasporas there.' He looks at Kate again and continues: 'There are around two hundred and thirty thousand Ukrainians in Argentina today, almost half of them living in Buenos Aires. I had to look through our registers, and then check the lists of arrivals of immigrants at a special reception point in the barrio Retiro. Yes, I have found your man. He arrived in Argentina in 1897.' The General is emphasising every word, as if he were giving orders. 'He was one of the founders of the Ukrainian settlement of Apóstoles. It is quite an interesting place, by the way. The population of sixty thousand has managed to preserve the language and customs even in the third generation. They have a yerba maté festival there every year, around now. Will you have time for a visit? It is quite a long way away, but . . .'

'It depends whether the descendants of Grygor Polubotko live in Apóstoles or in Buenos Aires.' Kate steers Pablo to the purpose of the meeting.

'Well, there are not really many descendants left.' The General withdraws to his position. 'Life in a subtropical jungle was not that easy. Grygor had a son and a daughter. His son died very young of some tropical disease, his daughter married in Apóstoles and died in childbirth. His only direct descendant is his grandson, Pedro Polubotko, who still lives on the outskirts of Buenos Aires.'

Pablo looks at Andriy's flushed face. 'I would not get too excited, though. He is an alcoholic. Apparently, he owned a successful business, a big metalworks, but he put all his money into the Ukrainian financial Kooperatyva and lost everything during the crisis of 1982. He hasn't been able to rebuild his business or himself ever since. So he moved from the metalworks to a tin house.'

The General chuckles at his own joke. 'He lives in Villa Jardin, in Lanus, just outside the Federal capital. Don't be fooled by the name. It is not a garden at all, but a *villa miseria* – a shanty town: abandoned factories, polluted river, slums. There are bus connections with the Federal capital, but I would not recommend that you go there, if you can avoid it. I certainly would not be able to join you. You see, the inhabitants are *angustiados* – full of anxiety and not very ...' He searches for the right word '... not very cooperative. Oh, when you called, Kateryno, you mentioned to me that Polubotko had distant relatives in England and had inherited some money. How much is it, may I ask?'

Kate is about to explain, but Andriy quickly says something in Ukrainian, and then translates for Kate. 'Around a hundred thousand pounds.'

Pablo smiles. 'It could make him a very happy man, if anything can now. When you talk to him, could you mention that we helped to find him? We rely heavily on donations, you see. Our problem here is that there are too many separate Ukrainian organisations – different parties, various religions. We need to create a strong united body, not two dozen small associations. That is what I am trying to do ... Oh, look at the time. If you will excuse me, I must go. I have a meeting at the Catholic church in half an hour. I hope to see you again before you leave.' He stands up abruptly, shows his yellow teeth again, adjusts his blazer, and marches out of the lobby.

Kate is glad to see him go: a good cup of coffee is all she needs now to shake off that post-long-haul feeling, but Andriy is already hovering over the map like a hawk.

'I have found the place, and the bus route. The fare, according to the guidebook, is only seventy *centavos*.'

He looks at Kate and she notices for the first time that the irises of his eyes have tiny brown dots in the field of green, as if his freckles have strayed from his nose, never stopped invading. She surrenders, puts her dark glasses on to shield her fatigued eyes and misplaced emotions.

They get off the bus in the centre of the Villa. Why was Pablo so negative? He's never been here, obviously. The brick houses with corrugated-iron roofs are painted in off-beat spring catwalk colours. The teenagers hanging around the video rental store have the world-standard belligerent, carefully unkempt, posing look. The owner of the fruit and vegetable stall must have used the traffic-lights for inspiration, since he has tomatoes and red apples on one side, avocados on another, with oranges and bananas in the middle. Overflowing boxes, bountiful clusters. The cardboard sign: *Hay Castana* informs passers-by that chestnuts can be bought here too but, decides Kate, cannot be displayed, because dark shrivelled piles would destroy the semaphore harmony.

A couple of chequered-capped old boys are playing draughts on the bench near the bus stop. They are taking the game seriously, scrutinising the board, rubbing their chins with gnarled hands for some time before each move.

When Andriy asks them for directions, the players look at the young couple glumly, as if they are expected to give away the country's military secrets. One of them raises his hand with a black draught, waves to the left, and then triumphantly advances the counter across the board to a winning square. What a staggering economy of effort, admires Kate.

She follows Andriy across the road. They dive into the side

street, where somebody has tampered with the sunlight switch. The dingy, narrow passage ends in a blank wall and a left-hand turn. They walk into an identical bleak alley, then another.

'Andriy, there is no way we could find anything or anybody here. And more importantly, how are we going to get back?' Kate looks hopelessly at the piece of paper with the useless address – the passages have no names. They are not deserted, however. The windowsills of some houses show off a spread of cigarettes and drinks. From time to time, vigilant homeowners check their displays and the space outside for those willing to buy and to gossip and those willing to acquire without paying. A winning combination of front-room trading and Neighbourhood Watch. Kate wonders whether the police in the Home Counties could be interested in the scheme.

The domestic kiosk in the third passage is guarded by an ample-bosomed matron in a sleeveless black dress. She is fanning herself with a newspaper, demonstrating the white contours of yesterday's sweat and fresh black stains under her armpits. Her misery is rewarded by Andriy, who buys a packet of cigarettes.

'I didn't know you smoked,' says Kate.

'I don't,' replies Andriy. 'She told me that we should go into this passage on the right. It is near the Riachuelo, on the river-bank, past the Centro Comunitario – the community centre – next to the abandoned military factory. A house with a "poster door". She said we'll understand when we see it. Come on.' He plunges into the alley, leaving Kate with no option but to follow him, trying not to step into the puddles seeping from the open drainage ditches. They are definitely getting closer to the river – the stench is stronger, the dwellings can hardly be called houses: rickety constructions of corrugated metal patched with plywood boards of all shapes and sizes. Here winter catwalk colours reign – the muddy brown of the walls, charcoal black of burned-out cookers, metallic grey of tin baths outside some of the homes. The baths are the only luxurious, solid pieces here.

'Here's a roadblock,' says Andriy, but Kate does not find the joke funny.

Three little girls are watching them from across the alleyway: all aged around seven or eight, all with black bunches dangling like spaniels' ears. One girl firmly holds the hand of a plump-faced toddler.

All three are wearing navy jersey tops and black knee-sagged leggings, with one sharp, screechingly pink centrepiece, one poverty-defying lacy dress over the dark clothes. The girl has white and pink Barbie trainers to match her Cinderella gown. The quick black eyes are looking at Kate and Andriy with the guarded curiosity of monkeys observing strangers in the jungle. There is no sweatshirt adjusting, no nose wiping. The group does not move, as if they are posing for a photograph, for a poster of some unknown high-minded charity, for a straight-to-the-bin leaflet, to be discarded along with other junkmail.

Kate rummages in her bag and digs out a stick of chewing gum, a dark blue airline washbag and four plastic-sealed crackers. It's not much, but it's a peace offering, a piece-of-decent-life offering.

The toddler starts towards Kate, attracted by the silver magnet of the chewing-gum foil. The pink princess deters him with a not very regal gesture, grabs his unbrushed black hair and pulls him back. He winces, but does not squeak. He is not an elected representative to accept gifts.

The flock leader steps forward, takes the offerings with lips stretched, as Kate guesses, in a smile. A second later, a saliva bullet hits Kate in the left eye. Then the pink warrior and her retinue disappear into one of the passages with a sense of the last word, of the completed defence mission.

Kate feels the hot spittle sliding down her cheek. She is so shocked that she does not even try to look for a handkerchief. Andriy wipes her face with the back of his hand, and then his hand on the back of his trousers. 'Let's go,' is all he says. And after a minute of walking in silence, he adds: 'You shouldn't judge her. These children are as unpredictable as a natural disaster – they *are* a natural disaster. They learn to fend for themselves from the womb. They are the gutter castaways in their element here; it is their world and nobody else's. Look, Kate. I think we have found the place.'

The 'poster door' is indeed, hard to miss. It consists of a piece of advertising display board with the portrait of an old gaucho covering the hut's entrance. Half of the gaucho's body is, probably, leaning against another shack somewhere in the rancid maze. The remaining one-eyed face, scarred by scratched or washed off paint, is contorted in a sinister grimace.

'And here, ladies and gentlemen, is a perfect example of a local security alarm, a powerful barrier against kids' gangs.' Andriy is sensing Kate's discomfort. 'I'll go first.'

They squeeze between the plywood and the corrugated wall and stop, adjusting to semi-darkness, to the reluctant light trickling through a glassless slit of a window. The room looks empty, so Andriy continues his tour. 'The accommodation is open-plan with a cool cement floor, ideal for the hot climate. In one corner you can see a console, which can be used as a table, with an earthenware mug of local design, an empty bottle and some – he winces – not particularly fresh food. Now let us turn to another corner

– what can we see there? A remarkably decent wardrobe, too grand for accommodation of this size. Perhaps you are wondering what could be hidden in it . . .'

Andriy is too showy, too cheery, too taut. Kate has never seen him clowning like this. If he is doing it to encourage her in this gloom, he is definitely achieving the opposite effect.

Andriy's tirade is interrupted from the third corner by a feeble guttural sound.

The creature (Kate finds it difficult to make out the gender) is lying on a mattress on the floor. The mattress is, in fact, a Lilo, optimistically covered in orange and turquoise squares. When was the last time its occupant sunbathed on the Atlantic playa?

The creature could have modelled for one of Goya's 'dark period' paintings – with its ashen, cadaverous skin, unblinking eyes staring into nowhere, wide-open mouth.

'And here,' Andriy whispers loudly to Kate, 'is a striking illustration of the damaging effects of alcohol on the human . . .' he pauses '. . . what was once a human being.'

She shudders. 'Let's get out of here. It's pointless. What would he know?'

'Wait. Stay here,' orders Andriy, and disappears.

Kate is left standing in the middle of the room. She is cursing her sentimentality, love of tangerines, solicitor's profession, the heat and, of course, of course, above all, this untamed, naïve, lanky, freckled, eccentric (she runs out of adjectives) Slavic boy who has dragged her into all this. The creature shows no other sign of life. Kate's horror lasts a full five minutes, until Andriy comes back with two bottles of tequila. The bosomy trader is having her lucky day.

Andriy squats next to the man, and tapping his hand gently, as if he were patting a sick dog, whispers something into his ear. The creature turns its head, looks at the bottles with its watery eyes and produces another husky sound.

'Come on, he is letting us go through his belongings.' Andriy charges to the wardrobe, not leaving her any time to think.

It is a shock to find two neatly folded, clean shirts on the shelf and a lonely navy tie on a coat hanger. 'A reminder of his previous life, a hope that one day he might wear them again,' guesses Andriy.

At the bottom of the wardrobe is a pair of well-worn brown shoes with scuffed toes, and a black briefcase with a broken lock. Andrew empties the contents of the briefcase on the floor. There isn't much.

A Bible. A key with a keyring in a shape of a miniature ball-bearing. A pewter cross. A postcard of a three-arched, three-belled church with an inscription in Spanish: *Iglesia Católica de rito bizantino Ucraniano de la Santisima Trinidad, Apóstoles.*

A little black booklet, gold-blocked *Republica Argentina. Pasaporte.* Kate opens it, looks at the photograph of a smiling dark-haired man with a dashing moustache, at the surname against *Apellido*, at the date of birth against *Fecha de nacimiento.* 'He hasn't aged at all, has he, Andriy?' she says sarcastically. He does not answer. There is a small wooden box with black iron bolts that looks like an Oxfam Fair Trade souvenir.

'The Will, or what is left of it, can only be in this casket,' says Andriy. There is not a shade of doubt in his voice. 'Ready?' Before Kate has time to nod, the box opens with a crackle. Inside is a piece of paper with letters she can recognise, but cannot read. Is that it? She feels a sting of disappointment. Well, what did she expect? Dungeons, ghosts, fanfares? Kate is not sure. She knows what she did *not* expect. A sweet spitting girl, a comatose alcoholic and a box that cracks like an eggshell.

Andriy picks up the box, rises decisively. 'Let's get out of here. There are better places to be in Buenos Aires after dusk.'

'We can't do that,' protests Kate. 'We are stealing this man's possessions.'

'Why don't we borrow the box from its proud owner, then? But first we need to explain to him all the legal implications, all about claimants, testators, Grants of Probate, executors and trustees, Will invalidations. Go on, take him through the process. He will be fascinated.'

Not bad for somebody whose first language is not English. At least he listened in London, thinks Kate.

Andriy continues: 'Look at him. His existence is a burned carcass of a life now, like the cars we saw outside. Just think how many kids can be fed, how many Chernobyls prevented. And when the money is claimed, we'll make sure he gets his share. Do you remember the condition of the Will? If the inheritance is claimed by the descendant, who does not live in Ukraine, he gets five per cent. Just think what five per cent will mean for him! Of course, we'll have to think how to make him presentable to the bank when the money is claimed . . .'

'*If* the money is claimed,' says Kate.

She is the first to hear the shooting. The sound grows, migrates, they are surrounded by deafening stereo effects: banging, hammering, drumming, cracking. There is no escape.

Andriy notices her pallor. 'You are not really scared, are you?' The sound resolution is high here – water hits the tin roof, echoes in the empty house. 'Look.' He grasps her shoulders and gently directs her to the window slit, to the descending transparent wall. 'See? It is only a thunderstream.'

'A thunderstorm,' corrects Kate. He is standing behind her,

holding her shoulders a little longer than necessary, perhaps. Breathing a little too close, into the back of her head, making warm air flow down to the hairs at the end of her neck. Is she imagining things? He cannot be interested in her, surely. She has never regarded herself as attractive. Everything in her was, is, will be ordinary: medium height, medium build, grey eyes, brown hair – sparrow colours. Is he just using the opportunity?

She tries to get angry with him, steps aside, asks: 'How are we going to find the way back to the . . .' she checks the map '. . . *calle* Warnes?'

'We should walk against the rain,' says Andriy evasively, and she realises the true meaning of his answer when they leave the hut. Though the rain has stopped, it *is* a real 'thunderstream' outside. The yellow water is brawling with the open drains. 'It gushes towards the river,' he explains, 'and we have to go in the opposite direction to the Riachuelo.'

The unsurfaced alley is now muddy and slippery. Kate skids and Andriy catches her, using his favourite elbow-gripping tactics, nearly losing the wooden box to the pungent deluge. She is pleasantly surprised that she is the heavier on his priority scales. Or maybe it is just an instinctive move, and he has simply lost his balance. The thought nags at her throughout their bus ride back to the centre.

The old bus is obediently following all diversions, waiting at the broken traffic-lights, crawling along the kerbs to avoid the deranged rush hour. By the time Kate and Andriy reach the central bus station, it is already dark.

They decide against a taxi – too expensive. The Subte is cheap and fast, but you cannot see much of the city underground. And so they walk, past the buildings of all architectural styles, past *librerias* – single-room bookshops, where people talk the café talk – past pizzerias and ice-cream parlours, where students bury their heads in books. Past the chipped-nosed angels in antique shops and big shopping arcades with angelic mannequins. In the evening, Buenos Aires resembles a fairground – it has the same illusion of a merry atmosphere, the same smell of barbecued beef coming from the open restaurant windows, prompting them that it's time to eat.

They choose a small, crowded bar with bright red chequered cloths, and squeeze into chairs at a low wooden table with a lethargic candle. While Andriy devours the menu, Kate looks for the source of the melancholy music. In the corner, somebody is playing a small accordion. The musician could successfully pose for the 'Welsh Farming Heritage' article in *Country Life*: ruddy cheeks, nose like a potato rejected by the supermarket. He has his left foot on a chair, the instrument on his knee, and is tapping with the toe of a pointed polished shoe. Engrossed in the music, he has closed his eyes, and is reliving his own personal, universally suffered emotions.

A smoky melody drifts through the sweltering air. Kate checks her guidebook. 'He is playing a *bandoneón*, first introduced to Argentina by German sailors. Usually it is the part of the orchestra that accompanies tango dancers.' She closes the book. 'Except that here we have no orchestra and no dancers.'

'Yes, we do.' Andriy tears himself away from descriptions of *empanadas*, *salchichas* and *parilladas*. 'They are dancing on the pavement – right behind you.'

It is not a show. They make a striking couple. She probably works as a secretary or an accountant, and has come straight from the office. She is wearing a knee-length, cream-coloured buttoned dress and an expression of concentrated effort. Her partner has rolled up the sleeves of his black shirt, revealing mason's muscular forearms. They look through each other; their legs are darting, like snake tongues, fighting for space. As if they are dancing at the edge of the cliff, and one false step would take them over the precipice. His knee is touching her inner thigh, the palm of his right hand is pushing her forward, dictating the moves. One – long step – infatuation. Two – lean back – abandonment. The potent cocktail of feelings is making Kate more and more drunk. She imagines surgeon's fingers on her back – sliding, touching, supporting . . . And later maybe even undressing her. She does not ask herself 'why' any more. She has accepted that there are some things in life you cannot explain. You just have to learn to cope with them somehow.

They walk back to the hotel in silence, feeling the intensity of the undercurrents between them.

She knows even before they get into the lift. Before he says, chokingly, 'Kateryna . . .' She is afraid to look at him, as if he can read in her eyes the answer to what is going to happen next. She turns to him and meets his lips, is sucked into the Black Hole of the Universe, where neither time nor gravity exist. She does not remember how they get into the room. Her body becomes fluid, all her senses concentrate on the tips of her fingers: the softness of his hair, the velvet of his skin, the coolness of the sheets.

Her weightless body accepts him slowly, as if she had always known him, felt him before and now is gently restoring the warm, long-missed familiarity of pleasure. She drifts up to the surface, gasps, and the Black Hole explodes and pushes her into the world, to her own voice coming from above, to his kisses, covering her salty, tear-streaked cheeks . . . And then she slips back into her trance, into the crevice at the bottom of his neck, where one reckless vein pulsates, calling her, telling her that he is there, her love and her life.

She wakes in the middle of the night. She can hear the music inside her. He is asleep, his knees tucked under him, head tilted forward on the pillow, as if he repeats a shape of a letter from an ancient, extinct alphabet. Like an S, but softer, more fluid. It was a vowel. Definitely a vowel, pronounced in one long sound, which began deep under the ribs, ending with a sigh.

She is welded tight into him, repeating his shape: her kneecaps into the back of his knees, navel against his spine, nipples in the hollow between his shoulder blades. They are two letters on a white sheet, making a magic, immortal word that means 'harmony', 'the beginning and the end', 'the flow of life'. She cannot say it aloud, but she listens to its sound. It is pure and simple, like a C-major scale. Where every note is new. Where every note is familiar.

She wants to check whether life behind the thick glass still goes on, so carefully detaches herself, slips out of bed, looks out of the window. The *avenida* below does not sleep: cars brake noiselessly at the traffic-lights, silent couples hold hands. The world listens to the melody inside her. And it grows, expands, she needs to share it, to sing before it spills. She thinks of the time difference. Four o'clock in the morning – seven in the UK.

She waits for an answer, and breathes out happily, quietly into the receiver: 'I am so much in love, *Babusya!*'

'I am so very glad to hear that.' The dear voice is distorted by a long-distance echo. 'You and Philip seemed a bit distant lately.'

'*Babusya*,' interrupts Kate, 'Philip is in New York. This is . . . No, I won't tell you, but you will like him, I am sure. Can we come to have lunch with you on Sunday?'

Chapter 12

'There is a visitor in Reception for you, Miss Fletcher,' chirrups Amy. 'Yes, I'll ask him to wait.' She puts the receiver down and looks at Kate with a professional, slightly tense smile. 'Kate, it is the third time you've come down to ask. There are no calls or messages for you. And you don't have to come here. I'll call you.'

He didn't ring yesterday. Or on Sunday. He has no mobile, so it is a one-way contact, or lack of it. She had to cancel their lunch with *Babusya*, had to mutter something to Philip when he called, and wait, wait, wait . . .

She doesn't just miss Andriy – the greater, better part of herself has an irrational, inexplicable craving for him, like that of a pregnant woman wanting to eat chalk. The remaining, empty part of her has to move, eat, sleep in Philip's bed. At least Philip is away, so he cannot see her clutching the corner of the duvet, hollow-eyed, watching the daytime TV shows. Now is not the right time for explanations. Though frankly, when *is* the right time?

Kate's mind provides some calming reasons for his lack of contact: he was working on an essay all night after their arrival, crashed out and has been sleeping for twelve hours . . . thirteen hours – fourteen. The reasons become slightly more worrying: what if he's caught a rare South American bug and is now unconscious in hospital, attached to a drip, unable to contact her? Or what if he's decided that what happened in Argentina between them was one big mistake?

By Monday morning she has run out of reasons. She becomes a haunting shadow, hated by Amy the receptionist. Just when she decides to check the timetable of the fast trains to Cambridge leaving in the next two hours, the phone finally rings, and Amy's triumphant, 'There is an urgent call for you, Kate,' makes her jump. But it is not Andriy. It's somebody else. Young, male, with a light stammer. Kate even has a laugh with him, when he is wrestling with her unusual last name. 'If it's a name you can't pronounce, that will be me,' she tells him. It is nice to share a bit of humour with a stranger first thing on a Monday morning.

And then he says: 'I am afraid I have some bad news about Andriy Savchuk.' And then he tells her. Kate's first thought is: April Fool's Day. What a sick joke. What a very, very sick joke.

She confirms the time and address, leaves the office, takes a train. She has read about this protection mechanism: in a state of shock, people often continue to move, talk, act for a while as if nothing has happened. The brain shuts the feelings down. Bangs a heavy lid on top of them and waits.

The fast train to Cambridge takes three-quarters of an hour – the longest forty-five minutes of her life.

The receptionist at the Admissions Office is polite and neutral. When Kate tries to talk to her about Andriy, she sounds like a recorded message: 'We cannot give you any information, I am afraid. You are not a relative.' Kate has to try a different approach. Though she feels out of place in her suit and heeled shoes in the middle of the courtyard, full of jeans and sweaters, her face is still young enough, so . . .

A girl in a white blouse and a grey pencil skirt walks decisively through the Porter's Lodge to her pigeon-hole.

'You look very smart,' remarks a porter. Small talk is in his job description.

'I've got my first job interview today.' Kate looks through the post, not at him. 'And I am *so* nervous about it!'

She does not find his pigeon-hole at first. She scans the names in red: SPIC, SPORT . . . It takes seconds to register that these are the pigeon-holes for societies, not students. Where arc the students' ones, then? Kate notices that there is another row around the corner. Luckily, the porter is busy telling off a student who has tried to drag his bicycle across the courtyard, so she rushes to the students' pigeon-holes, reading the names on the yellow background: Anderson . . . Lonsdale . . . Savchuk.

Andriy's pigeon-hole has two enveloes in it with his address: his flat is outside the college, in a postgraduate block.

Kate checks the tourist map she has picked up at the station – a distance for a bicycle ride, not for walking. She runs all the way to a red-brick Victorian terrace, in through the unlocked door, along the corridor, up the stairs, checking the names. Her heart stops before she does. The door with the name *Andriy Savchuk* is sealed. There is a piece of gummed paper across it with the *Cambridge Constabulary* stamp and a spiral of a signature. There is no point in knocking, but Kate still pounds at the door, hammering in her grief.

The door opposite swings open and a head peers out. The head has tousled, straw-coloured hair and dark, sparkling eyes and reminds Kate of the Scarecrow from *The Wizard of Oz*.

'There is no point in knocking the building down,' says the head with a slight Scandinavian accent. 'He is gone.'

'Gone where?' Kate clings to her last straw of hope.

'Gone-gone.' The neighbour raises her (by now Kate has figured out it is a girl) glazed eyes upwards. The Scarecrow has a drink-related speech impediment coupled with a concentration problem, so the conversation is very slow. 'Had an accident. Drowned when he fell off the bridge near Jesus Green. It was quite shallow, but he must have hit the lock gate and broke his neck. I overheard the police, when they were searching the room. They said there was heroin in his bloodstream. He never looked doped to me though. My neighbour from downstairs feels every rustle when doped. He bangs the ceiling every time I cross the room. I tiptoe, creep to the toilet – he still bangs. Never apologises, but I don't blame him – he doesn't remember a thing afterwards. I was so fed up once that I went downstairs, tried to get into his room, and you know what he said? That he could not open the door because it was dangerous and I should get away – the giants were walking over him.' The Scarecrow hiccups and gives the frozen Kate a sobered look. 'And who are you, by the way? I haven't seen you here before.'

Kate mumbles something about a conference, the speaker not turning up and the College not giving out any information, that she is one of the organisers and is only doing her job. Then she turns and walks away.

She remembers little of the next hour. A dodgy minicab taking her to the main hospital entrance, the outpatients receptionist, aloof and professionally sympathetic: 'It is right underneath our building, in the basement. Turn left.' The eerie lighting of the fluorescent room and the long walk along the corridor with frosted windows. Struggling to answer the stammering questions of the dishevelled DI. She cannot wait to get out of here, into the freedom of the grey Cambridge afternoon.

The outside world surrounds her with colours and textures, but she is not a participant any more.

A spectator of the 3-D blockbuster called 'Ordinary Life'.

An ambulance whizzes past her and screeches by the Accident and Emergency entrance on the left. Kate remembers that this is a hospital after all, a place designed to save the living.

A red-haired boy is talking to a Japanese girl in a shiny nylon jacket by the door of the research laboratory. His hands speak for him. He clenches his fists, brings them to his chest, then thrusts the palms open, like a magician in training. His spell seems to work because the girl smiles and nods, smiles and nods, like an oversized porcelain doll.

Next to them a girl, too young to be a doctor, tries to park her bright Mini under the sign 'Authorised University staff only'. The car objects with noisy bursts. Rust has stained its white stripes, but is still invisible on the green bonnet.

Kate drifts past the magician, the doll and the Mini, and suddenly doubles up. The punch in the stomach is so violent that she has to crouch right here, behind a police car. A hot wave rises to her throat, burning through her body.

God, she is not ready. For his death, for this agony. And for this new, unknown feeling of danger.

'If you f-f-find you have any items that belonged to the deceased . . .' the policeman had said to her.

Yes, he left her three items. No, he left her to deal with those three items, all on her own. Something from his dream. Something that will save his nation. Just handed her the box with the Will and his grandfather's documents as they got off the plane in

London. 'I trust you' was all he said – abrupt, as usual. She is in this world without him, but with his secret.

As the train back to London pulls out of the station, Kate finally presses her forehead against the carriage window. Slashes of horizontal rain cut the view into dozens of distorted pictures, into flashes of green Hertfordshire fields with bare, dark patches. She remembers the brown dots in his green irises, his unsettled smile. The Russian Orthodox priest once told her that a soul, having left the body, will leave the Earth on the fortieth day. So he is here, with her, urging her to complete what they started.

Will he protect her during those forty days?

She pleads with him not to leave her just yet: 'Could you give me five more minutes, only five minutes to compose myself? Maybe you could stay for a couple of hours until I get home? Join me when I catch the flight . . . Do you think they will arrest me at the airport? Are they watching me now?'

But she has no choice. She has to go. To find the rest of his soul. Even if it destroys her.

She calls the office. She feels she cannot speak so he helps her out – as always, in his aloof, ironic manner. He uses her voice to call the office and talk to Sandra, their Department Secretary: 'No, I will not return to the office today, I'll go straight home to pack. There is a late flight tonight, I need to catch it. Please book the hotel . . . Yes, and ask them for a meeting. Thank you for all your help, Sandra. I will be back in a couple of days.'

He even provides Kate with the reasons for her rushed departure – something about urgent family matters. After all, Andriy was almost family, wasn't he?

*   *   *

Kate thinks about the fatal coincidences in Andriy's documents. Everybody who chased this wretched Will seems to be doomed. She tries to follow her logic.

The Ambassador to Vienna was arrested and shot as a traitor to the nation before the *Bolshaya Chistka*, the Great Purge of the 1930s, when over fifteen million people died in the hard labour camps of Northern Russia. But this Ambassador was from the wrong background to be a representative of a socialist state, and was trying to ally himself with the enemies of the Republic.

She remembers other stories Andriy told her:

About the Chairman of the Congress of Cossack Descendants who died a day after the congress. Nothing strange there, he had an acute form of tuberculosis.

About the lawyer, sent by the Congress to London to claim the inheritance at the beginning of the century, who never came back. But then there was a rumour that he did a runner, decided to stay in London with the money, collected by the Congress.

There were reasons, explanations for each of the cases. What would be the reason for Andriy's death? Is she the right person to find out? The sooner she hands the documents to someone else, the better.

Six hours later, on the plane, she puts Andriy's fragrant file on her lap.

Apart from the typed letter from the Ukrainian Ambassador to Vienna, confirming the meeting with Grygor Polubotko, and a handwritten copy of the Will, which Grygor presented to the Ambasssador in 1922, there is one more document. A copy of a report, dated December 1724, by the Russian Secret Police on the interrogation of Yefrem, the sentinel at the Peter and Paul

Fortress, about the meeting between the Emperor of All Russia, Peter the Great, and the Cossack Treasurer Colonel Pavlo Polubotko. The waxy paper is covered with unfamiliar curls and dots, but Kate knows it by heart, from Andriy's calligraphic, accurate teacher's copy.

She pulls Andriy's copied pages out, reads them again, just to look at his handwriting:

Peter and Paul Fortress, St Petersburg
December 1724

To the Head of Taynaya Kantselyariya General Yamshchikov.
The questioning of the Alexandrovsky Ravelin sentry, Yefrem
Malakhov confirmed the following . . .

Yefrem often thinks how lucky he is. When he returned scarred, wifeless and childless, after twenty years of fighting for his country in the battles against Sweden and the Ottoman Empire, Mother Russia loved him back. Yefrem was allowed to serve the great Empire here, in its heart. Everything about the new capital is glamorous and spellbinding – the milky dusk of early summer nights, the streamlined Italian perfection of the buildings on the Neva embankment, the babel of Italian, Dutch, English and French in the coffee-houses – the new foreign alternative to the vodka-reeking *kabaky*. Nothing like old Moscow where, as he remembered, the ornate chambers of the Kremlin, the spiky domes of St Basil and the golden onions of the monasteries reigned over the dark, drunken poverty of huts and muddy roads. He is proud to be a sentry at the new Peter and Paul Fortress that is piercing the northern skies with its golden needle. The only problem with the fortress is that, built on a strip of marshes, close to the sea, it is often flooded and sometimes the prisoners die in the freezing dampness of the cells before being sentenced – but this has nothing to do with Yefrem. He is only a guard, a small man, serving his Tsar and Great Russia.

He senses the visitor before he sees him. A man strides briskly across the courtyard, towards the red and white stripes of the sentry box, leaning forward against the wind. Yefrem has never seen him that close.

His white scarf, made of the finest Dutch cloth, is hastily catching up with the tall body, his movements are filled with unstoppable determination and ruthless energy. Yefrem flinches and hurries towards the nocturnal caller. He is praying silently, asking God to save him from an outbreak of the visitor's rage.

'The keys!' snaps the night guest.

Yefrem does not need to ask questions. He knows exactly who has to be seen.

The prisoner Pavlo Polubotko, a Ukrainian Cossack Colonel, is terminally ill. The priest has given him absolution already. Thirteen months of thorough questioning by *Taynaya Kantselyariya*, the notorious Secret Police, and the freezing torture of the cell contributed to his ailing health. The guard has also heard that the sentence has never been passed, and it was rumoured that the Cossack was not guilty of treason . . .

Pushing open a heavy oak door, the visitor has to duck: the doors of the fortress, which was named after him as much as after the Apostles Peter and Paul, were not designed for somebody so tall. Or maybe, the doors were built to show that he was the tallest as well as the wisest, the Tsar of all the Russias, Peter the Great.

The Emperor takes a candle from Yefrem's shaking hands and

stops for a second, allowing his senses to adjust to the thick, rancid darkness of the cell.

Through the half-open door Yefrem can see the old Cossack. His sallow, withered skin is set on the cheekbones, saliva is dribbling from the half-open mouth – the Colonel looks dead already. The only sign of life is a wheezing whistling sound. 'The hissing of a dying snake,' Yefrem heard the Tsar saying.

Yefrem is not sure what to do – to go back to his sentry box or remain here, guarding his Tsar. His curiosity is stronger than the sense of duty.

'You should not have come, Tsar Peter.' With an obvious effort, the Cossack Colonel tries to raise himself from the bench. He is still a warrior, he needs to stand in the presence of his sovereign.

'I never wanted it to go this far, Pavlo.' Yefrem is surprised to hear the Emperor's apologetic tone. 'But I had no choice when you and your traitor friends came to me with your ridiculous petition. What insolence – asking for more independence, for petty privileges and accusing the Emperor of unfairness in front of his own subjects! I did not need to be reminded that out of twelve thousand Cossacks, recruited for the Persian campaign, hardly a thousand survived, but this was the price one had to pay for victory. I had a chance to read the interrogation records. I could dismiss the accusation by the priest Havrylo, that you had seized the monastic lands for your own use. Everybody knows how religious you are.

'The second accusation, however, is far more serious. Secret agents reported that you were in contact with a certain Hetman Orlyk, a dangerous plotter, protected in Sweden by Karl XII. Such a betrayal, even if only suspected, had to be punished.

'I am not here to apologise. I simply want you to explain the disappearance of the Cossack army treasures. What happened to the gold? You were elected a bursar for your honesty.'

'You should not have come, Tsar Peter,' repeats the Cossack with obvious effort. 'The priest has just gone, and my soul belongs to God. Nobody can stand between me and the Almighty now. But you have always thought of yourself as God, haven't you? Your soul is so clouded with hatred that you cannot see the obvious. My nation has given you so many lives, and you are still taking, always taking – and we would be ready to give, if we were treated as equals, not slaves. We trusted you, adored you, and all we received was insults and innumerable misfortunes. My last words for you are: It is easier to rule the nation by admiration, not by terror. Your rule won't last; the anger in your heart is unworthy of a Christian Monarch. As two Christians, we shall face God soon, as Peter and Paul did in the Bible. My soul will be waiting for you for forty days – we should face the judgement of the Almighty together.'

Yefrem is bewildered by the Cossack's speech. The man is obviously out of his mind to dare to speak to the Tsar like this. Yefrem hears a thud and rushes to the cell. He can see the Emperor shoving Pavlo against the dank, slippery wall.

'What have you done with the Cossack gold, Pavlo? It doesn't belong to you. It belongs to Great Russia, to the Empire! You cannot take it with you anyway.'

Kate's finger follows Andriy's neat dots and crosses:

Peter the Great, the Emperor of All Russia, died in January 1725, exactly forty days after the death of the Cossack Treasurer Colonel Pavlo Polubotko. Pavlo's speech, retold by Yefrem, became a legend.

The Cossack gold has never been found. There were claims that the gold was deposited with the Bank of England by Polubotko's son in 1723.

The gold, according to Polubotko's Will, can be claimed by his descendants in any generation. There are two conditions: that Ukraine has to become an independent state, and that the descendant has to live in Ukraine. If the descendant lives abroad, he can claim 5 per cent of the inheritance, giving the rest for the benefit of independent Ukraine.

According to The Guinness Book of Records, *Polubotko's gold with interest accrued is the world's second largest unclaimed inheritance.*

In August 1991, Ukraine officially declared its independence, much to the surprise of the whole world and the dismay of its immediate neighbours. On the agenda of the first historic session of the Ukrainian Parliament, Verkhovna Rada, there was a motion to present all the necessary documents to the Bank of England, so that the Cossack gold could be claimed back for the benefit of the newly independent nation, almost three centuries after it had been deposited in those far-off London vaults. Either not all the documents were in place, or the Parliament had indeed more mundane and urgent problems to resolve for the survival of the new state, but the proposal was put on the backburner 'Do krashchyh chasiv' – 'Till better times', as Ukrainians would say.

She is interrupted by a deep, neglected cough next to her, and looks at the passenger – a boy in a navy blazer with a coat-of-arms embroidered on the breast pocket. Probably a boarder in an

English school, going home for the Easter holidays. Travelling alone, he has followed all the necessary precautions – seat belt tightly snapped, the uniform blazer all buttoned up, the tie knot tightened. His face is a mask of concentration on the Gameboy. Only his neck is a giveaway – a thin, fair-skinned neck, coming out of the soiled shirt collar like a timid February daffodil shoot. It will take his mother several days to shake him out of his shell. Soaking, nourishing, feeding, spoiling him rotten, she will peel off layer by layer – first the unfresh clothes, then his 'I-know-not-many-children-have-this-opportunity-and-so-I-should-be-grateful' attitude. When he finally succumbs, shyly laying his head on her shoulder, he will nuzzle into her neck and weep. With joy breathing her oh, so familiar smell; with fear, that this closeness is only temporary; with the blissful feeling of being defenceless and yet unreservedly, unashamedly safe. The feeling Kate needs so badly now.

'What game are you playing?' Kate tries to knock into his armour.

The boy looks at her through his overgrown fringe. 'Super Mario Brothers. Deluxe,' he adds proudly.

She asks: 'What's it about?' and thinks, Why are you bothering him? Leave the child alone!

The boy must possess a telepathic skill, as his tone is reluctantly polite. 'Mario needs to hit some enemies, you see – some of those annoying little mushrooms that exit the screen. Not personal enemies, just bad heroes. He has to jump, kick, run and rescue Princess Peach from the evil clutches of a huge dragon. I am in the middle of a chase now.' 'So am I,' Kate nearly says. 'I have got eight hundred and fifty-three points, and I would love to get to a thousand. Now, if you would excuse me . . .'

Not a bad speech for a Ukrainian ten year old: short and to the point. They certainly teach them some manners in these public schools.

Kate decides to look busy too and opens her diary. She has three entries for today: *Marina (final) – green dress. Fiona (cat). NY tickets.* All very important, key things, which she shouldn't have forgotten, wouldn't have forgotten in her previous life: a final fitting of a bridesmaid's dress for her friend Marina's wedding; talking to her neighbour Fiona about feeding her cat while she is on holiday in Spain; changing the flights to New York. But they will all have to manage without her. She is in a different reality now, just like this boy next to her.

The pilot is informing his passengers that they are flying over Poland. She looks at the neat chessboard of the fields below – some are still covered in snow, some are richly black. She has made her first chess move: flight London to Kiev. This is just an opening move, an invitation to a more complex gambit, to a sophisticated combination. Will she be able to play it? Will she choose the moves of a pawn or those of a queen? Her chess skills are rudimentary.

The pilot carries on talking – he must feel lonely there, with only his crew and the clouds to entertain him. He tells his passengers that the tail wind is quite strong, so he expects to land in sixty minutes. She has an hour to devise her plan of action. An hour to find the kind of strength she's never had. Sixty minutes 'till better times'.

PART 2
The Edge

Krai (Ukrainian; noun, masc.) – land, country
– limit, edge, border

Chapter 13

TARAS

Kiev, April 2001

The city has changed, as if somebody has replaced a black and white snapshot with a glossy colour print. He remembers the visit to Kiev before, back in his student days, when the palette of grey shades was enlivened only by the red and white lettering of Soviet posters, encouraging workers to improve their productivity and to implement the five-year plan in three years.

In May, the propaganda reds of the Labour Day demonstrations were toned down by the bridal freshness of chestnut blossom – but that joy was short-lived. The faces, the buildings, even the golden domes of the monasteries and churches were covered in a grey patina.

Now, strolling down Kreshchatyk to the main square, Taras is in the setting for a very different photo shoot.

A giant blonde is winking at him from the shampoo advertisement covering three floors of the department store; a cowboy aims his lasso at Taras to drag him into 'Marlboro Country'. The granite-clad main square, formerly the base of a colossal Lenin monument, is now the realm of roller-bladers and skateboarders, demonstrating their skills to envious crowds. The spring air is damp, but the street cafés already compete for customers, their multi-coloured umbrellas advertising every possible soft drink brand. Taras chooses a café where all the tables, chairs and umbrellas are bright red. A flock of teenage girls is chirruping next to him. They are celebrating their recently discovered sexuality, proudly parading their lime and pink jackets and mini-dresses, Turkish and Chinese market copies of black and cream designer models from the recently opened boutiques.

The service in the café is very slow – in fact, there is no service at all. Taras gets up to queue at the counter for his Cola and is treated to the street soap opera. The waitress holds on to the telephone receiver as if it will save her from drowning in the mascara-coloured streams running down her face.

'What do you mean, nothing personal?' she shrieks. 'We have been together for three months, you met my parents . . . Come, *zaychyk*, we'll talk' – she changes her tone, calling her boyfriend 'little bunny' in her desperate plea for love.

She reminds Taras of the conversation he had with his boss a month ago. The day before his trip to London, Karpov called him into the office. After the final brief, he added, looking above Taras, at the fresh crack on the wall: 'You were at university together, you said. I hope there is nothing personal in this, Lieutenant.' Karpov would never know or would pretend never to guess that for Taras all this was, is, will be personal.

When did it start? Perhaps that day when he pulled file N1247 off the shelf and read the word ЗОЛОТО in the upper left corner. He has read the files entitled *Gold* before.

The first one was the file N1442/b. The journalists would blow up the archives for a story like this: about the Tsar's family gold, hidden abroad during the First World War; the Tsarina's rings, sewn into the hems of the ladies-in-waiting's dresses and the royal 172-diamond tiara, smuggled to London in the doctor's suitcase with the false bottom. Taras had to classify the file as *Not For the General Public* and send it to the *Spetskhran*, the security vault, but frankly, it was disappointing. The 'eye-witnesses' were, in fact, rumourmongers, and the evidence tasted like vanilla-flavoured gossip.

File N2113, *Gold reserves of the Russian Empire, Stored in Japanese Banks*, Taras classified as *Pending*. It was only a matter of time before this file would be used: the copy of the agreement between the White Army General Rosanov and the Yokohama Siokin Bank, signed in 1921, was there, awaiting presentation. The confident handwriting of some mega-senior official on the cover (*Can be used as a weighty lever in the Kuril Islands conflict negotiations*) prompted Taras's classification.

Then there was the *White Army Gold* file, N1872. Three tons of gold coins, hidden by the Kolchak army in the Siberian *taiga* in the early 1920s. It made exciting reading: local hunters, Red Army officers, and later, in the 1950s, a secret KGB expedition, all searching for these coins in the Hanty-Mansijsk region. But with the *taiga* stretching for thousands of kilometres, they can search for another hundred years, decided Taras, and he classified the file as *Open Access*.

The file about the Romanian gold train, which disappeared during the 1917 Revolution, at least had a happy ending. Somebody dealing with it before Taras had scribbled *CASE CLOSED* in big block letters and then, in English, *Three Times Lucky!* Taras knows why. The gold was found and returned to Romania in three batches – in 1934, in 1948 and finally in 1964, twenty-four tons in all.

The most inspiring case was Schliemann's gold, of course. These were the Treasures of Troy, brought into the country from Germany by the Soviet Army after the war. He remembers the file well. It promised travelling, action, promotion. Taras presented the findings to Karpov and, as a result, was even included in a team that was planning the return of the gold to Germany as a gesture of good will. But somebody at the top made a wise decision that gestures of good will should not be over-generous. The treasures are priceless, no doubt, but they have a high enough price not to become freebies. So the whole plan ended with a token gift. Most of the treasures remained in Russia to be displayed in a lavish, widely publicised exhibition. It is on at the Pushkin Museum now – Taras has seen the posters.

No, it all started much earlier, even before he became a student. Perhaps that early June, at the end of his conscription service, when he was turning twenty. The end of Far Eastern humid heat, the bullying and the oily millet. Two years, two grinding years – at the age when he should have been having the time of his life. But then, most Soviet boys had to go through this, unless they had influential parents to get them an *Exempt for Health Reasons* certificate when they turned eighteen. Even the invincible mosquitoes could not change the festive mood of those for whom the heavy smell of the tank oil was soon to be replaced by the musty, sweaty stench of a slow train taking them home. Taras was called to see Colonel Serov, the Tank Regiment Commander. The Colonel was sipping his tea laced with cognac, glowing more than usual.

'Well, Private Petrenko,' his tone was brimming with fatherly concern, 'what are your plans for the future?'

'I'll think about them when I get back home,' answered Taras, puzzled by this sweet-talking from his Commander.

'You know, to achieve something in life, you should study hard.' The Colonel was full of patronising generalities. He was practising them daily on soldiers and officers alike. 'And we could help you to get a place at university. What would you say to that?'

Only then did Taras understand the 'we'. There was another man in the office, a Major, who had so far shown no desire to acknowledge the soldier's presence. Taras was taken aback. Why should the Colonel help him? Especially after recent events . . . He was not that keen on university, but what would he do otherwise? Return to village life, where the biggest excitement would come from drunken fights on Saturdays? No, he wanted to be a winner, and if to get to the top meant he needed to study, he would give it a try.

Taras managed a grateful smile. 'I would appreciate it if the Army could help me with my education, Comrade Colonel.'

'We will, Taras.' For the first time in two years, Serov called him by his first name. 'But that would require a certain commitment on your part as well. You will have to join a particular military organisation and perform your civil duty. Do you understand what I mean?'

Ah. Now he understood. He was being recruited for the KGB, chosen for his strength and abilities, given the chance to join the real power.

'If you need to think about it, we—' continued the Colonel.

'Thank you, *Tovarysh Polkovnik*,' interrupted Taras. 'I have thought about it.' He did not say how often. Steady. He shouldn't seem too keen.

'Are you absolutely sure, young man? It is a serious commitment. Your whole life will change and—'

'I have decided, Comrade Colonel.'

Private Petrenko had never interrupted his Regiment Commander before. Now he has done so twice in a minute.

The Major stood up from his corner. 'Well done. We need to talk about the arrangements, Private Petrenko. Wait outside for a moment.'

Not that Taras was into eavesdropping, he simply could not help overhearing. The Colonel started talking before he closed the door: 'Frankly, I think he is all yours, Sergey. He is strong, he is bright and, most importantly,' the Colonel paused, 'he's a clean sheet. He hasn't been taught anything you would need to change. You've made the right choice. Now, vodka or cognac?'

'I think you are right,' replied the Major. 'He has potential, this boy. It is quite smooth, this cognac – is it Armenian? I have heard that every now and again, the cognac plant N1 in Yerevan sends a special reserve bottle to England, to the Queen Mother. Do you think it's true?'

Taras waited outside the door for some time, until they had finished the bottle.

In August, after a four-week crash course of revision, Taras became a student in the History Faculty of Lviv University. Though he studied assiduously, he found it tough going after two years of Army drills, and felt that his entrance exam marks were higher than the knowledge he showed. His mentor had kept his first promise. Now it was his turn.

The History Faculty of Lviv University was not a random choice. Lviv did not become part of the Soviet Ukraine until 1939, and still had memories of its Central European past and a better lifestyle: lions gazing from the balconies of the arched mansions, trams rattling through the cobbled streets of the old city centre. Atheist propaganda could not empty the enormous Catholic Kostyol, and coffee shops at every corner invited passers-by to try 'a cake like Mamma used to bake' taken with strong coffee, brewed in a small pot on hot sand, Turkish-style.

People here were less scared to express their opinions openly, and their understanding of the historic events of 'Western Ukraine joining the Soviet Union of its own free will and desire in 1939' was quite different from the one in the school history textbooks. Russians were openly hated here, and Russian-speakers, asking directions in town, were often ignored. As far as the KGB was concerned, students of the History Faculty of Lviv University were dormant dissidents and Nationalists, and had to be identified early.

Taras was older than most of the students on his course. He was unmoved by the naivety of their youth, their childish dreams and crushes. He had his Supreme Goal: he had to fit in and become popular. He was learning to laugh at their jokes, to watch the same movies, to listen to the same bearded physicists-turned-bards. With his unique Army experience (everybody else came straight from school), his Western Ukrainian mountain accent and open smile (well practised in front of the cracked stained minor in the university hostel toilets), he was accepted by his fellow students as an elder brother. Less sophisticated than the city intellectuals, perhaps, but sincere and fun.

When Taras proposed the organisation of a political discussion club, everybody supported the idea. The Dean of the Faculty allocated a lecture room on Wednesday evenings, *So that the students can study, have better understanding and approve the policy of the*

Communist Party and denounce the pretentious Western propaganda said his memo, pinned on the Faculty noticeboard opposite the Dean's office. The Wednesday Club became a forum for hot discussion and even occasional doubts about the right course of Communist Party policy. The boldest, the most controversial ideas were always expressed by Taras Petrenko.

Nobody, not even his room-mate, ever suspected that every single word of his challenging speeches came from texts supplied by his KGB tutors. Every Thursday morning Taras handed a detailed handwritten report of the latest club session to another jogger during their chance encounter along the secluded leafy paths of Striysky Park.

Another active speaker at the club meetings was Andriy Savchuk, or Andriyko, as everybody called him. He was knowledgeable and popular, and his family history gave him an additional heroic aura. His grandfather, a famous historian, well-known in the West, was accused of extreme Nationalistic ideas in his own country. He was not arrested, however. Western radio stations, their broadcasts not fully jammed by sophisticated Soviet devices, started a massive media campaign to protect him. As a result, he was not arrested, but instead he was not allowed to publish anything, or to lecture anywhere, and was wasting away quietly in the Archives, his work carefully monitored by two minders.

Andriyko was an obvious target for the KGB's keen attention and a 'natural' choice for Taras's best friend. When Andriy graduated with Honours, scooping the top awards at the annual students' research conferences during all five years of his university course, everybody expected that he would be offered a lectureship at the university. There was a rustle of surprise when at the graduation ceremony the Dean announced *raspredelenye* – job assignments. Andriyko was given a place as a school history teacher in a small town not far from Lviv. The next big surprise was the announcement that Taras Petrenko was offered a postgraduate place in Moscow at the famous Institute of History and Archives. Yes, Taras was a great chap, no doubt about that, but not really very academic. Perhaps, his friends thought, the fact that he had organised the hugely successful discussion club had had an impact.

After all the farewells, hugs, and promises to write and get together each year, Andriy went to a provincial school, Taras to Moscow. He was genuinely upset at not being able to leave his friends his address, as he did not yet know which hostel he would be living in. He could not tell them that the hostel would be not in the centre of Moscow, near the Archive Institute, but on the outskirts, on Michurinsky Prospect, next to the KGB Academy.

Or maybe it all started when he met Carmen?

When they *both* met Carmen. Everything about her was loud, exotic, luscious: her deep husky laugh, her scarlet pout, her swinging gait, her Cuban accent. She lived on the same floor as Taras and she was the one to ask him out – in the kitchen, over the boiling kettle: 'Let us see a film together, Taras. *Vamos* tonight, no?'

Who could resist her, mixing in Spanish words, licking honey off her fingers, in her snazzy micro-gown and homely red felt slippers? Show me a man, a hot-blooded young male, who would not agree to have a cup of tea with her afterwards, especially when she mentioned to him, tossing her raven-black mane, that her room-mate was away, visiting her parents? He admitted to her that she was his first woman, but never told her that she was 'the one and only' – never had a chance. Why did he invite her to the next Wednesday Club? Just to impress her? She was impressed all

right. Left that evening with Andriy, and they remained inseparable for three years, until she returned to Havana.

No, he knows when it really started.

It was that sunny, frosty Sunday afternoon, when Andriy invited
him to lunch with his grandparents. The day when Taras pressed
the button of the doorbell and listened to that melancholic waltz
for the first time, when Sara Samoylovna opened the door and he
stepped into the world of books and coffee aroma. It was Andriy's
family clan gathering – aunts, nephews, elder brother, with Sara
Samoylovna reigning over it: as peacemaker, entertainer, earth
mother. It was the most ordinary dinner – borshch, pork with
pickled cabbage, poppy-seed cake. And because it was so normal,
so unlike his family, he resented it even more.

Taras was seven when his mother disappeared. Rumour had it
that she escaped, as she could not take her husband's drunken
jealousy and beatings any more. Some said that being a robust,
good-looking girl, she could not think of anything better than to
offer to the factory workers in town her . . . 'God forgive me for
even thinking about this!' whispered the village women, rapidly
crossing themselves. But nobody really knew whether it was true
or just a thread of petty jealousy, woven into fatuous chatter, merely
to add some excitement to the drab routine of village life.

His father Mykola, a forest warden, had drowned his sorrows
in the murky mooonshine supplied in abundance by the soft-
hearted *vorozhka* Baba Marusya, the village witch. The boy was
looked after by the hunchbacked Baba Gapa, their neighbour,
whom Mykola would occasionally, in his sober days, help with
her vegetable garden. When Taras was ten, his father was found
dead in the woods: he had tripped on a muddy, rocky path and

rolled down the hill, his head smashing against the stones. Taras was lucky enough to escape the orphanage. He attended the village school and Baba Gapa continued to feed him, but somehow he was always hungry. It was a craving for an ordinary family life, for a family meal, for making a *diduh* – a pagan straw 'spirit' – for Christmas and painting *pysanky* eggs for Easter.

When Andriy's grandmother offered Taras another slice of the poppy-seed cake, a lump in his throat stopped him from answering. He was grieving for the loss of something he had never even had. He had been unfairly cheated of things taken for granted by this family. They were experiencing his unfelt emotions, enjoying uncon- ditional love, which was meant to be his, just his.

Poor Sara Samoylovna, old darling starling! She twittered the disaster upon herself.

She should not have told Taras about the diary, about the papers Andriy had found stuck under the oilskin cover, she really should not have! If only she hadn't mentioned the fact that Andriy had taken the papers with him to Cambridge, that he planned to start his own investigation. If only she hadn't banged on and on about how excited Andriy was about them . . .

Taras considered Plan A first: '*I am on a research trip in London for a week – what a chance to see my old uni mate.*' A pint in a pub, then another one, then a conversation could lead to the research Andriy was doing, then to other, more significant topics.

But deep in his heart, Taras knew that Plan A was never going to work. Andriy's family was always watched, he was used to secrecy, it was in his blood. He was always careful with words. His friends (including Taras, nudged by his mentors) used to tell him that he never invited anybody into the invisible circle he drew around him, but it was great to be with him when he stepped out of it.

The chance of Andriy telling his university friend about the documents was minuscule. In fact, less than that – zero. Which left Taras with no choice but to follow Plan B.

Not that killing Andriy was easy. It was a logistical nightmare, for a start – to find a pub busy enough for them to get lost in the crowd, to work out the amount of alcohol needed to have the desirable effect once it was spiked, all the timings . . .

Even with army training, where killing was drummed in as a quick survival reaction, fuelled by the adrenalin of the fight – almost intuitive, a natural skill, just like driving or flying a plane – killing does not come naturally to Taras. He needs to be detached, totally detached.

He remembers the discussion at the Academy, when Surikov asked them to write their own definition of cruelty. Orlov, their group comedian, wrote a quick line: *Cruelty is a cruel act.* Gorchakov, their sophisticated philosopher, gave the definition of cruelty as *Causing pain or suffering on a weaker being without pity or remorse.* Taras wrote *Unjustified violence.* He is not cruel. His violence was totally justified.

The hardest task of all was to forget that it was all personal, to follow Rule N2 from the 'Know Your Enemy' course: *To fight the enemy, you have to focus on the tasks, not on your anger or resentment. The emotions will cloud your judgement and lead to mistakes. Self-discipline is the key.*

So he *did* focus on the task. Spiked a drink in the crowded pub, supported Andriy on the ropewalk so that he would not fall into the river – everybody could see that. Walked under the balconies, then stopped opposite the willow tree to sit on the bank and have a long, long chat, waiting until it got darker and quieter and the crowds had subsided.

By then his drunken friend was brave enough to cross the bridge walking on the banister. ('Remember, Andriy, how we used to fool around during our summer teaching practice outside Lviv? This bridge is wider, surely, and it's so easy to get on the banister – use this latticed ironwork. Don't worry about balancing, don't worry at all – just hold my hand . . .' As Andriy climbed on the banister, Taras supported him until he'd walked ten, maybe fifteen steps (counted by Taras during the day) until he reached the perfect place, a waterfall below. It wasn't a push, not even a nudge, just letting Andriy's hand go so that he lost his balance and fell into the perfect triangle of the waterfall . . . Maybe just a concussion, if not a broken neck, would have done it, dragging the body into the weir.

Not everything went according to plan – he got into Andriy's room unnoticed, wore gloves when he searched the room, but he still could not find any documents. 'Disappointing, but not fatal,' as Karpov would say. You take the only person who knows out of the equation and you achieve your objective. With Andriy's love of secrecy, he would have found a unique hiding-place, known to him only. After all, the task Taras had was not necessarily to find the documents, but to make sure that nobody else would ever find them.

He feels sorry for Sara Samoylovna though, he genuinely does. Poor Sara, she has never been to Australia. She does not even know yet in how masterly a way she has launched a light, ochre-coloured boomerang. Taras watches it spinning in the air, parallel to the ground. Here it inclines to its flat side, rises, ready to injure the prey. Then it will curve to the left and glide back to the thrower. They say that small boomerangs are ideal for hunting small birds.

Small birds and old ladies.

He has a knack with them, he has discovered. Take the meeting he had this morning with the old Professor, for example. Visiting her, he decided, was important, especially before the second stage of the operation: she certainly knew most of the details of the gold story. According to the file, she would know about Oksana, too.

Arranging the meeting was easy: her name was famous, even though her publications were rare and controversial, and she was always happy to receive visitors. This morning she was only too keen to share her knowledge with a young, enthusiastic researcher. Taras had to admit, the Professor had an amazing memory for her eighty years. She remembered so many dates, so many facts about the Cossack Hetmans, that after two hours even his professional patience was running out.

Taras had already studied every letter of the framed Harvard Honorary degree on the wall, every background detail of the photographs of a smiling, toothless boy (must be her grandson ... or great-grandson?), counted the piles of paper on the floor by the desk, rubbed a rusty tea stain off the rim of his cup to reveal a faded golden inscription: *To one of the greatest historians of our times from enchanted students on her 70th jubilee*, but there was still no end to the illuminating lecture on 'The role of Cossack Councils in Military Decision-Making'. He regretted that the title of the PhD topic he had invented, in order to invite himself in, had turned out to cover such a substantial topic. He should have thought of something minor, less relevant to her research. Prize idiot!

'My dear boy, you should also try to look at the approach of the Cossack councils to choosing new chieftains,' the Professor carried on. She showed no signs of slowing down whatsoever. 'The

Cossacks would gather at the square on the first of January, eat, celebrate, and then shout the names of the candidates, and those whose names were shouted loudly enough had to leave the square and wait for the results of the voting. Interesting approach to democracy, don't you think?'

'*Pani* Maxymovych,' he managed to interrupt her, drumming his fingers over the box of chocolates he had brought her, 'what do you think of all these stories about Cossack gold? Does it really exist?' He deliberately chose *pani*: the elegant, Western Ukrainian address, almost *Lady Maxymovych*. No woman is averse to gentle flattery, even if she is a world-famous eighty-year-old professor.

Clearing her throat, she looked at him through her thick lenses. 'You are a historian, my boy. By now you should see the difference between chasing sensation and recognising historical facts. During my long life I have only had two encounters with this story. In the sixties, I think it was in 1962, when I was working in the Archives, two men from Moscow, from the KGB . . .' she whispered the last three letters, obviously still in awe and fear of the organisation '. . . came to visit me and asked questions about the descendants. They mentioned the letter, received from the British Treasury solicitor, asking for the descendants' names and addresses, and for a simple family tree showing how this relationship was traced.'

Of course I know about that! I have read the report about that meeting with you in the file – why do you think I am here? thought Taras, while the old historian carried on: 'The second time, in 1972, when I was allowed to work in Paris . . .'

'So, have you found the descendants?' interrupted Taras hastily. He was worried that the memories of *la belle France* would divert the Professor's thoughts away from the single thing he came for.

'Well, there were so many of them, Taras. Have you heard about the Congress of Descendants in 1906, then?'

Oh, I have studied the list of participants and the Resolution for about two hours, *pani* Maxymovych. Page seventy-five to one hundred and fifteen of case N1247, thought Taras. However, he shook his head and said aloud, 'No, I've never heard of it, Professor.'

Her energy amazed him once again. She bounced off her chair, leaned over to the second file in the third row of her twenty-four files on the floor (Taras counted them twice) and pulled out a piece of paper.

'Here!' She looked ten years younger in her jubilation. 'It's all here, Taras.'

He looked at the copy of the Kiev *Evening News* for 15 January 1906, and scanned the familiar lines again:

An amazing event in our town! Today the hall of the Girls' Gymnasium N2 held the Congress of Descendants of the Cossack Hetman Pavlo Polubotko; 480 descendants from all corners of Great Russia – from Kharkov, Poltava, Saratov, St Petersburg, Khabarovsk – participated in the Congress. What a mix of classes and dialects! An advocate from Odessa, Nikolay Polubotko, was elected the Chairman of the Congress. His speech (see below) caused a standing ovation:

'My dear, dear friends! I would like to address you as brothers, as all of us here are followers of the ancient Cossack fraternity.

'Last autumn, the Tsar's manifesto gave us hope. The Ukrainian faction at the first Duma has already raised the issue of territorial and political autonomy. Two months ago, we all welcomed the new law on the freedom of the press. Soon we will have the right to rule our own nation. But are we ready for our independence? We speak

the language forbidden in the streets; we have only two national newspapers, no Ukrainian schools. We need money to revive our national culture. Our Congress can and will do something about it. The gold our ancestor deposited in those deep London vaults could assist us in building the new Ukraine. I think you would agree with me, that we should pass the resolution to claim the money back for the benefit of the independent Ukrainian nation.'

The delegates of the Congress chose Nikolay Polubotko as a messenger to deliver the appeal to London.

'You know, Taras,' the Professor's tone was solemn and deliberate, 'he disappeared in London, this lawyer. Took the money the delegates collected for the investigation, and ran off.' She removed her glasses and wiped the lenses vigorously, as if this would improve her vision.

Taras was glad she could not see anything at that moment. It was hard for him to hide a smile. He just imagined her face if he had told her the truth: 'No, Professor, he did not run off with the money. He never even got to Britain, your Nikolay. One of the delegates, a School Inspector from Kiev, was given a choice, you see. Either he could hand a letter about the movements of the descendants' envoy to the police agent during the "chance" encounter at the new public library, or a letter about "his anti-monarchist views, expressed at the Congress of Cossack Descendants", would have been sent immediately to the Ministry of Education. By the way, the library where the letter was handed over was called "Pharmacy for the Soul". The Kiev Department of the Secret Police certainly used irony well. Following the Inspector's report (page 89, case 1247) Nikolay Polubotko was thrown out of the train on the Polish–German border; his body

was never found. It would have been so inappropriate and incon-
venient to have the Ukrainian independence issue discussed in
the first Duma and presented to the Tsar once again – wouldn't
it?'

The Professor put on her glasses and resumed her quest for
descendants.

'Surprisingly,' she went on, 'there were no inheritance claims
after that. At least, no claims I know of. Remember – the times
were dark, the evidence was insubstantial, the necessary documents were inaccessible. There was one girl though, whom I can
remember very well and who, I would say, had more chances than
the others in claiming the inheritance. She was my student in the
sixties ... Oksana, that's it, her name was Oksana. She was the
daughter of a famous mathematician, who perished somewhere
in Stalin's camps.' She changed her voice to a whisper again.

'Bright girl she was, quite outspoken for her age, but then she
was from that first Soviet generation that was led to believe – for
a very brief period of time – that they were allowed to speak their
minds. Well, Oksana was trying to claim the inheritance to rehabilitate the names of her grandfather and father. She was a great-
great-great ... Anyway, I've lost count, but the legend lived in her
family for generations. We often talked about Oksana's Cossack
roots – she even invited me home to see the artefacts. Of amazing
historical value they were: a portrait of Pavlo Polubotko and a
small silver candelabra which, she said, used to belong to the
Cossack Hetman, several letters from the Hetman's son Yakiv.
Amazing how the family managed to save all this – despite all the
searches and arrests that took place. They might have had the original Will, even – I don't know, they never showed it to me. I
remember that I tried to persuade Oksana's mother to give these

items to the museum, but she was adamant that they would need them as proofs.'

Pani Maxymovych was not telling Taras anything new. Her memories merely confirmed everything he had read in the report of 1962.

He coughed politely. 'Do you know where I can find Oksana?'

'Oh, my dear boy, I have met and lost so many people in my life, I cannot keep track. She did not graduate, that I remember well. The Dean told me that she married her fiancé and moved to Moscow with him. Whether she finished her studies there, I don't know, as I have no idea what her married name is. Where was I? Oh, the engravings! I have this fascinating collection of engraved portraits of Cossacks I was going to show you . . .'

But Taras was already pushing his chair back. 'Thank you so much, *pani* Maxymovych. I'll have a look at the portraits next time, if you will allow me to come and see you again.'

The old lady sighed. 'What is this sudden obsession with Cossack gold, I wonder? The Parliament declaration, newspaper articles, TV programmes – even today you are the second person to ask me about it. A lovely English girl came this morning, and—'

'A lovely English girl?' echoed Taras. He settled himself back on the chair again.

'Oh,' the old historian kept talking, not looking at Taras, folding and putting the papers back into the file, 'a PhD student from Cambridge, researching Cossack history. Sweet girl, quite shy, looks a bit tired. Works hard, obviously. It was quite enlightening to find out that somebody in Cambridge was interested in such a topic. We could not talk much, mind you. I learned French at school, you know, so we used that to communicate, along with my dozen words in English and her surprisingly well-accented ten words in Ukrainian. I gave her my article to read – I am planning to publish it this year, for the Tenth Anniversary of Independence. Don't know what newspaper to hand it to, they are all so shallow these days, so vulgar! Anyway, the article is about the Cossacks' foreign legacy, so it could be useful for her research. It is in Ukrainian, but she might find somebody to translate it for her. We agreed to meet tomorrow, when my daughter, an English teacher, would be here to interpret.'

Taras could almost feel his brain clicking, working on overload, analysing the information he had just received. He was not at all comfortable with the idea of this other visitor. Should he leave his pen, or the notes of today's discussion on the floor by the chair, so that he could come back again tomorrow morning and meet this English student? But his pen was only a cheap plastic one and his 'notes' consisted of five lines, scribbled down out of boredom. Damn . . .

'By the way,' the old professor's voice suddenly buzzed with excitement and affection, 'you mentioned that you graduated from Lviv University. Did you have a chance to meet a celebrated historian there during your studies?' She gave the name of Andriy's grandfather.

'No, I don't think so.' Taras looked straight into her thick lenses. He was very careful with his words. 'But I have heard a lot about him. Why do you ask?'

Her smile was more childish than senile. 'He was a remarkable man. An encyclopaedic mind. I used to know him very well. In fact, we were at university together before the war, and more than just friends.'

Taras felt an unpleasant heaviness in his chest. Of course, she was not just '*Pani* Maxymovych', she was 'Professor *Vera*

Maxymovych'! He recalled Sara Samoylovna's words: 'Vera was a girl my husband was going to marry before the war. They studied together, and then she remained in Moscow. Amazingly, after the war we became great friends.'

And to think that Vera Maxymovych might call Sara Samoylovna, and mention his visit . . .

'Ignoring coincidences is the first step towards failure', were the favourite words of Colonel Surikov at the Academy. They are Taras's favourite words too. Rising decisively, he said, 'May I have a glass of water before I leave? Don't worry, I'll find my way to the kitchen.'

Chapter 14

Kiev, Lavra Monastery, April 2001

How can he tell the difference? Some must be pilgrims, others tourists. All the women wear headscarves, and most of them are crossing themselves quickly. And all of them are looking down, as if the truth, the spirit, the strength they are seeking is hidden under the massive lead gates. Why aren't they looking up? The divine is all there – the golden onion domes of the monastery, peeled by the sun, glittering in the still air. He is the odd one out – a young man in the crowd of middle-aged female believers and visitors, but he does not mind. He is on a mission.

It is certainly not a mission of which Karpov would approve. 'Do explain the logic of pursuing this in the middle of Stage Two of an important operation, Lieutenant Petrenko. Go on,' he would have said, lifting his head, aiming his chin at Taras.

Luckily, with six hours' waiting time before the beginning of the next operational phase, Taras has no one to answer to. He owes this mission to himself, and to himself only.

'Your own fear is your ultimate betrayal'. For once Taras agrees with Colonel Surikov's pearl of wisdom. He still shudders when he thinks about his previous visit to the monastery twelve years ago and about *that* 'ultimate betrayal'.

It must have been an effect of the lecture about the mystery of the caves just before the university research trip – one of the rare university lectures he actually enjoyed. The slides are still clicking in his memory: construction dates, numbers, photographs of various churches . . .

The first slide was a cluster of whitewashed buildings with golden onion domes spreading over the green hill. What a sight, thought Taras then. He remembers the opening text well: *Pechersk Lavra, the oldest Russian Orthodox monastery, was founded in 1071 in the subterranean caves. Hence the name, deriving from the old Russian* pechery *for 'caves'.*

Click, next slide – a photograph of the underground chapel, followed by a commentary from Professor Symonenko, their research tour organiser:

'*Zatvorniki*, the hermits, were often buried alive in the caves in an attempt to secure holiness more quickly. A tiny window was left for air, water and bread. The caves also acted as a cemetery for two centuries. The bodies of the monks, buried in the caves, often became mummified by the will of God, or by some strange whim of nature. The first explanation was obviously more acceptable to the monastery, and soon Lavra became a place of pilgrimage, with numerous churches and underground chapels for quiet prayer.'

The third slide was slightly more disturbing – narrow, dim corridors; candlelight, reflected in the glass of the coffins in the arches.

'These are the famous caves, the mysterious underground labyrinths, which are still not fully researched . . .' Symonenko lowered his voice and paused for maximum effect. 'Only two out of the hundred and thirty kilometres of corridors are open to the public. Any attempts to explore the caves further have resulted in a number of baffling disappearances. Those lucky lost souls who were found alive, eyes wide with horror, showed signs of significant distress . . .

'So, my dear fellows,' concluded Symonenko cheerfully, 'during the visit to the caves, do stick with the group, and if you have any desire to get lost – you'll have to live with the consequences.'

A week later, together with the other students, Taras inched along the airless underground passages, clutching a taper, peeping into the handkerchief-sized windows of the mummified hermits, listening to the mumbling echo of the pilgrims' prayers in the subterranean chapels.

It started with a smell. The stale, mouldy smell of unaired old buildings. Here, mixed with a whiff of incense, with the greasy smoke of cheap tapers, it was suffocating. It was getting deep inside his lungs, bringing panic with it. Taras slowed down, despite the protests of his fellow students, shuffling along the passages behind him. The light of the taper in his hands was dancing faster, and he felt a trickle of sweat running down his face. He turned his back to the dank wall, and tried to squeeze past the flow of pilgrims, edging his way towards the exit. The embalmed bodies seemed to get closer, the ceilings were getting lower, and Taras's world narrowed into a faint hope of daylight at the end of the umpteenth passage.

When he finally pushed his way out and burst into the white and azure church, built above the exit from the caves, he collapsed on the lead floor, breathing heavily, squinting at the rays of sunshine, and oblivious to the crowds around him. He has never forgotten that day, or the promise he made to himself then: to walk through the caves again and conquer his fear.

Taras remembers that there is a panoramic platform behind the refectory church. A minute later he takes in the whole view: the islands in the middle of the river with their empty sandy beaches, the busy flow of traffic on the bridge across the Dnieper; the cranes stretched over the new skyscrapers on the left bank. For a nanosecond he regrets his decision – it would have been so much nicer to spend the remainder of the day in the park along the river. He deserves these several hours of a break, he really does. His gaze avoids the one thing he came for – the green roof of the building below: the prayer house for the pilgrims by the entrance to the caves. He tries not to think about all the awful things that might happen. What if he couldn't get out of the caves quickly enough? What if his heart stopped there and his body was trampled upon, crushed in the dark by hundreds of pilgrims before he was discovered?

Sharpen up, Taras, enough daydreaming. He quickens his pace. To distract himself, he decides to count the wooden steps of the gallery, leading to the entrance to the caves. 'Fourteen, fifteen', he whispers to himself, pausing for breath. By the time he says, 'One hundred and seventy-two,' his palms are treacherously clammy. He catches the whiff of the familiar 'moss mixed with incense' smell and feels so lightheaded that he has to stumble to the pilgrims' font by the entrance and splash his face with icy water.

Steady, Tarasyk, he thinks to himself. There must be an explanation why this smell triggers such a blind panic. He calls himself Tarasyk, as his mother used to call him before she disappeared, as she called him when . . . The memory hits him: the mouldy walls, the darkness and his mother's voice from above: 'Tarasyk, where are you?' He is trying to answer, to call her back, but he is limp with fear, his skin is covered in goose bumps and he has lost his voice . . .

How old was he? Four? Five? They were playing hide-and-seek in Baba Gapa's garden when he decided to jump into her *podpol*. Every house in the village had a similar cellar, used as a cold store for vegetables, curd cheese and butter. He was so proud of himself, when he managed to close the heavy lid. The panic came later, when all his friends ran away into the kitchen garden, and he realised that he could not push the lid back. He scratched the wood, grazed his shoulder to raw skin, screamed to huskiness, but nobody came, nobody could hear him. He was going to die here and they would only find his body when Baba Gapa needed to get some butter out. He crawled into the corner, sobbing in desperation, his leg brushing against the damp wall and his toes hitting the cold glass of a jar.

Baba Gapa found him that evening, when she opened the lid of her *podpol* to put some curd cheese in. Taras was pulled out, straight into his mother's tender: 'Oh, thank God, Tarasyk, the whole village is out looking for you!' and his father's curt, but relieved: 'I will kill you, you little bastard!'

He was smelling of pee and sour cream, his cheeks were covered in a yellowish crust, but a relieved smile was glued to his pale lips. He was so happy to be alive, even beyond the suspicion that a moment later his father would beat him to death.

Taras splashes his face again. 'You identified the trigger for yourself, Lieutenant Petrenko. Now all you need to do is to face your fear,' Surikov from the Academy would have told him.

A young monk with a goatee marshals Taras towards the lime tree, where a tour guide in a black soutane is waving a souvenir brochure over his head, gathering his flock. Taras notices a thick black cable running along the walls down to the caves, and realises what is missing – he has no taper in his hand. Bulbs are hanging over the glass coffins, lighting the arches by the subterranean churches; glowing arrows point in the direction of the exit from every corner of the winding passages. The monk guide asks the group to slow down and stops by a small coffin. The mummy is completely covered by a red velvet cloth, only one deformed hand being visible, the knuckle bone exposed under the cracked parchment of skin.

'So,' the monk chants a familiar script, 'Feofan lived such a holy life that he was declared a saint when he was still alive. However, he sinned soon afterwards, leaving the brethren with a difficult choice. A wise solution was soon found. When he died three years later, only the saintly part of his body was buried here in the caves, while the part which had sinned was left in the common grave outside the walls of the monastery. I will let you guess for your-selves which sin he had committed.' The chorus of laughter echoes along the corridors.

The electric bulbs instead of the candles, the souvenir kiosks and the guides in their long soutanes make the caves look like a theme park. The curse is lifted, leaving Taras disappointed. The trip to the caves has been a waste of time.

He strides across the courtyard, past the newly built Assumption Cathedral, past the leaning belfry to the forged gates. By the exit he notices a small poster with an arrow, which invites everybody to *come in and see the unseen*. The old cashier in a purple scarf is sitting on a rickety chair outside the exhibition hall. She flashes Taras a gold-crowned smile: 'The exhibition is included in the price of the ticket. Come, have a look.' Her tone promises a miracle. Well, people visit Lavra for its wonders, after all. With her flowery scarf and faded, darned cardigan, she reminds Taras of Baba Gapa. He walks in, reluctantly.

At first he does not understand what is on display. The room is stark, futuristic, with twelve symmetrical glass discs on the walls. Taras leans over one of the discs and sees a golden caravan, shimmering under the midday sun. Four camels, moving towards a pyramid and a palm tree. He moves away from the disc, and the picture disappears; there is nothing but a thin silver line with a golden dot behind the glass. Some sort of a hologram? He checks the disc again. The camels are still there, still on the same path to the oasis.

Taras scans a sign on the wall, surprised by its impassivity. The inscription coldly informs him that the composition, made of gold, is placed in the eye of an ordinary needle and can be observed under a microscope only. No exclamation marks, no mention of the amazing skill of the artist, no reference to a 'miracle' anywhere.

Fascinated, Taras moves between the discs. There is the smallest book in the world, with the pages stitched by a cobweb, then a flea in golden boots . . . Only now does he notice that there is another visitor in the room. A girl, oblivious to the fact that she started from the wrong end of the exhibition, is moving towards him, spending no more than a few seconds over each display case.

Taras scans her, true to his professional habit, taking her in with one look: a square bag bulging with folders, no camera. Wearing black trousers, not jeans, and a camel coat. Probably a foreign student or a researcher, definitely not a tourist. Her body is all sharp angles – her chin, her nose, her elbows. She moves with the amazing slow grace of a slender giraffe. Her brown hair is pulled into a pony tail and, as she leans over a microscope, Taras notices a mole on the left side of her neck, just below her ear. She steps towards the next microscope without noticing Taras behind her, and the heel of her boot lands straight on his toe. She loses her balance and nearly falls back, but Taras is already there, offering her his shoulder, supporting her elbow, picking up her oversized bag from the floor.

She mumbles sorries and thank yous in English and accented Ukrainian under her breath, lifts her head, raises tired, lacklustre eyes, and that's when it hits him.

There is something oh, so familiar, so vulnerable and tender about her.

So, Taras, this is what the girl of your destiny looks like, he thinks. She is taller than he imagined her, skinnier.

He is totally unprepared for the new wave of emotions that has knocked him over in the middle of a stark exhibition hall. He has been ambushed by a girl who looks at him apologetically, biting the corner of her lip, clutching a crumpled handkerchief in one hand and clinging to the clasp of her bag with the other. How can anybody look so determined, and yet so hurt and exposed? For the first time in his life he does not want to defend himself. He wants to protect her.

They are next to the microscope with a rose inside a polished human hair, and Taras says, 'Isn't it amazing?' just to say something, to gain time, to keep her here, with him. She does not answer. 'I wish I could give you a real rose,' he tries in English, but the girl either does not understand or does not hear him. She looks past Taras, and slowly, as if sleepwalking, drifts towards the exit.

He stands there for a minute or two, listening to his heartbeat, trying to put a name to what he has just experienced. When he rushes out, into the cold air, past the gold-toothed granny, the girl has gone.

Taras assesses the situation. The museum is by the main gate.

She could have gone further into the monastery precincts, which is unlikely, as her camel coat would now be visible against the white walls. If she has left the monastery, she is most likely to have turned right, with the flow of tourists.

Taras decisively turns right, and marches along the street to the square with an obelisk and a modern Pisa Tower of a badly built hotel, towards the metro station. He scans the bus passengers and passers-by, dives into the underground crossings, circles the square. All in vain; he has lost her. In his exasperation he has marched quite far, down to Podol, to the open spaces of the Contractova Plosha. He stops to catch his breath by a low two-storey building, with the ground-floor windows sunk so deeply that the windowsills can be mistaken for doorsteps.

The front is covered in memorial plaques *celebrated poet, legendary Cossack hetman, eminent scholar, renowned composer* – apparently, all the famous people whose names he does not recognise *studied here, at the Kyiv-Mohyla Academy, the oldest educational establishment in Eastern Europe.* So that's where she went! Not the girl he is chasing now, but the girl they were pursuing in 1748.

His file on Sofia is deep in his briefcase, but he does not need to take the copied pages out. He remembers them well.

On devitsa *Sofia Polubotko we have an honour to report the following. Has a predisposition to take risks and possesses a certain level of education. At the age of 16 became a student of Kiev-Mohyla Academy in Kiev, masquerading as her brother Panas. Currently staying in France, with the family of Count Orly, also known as Cossack Hryhory Orlyk, the enemy of the Empire.*

Chapter 15

Champagne, France, June 1748

The silence is becoming awkward. Sofia needs to break the ice fast, while it is still a thin layer of the first ground frost. She knows that one careless word or wrong move will ruin everything.

She has expected Count Orly to be something like her father – big, broad-shouldered, with a black moustache – but the servants have called to the door a suave, unsmiling Frenchman in a green damask waistcoat and purple velvet breeches. His heavily powdered wig sits just behind his hairline, his own grey hair brushed back over it to conceal the join.

He invites Sofia in with a nod and she follows him into the enormous, bare-walled kitchen, full of copper pans and wine presses. Vasil stays behind to unload her *skrynya*. The Count watches her, silent.

'*Et alors?*' he finally says in French. In French? She did not expect him to speak French to her! *And* she has forgotten her dictionary.

She tries to start a conversation in Latin, regretting for the first time not learning the language properly at the Academy. She wants to explain to the Count that she has brought something for him, but mixes up the words. The Count is watching her, not offering any acknowledgement. What is she going to do? This man is not going to help her, that's obvious. But she cannot face the journey to London on her own . . . She runs out, swallowing tears mixed with resentment.

Vasil is waiting for orders outside. He has dragged the *skrynya* out of the carriage, but has not unharnessed the horses. They are clearly not welcome here. Sofia gets her father's letter out of the *skrynya* and, after some hesitation, pulls out a linen *rushnik*. The festive towel, so lovingly embroidered by her mother with red and black flowers, is now grey with road dust and even more crumpled than her blue coat.

Well, Sofia thinks vindictively, this is just the right present for somebody who started off the agony of this journey with his wretched letter to my father, and now refuses to recognise me. But when the Count sees Father's letter, he turns to Sofia with a broad smile and says in slightly accented Ukrainian: '*Zdorov, dytynko!*' He calls her 'dear child' in her own language, and she feels the warm wave of relief washing away the tensions of her travel.

The Count leads her into the hall. If she were not so tired, Sofia would admire the suite of rooms they walk through, the snail of a staircase and the blue printed silk on the walls of her bedroom. But she *is* tired. Desperately. Profoundly. 'Oh, I must tell Vasil to . . .' She sinks into a heavy, dreamless sleep.

The sun is playing with the specks of dust, teasing her. She must have slept through dinner and, probably, breakfast. She looks out of the narrow window. The view to the right is dominated by the curves of a massive turret. Below, two black swans are floating on the dark water of the moat, like giant question marks. Sofia decides to leave the room in search of people and answers.

'A-a-ah, Sofia!' A lady in a purple velvet dress is waving at her from the bottom of the stairs. The Countess, guesses Sofia. Her legs are unsteady again, but this time because she is nervous.

Count Orly saves her. 'Good morning, *dytynko*! This is my wife, Hélène.' And adds, 'She loves talking.' The Countess, as Sofia discovers, also loves talking quite fast. She shows Sofia round the château, shaking her head sorrowfully, pointing at dilapidated walls and crumbling stone. Sofia guesses that the château is more than a century old and in need of repair, and Hélène is upset about the lack of time or money for restoration. More likely, lack of time, she decides, admiring the heavy gold embroidery of the Countess's dress. She wonders whether she will need a dress in London. There are some festive clothes in her *skrynya*: a richly embroidered silk shirt, blessed in Chernihiv Cathedral by her mother; a tight, beaded waistcoat, a black patterned woollen skirt, and red-heeled boots, made of the softest Moroccan leather . . . But no dress.

As if reading her thoughts, at lunch the Countess is talking about fashions. The Count translates reluctantly: 'The fashions in Paris change so fast that if a woman spends a month in the country, she comes back to find that her clothes are already out of date. I have several dresses that I would never dare to wear in Paris again, but which would still be in the height of fashion in London. You can try them on, Sofia.'

When she is helped into a green brocade dress with a quilted yellow silk petticoat, Sofia gasps. Not just from admiration. The whalebone bodice is biting into her ribs, making it almost unbearable to curtsey or turn. She looks at herself in the mirror. Field

Marshal Razumovsky would have taken her for a lady of the court now.

The Countess escorts her downstairs for coffee. Sofia is given a dainty blue and white cup, made, as the Count explains to her, from the famous Chinese porcelain. It has the flawless whiteness of the first snowdrops and a smooth, silky feel. The new dress is making Sofia's movements clumsy, and the brittle treasure suddenly slips out of her fingers. Looking at the chipped cup on the floor, Sofia is drawn into a whirlpool of guilt and embarrassment. She wants to run away, to apologise – but cannot say anything in French. The Count saves her again. He finishes his coffee and throws the cup on the floor with such strength that it scatters into small fragments.

'It is good luck to break something, Sofia,' he comments, laughing. 'And we will need all the luck we can get in London. We are leaving tomorrow. I should really be giving you several days to rest, I know, but the matter is becoming more and more pressing. Are you ready, *dytynko*?'

She smiles and nods, forgetting for a moment a broken cup, a whale bodice and even the potholes of the French roads: 'Of course I am ready!'

Abandoned her studies to go travelling across Europe on a secret mission, stated the Secret Police report. Taras is tempted to push open the heavy door of the Academy, wander along the corridors, mingle with students, imagining her here, in the library. But not now. His flight is in three hours, from a small airport across the city. It means bumping along on a minibus for an hour, then taking a shuttle.

You'll have to wait, Sofia, he thinks. Sorry, but I need to see Oksana first. It is not going to be an easy meeting. Not easy at all.

Chapter 16

Dnepropetrovsk, Eastern Ukraine, April 2001

He should have chosen a train. An uncomfortable overnight journey, yes, but there wouldn't have been any of this rumbling noise from this shabby AN-24 plane. A new airline, he had thought – great – with quick, cheap local connections. Now he is discovering the hard way that 'cheap connections' means just that. A new airline has acquired turboprops that look as if they have been written off. A plane crash is not a part of his plan today. At least, he hopes they will stick to the 'quick local connection' part of the deal, and he will be there in an hour. The seat next to him is empty. He takes the copied pages out.

Report on the interrogation of Oksana Polubotko
Second-year student in the History Department of Kiev University
March 1962

'Your name.'
'Oksana Polubotko.'
'Date of birth?'
'Twenty-third of March 1943.'

Taras skips familiar questions and moves to the last page.

'What do you know about the inheritance?'

'That some gold was deposited in London. The inheritance could be claimed by the descendants in any generation.'

'Did your father try to claim the inheritance?'

'Yes. In 1953, just before his arrest. He said he was doing it to rehabilitate the name of my grandfather.'

'Have you tried to claim the inheritance?'

'Yes. I sent a letter to *Injurcolleguia* three months ago.'

'What are your reasons for claiming the inheritance now?'

'Well, there were so many articles published last year about the truth of Stalin's thirties that I thought . . . just wanted to prove that the money is really there, that my grandfather was not an English spy, and that my father did not try to falsify the documents to claim the inheritance. What is wrong with trying to clear their names? For the sake of my mother, for the sake of my future children. It is important that—'

'Enough. Do you have a document confirming that you have the right to this inheritance?'

'No. My father said that the Will itself was in the Bank of England and that we only needed to prove the ancestry.'

'What do you have to prove it?'

'We have a portrait of the Cossack Hetman, his letters, the letters of his son and a silver candelabra with the name of Pavlo Polubotko engraved on it. My father worked on the detailed genealogical tree, proving that we are direct descendants. The elder son of the Hetman was my great-great-great—'

'Have you ever tried to get in touch with any other descendants?'

'No.'

'Are you in possession of other documents concerning the inheritance?'

'No.'

'Have you ever received any letters or documents from London?'

'No.'

Taras knows what happened next. He can see it.

The Fish was writing something. No more questions. She was almost pleased to see other people in the room. They told her that she needed an injection to relax.

There was a burning, tingling sensation in her arm. And then blood rushed to her ears and an avalanche crushed her, dragged her, tore her. She tried to scream, but her tongue was too big for her mouth. It fell out and, aghast, she watched it grow longer, thinner, transforming into a tentacle. Her arms became tentacles too, supple, agile. They were reaching the dark corner of the room, winding around The Fish, strangling him. The Fish was wriggling, his distorted, slippery mouth locked in a smile.

The roar of the fan was now filled with the howling of sirens. She was out of the room, in a dark lift, plunging down at an unbearable speed. Neon lights around her were flashing faster and faster, fusing into a blazing kaleidoscope. And then she fell into a soundless, indifferent darkness. She would never see the face of her interrogator, she would never know what he had written.

But Taras knows. He sees him very clearly: a leaner, younger, single-chinned version of a man he knows well. He is hunched over the desk, chain-smoking (one habit he gave up years ago), covering the sheet with familiar spiky handwriting.

Report on the Interrogation of Oksana Polubotko, born 23.03.1943

Kiev, 18 March 1962

Conclusions and resolutions

To be kept under supervision.
Isolation recommended.
Provide survival, in case the identity needs to be used in the future.

Below, underlined, in block letters: GROUP B PATIENT.

An inconspicuous signature in the bottom left corner with the oh, so recognisable and sinister, razor-sharp zigzag at the end: *Interrogated by: Investigator Karpov.*

It had not taken Taras long to check which hospital they had put Oksana Polubotko into. The RPB, or *Respublikanskaya Psihiatricheskaya bolnitsa spetsialnogo naznacheniya*, was the third largest mental hospital in the Soviet Union – after the Sklifosovskiy Institute in Moscow and Kresty in St Petersburg. Situated in the centre of the Ukrainian city of Dnepropetrovsk, it contained around a thousand patients from Moldova, Ukraine, Belarus and the Caucasus.

It was easy to find Oksana, but to get inside the hospital was much more difficult. The RPB Hospital now belonged to the Ukrainian Committee of National Security, rival to the Russian FSB. Luckily Colonel Nikonenko, the *Glavvrach* currently in charge of the hospital, had been a year above Colonel Karpov in the Academy.

'Do pass the Chief Doctor my best regards, Taras,' Karpov said in Moscow, handing him the permit for *Oznakomitelnaya poezdka*, a 'familiarisation trip'.

'And take your time, really familiarise yourself with the hospital, get to know the staff, observe the patients. No need to rush,' he added, putting his hand on Taras's shoulder. The tone could have been caring, almost fatherly, but the heaviness of Karpov's paw left Taras in no doubt – there was zero tolerance for mistakes here.

Taras knows his boss well. Karpov is not drawn to money, is not keen on stirring up international scandals. Vanity is not his deadly sin either. This case simply disrupts the orderliness of his life with its non-ending. He does not mind whether the ending is happy or tragic; he simply needs to close the page.

Well, Taras can guarantee that. He understands what Group B patient means. He chose the topic *Analysis of the Dissemination of Dissident Literature and anti-Soviet Propaganda* for his course paper at the Academy, and as a part of the research, had to fill in numerous forms to allow him access to the information on political prisoners, 'looked after' in the mental hospitals around the Soviet Empire. He had never had the chance to visit one of those hospitals though. Never thought that this chance would come, ten years later.

Group A patients were injected with drugs that would paralyse only their will, not their body, and sometimes lead to temporary loss of memory. This group of patients could still recover. They could be questioned and even released later. Their further desire to rebel was treated with Borax injections, causing high fever, convulsions and excruciating coughing spasms.

Group B patients had two different sets of drug administration cards. One set, with a list of vitamins and stimulants, was kept at the nurses' central post. Another set of records was held in the safe of the *Glavvrach*. These records showed that Group B patients were continually injected with small doses of the neuroleptic drug aminasin. The damage was gradual and irreversible: coordination loss, paralysis of mouth muscles, causing constant dribbling, and mood swings. Teturan injections blocked the blood ferments, depriving the cells of oxygen. Group B patients turned into obedient, brainless, inert robots, excellent for monotonous manual tasks, existing in a dark and lonely world of their own.

He cannot see the building from the road. The wall is high enough to commit suicide from. He knows that the hospital used to share its territory with the prison. The prison was moved a long time ago, but security remains tight – an electric fence, two sets of gates, two warrant officers in the guardroom. Taras has to leave his passport and ticket behind, unclasp his watch and empty his pockets. God, he thinks, just entering this place can make you disturbed and edgy! He steps into the inner courtyard.

A bulky, puffy-faced man is waiting for Taras at the entrance. 'I'm Yuri,' he introduces himself, breathing alcohol and stale cigarette fumes, infused with mint, over Taras. 'The Chief asked me to escort you. I am a doctor here, just doing the physio, nothing more.' He stops before saying too much. As they walk to the main entrance, the crunching under their feet echoes across the well of the courtyard. Taras notices that the gravel is peppered with white pills.

'What are these?' he asks.

'Some of the patients are not very keen on taking their medication, you know.'

Taras doesn't know, and Yuri is not keen to explain. 'I am leaving soon,' he says instead. 'They lured me in with a good salary five years ago, but now I know why they need to pay a lot to keep us working here. I used to be a sports doctor, working with swimmers – fit, strong young guys . . . What's wrong with you, by the way?' he asks Taras, pointing at the bandage on his left wrist. Taras notices that Yuri's hands are trembling.

'Too much boxing, not enough training,' he says, the first thing that comes to mind.

'Really?' Yuri's surprise is genuine. 'It is not a typical boxing injury at all. What happened?'

Silly mistake, thinks Taras. He should have prepared a story. Thought of a plausible reason in advance. But how on earth could he expect to be accompanied here by a sports physiotherapist?

Luckily, Yuri has already returned to his own traumas: 'Working here can hardly be more of a contrast with my previous job, really. It takes all your strength to keep sane here, and the rest. My wife left me, I enjoy vodka far more than I used to . . .' Yuri stops and Taras notices that his tone brightens and loses its bitterness. 'Only forty-seven days to go now. I am moving to Crimea, to work as a doctor in a village there. The smell of dry herbs in the steppes, horses, stars and a small vegetable garden – maybe I'll even be able to forget this place. I'll try very hard, at least.' They walk in silence, until Yuri is obviously relieved to hand Taras on to Svetlana, a once-pretty thirty-something nurse.

Svetlana takes him upstairs, pointing things out along the way in the voice of a professional tourist guide: 'The hospital was built at the time of Catherine the Great. As it was a prison, the walls are one metre thick. We have four floors here; women are in a separate block. Two warrant officers and two nurses are always on duty on each floor . . .'

The first thing that hits him is a persistent, strong stench – a mixture of urine and vomit. Then the noise. A constant hum of inarticulate bellowing, sometimes interrupted by screams. And then he sees them. The wards don't have doors – just metal barred gates.

Svetlana feels quite at home here: 'We keep between five and twenty patients in each ward. The lights are always on. No doors, as you can see. It is much easier to check on them like that.'

'How do you administer drugs?' Taras manages one polite question, trying to breathe through his mouth at the same time.

'Oh, we have strict procedures here,' continues Svetlana. 'Actually, you will be able to watch it all yourself in half an hour. Everybody, from the nurse to the head of the hospital, is personally responsible for any breach of procedure. The medicine cabinet, for example, can be opened by authorised personnel, only if two people are opening the cabinet together. This rule ensures double control and reduces the risk of unauthorised access. Then a patient is administered his or her drugs, again by two people – a nurse and a security officer. The officer requires the patient to open his mouth and checks it thoroughly with a spoon to make sure everything has been swallowed.

'We used to have problems with Group A patients from time to time,' confesses Svetlana. 'Some of them still managed to hold the drugs down with their tongues, then throw them out of the window or induce vomiting the moment they could get into the wards. Luckily, we don't get many Group A patients nowadays.'

Taras remembers the snow of white pills crunching under his steps in the courtyard, is about to joke about the cleaning staff inefficiency, but then decides against it: maybe there are more Group A patients kept here still than Svetlana leads him to believe.

Half an hour later, watching the row of human beings obediently opening their mouths to swallow the vitamins and other drugs to stimulate their systems, only to be later injected with the drugs that are slowly killing them, Taras understands why in the seventies the Soviet Union was thrown out of the World Psychiatric Association.

A fragile creature in a faded flannel gown stumbles towards the medicine cabinet. 'This is Oksana,' says the nurse, 'our oldest patient.' There is a note of pride in her voice. 'She has a very strong heart. Many younger patients die here, but she still carries on.'

Come on, Svetlana, she is not *that* old, thinks Taras, looking at the hunched, wrinkled creature with wispy, cropped hair. She looks eighty, though he knows she is only just fifty-eight.

Oksana turns to the warrant officer, points her gnarled arthritic finger at Taras and says, 'Tak . . .' The warrant officer ignores her, so she turns to Taras. He feels uneasy – she seems to look at him with a flicker of recognition in her clear blue eyes as she says, with seriousness and weight, 'Tak . . .'

Taras turns to Svetlana. 'What is she trying to explain?' he asks.

'Oh, not much,' replies the nurse. This is the only thing she has been saying for years.

'Does anybody visit her?' asks Taras cautiously.

'Nobody at all from the time she came here – which was the year I was born,' Svetlana chuckles, looking straight into his eyes, and in a split second Taras realises that his challenge may become just a touch easier.

He thought it would take a couple of days to work it out, but he might as well try it now. He has to work fast. His window of opportunity will only last for a minute or so. He smiles at Svetlana, returning her gaze, rubbing his right bandaged wrist with his left hand.

'Too much time in the gym,' he explains to the nurse, 'and a sprained wrist as a result!' He feels the bump under the bandage. One tiny pill that would kill a person with a strong heart. Guaranteed.

'Maybe, Svetlana, you could find some special medication for me?' Taras gently, but firmly, pulls the nurse towards him. She turns away, blushes and swiftly puts her hand with the wedding ring into the pocket of her white gown. In this flirty commotion she does not notice that the young Lieutenant adds a tiny white pill to Oksana's plastic tray. The warrant officer, occupied with checking somebody else's mouth, does not notice anything either. Taras lets the nurse go and stands there for a moment, watching the patients taking their pills.

His mood improves with every step that takes him away from the hospital gate. He told Svetlana that he would be back tomorrow, to 'continue his familiarisation tour', but he would call the hospital in the morning to say that he was urgently needed back in Moscow. He should have got a Magician's First for the trick he has just pulled. He is even more proud of the fact that he has saved Oksana from further suffering.

Kindness for Taras is not about fancy words. It is all about actions. Oksana would die quietly, and nobody would bother to perform a post-mortem on a Group B patient of the RPB Specialised Mental Hospital.

Chapter 17

Boryspil airport, Kiev, April 2001

The magic does not get much better than this. A gloved hand, hovering in the white air, waves the wand, and a red glossy square appears from nowhere. The hand waves again, and the square is transformed into a door, and with the third wave – into the side of a red Toyota Jeep. This time, the magician wearing the police uniform becomes visible. Not to take compliments, but to direct the owner of the Toyota to the car park by the entrance. Judging by his tense expression, this fog is not just a temporary nuisance for him. It is an accident, waiting to happen.

The architect must have had this weather in mind when he designed the departure lounge – a UFO-style disc hovering in the dense, wet, white air, flying into nowhere. Inside the disc, the theme is reinforced as the Departures screen glows ominously repeating the same word on every line:

'Delayed . . . Delayed . . . Delayed . . .'

Taras wonders whether the flights from Dnepropetrovsk to Moscow will always need to be transited through Kiev. He is on his way home, he has completed the mission, and he can allow himself to be just a little impatient. He has read and reread today's newspaper. He has stared out of the window and he has thought through his report to Karpov. Now he has nothing else to do but to follow the great principle, favoured by Colonel Kaletsky, their lecturer on Political Analysis in the Academy: 'Save your efforts, don't fight the inevitable, just accept, relax and enjoy.' Actually, there's a thought. He could play the game Kaletsky has taught them: look at the newspaper headings, guess what activity goes on behind the news. Read into the lines, not between the lines. Look at the bigger picture. *Let's try it, Lieutenant Petrenko, starting at the top of the front page.*

Taras picks up a newspaper again. On the front page is the political news, beginning: *Safe journey to Europe. The President's tour of three European countries starts next week. After visiting France and Germany, the trip will culminate with the talks in London.*

It should read: Another plea-for-money trip for the Ukrainian President. He is struggling, needs further loans to boost his prestige before the elections. Whether these countries will give him the money is another matter.

Another trip is going well though, judging by the next article, headlined, *Russian President visits Ukraine on his way home from France,* and continuing: *The Russian President has brought the French cold weather with him, but it doesn't stop the warming up of Ukrainian-Russian relations. The Ukrainian and Russian Presidents discussed the issues of the Common Economic Space, the common use of the sea ports, and other matters. Both Presidents confirmed that all the previous misunderstandings are a thing of the past.*

And in the same paper, but from its Economic Correspondent: *Ukraine on the crossroads. The geopolitical position of our country in the centre of Europe means that it is fast becoming a leader in the development of the transport transit corridors . . .*

Read: ... fast becoming a leader in the transit of drugs and trafficking of people. The corrupt customs system not only allows it, but thrives on it. Numerous ports on the Black Sea and under-equipped Customs and Border services make Ukraine a target of the trafficking crime groups.

International news: NATO is planning to conduct another set of Alliance exercises this summer at the training fields in Yavoriv, Western Ukraine.

Read: Back to the title of the second article. The geopolitical position in the centre of Europe is also the strategic military position – isn't it?

Sport: Our boys are not having a good season. The match Dynamo played yesterday with Juventus proved it again. When are we going to be in the league of major European players?

Read: We have sold all our best players abroad to the major European clubs. What other results can you expect from the remaining team?

The last page has a black-framed portrait of an old woman he last saw only a few days ago in her small flat in Kiev.

How sad, thinks Taras, looking at the photograph.

There is an obituary below:

Our prominent historian Vera Maxymovych was found dead by her daughter in her apartment yesterday. The Coroner confirmed that the cause of death was carbon monoxide poisoning: Vera Maxymovych had closed the damper of the old-fashioned gas boiler in the kitchen by mistake. She was eighty-one. 'That's what old age is like,' commented her grief-stricken daughter. 'Mother remembered the past in vivid detail, but was gradually losing touch with the present.'

With Vera Maxymovych we have lost one of the greatest

A.K. Shevchenko

historians of our times. Her name, Vera – Faith – was, indeed, symbolic. She always had faith in the rebirth of our nation, was a keeper of the national memory. Her audacious article Ukrainian Trump Card in the History of the World *was quoted and handed over during the darkest times of the Soviet censorship. We admire the astrologists for their ability to see the future. We will remember and admire Vera Maxymovych for her incredible talent to see the past through the darkness of centuries and the plethora of Soviet propaganda.*

Taras smiles at the Professor's portrait: 'Thank you, *pani* Maxymovych!' he says silently. 'Thank you for confirming this yet again. This operation for me is not about settling old scores or the chance to get a promotion. It is about holding the Ukrainian Trump Card.' He folds the newspaper carefully.

Not everything in the last two months has been going according to plan, and he could not find the wretched documents, but at least he has done everything possible to eliminate potential problems. The Ukrainian President will be in London in a week. The timing of closing this case, completing the operation, could not be more perfect. By the way, on the subject of timing . . . Taras checks the Departures screen. No changes there.

Around him, on the rows of seats punctuated by souvenir kiosks, bars and coffee shops, the world sits united. Next to Taras, a middle-aged man with a folder entitled *World Ophthalmology Convention Bratislava 2001* on his knees listens intently to a young blonde in a minuscule skirt and a fur jacket, who describes to him the dangers of living in Spain.

An American missionary in a faded anorak moves his lips, scrutinising his Bible, next to a distinguished-looking priest, reading

206

a newspaper in an alphabet of hooks and waves. Georgian, most likely.

A man in a dark suit and bright red tie is tucking into a gargantuan piece of chocolate cake. He is bald and round, just like a dough ball, and his face is lit by a childlike joy. He is in seventh heaven, floating over the fog, ignoring the Departure screens and the world around him.

Four spotty teenagers in identical tracksuit tops with the blue and yellow slogan *Athletics Youth Team Ukraine* on the backs are having a laugh with a pale girl in a wheelchair. The girl giggles noiselessly, covering the tubes coming from her nose with thin fingers.

A kilted football fan is exchanging stories with a tanned man in an origin-revealing T-shirt: *Australia . . . Feel on top of the world!*

Judging by the number of empty beer cans and empty crisp packets on the table, they don't mind the delay at all, and the irony of the neon sign Bar Fortuna does not bother them.

A girl at the table next to them is staring straight at Taras. A familiar, tired, pale face. She recognised me, he thinks. He waves to her, but she does not wave back. He understands why: she looks straight *through* him, just as she did then, in the museum. This must be her waiting strategy: staring into space, rocking absent-mindedly side to side, palms squeezed between her knees. Her long neck is moving with a nanosecond delay to her body, and it looks as if she is rehearsing the movements of a dance, saving her energy for the real thing, listening to the melody in her head.

Two meetings in three days is more than a coincidence to ignore.

This time I am not letting her go, thinks Taras. He will buy her coffee and they will have a chat – nothing significant, something about the fog, their final destinations, how long they have been in Kiev. Taras gets up and slowly walks to the kiosk to join the long coffee queue. Five minutes later, still in the middle of the queue, he is tempted to check whether she is still there, but decides against it. The fog is wrapped around the airport so tightly, the seats inside are at such premium, that she would hardly try to escape from the Bar Fortuna.

Chapter 18

KATE

Kiev, April 2001

The city has changed, as if somebody has replaced a black and white snapshot with a glossy colour print. Four years ago, when she visited Kiev for the first time, the city was covered in a grey patina – dirty slush on the roads, oppressive Soviet facades, sullen faces and shapeless coats. She remembers that winter trip vaguely. In fact, she has deliberately tried to erase it from her memory. One of her clients had bequeathed his collection of icons to the Pechersk Lavra Monastery, and Kate was sent to discuss the details of the transfer. In fact, she sent herself. It could all have been done by phone and fax, but she felt 'schmaltzy' – her Jewish friend Tara's favourite expression. Yes, 'schmaltzy' would definitely be the right word. She was too sentimental, nostalgic and curious about her roots, though not too keen to try the Ukrainian lard, real *schmaltz*. They call it *salo*, as far as she recalls.

That whole trip was a fiasco, starting from the moment when Kate refused to put a hundred-dollar bill into her passport, despite the broad hints dropped by the customs officer about a 'foreigners' tax'.

Yeah, right, she had thought. Are you going to give me the

receipt? I wonder. And why is the copy of the relevant legislation not displayed anywhere – and in English? I am a solicitor, after all, representing the law. My job description does not cover bribes!

Actually, a hundred dollars is not that much if you want to avoid the scrupulous inspection of your mismatched underwear, sniggering customs officers and total humiliation, she thought an hour later, struggling through the dim and smoky Arrivals Hall to the exit. The crowd carried her into a circle of middle-aged men, dressed in uniform black leather jackets. They were breathing a Greek-sounding incantation, *'Nadataksinadataksi'*, repeatedly into her face, trying to get hold of her hand and her suitcase. Luckily she had heard somebody outside the circle shouting her name, and struggled through the crowd. On the way to the city, sitting in the old Volga provided by her hosts, she got it: the chanting cult was a group of private drivers, looking for fares. And desperate for work, judging by their grip on her luggage. Their chant *'Taksi? Nado taksi?'* simply meant 'Do you need a taxi?'

The centre of the city had looked dark and hostile, and Kate decided to postpone the sightseeing until next morning: her meeting with the Monastery's Prior and *Injurcolleguia*, the National Inheritance Agency, was not until three o'clock.

At the hotel she was met by the stern-faced floor lady. *'Chai? Tea?'* she demanded. Kate had felt that with one more question, perhaps an offering of sugar from this woman, she would confess anything. She shook her head and slipped off to the restaurant. Though the hotel brochure had stated that the restaurant was on the second floor, she couldn't find it for a good ten minutes, until the floor lady, who was watching Kate's embarrassment with amusement, asked her: 'Restaurant? Want restaurant?' When Kate nodded, the floor lady took her hand, like a proud guide for the blind, and led her to the brown door with the sign, saying PECTOPAH. Kate had looked at this door before, bewildered by the meaning of this enigmatic word. Didn't guess that it was 'restaurant', written in Cyrillic.

The last straw came when a haggard waitress finally brought a starving Kate a steaming plate of borshch. After the first two spoonfuls she had to admit that the only thing this soup had in common with the borshch her *babusya* used to cook, was the name. For once in her life she had praised herself for being chaotic – for there, lurking in the depths of her handbag, was salvation in the shape of an old Kit Kat.

When Kate ventured outside next morning, it only took her ten minutes to realise that a dippy English girl on a sightseeing mission, shuffling through the snow in high-heeled shoes, with no hat or mittens, might bring tears to people's eyes. Not in this country though. The faces of the passers-by under the fur hats seemed as frozen as the pavement she was battling along.

In another life Kate would have found a dozen convincing reasons not to visit Kiev again. Now she had a single reason to do it.

Surprises start the moment she leaves the plane. The refurbished airport is welcoming her with neon blue and yellow signs in English. The queue to the booths under the sign *Passport Control* is full of chatty, brightly dressed, long-legged mothers with school-aged children. No heavy fur coats, lots of smiles.

The border guard does not smile, however. He frowns as he checks Kate's passport, shakes his head and waves her away with a categorical '*Tudy!*'

Tu-dy. To . . . where? By the time Kate guesses that *tudy* might mean there, the border guard repeats, '*Tudy, tudy*,' impatiently and points her in the direction of the booth in the corner, where two of his unsmiling colleagues are already waiting for her. Ah. Her chess game is over after just one move. She admires the efficiency of the British Police and the speed of international communications. When the dishevelled policeman in Cambridge asked her not to leave the country, he really meant it – strongly enough to have her followed, to send a message to the border guards in Kiev. Are they going to question her here or just send her back, courtesy of the Crown?

Kate hands over her passport and her fate to the border guards at the booth.

'British?' asks one of them, skipping through the pages of her passport.

Kate nods. Isn't that obvious?

'You need a visa,' he says in English.

Of course she does. Not much relief there. Even though the British police are not as efficient as she thought, she will be deported now anyway. Last time it took a week of waiting, followed by two hours of queuing at the Ukrainian Consulate to get a visa. OK, she has forgotten about the visa today, she has had her reasons, but how did the girl at the Gatwick check-in desk miss it? She should have known.

The border guard conveniently provides a solution. 'You can buy the visa here, at the airport. It will cost you eighty US dollars.'

This time, the exchange is well documented. Her dollars are promptly taken, and she receives a stamp in the passport, a receipt and even some change. She is free to go. To make her next move: Customs.

A pretty, heavily made-up customs officer returns her passport with the hundred-dollar bill still inside. 'Anything to declare?' she asks Kate, fluttering her Barbie eyelashes. Kate does not answer. She inhales deeply, trying to control her mounting panic. God, she hasn't thought about that. They are going to search her luggage, aren't they?

'Anything valuable?' continues the girl. 'Gold, currency, paintings?'

No, thinks Kate. Only the future of your country.

Barbie's manner is quite amiable – she must so far be unspoiled by the powers given to her by the state.

'The only gold is this ring I am wearing,' begins Kate. 'I also have two hundred dollars in my wallet. Do I need to note that in my customs declaration?'

But the girl has already waved her on, fluttering her lashes at the next passenger, a basketball-player-sized American behind Kate.

She recognises the *nadataksinada* circle and nods to the most friendly-looking driver.

'My name is Nikolay, Nick,' he smiles, introducing himself in English. He explains that he used to be a schoolteacher, but decided to go into business: had borrowed the money for the car from his friends and now works as a driver, paying a third of his profit to the people who lent him the money.

'Let me take care of your bags,' suggests Nick, opening the boot of a battered blue Volvo. Too late. Kate has already dragged her overnight bag onto the seat next to her and is firmly clutching her handbag. The last thing she needs is for the papers to be stolen now. Especially when there is such a stark warning sign by the airport exit, glaring at Kate with all its spelling mistakes: *Administrasion does not bear responsobility for luggage that is not looked after.*

The city is awash with light. As they cross the river to the centre of the city, Kate is mesmerised by the view. Green beams of light criss-cross the figure of the stern giantess with sword and shield ('Official name *Heroic Motherland*, but we call her *Ghostwoman*,' jokes Nick); the golden domes of the monasteries hover on the illuminated hill next to it.

Kate's hotel overlooks the main square. The walls are freshly painted, the reception area looks modern and inviting. There is still a floor lady, but she is smiling! Kate does not dare to ask for tea though, fearing that the amicable mirage will disappear.

The hotel room is newly refurbished, probably by a colour blind designer. Blue curtains with pink tulips are complemented by a green carpet and heavy brown cover on her bed. No wonder that Raphael's plump angels on the framed poster are puzzled! To give her eyes some respite from the colour clashes, Kate looks out of the window at the main square and understands that the hotel designer's artistic principles are more common here than she thinks. Several mismatched monuments are competing with each other, crowding the square. A statue of a girl with golden wings, perched on a massive column, is right opposite Kate's window, her face turned away. What is her expression like? wonders Kate. Is she solemn? Is she smiling? Why does she have wings? She decides to venture into the square, to look the statue in the face. The 'in the face of danger' expression jumps conveniently to her mind. She stands by the window for some time, taking the whole view in: the semicircle of austere buildings, softened by the orange glow of streetlights; the green and blue flickers of advertising signs on the roofs, multicoloured fountains and a brightly lit church, competing with the TV tower on the horizon. Fear does not fill her yet, just starts stirring under the lid of numbness. Is she watched here? Was somebody – *that* somebody, the secret force that killed Andriy – following her all along, instructing the Customs Barbie Doll, pushing forward Nick the driver, teaching the floor lady to smile? Is all this friendliness just a show before they pounce?

Kate rubs her forehead, trying to erase those ridiculous thoughts.

In any case, they wouldn't touch her here, surely – not with all of these lights, not in front of all those strolling witnesses? The square is only a couple of minutes away, down the hill and through the underground passage.

The militiaman in the lobby looks her up and down and decides to let her out without questioning. I hope he'll let me back in the same way too, thinks Kate.

The underground passage brings her into a different city: dimly lit, full of cigarette smoke and the cacophony of unexpected sounds – the clinking of beer bottles, husky laughter, snatches of unfamiliar music, the demanding intonations of beggars of all shapes and ages.

God, such contrasting worlds only ten steps away from each other, thinks Kate, squeezing her way through the crowds, past the endless kiosks selling plastic Chinese versions of every possible consumer product. Never mind, I am almost there. In a couple of minutes I will be basking in the orange glow. But her path is blocked. A teenage gypsy girl stands on the bottom step, a baby gummed to her pale breast. She does not move, does not let Kate go past her, just stands there, her right hand thrust towards Kate – silent, intense. Kate takes a step to the left. The gypsy girl mirrors her move, thrusting her hand nearer to Kate's face and dangerously close to Kate's handbag. Kate backs off and hastily retraces her steps: back through the smoky passage, up the stairs, to the granite platform in front of her hotel.

She stops, catching her breath, only to feel a violent push at her left shoulder as somebody tries to knock her bag off. Kate pulls it sharply back and turns her whole body towards the attacker. But there is no attacker. A teenage skateboarder, whose path Kate had crossed, brakes sharply and shouts at her. For once she is pleased that she does not understand the language, though the way he spits on the pavement after his curt speech leaves no doubt as to the meaning of his words.

She turns left, away from the square, into a quieter street, past an azure-white building showcasing fifties' style photos of glamorous women with phony smiles. It must be a theatre. Judging by the crowds outside, freshly cologned and perfumed, today's performance is about to begin. An unshaven man steps in front of Kate and shoves tickets into her face in the ultimate persuasion attempt. She side-steps him and hastens up some steps in search of an even quieter corner.

What a place! Just as she thought that it had become friendly and welcoming, there's danger looming at every corner. Or is she just being hyper-sensitive?

A massive grey building on the left looks like nothing she has ever seen before. It is moving, flowing, alive, like a castle made of quicksand. Such a tormented house! Its six floors at the back are desperately clinging to the hill slope, emerging as three floors at the front. Frogs grimace on the roof, sea monsters sneer from the columns, an octopus spreads its tentacles. She wonders what it would be like to jump off the roof. If she did it at the back, she would roll down the soft slope, scratched by the dry branches and broken bricks. She would have numerous fractures and lacerations but would probably survive, cushioned by thousands of last year's rotting leaves. If she chose to jump from the front, her body would hit one of the rhinoceros horns above the door, or would be impaled on deer antlers by the entrance, or struck against one of the hard concrete edges.

Kate stops and scrapes her hair into a tight pony tail, pulling herself together in one quick movement. It is much quieter here: no sirens, no drunken screams. Too quiet, in fact. Most of the windows are dark – it must be an office area.

A lonely bread van is unloading at the bakery. Kate moves closer, hoping to ask for directions and maybe, just maybe, to offer some of her change for a fresh bun – she is starving. Two burly men work in unison: strong hands, one quick move, covered crate out. Kate is just about to ask for directions, when one of the workmen turns and looks at her with such icy hostility that she freezes and decides that there is just enough light to check the map herself. To her relief, she is not far from the hotel at all: turn left, then left again.

Dusk is an interesting time of the day, she thinks. All the contours are smudged, and even your feelings are blurred. You don't know any more whether you are scared of being lost in the unknown city or whether it is the primeval, animal fear of being followed.

It dawns on her that, apart from Sandra, and those whom she fears might be watching her, nobody else in the world knows where she is. The street seems narrower and darker now. As her own echoing steps are the only sound here, the drunken songs of the underground passage suddenly seem far more appealing.

She hears the voice before she sees him. There is a stern immediacy in his tone, a demand to surrender. She can even recognise the words: *Idy sudy negayno!* Come here immediately! That's how *Babusya* used to call her to Sunday dinner. But *Babusya's* words were coloured with warmth and concern, maybe with a touch of irritation when Kate was too deeply engrossed in her world of make-believe. This, however, is an order. She cannot see him. He is in the dark somewhere, shouting the words she can understand. Expecting her to obey, and to obey immediately.

She can run back down the stairs, to the square full of racing teenagers, but he can probably run faster. It is his territory, his city – he can skip those steps in the dark. She can try to answer back, but she is so panic-stricken, she has forgotten all the other words *Babusya* used to teach her.

The order is repeated, and she can see a silhouette now: a short, stocky man, one arm tensing up along his body, the hand clenching into a fist, the other impatiently swinging the rope. His voice is quite young; she expected him to be leaner and fitter, but maybe he is from the old KGB, maybe retired – why should they waste the efforts of young officers on her? And what is he going to do with the rope?

He is about ten steps away, under the chestnut tree. Still far enough for her to think, This is how fear tastes: metallic, a heavy taste, no saliva, no bitterness. She takes a split-second decision he least expects – she runs towards him and pushes him out of her way. As she sprints, the stunned, shocked face of an old man stares after her in the diminishing evening light. He does not follow her. Puzzled, she slows down, looks back.

The man is still there, under the tree, bending down with his rope, attaching it to something on the ground, repeating his muted order. The intonation has changed though. His tone is a mixture of mild rebuke and endearment at the same time. Kate collapses on the pavement, shaking, tears in her eyes. The man walks past her, not bothering to give her a second look. He is too busy scolding the rebellious Scottish Terrier he has just put back on the lead.

No treats tonight, that's for sure. If he had turned, he would have seen that strange girl still sitting on the kerb under the chestnut tree, rocking backwards and forwards, and digging her nails into her knees.

Kate cannot stop laughing.

Chapter 19

How can she tell the difference? Some must be pilgrims, others tourists. All the women wear headscarves and cross themselves quickly. And they all look down, as if the truth, the spirit, the strength they are seeking is hidden under the massive lead gates.

She is the odd one out – no headscarf, and she is looking up. Why aren't they looking up? The divine is all there – the vast dome, every inch covered in paintings, the archangels looking down at her and a spinning wheel of light, streaming through dozens of narrow windows below the dome. She hears the bells ringing: the drone bell setting the beat and the treble bells creating the patchwork of melody, summoning everybody to the service. She follows the flow of believers: past the long table with loaves, eggs and honey left for the monks, past the bronze candlestand, with its reflected glimmer of thin orange tapers, closer to the altar where a young priest whispers a prayer. The almond-eyed Madonna looks down at her from the white, richly carved icon stand. Kate breathes familiar words, repeating them after the priest and the choir.

In the air, infused with incense, glowing with lights and prayers, the Madonna seems to move her head – not even a nod, just a minuscule illusion of movement.

'I know,' murmurs Kate, 'I know. I am going to do it, I'm nearly there.'

It is amazing how the time drags on here. She has spent nineteen hours in this country already: watching the square, tossing and turning on a hard mattress at night, taking a taxi to visit the old Professor. 'There is one person who knows more about this story than anybody else,' Andriy had said to her on their way back from Buenos Aires. 'It is a shame we cannot go and see her now. Maybe later, one day. Will you remind me?' He scribbled the name on the back of one of the pages in the folder. Surprisingly, he knew the address by heart, too. Kate meant to ask him why, but never did.

Her meeting in Lavra was not until two o'clock, so she took a taxi to see the Professor, as Andriy had suggested. But 'go and see' was all she could do: the old lady was very friendly, but their conversation was minimal. All she seemed to have understood were the words 'Cossacks' and 'Cambridge'.

Kate had so much time left after that meeting, that she ended up wandering around Lavra, visiting every museum and every church she could find.

She looks at her watch. Time to return to the gate. At last!

A young man in a black cassock is already waiting for her. 'Kate? The Prior is expecting you. My name is Brother Serhiy. I am going to interpret for your meeting with the Metropolitan, if you don't mind.' He has a rich baritone voice, and speaks in a chanting, melodic manner. He must be a soloist, unless all the choristers here are that good, thinks Kate. His English, with a touch of American drawl, is amazingly accurate.

'Where did you learn to speak English?' she probes, after some hesitation. She is obviously not the first one to ask, as he replies instantly, in a tone that cuts out any further questions, 'I read Politics at Harvard, on a Ukrainian scholarship. Got disillusioned. Politics is quite a narrow subject, while God is everywhere.'

They reach the Prior's residence in silence.

The Prior is waiting for her by the entrance. Kate is relieved to see his familiar, smiling face. 'Kateryna, how nice to see you again!' he exclaims cheerfully, but then lowers his voice, concerned. 'What is it all about – your panicky call, the request for the urgent meeting with the Metropolitan? God must have heard you, as the Metropolitan is here in Lavra today, to check the preparations for the Easter service. You know how to address him, I hope?'

Kate looks at him surprised. Shouldn't she just call him 'Metropolitan'?

The Prior carries on. 'You realise he is not a Bishop – he is the most senior person in the Church, like your Archbishop of Canterbury. Actually, in the Slavic Churches metropolitans rank above archbishops. He is the Metropolitan and the Most Blessed, he is often called *Vladyko*, His Beautitude, *Vashe Svyashenstvo*.'

They move together into the building, with Brother Serhiy a few steps behind.

'Be brief and to the point,' whispers the Prior. 'I don't know what you are going to say to him, but it'd better be worth it, Kateryna – I've put my neck on the rails.'

'On the line', Kate is about to correct him, but decides against it. The Prior turns to her before opening his office door. 'I will be at the meeting, but cannot translate for you: subordination issues. Brother Serhiy is very good, as you already know. You can trust him. You have ten minutes, Kateryna. God help you.'

The Metropolitan is sitting at a massive table, covered with dark green cloth. His face is half-lit by a malachite desk lamp, distorting the features under the white mitre. With his long beard he would have resembled Santa Claus, had it not been for his grave, guarded look. Santa Claus without the twinkle. Makes all the difference. No gift-giving, no for-giving, just a heavy suspicion of your sins. He greets Kate with a reserved nod. She wonders whether it is true that senior Orthodox clergymen, 'the white clergy', are not allowed to touch a woman, even to shake her hand.

The Metropolitan does not say anything. Kate sees it as her opportunity to speak. She opens her mouth then realises with horror: of course she does not know how to address him. 'Dear Metropolitan? *Vladyko?* Your Godliness?' She settles on 'sir', hoping that Brother Serhiy, her interpreter, has diplomatic as well as linguistic skills.

'Sir,' begins Kate, 'Pearson and Butler, the legal firm I work for, is in possession of our client's Will.' A *client's Will?* Who is the client, then? An eighteenth-century Cossack? Or his noble descendant, an Argentinian alcoholic? What if he asks? Kate begins to speak faster, in order to deny the Metropolitan a chance to interrupt her.

'According to this Will, sir, a substantial inheritance is to be passed to the Independent Ukrainian state. However, we are under strict instruction from our client' – oops, forget the word 'client', Kate! – 'to submit the documents to the President, and to the President only.' Kate is surprised by the firmness in her own voice. She did not rehearse it, did not think it through. And how did she manage to be so brief?

The Metropolitan nods, acknowledging her words, but does not say anything.

The Prior, subdued in the presence of the Metropolitan, decides to give Kate a belated introduction. '*Vashe Blajenstvo*. Pearson and Butler solicitors did work for us in the past. I met Kateryna for the first time four years ago. A collection of icons on the ground floor of the Treasury Museum was donated to us with her help. She is a trustworthy, professional solicitor and a great friend of our country.'

I wish Carol could hear that, thinks Kate.

The Metropolitan's stare is heavy with doubt and suspicion. 'You said it was a substantial inheritance. What sums are we talking about?'

Kate does not answer.

'He means – how much is it?' prompts Brother Serhiy.

I know exactly what he means, thinks Kate, and pronounces the number aloud for the first time. It is surreal, almost a category, an abstract notion.

There is a long silence. Finally the Prior brings himself to voice his opinion.

'*Vashe Blajenstvo*, if you would allow me . . . I think that if the President is made aware, that you – that the Church – has provided assistance in this matter, then, with God's help, he would make sure that the Church is not forgotten when the money is received.'

The Metropolitan pins Kate to the floor again with his heavy stare. 'Have you got the documents with you?'

Kate has the papers in her bag, but something stops her as she is about to nod. 'No. They are not in my hotel either. I have them stored in a safe place. As I said, I can only discuss the documents with the President.' She cannot think of any safe place in Kiev, and pauses. The pause gives additional weight to her words and decides the outcome of the meeting.

The Metropolitan speaks slowly, tapping the green tablecloth with his palm after each sentence, each word absolute and irrefutable. Even the Harvard graduate's translation cannot soften the meaning.

'The Church could really benefit from additional donations. We could attract more young people to the temples. There are too many temptations around for them – drugs, casinos, striptease bars. Strong spiritual leadership, spiritual education is what they need. We should open their hearts to trust and love.

'The politicians are shouting enough about saving the nation; we are here to help a person, a lost soul. Jesus does not call upon us to save humanity, He calls upon us to save a human being.

'You do understand, however, that what you are asking for would be a breach of protocol? Anybody could walk in from the street with a request to see the President and make a claim about some secret papers! But taking the Prior's reference into consideration, I'll see what I can do. The President is coming back from his visit to Latvia tomorrow. Contact my office on Wednesday.'

The Metropolitan nods slowly. End of the monologue, end of the conversation, end of the meeting. It is obvious that preaching is his true vocation, rather than alleviating the suffering of others. She leaves the room, turns, expecting to say her thank yous to the Prior, but the door is already closed, cutting off the Prior and the Metropolitan. Kate wonders whether this is their rare chance for a private talk or the subordination issue again. Brother Serhiy accompanies her out in silence. 'I'll call you and collect you from the hotel on Wednesday,' is all he says as he lets her out of the building.

Only now Kate understands. On Wednesday? They expect her to stay here until Wednesday!? Forty-eight hours more of this?

At least the President wasn't away on a tour of Asia or somewhere. Otherwise she would have had to stay here for . . . for how long? Should she be here at all? Kate is annoyed and Andriy is the only person to whom she can address her indignant speech. It's a monastery: everyone around her moves their hands to cross themselves, everybody mutters prayers, so a gesticulating girl, talking to herself looks pretty normal around here.

'Listen, Andriy, how could you land me in this?' Kate whispers indignantly. 'Why do I have to take forty-eight hours of *my* life to change the lives of all these people here – a kissing couple on this bench, a *babushka* in a purple scarf at the ticket desk, a toddler padding along the cobbles to his pram, an interpreter with a goatee? You betrayed me, that's what you did. And don't give me that sweet boyish smile of yours – you knew the dangers. It's not really *my* problem, but it is *my* very real fear though, and *my* life! Only today, when I pronounced the number out loud, I realised that this money will be taken away from my country! Is what I am doing wrong? What if this folder of yours creates a national crisis in my country? God, whose advice do I seek? I've had enough of it all, honestly. I should just leave the folder here and walk away, take a taxi to the airport. It would be so easy, just three moves: unzip the bag, pull the file out, leave a wooden box on this sunny bench.'

She feels just like that miniature man she saw treading decisively along the spiral wire in the microscope museum this morning. The inscription in five languages gave an explanation:

The balance spring, taken from a miniature watch, indicates important, crucial moments of life. The size of the man walking down the spring is 5 microns.

So there he was, all five microns of a man, balancing on the spring, marching through 'the crucial moments of his life'. She has nearly lost *her* balance already, hasn't she? Literally, as she stumbled over another visitor in that museum this morning, nearly fell, dropped her bag. Luckily, he caught her by her arm, picked up the bag and held her elbow a little longer than was needed. And he said something to her ... what was it? Ah, yes. 'I wish I could give you a real rose instead,' referring to the rose inside the polished human hair in that museum. Sweet, actually ... Kate wonders whether she should have enlisted his help. Or at least talked the situation through with him.

Forty-eight hours! God! She will need to kill the time somehow. She flicks through the city guide: ... *Podol, an area by the river, is an ancient district of craftsmen and merchants. The name means 'the lower part, the edge, the hem of a dress' and indeed, this ancient district, stretching to the banks of the Dnieper, has bordered the palatial city on the hills for centuries. Several streets descend from the Upper Town to Podol. The most popular one is called . . .* She knows what it's called. How many times has she practised this name?

The street has become a cult place for Kievans and visitors. There are several reasons for this. Kate has her own reason for getting there. Not several, just a single one. She checks the map – it is a long walk, but straight down all the way, mostly through the leafy park alleys. She might even meet more dog-walkers for some extra adrenalin.

The centre of Podol, Contractova Plosha, greets her in the full make-up of freshly painted buildings, invites her into dozens of restaurants and shops. But she chooses an uphill struggle instead. She will not admit to herself the real reason for climbing up this steep, cobbled street, not until she almost reaches the top of the hill. She stops again, pretending to read the memorial plaque on the wall, but in fact pausing for breath, trying to remember her last visit to the gym. No wonder. She continues her peak conquest, slowly but surely, scanning the booming street trade along the way: brightly painted wooden souvenirs and pseudo-antique icons, artisan clay pots, embroidered towels, watercolours and oil paintings of all shapes and sizes. She stops again, this time in front of a large canvas with aggressive colours, stretched on a rough, unvarnished wooden frame. A scarlet dog sleeps under an unevenly shaped table covered with an unnaturally white tablecloth. There must be some significance in the objects chosen for the still-life composition on the table: an antique chalice with wine, prickly black seeds, a mouldy walnut. A white bird sleeps next to the walnut, its head under its wing. The dark-blue background is a clamour of various shapes and faces.

A shadow with long, greasy hair appears from nowhere and starts a monotonous recital: 'Let me explain to you the symbolism of the painting. The dog is your life energy. It is protecting the white cloth of your life, your ideas, locked in a walnut and the seeds of the future. There is the dark magic of life in the chalice, and the white bird is your dream, your undiscovered self.' He says 'yoooo', dragging out an accented breath, looking past Kate. For him she is just another member of a tribe of buyers, prepared to pay for his soul and creativity.

She admits to herself then that it was all about Andriy, this uphill struggle, the artist's accent, the name of the street – *Andriyivsky Uzviz*, Saint Andrew's Church on top of the hill. She buys the painting.

Back in the hotel room, Kate mirrors her own life against the picture. The red dog of energy has left her, leaving a bleeding trail across the tablecloth. The magic chalice of life is empty, the dream bird has gone, and there is nothing she can do to salvage the stained fabric, shrivelled walnut and abandoned seeds.

This is not her main problem at the moment though. She should have thought about it before. She should have, but she didn't. It should have been obvious when she was buying this 'dog saga' – the painting is too big. Not too big for her bag, just too big for anything: for the plane, for the flat, for carrying around. Still hoping for a miracle, Kate flips her bag open and pulls everything out. It is then that she notices a small parcel, wrapped in brown paper, stuck in the left corner. Oh God, how could she have forgotten? How on earth is she going to deal with this?

She counts the hours remaining to Brother Serhiy's phone call. Well, she could just about make it. If she moves fast, if there are tickets, if . . . She interrupts herself on the seventh 'if', and starts throwing things back into her bag.

She has one more thing to do for Andriy, one more delivery. It is not going to be an easy meeting. Not easy at all.

Chapter 20

Lviv, Western Ukraine, April 2001

Why didn't I try to catch the plane? It would have been so much easier! Only a forty-minute flight – yes, in a noisy, uncomfortable AN-24 – but at least I wouldn't have been stuck here for twelve hours. Why did I follow the advice of the hotel travel agency? She keeps cursing herself, annoyed.

The train is surprisingly clean. The uniformed girl has just brought tea in an ornate aluminium tea-holder for Kate and her fellow-traveller, a fussy woman in her sixties. She has not stopped talking for the last two hours, and Kate could repeat her story to everybody by now. She has understood enough of it – the odd familiar word, the facial expressions, plenty of gestures: the woman lives in Lviv, and has been in Kiev, visiting her daughter and her two-year-old grandson, who is such a delight and so very clever (out comes a photograph of a toddler, a wave connecting his head to the book Kate was planning to read), just like her late husband who died from a heart-attack three years or three months ago . . . (a kiss, fingered number three, a hand to the heart and a quick cross over her husband's photograph); she does not like her son-in-law, always chasing a quick buck, hunting around the new clothes markets in his leather jacket – he might even be involved in a racket or something. A clenched fist shaken at an image of quite a homely-looking young man, slightly plump, with a crew-cut, holding a smaller version of himself on his lap. Hardly the image Kate had, when her compartment neighbour kept repeating the words 'mafia' and 'business' and waving the penknife she was cutting the sausage with. Or maybe the mafia was after his business and that made her unhappy – Kate could not understand this part of the story.

She declines the brightly wrapped chocolates, chicken leg and tomato, offered in this order, and turns to the hills and white-washed villages. A girl, standing by the black cow, watching the train, takes off her coloured scarf and waves at Kate. Could she have been Andriy's pupil? A path running up the mountain to the woods – did he ever walk here? Did he take his class to the white-walled castle on top of the hill?

She gets off at Lviv station, straight into a fifties' film set: huge glass ceiling, steam trains. She wanders the streets of his city, listening to the tram rattle, breathing in the aroma of coffee from the open doors of the cafes. But she is not here for coffee at Rynok Square, however strong it might be.

Kate gets into a taxi and shows the driver the address, written on the cover of a small brown envelope in Ukrainian, in Andriy's handwriting. She doesn't even know how far she has to go. Five minutes later, the driver stops outside a mansion with bas-reliefs of lions over the arch. The mansion has been divided into flats, and there is a shop with bars in front of it and a sign, РЕСТОРАН, on the ground floor. She knows now what РЕСТОРАН means, though she is not sure whether the entrance is barred to deter teenage vandals or famished visitors.

She steps under the arch, reaches the second-floor landing, extends a finger to press the button, and stops. Maybe Carol was right when she claimed that Kate was 'good at logistics, hopeless at logic'. She is always right, of course, she will tell you that herself, but her opinion certainly fits this occasion. Kate organised the logistics brilliantly, got here quickly – but what is she going to say? How are they going to communicate? All those questions she wanted to ask, all those words of condolence she wanted to say . . .

She sits on the landing for some time. The door on the floor above creaks open, followed by shuffling and coughing. She looks up. A wrinkled creature in pyjama pants and a woollen jacket is negotiating the stairs. Kate understands that in a minute she will be a major obstacle, delaying the life-prolonging quest for fresh air. The quickest and safest way to remove herself from the figure's path (she cannot tell whether it is a man or a woman) is to get into the flat. She presses the button. The bell replies with a Strauss melody, too airy for today, too wrong for this place, and the door is opened immediately, as if somebody were already standing there, waiting. As if those inside are as shocked by the incongruous joviality of the melody as Kate is.

A small, grey-haired woman with the brown eyes of a wise, tired bird lets Kate in. She does not ask anything, as if she is used to the constant flow of visitors. Kate follows her into the apartment and understands why.

Andriy is waiting for her in the room. She walks straight into Andriy's eyes, into his ironic smile. But it is not the Andriy she knows. Oh God, she thinks, the tense is wrong – it is not the Andriy she *knew*! It is a photograph of a younger, softer Andriyko, still open to everything life is about to offer. Or maybe he looks younger because the photograph is lit by a warm yellow halo from the taper, burning next to it. A black diagonal line is running across the right corner of the portrait. Beside the photograph, on the embroidered red and black towel, just like her *Babusya*'s, there is a small glass of water, covered with a piece of bread. For his thirsty and hungry soul, while he is still here, with us, guesses Kate.

Kate's hostess sits on the sofa, her back straight, her hands placed carefully on her knees. She is dressed in a black lace blouse with a white cameo brooch, her wispy hair neatly fastened by a tortoise-shell comb. She looks like a Spanish Countess from an old painting: immaculate, composed, noble in her grief.

Kate takes the photograph out of her bag. It is the only one she has of them together – in the cafe in Buenos Aires, with a lethargic candle between them. She remembers a disgruntled waiter, who tried to explain to Andriy that he was too busy serving *asados* and he was not there to take photographs, Andriy pretending not to understand him, asking him to try again, so that they would have two Polaroids, one for Andriy and one for her.

Kate's hostess looks at the photo and clasps her hands. She then holds Kate's hand, and in the husky voice of a seasoned smoker tries to tell her something important, something that matters. She points at the shoe box on the table. It is full of photographs of Andriy. Kate guesses that she is being offered some. She picks two. The first is of Andriy with a fishing rod, at the riverbank. He is still a boy here, aged about thirteen, at ease with nature and himself. Another one is from his graduation. Andriy is the only one smiling in the first row. That's him to a T, thinks Kate. Nonchalant and ironic, however solemn the occasion.

Andriy's grandmother brings a cup of coffee from the kitchen and manages to put it on the table in front of Kate without splashing, even though her hands are trembling so much that a coffee spoon falls on the floor with sorrowful jingling.

Kate holds out a small brown parcel. 'Let me post it for you,' she had told Andriy. 'We send lots of stuff to Ukraine regularly, we have special rates. It will be a quick guaranteed delivery to your granny.'

'See?' she tells him now, looking straight into his eyes. 'I promised you a guaranteed personal delivery!'

Sara Samoylovna unwraps the parcel. It is a bird, carved from pink stone. A kingfisher.

Kate tries to explain that this is a typical Argentinian semi-precious stone, called Rhodochrosite, that Andriy bought it for his grandmother in a boutique at San Telmo, in Buenos Aires, but soon gives up. Andriy's granny strokes the bird gently, as if it is a nestling, and places it next to Andriy's portrait. She takes Kate's hand in her dry, small palms, and they all sit together watching the light of the taper. Kate, a tousled sparrow, Sara Samoylovna, a grizzled starling, and a pink kingfisher from Argentina. Three birds perched together in their grief. Kate is suddenly pleased that they don't speak the same language. She cannot ask Sara all those questions about drugs and lies, but she does not need to. The shoebox with the photographs has given her all the answers. Discovering Andriy's life through countless frozen images, meeting his open, ironic stare, smiling back at him, she knows now that it was not an accident, whatever the police in Cambridge will conclude. And it wasn't a suicide either. But she could never, even if she knew how to say it in Ukrainian, say to Andriy's grandmother those terrible words, 'unsolved murder'.

They sit together in silence until Kate's time is up. She shows

Sara Samoylovna the train ticket, and a taxi is called to take her to the station.

When Kate gets into the carriage, two men in vests, her fellow travellers, are already there. They must have been there for some time, since they are in the middle of a card game, and their second bottle of vodka. She nods, and is just about to climb into her upper bunk bed, when one of the men winks at her and fills a glass with vodka. She shakes her head, but he insistently shoves it in her hand, bubbling with good humour and his idea of hospitality. Kate reluctantly takes a sip. The spirit burns her, numbing another pain. For an instant she can relate to those who praise the healing powers of alcohol and join Alcoholics Anonymous later. She ends up standing by the door of the compartment, listening to the male banter. Her fellow travellers are oil engineers who work on the rigs for a fortnight at a time, and spend the rest of the month at home with their families (kids' photos promptly brought out, wedding rings lovingly patted). She stands there for some time, watching their game, trying to understand the rules, and even accepting another glass of burning liquid before climbing up onto her bunk and falling into heavy, dreamless sleep.

She wakes to a smell of petrol. She is still drowsy, but cannot breathe, cannot open her mouth. Somebody is suffocating her. She tries to move, to sit up, but there is something heavy on top of her, pinning her down. When she understands and tries to scream, it is too late – the sound is smothered, lost in a petrol-impregnated palm, covering her mouth. It is too late to be afraid, and her brain registers the situation with the cold logic of a police investigator: a drunken, smelly man is on top of her, trying to pull her jeans down. She wriggles madly, fighting for breath, hitting the wall, sliding her nails into the sweaty flesh of his shoulder. There is no sound from her rapist, apart from husky, rapid breathing in her ear. Suddenly he gives out a loud animal grunt and turns floppy and soft, like an oversized teddy bear. He slides off her and it is all over, as quickly as it started, and he is back on his bunk bed below, and her jeans are still intact, and his drunken friend is snoring opposite her would-be rapist, on the bunk underneath her.

She knows what to do now. She will wait for him to fall asleep and then she will slide the door of the compartment, sneak out of the carriage and ask for help. But she doesn't. Instead she turns to the thin wall of the carriage, shivering, and curls up, pulling her knees to her chest and fixes her eyes on the green pattern. She must have fallen asleep again, because the next thing she knows is that the train has stopped, and her back is cold, because there is a draught. The door is dragged open. They must have arrived. Her back senses the activity behind her – bags being lifted, people leaving the carriage. Suddenly she feels the sheet being pulled off her slightly. Something wet touches her skin and a piece of paper is placed on the pillow in front of her nose. If there is anything funny at all in this situation, this is it. He has planted a wet kiss on her arm before leaving the compartment. Left her his name and a telephone number.

They have long gone, but she lies very still, facing the wall, until somebody else touches her. This time it is brisk, insistent. It is the conductor. Where was she when Kate banged on the wall? Having tea?

She concentrates on her physical actions. Her brain is like a computer, functioning in safe, read-only mode. Her elbow is sore – she must have grazed it last night, against the wall. She has the sheets up to her chin, but the patch on her thigh still feels sticky – is it his sperm? She registers coldly that she must get another pair of jeans from her bag and put them on before leaving the train. She follows the actions with mechanical precision – sheet off, bag unzipped, jeans changed, old pair into the plastic bag, to be thrown away into the rubbish bin on the platform.

She accepts the taxi driver's offer to take her to the hotel for an indecently inflated price, marches past the stern militiaman, gets her key from the floor lady. In the bathroom she coldly registers the rusty dripping pipe and the stained cloth underneath and a spelling mistake on the paper sign DISENFECTED on the toilet seat before throwing up violently. She starts to shiver, but cannot close the bathroom door for a while, then realises that she needs to remove the bathroom rug first. She gets into the shower and, after several pointless attempts to hang the shower head on the hook, realises that it will never work: the hook is too high, the shower hose is too short. By the time she opens the tap which says 'cold' and steps away, waiting for the boiling water to cool down a bit, she has fully mastered the logic of this place. She stands under the water stream for what seems an eternity. Her mind, like an overloaded computer, sends her short final commands. Get out of the shower. Towel. Sleep. It is almost over. Almost.

Chapter 21

The magic does not get better than this. Somebody has waved a wand, and the whole airport is now wrapped in cotton wool. The milky cover acts like a plaster, healing raw emotions and painful memories. The passengers move in slow motion and even the loud-speaker seems subdued, repeating the same word apologetically: 'Delayed . . . delayed . . . delayed . . .'

Kate looks at the Departures screen. She is three hours away from freedom and normality, from leaving this place. She has learned a lot here: that fear has a metallic taste and smells of petrol and vodka fumes; that grief in this country has the glow of orange church tapers; that danger can be only ten steps away. She also knows now that she is strong enough not just to climb a steep hill in one breath (well, almost), but to fight off a rapist (OK, a very drunk one, but still), that she is confident enough to handle meetings with this country's top clergymen and even the President.

The whole day went by in a blur. From the moment of the morning phone call that brought her back to reality (her heavenly assistant, Brother Serhiy, was waiting in the hotel lobby), she was just a leaf, blown around in a whirlwind of events: the second meeting with the Prior, a car trip taking her to the President's Administration building, a walk through the endless corridors of power with interminable security checks, and finally, the meeting with the President himself.

She must have felt something when she presented the Fairtrade box, Andriy's documents and her copy of the Bank of England ledger page with the registration number to the President, but she does not remember what she felt, actually, or how she even got back to the airport. The only memory she has is of the constant presence of the President's English-speaking assistant with her, all the way to the airport, all the way to the check-in desk. He was bald, smooth and round, like a dough ball, his red tie was too shiny, and his English was not as good as Brother Serhiy's, but at least she was not on her own; she was looked after.

The President is smiling at her gratefully from the seat next to hers, from the front page of the newspaper, published for foreigners, with good intentions in bad English. It is obvious why some marketing genius decided that the newspaper should be distributed to the passengers of this particular flight. The title above the President's photograph is *Safe Journey to Europe*. The official tour of European capitals starts in two weeks, culminating with the meetings in London. She closes her eyes. The timing could not be more perfect.

The President asked her why she was doing it.

'I am a lawyer, it is my duty. I am following the instructions of my client,' she told him.

'What can you tell me about your client, then?' asked the President.

Ah, she had expected this question. This time she is well-prepared. 'Not much.' She shook her head. 'There was a confidentiality clause in the bequest, I am afraid.'

And what *could* she tell him, really? How could she talk about Andriy? About the gentleness of his touch, still felt on her skin, about the smell of his hair, like freshly mown grass drying in the sun?

She should have been more professional, of course. Should have used the trite, general phrase: 'I am doing it for the prosperity of your country, doing it for the new Europe,' or something like that.

She could not tell him the real reason. There it is, glaring at her again from the familiar notice on the column above her table: *Administrasion bears no responsobility for luggage that is not looked after.* That is how she feels now. She has transferred the burden of responsibility to this country, and she does not really care who is going to look after that enormous 'luggage'. She feels like a wizard from a children's picture book. She has lifted the curse of fear, which lasted for centuries, stopped the trail of murders and betrayals. She remembers Andriy's list of people, who died or disappeared in connection with the Will.

Whatever the curse, she does not have to worry about it now. What is there for her to be afraid of? She bears no 'responsobility', she is quite comfortable at this grey Formica table, under the red neon *Bar Fortuna* sign. She is at the right place to eat her chocolate bar, according to the printed notice on the table that informs her: PLACE FOR HAVING MEALS; so all she has to worry about at this moment is whether to peel and eat a tangerine now or wait for a couple of hours. Kate brings the aromatic ball closer to her face and inhales the familiar tangy smell.

'Coffee?' It takes a couple of seconds to sink in. It is not just a question, it is a suggestion, an invitation, and it is addressed to her. Kate slowly places her tangerine on the table and lifts her head.

The question is repeated, but this time in a more extended, heavily accented version: 'Will you like a cup of coffee?'

A young man in glasses is standing by her table with two plastic cups. His face looks vaguely familiar. Kate gives him a closer look. He could be mistaken for Andriy's elder brother. He is taller, and his shoulders are broader, but the metal-framed glasses, the shy smile are the same. The eyes are very different though – these are a piercing grey, not green for a start, and there is something in his gaze . . . She saw a wolf at Longleat Park once – proud and defiant, observing his pack, ignoring the safari park traffic – and the eyes were very similar.

'I saved you from falling in the Lavra Museum a couple of days ago,' the young man offers a prompt.

'Oh, when I stepped on your foot,' remembers Kate. This time she returns his smile.

'It looks as if *we* are stuck here for some time,' he says, accenting the 'we'. 'Are you waiting for the Moscow flight as well?'

'No,' replies Kate. 'I am flying to London. Well, not flying anywhere yet!' And before she knows it, the cup is on her table and the young man is sitting next to her, smiling.

She picks up the plastic cup and nearly drops it, feeling the tingling at the tips of her fingers. The burning sensation travels to her throat, melting the frozen emotions. One more second and she will burst into tears. Or talk. Yes, talking might help.

'Sorry, I did not warn you – it is very hot,' says her coffee-mate.

Kate looks at him. He is the first person she can talk to in this country, however bad his accent is. The Harvard graduate in Lavra does not count; he chose not to listen to her most of the time.

Suddenly there is a torrent of words. She talks to him avidly, not sure whether he understands her well, but he is serious, and he listens attentively.

'I lost somebody very dear to me recently,' she tells him, 'and made a commitment to the person I lost – a commitment that was very, very difficult to fulfil. Do you know how hard it is, when you are all alone and the world is against you? Do you think it is possible to carry on living like this?'

'It is a difficult question to answer.' His eyes are compassionate and understanding behind his glasses. 'I don't know what happened to you, I can only guess what you are going through.' He leans over and touches her hand. His fingers are soothingly cold. 'All I can say is that you must be strong enough to live with this commitment – not just for yourself, but for the person you have lost.'

'*Passajyry do Londona . . . Passengers for London . . .*' The loud-speaker sounds much more cheerful. Gate 8 is flashing on the Departures screen.

'Thank you for listening,' is all Kate says. And then, unexpectedly for herself, she adds: 'Do you ever come to London?'

He nods.

She fumbles in her bag for one long embarrassing moment, knowing that if she continues her search for the business card, she'll miss her flight. She tears off a piece of the newspaper and scribbles her number on the white edge. 'Please call me if you are ever in London,' she says, handing it to him.

He studies it for a moment. 'It is six or eight?' he asks, pointing at Kate's scribbles.

'Eight – and this is eight as well.' She reads out the whole number.

'It is nice,' he answers. At first she thinks that he means, 'It was nice to meet you,' but then guesses that as his knowledge of English grammar is not up to much, he probably means, 'It would be nice.'

'Will you call me then?' she asks again, biting the corner of her lip, trying to counter-balance the weight of a wrapped painting with her bag.

He looks at her gravely, eyes dead serious behind his glasses.

'Yes, I will call you when I am in London. I promise I will.'

PART 3

The Wisdom

'The true mystery of the world is the visible, not the invisible.'
Oscar Wilde (1854–1900)

Chapter 22

TARAS

He should not have paid her to stop; he sensed that she wouldn't. She took the money, paused, wiped her nose, coughed and started all over again, watching him defiantly. *'Nie-e-se Ha-a-a-lya . . . vo-o-odu . . .'* Her frostbitten hands are singing with her, following the flow of the melody. She is no older than twelve, this girl, singing a Ukrainian song from his childhood, his last memory of his mother.

'Da-ay vo-o-dy . . . napy-y-tsya . . .' She makes it sound so forlorn, even though there is hope and boyish expectation in the words: 'Give me some water, Galya, let me have a look at you, beauty . . .'

This corner has been her spot for three months now. She sings by the exit, oblivious to the underground world of *perestroika* survivors: pensioners selling newspapers and their hopes for a safe old age; former engineers selling cigarettes and their pride. There are always some coins in a shoe box in front of her – her levy to her alcoholic mother for letting her live at home, for not selling her to the streets.

He sighs, leans over to put another coin into the shoe box and is knocked over by a bulky red-faced man, carrying a huge box.

'What the fuck do you think you are doing, fucking standing here, blocking everybody's way?' Taras is stifled with fumes of stale alcohol. 'This is the fucking underground passageway, not the Rossiya Concert Hall.'

Welcome home. This *is* home now, after all, this heaving area of identical tower blocks, not the thatched *hata* in his remote village in the mountains. He will never return there. Too many whispers still lingering in the air. Too many unforgiving enemies waiting for him, bearing the scarred memories of his notorious punch: the knuckles of his clenched fist hard against the bridge of his rival's nose. Instant bleeding, blinding pain, fight over.

'What will become of him?' Baba Gapa used to ask the neighbours, making swift, shallow crosses, always adding: '*Gospody pomojy*,' asking God to help Taras to find a straight path in life.

When Taras was eighteen, the age of conscription, the postman handed him a *povestka*, a yellow paper ordering him to report to the military enlistment office of the nearest town at 09.00 on 5 May. He was delighted. At last, his chance to see the real world.

It did not take him long to learn that in this real world there were people much stronger than he was, and that the rules were different.

As Taras was familiar with tractors and farming machines, he was sent to an elite Far Eastern Tank Division. After four months of fitness training in the *uchebka*, the training centre, he stepped into the barracks of the Tank Unit where he was to spend eighteen months of his life. He liked the divisional quarters from the moment he walked through the green gates with the massive red stars on them. He liked the order and the cleanliness of the swept tarmac, the patriotic posters and an old T34 tank on the grey concrete base. The smell of freshly cut grass and the whitewashed borders of the flower-beds reminded him of his village.

He stood at the entrance of the barrack room for some time, getting used to its dusky light, its rows of double bunks with their neatly tucked coarse grey blankets. He was wondering whom to ask about his bunk, when three soldiers approached him slowly. Instead of greeting him, one of the trio kicked him in the stomach – a sharp, well-aimed stroke, straight into the solar plexus. He was hit again and again till he fell on his knees and crouched on the floor, covering his head, like a blinded, wounded animal. Another soldier took his kitbag away, tore the pages from his thin address book and stepped on his toothbrush with his heavy boot. Nothing was said throughout the entire ordeal.

That was Taras's first acquaintance with the 'Kings' – three Chechens in the middle of their second year of service: Rustam, Akhmed and Mayrbek. This ruthless trio from the same Chechen village was not bloodthirsty, just curious to see how far they could drive the new recruits before their will was crushed and they became obedient zombies. Curiosity was soon replaced by boredom, as it was rare that a new soldier would try to rebel after the 'button training'. The third metal button of a soldier's blouse was methodically crushed and flattened into the new recruit's chest, leaving a scarlet bruise. The whole unit had succumbed to the Chechen demands, hiding hatred and humiliation in the deepest corners of their hardening soldiers' souls. But now the Kings had a new nut to crack – this Carpathian mountain boy with the cold, defiant stare.

On his first night he was thrown out of his bunk bed by Rustam and told: 'Fetch your toothbrush and polish my shoes. That's an order!'

Taras's knuckles turned white, gathering strength, and in a second Rustam's nose was bleeding. The incident caused quite a stir. Nobody in the barrack room had ever dared to look straight into the Kings' eyes, let alone fight them. Rustam did not hit Taras back; that would have been too easy. Instead, he chose five first-year soldiers to do the job for him. Next morning, when the unit paraded for roll-call and the sergeant shouted the name, 'Petrenko!' into the bracing October air, nobody answered. Taras was found semi-conscious in a pool of blood on the floor of the barrack room, between the rows of bunk beds. He was sent to hospital with concussion and two broken ribs. Naturally, everybody claimed to have slept soundly that night and was blissfully unaware of what had happened.

When Taras returned from hospital, he was left alone for three nights. Nobody talked to him either. On the fourth night he woke up, feeling something wet on his skin. One of the Kings stood over him, urinating on his face. Everybody in the room watched in silence. Taras could take the pain, but not the shame. The Kings knew that this fresher would fight, and this time they did not want to leave the pleasure of torturing him to somebody else.

They dragged Taras to the barrack-room door. Rustam forced his right hand into the hinged side of the doorframe. Akhmed started closing the door slowly, crushing Taras's fingers, watching his face intently, ready to seal his mouth with his huge palm, to muffle any high-pitched sound. But Taras did not scream. The pain was so excruciating that the blood immediately rushed to his ears with the swelling sound of a waterfall. Green dots in front of his eyes started flashing in a tribal dance of pain. Somebody inside his brain was tightening the wire, tighter, tighter, until he was completely blind, bloodless, lifeless – but still he did not scream.

Next morning, with three bandaged broken fingers, he was called to see Colonel Serov, Commander of the Regiment.

The Colonel was sipping his tea laced with Armenian cognac.

'Private Petrenko,' he started slowly, 'the report from the Training Centre describes you as a good soldier, an excellent tank mechanic. It would be a shame to lose you – either to another unit or, indeed, to *komissovanye*, early dismissal from the army. But,' Serov leaned forward, adding more weight to his words, 'you are asking for trouble. The officers cannot change nappies for every-body in the barracks. Army time is not party time. You *could* write a transfer request, and we *could* assign you to another unit,' the Colonel went on, measuring every word. Taras knew what this meant: the investigation team from the Centre, problems for Serov and more trouble for him.

'I don't have anything to say.' Taras was looking over the Colonel's head, at the drab yellow paint on the wall. 'I fell over – that's all.'

'Then how do you explain three broken fingers?' The officer was obviously irritated by his answer.

'I have told you, Comrade Colonel, I tripped over and fell awkwardly,' repeated Taras, still staring at the dingy wall.

'Well then, just watch how you go, Private Petrenko,' sighed the Colonel, 'because if you fall over and break something again, you have only yourself to blame. Is that clear?'

'*Tak tochno, tovarisch polkovnik!* Sure, Comrade Colonel!' replied Taras, and left the room.

He knew what Serov was thinking. Everybody had been through *dedovshina*, the recruits' bullying routine, during their first year in the Army. To make it to the second year one had to grit one's teeth and obey the orders of the older Privates and Sergeants. Obey and you survive, rebel and you are out – that was the Army way everywhere, wasn't it?

It seemed that Taras had to learn his lesson the hard way.

Taras did learn, but it was a different lesson: 'If you cannot fight back with your fists, use your head. Wait and plan. Think, and you will win.'

He polished Akhmed's shoes with his toothbrush, wiped the toilet floor with his handkerchief in the middle of the night, and the Kings soon lost interest in him. His brief battle was lost, as far as they were concerned. Only Taras knew that soon, very soon, the debt would be repaid.

For several weeks the Tank Unit was under constant pressure. Visitors from Central Headquarters and observers from other countries of the Warsaw Pact were expected at the divisional manoeuvres, planned for the end of the month.

The Commander of the Far Eastern Tank Division had his chance to show off, to get promotion. It was decided that the distinguished guests would be shown the rapid deployment capabilities of the Tank Division during the manoeuvres. The new T72 tanks were checked and double-checked, officers and their NCOs repeated their battle orders again and again, and Serov's regiment was already briefed for action. Nobody, not even the Commander, knew the exact date and time of 'H Hour', the time when the manoeuvres would commence.

It all began at three o'clock in the morning. Taras's regiment had to cover the left flank of the Division's mechanised assault units, and move in after the anti-tank missiles had cleared the glowing red 'enemy' targets.

The battle was a real showpiece, and everything was going as planned. So, when Colonel Serov heard the news, at first he thought it was just a bad Army joke at an unsuitable time. One of the T72 tanks had moved into the line of fire of the anti-tank missile batteries. Its rear subdued battle red lights were mistaken for moving unmanned 'enemy' targets and the tank was hit twice, at the base of the turret and the external fuel tanks. The tank crew had no time to open the hatches to escape and died inside the heavy machine. ('Why?' shouted Serov, adding a dozen swear-words. 'There are three hatches; it only takes six seconds to open the top one!')

Worse still, the crippled tank was guided by the best crew of the regiment. The commander, driver and gun-layer were the three Chechen Kings.

The soldiers who had fired the anti-tank missiles were severely reprimanded for negligently discharging their missiles, but the case never made it to the military tribunal. The blame was attrib-uted to Rustam, the Tank Commander who drove the T72 into the target area with his rear lights on before the whole regiment began the operation.

The investigation could not determine why Rustam did it, but it was obvious that after the missile impact and fire, the Commander was probably too seriously concussed to open the top hatch; the driver's hatch was jammed by the missiles' impact and heat. The gunner had probably panicked or had been too seriously injured to open the lower hatch, so the life-saving six seconds were lost. The investigators concluded that the break-away tank could not be warned that it had moved early, due to radio silence being imposed to prevent communication inter-cept of the early part of the manoeuvres. It was an unfortunate accident, but every year the armed forces had an unofficial 'allowance of death and injury during exercises', and this case just melted into the statistics.

There was one conversation, however, which could not fit into the rows of casualty numbers in the reports. Two days before the beginning of the exercise, during the short lunch-break, Taras turned to Rustam, who was sitting next to him on the edge of a muddy tank track.

'Hey, did you hear, Rustam? The Colonel said that the first tank to move in during the night-time attack would be commended for its reaction, and the crew would either get ten days' leave or final discharge from the Army one month ahead of schedule. Wouldn't it be great? You have only got three months left. The H Hour for the whole operation has been moved forward by ten minutes, by the way. I overheard Serov – now, there is your chance, isn't it?'

His tone was casual, in fact, intensely casual, as Taras had thought about this conversation for days on end. He thought about Chechen pride and impatience; about the highlanders' love of horses, passed to the T72 steel horse; their desire to return to their native village as heroes.

When servicing the tanks, Taras tried numerous ways to over-tighten the latch bolts, so that they would get jammed on impact. The timing of the conversation was important, too. Around Taras, hungry soldiers were too busy scraping the remains of their oily buckwheat from the bottoms of their aluminium mess tins to be interested in anything else.

He is washing his hands for the first time this evening. Or has he done it already? With all those reminiscences, he has reached the flat on auto-pilot.

A cheap Indian tea bag, boiled water, two white cubes of sugar in. He arranges the cheese slices on his sandwich in one thin, even layer and looks out of the window. What is on today, at the soap opera of the tower-block opposite?

Sixth floor, the window opposite. She has a visitor. Cognac bottle on the table, a box of chocolates, left unopened. It is the first time in a year that Taras has seen her pulling the curtains in her bedroom next door. Good luck to her, she has been waiting a long time.

Fourth floor, three windows to the left. Shuttle Mother is back. The girls skip around the holdalls, trying on their new T-shirts. Their mother is watching them, slumped in the armchair in the corner. He cannot see her face, but she must be smiling, he is sure of it. The sofa-ridden husband is nowhere to be seen. Maybe she threw him out. Unlikely, since she needs him to be at home with the girls when she disappears off on another Turkish expedition . . . The man must have escaped from this fleeting girlie joy to have a drink with his mates. Using the money earned by his wife, of course.

Fifth floor, two windows to the right. Does this pensioner never leave his room? He is permanently cocooned there, deep in his thoughts, leaning over his papers. Taras wonders who pays his electricity bills.

He is so used to his nightly checks of the block opposite that he will miss this evening routine when he gets his promotion and moves to a bigger, better flat, closer to the centre. For him these are not just the windows into another life. These people have become his surrogate family now, since he has no other. He switches the radio on.

A pleasant voice is greeting him, giving him the summary of the evening news.

Russia hopes to continue its winning start to World Cup quali-
fying after last week's win over Slovenia.

The annual Golden Mask National Theatre Festival Awards ceremony took place today.

The United States declared four Russian diplomats *persona non
grata* and ordered them to leave the country in connection with
an FBI agent charged with spying for Moscow.

Soon he won't just listen to those bulletins. He will be there,
creating them. He is already behind this one: 'The Ukrainian
President is on a tour of European capitals.'

They cannot add 'and will return empty-handed', since they
wouldn't know – but Taras saw to that.

He submitted his report today, after working on it over the
weekend. His meeting with Karpov on the results of the operation is tomorrow. If Karpov does not offer him the promotion,
should he suggest it himself? A transfer to a Sabotage and
Subversive Activity branch, ideally. Karpov knows somebody there,
surely? He has chums everywhere. He will give Taras a reference:
he has a good track record, after all. True, they might claim that
he did not attend the prep course at the intelligence school N101
in Balashikha, plus they might say that he is too old for it now –
but he will quote Colonel Surikov to them: 'A sharp mind is better
than sharp eyesight.'

Taras stretches out on his narrow sofa, feeling the springs under
his spine. What were the words of that new single, which was on
the radio today before the news:

'*Dance with me, destiny – for joy, not sorrow. Dance with me,
destiny, change my tomorrow.*' He smiles, not opening his eyes.

Tomorrow. His life will change tomorrow.

Chapter 23

Moscow, Tuesday 10 April 2001, 2.00 p.m.

It is two o'clock when Taras is called to the office of Colonel Karpov. He marches off at an expectant pace. His steps echo along the empty corridors, setting a strong, optimistic beat. There is nobody around, so he can even whistle quietly here.

Karpov does not greet him. His watery eyes pierce Taras, his thin lips pursed into an even thinner line. 'Very good report you have written, Taras, very detailed, very thorough.' He pauses and coughs, clearing his throat. 'Shame about the contents though.'

Taras does not understand. He tries to read the meaning in Karpov's eyes, but his boss is not looking at him.

'Before we discuss your report, Petrenko, I would be interested in your comments concerning *this.*' He pulls out a bottom drawer and places two photographs in front of Taras.

Taras's thoughts are tangled into one tight ball. How could I not have spotted anybody – but then, with all those crowds . . . Did they follow me in Kiev only, or all the way? How much does Karpov know?

'Well?' says Karpov, after a prolonged silence. 'Was it a pleasant date?'

'She was just a fellow traveller,' answers Taras firmly. 'Our flights were delayed and we had coffee together. She did not even tell me her name.' That was true, actually. She was in such a rush that she only managed to scribble her telephone number.

'I did not realise that coffee mornings were included in the operational plan,' says Karpov frostily. 'Let's assume for the moment that it *is* true. Then maybe you could explain *this* to me?' He places a sheet of paper in front of Taras and waits.

According to informed sources, one of the issues intended for discussion by the Ukrainian President with the British Prime Minister is the presentation of appropriate documents to claim back the Cossack gold deposited in the Bank of England for the benefit of the independent Ukrainian nation.

For the second time in his life Taras hears this sound. The hissing sound of danger. The first time he heard it was in the Far East, at the beginning of his second year in the Army. His NCO, Oleg, took him into the dawn expedition to get a tiger lily, an orange flower with black stripes, for the wife of a visiting Moscow General. The locals used to say that to get the lilies one had to go through three stages of hell, past three circles of snakes. Taras found it impossible to believe, and was quite surprised when Oleg told him to put on the oiled rubber apron, thick rubber gloves and boots kept in the division in case of nuclear attack.

They started the expedition at dawn. Taras was admiring the deserted hills, covered in purple carpets of flowers, when he felt, rather than heard, an odd whistling noise. He saw Oleg beating a tiny, pale-brown ribbon. Then another one. And another. Only when the noise stopped did Taras realise these were snakes.

'First circle done,' smiled Oleg cheerfully. 'We are moving into the second one now.'

Taras licked his dry lips.

At the second circle, the snakes were bigger, darker, and much more graceful in their lethal movement.

The third circle he remembered only too well. He often had vivid dreams about it. When they got to the top of the hill, had almost reached the orange flames of the lily, he saw her. She was beautiful. Green velvet skin with black spots, shining in the first rays of the rising sun. She was watching the humans with an air of supremacy. It was her kingdom and her treasure, and she was not going to give it up without a fight. The lonely hissing sound was loud and clear in the morning air. 'This is where the fun starts,' whispered Oleg, winking at the now pale Taras. An instant later, the Snake Queen was wriggling on the hook, trying to spit her lethal curse at the humans.

'Pick the flower,' commanded Oleg. Taras did not move. 'Fucking hell, pick the lily, Taras!' This time, Oleg was not winking or smiling. He required immediate action.

Taras slowly cut the flower stem as close to the ground as he could. The flower was still alive, burning his hands with its orange petals, when they got to the barracks . . .

If ever there was a fourth circle of hell, Taras is standing in the middle of it now, listening to the hissing turning into white noise inside him.

'This issue on the agenda of the President's talks – it requires a running commentary, don't you think, Petrenko?' Karpov taps his fingers.

Taras does not understand. The phrases in front of him are blurred into one sentence. And what a sentence it is. A death warrant. He is frantically searching for an explanation in his head.

'I had a drink with General Ipatyev yesterday,' carries on Karpov, 'and I mentioned to him your recent exploits.' For the first time Karpov's icy tone is touched by emotion – but not the one Taras has expected today. 'This morning, Ipatyev invited me to his office to show me this – a transcript of the telephone conversation. God only knows how his boys managed to get it! Freshly recorded yesterday. "Talk of the devil," Ipatyev said sarcastically, handing it to me. He meant *you* as a devil, presumably, Petrenko!'

He places another document on the table in front of Taras. The letters are treacherously jumping off the page, disappearing off the lines:

This conversation took place on 9 April at 16.00 Greenwich Mean Time in London.
Official A (Office of the Prime Minister)
Official B (Bank of England)

A. This business of the inheritance . . . The agenda for negotiations, which the Ukrainians have presented to the British side, does not hint at it. I think they plan that the President will deliver the message unexpectedly, under Item Seven on the agenda: 'Other matters'.
Do you think the Ukrainians have the right to claim?

B. Provided they have all the documents – and I assume that the President would not raise this subject otherwise – I am afraid that yes, they do, sir.

A. What sort of sum are we talking about?

Long pause.

B. According to our calculations, with all the interest accrued over the years, it is over two hundred and seventy billion pounds.

Long pause.

A. We'd better be well prepared, then. Of course, we will assure the Ukrainian President that Her Majesty's Government will do everything possible to help him recover the funds. The PM will express his understanding of the Ukrainians' desire to claim the funds now, at this historical and unfortunately, not the easiest of times in the development of their newly independent state. But we also need to give a subtle warning that claiming an inheritance could be a lengthy and expensive process, perhaps taking years and costing millions in legal fees. Bearing in mind the sums involved here, I am inclined to believe that this inheritance case might fit that scenario. As far as I am aware, the presidential election in Ukraine is next year, and in this situation, spending the funds on the legal fees in Britain might not appear to be entirely justified.

It might also be worth mentioning that if Ukraine, with the support of British friends, joined NATO, the President could focus his efforts on securing a peaceful future for the nation. A good one for the pre-election speeches, don't you think?

B. Sir, I looked at the Ukrainian budget deficit and inflation figures for this year – they are abysmal. The country desperately needs this money. I feel they would be foolish not to claim; this is their chance of survival, their chance to break away from Russia.

A. Thank you. I shall add your comments to the brief on our preferred line to take.

'Your running commentary, Petrenko, is not loud enough for me to hear. Am I getting on a bit, or do I take it that you have nothing to say?'

Karpov can be sarcastic, thinks Taras. Not now though. Today he is caustic.

Taras feels a hot trickle of sweat running from his temple down his left cheek. He does not bother to wipe it away. Just like that. A diplomatic scandal, involving three countries. No doubt his name will be revealed, more questions asked.

'It is just not possible.' His voice is listless, as if he is pushing every sound through a lead barrier. 'You know the story, Comrade Colonel. There were only three documents missing from the file – I checked all the records thoroughly. According to the list of contents, they were *The Interrogation Report of Pavlo Polubotko, the Cossack Treasurer; Report on the Descendant Claiming Possession of the Will* and *The Copy of the Text of the Will.* Now, the descendant who tried to claim the inheritance is no longer with us, and neither is the only other person who might have tried to dig further – Andr— This second person has been stopped from finding the original Will. And without the presentation of the Will, the inheritance cannot be claimed.'

'Are you sure that you haven't found any documents in Cambridge, Lieutenant Petrenko?' Karpov's eyes become two narrow slits. 'God knows what you were doing in Britain and what game you were playing, because my sources also confirm that the Will arrived in Ukraine from Britain. Brought by a British solicitor. Female.' The Colonel is punching every word.

'I cannot understand how . . .' Taras stops. He suddenly realises that he has made a classic mistake, not permissible even for a beginner in the Academy. He remembers the text of the 1962 report: *The only direct descendant,* **living in Ukraine** *and claiming the inheritance at present is Oksana Polubotko.* He has never considered why these words should have been underlined. His vision was blurred by a personal vendetta. He did not check any claims from the descendants *abroad*; he followed one lead, never looked any further afield. Easy and unforgivable.

Taras tries to swallow a hard lump in his throat.

'Well, you'd better go and write another report now. There is a lot to be explained.' Karpov is not looking at Taras any more.

Taras does not return to his desk. Nor does he plan to come back to write the report tomorrow. His steps echo in the giant lobby, a powerful Genie watching him from above.

He walks out and stands for a minute, squinting at the bright spring sun. Moscow is buzzing around him. He has forgotten how vast this Square is. Or maybe he has never even noticed? At the red lights, Bentleys and Mercedes 500s are stuck next to battered Ladas, all equal in their waiting. Street beggars scurry around them with surprising agility. American tourists, glued to the window of the tour bus, are clicking their cameras, taking pictures of the 'heart of the evil empire', as they love to call the building where he works. Correction: the building where he used to work.

Taras decides against the metro and the packed route 211 minibus and starts a long walk home.

By the time he gets to his tower block, it is already dark. His ankles ache after the unusual amount of exercise. And it's not over yet, discovers Taras. The lift is not working again. He will have plenty of time to think on the way up to the seventh floor.

As he gets to the sixth floor, he hears a whining noise. There is no bulb on the landing and the light, coming from the floor above, is quite dim, but Taras can see that it is not a dog. A small skinny boy in vest and underpants is crouching, whimpering, on a soiled rug outside flat N62, smearing snot and blood from his broken lip all over his face with the back of his hand.

'What are you doing here, Vasya?' asks Taras, and instantly regrets it. What a pointless question! It is obvious what he is doing here. The sound of a violent, drunken argument is coming from behind the flimsy door. The boy has run out to escape his father's fists, just as Taras used to. Only he did not have the rug to sit on and the roof to hide under; he had to run into the woods or across the damp vegetable garden into Baba Gapa's shed.

Taras walks past the boy, not saying another word, not slowing down. He opens the door of his own flat one floor above, marches to the bathroom and washes his hands for a long time. Then he starts his evening tea ceremony: butters the bread, evenly arranges the slices of cheese on top. He decides to make his tea weaker today and, after some hesitation, adds another spoonful of sugar. Then he puts the door key into his pocket and walks out, balancing a plate with the sandwich and a cup, trying not to spill the tea as he negotiates the steps in the dark. When he reaches the floor below, Taras carefully places the plate and the cup on the concrete floor of the landing. He takes a neatly folded handkerchief out of his pocket, thoroughly wipes Vasya's grubby cheeks, and folds the handkerchief back again. Then he sits on the stairs in silence, watching Vasya eat. The boy is not whimpering any more; all his efforts are concentrated on swallowing the food fast, just in case his mother opens the door. Taras leans over, and sticks the banknote into Vasya's holed dirty sock: 'Come on, Vasya, hide it well. For food, not toys – remember? They will sell or break the toys, you know.'

Vasya looks up at him and Taras notices that his left eye is swollen and the left corner of his top lip is twitching. He wonders whether it is a nervous tic he has developed or the result of a blow. He rises decisively.

Taras keeps pressing the doorbell for a long time. The shouting stops. When the door is finally opened, he pushes Vasya's drunken mother aside and strides into the kitchen, skirting the collection of bottles in the shabby hall.

Vasya's father is sitting at the table with his back to Taras, staring out of the window. His elbows are on the table, his chin resting on his knuckles. A picture of domesticity. Taras gently takes one of the man's hands away from his face, then in one quick movement twists his wrist, looking straight into his startled eyes.

'Touch Vasya again and I'll break your arm,' is all Taras says. He knows there is not going to be a next time, but he also knows that the pain, connected with the threat, will go straight to the subconscious, and the memory of it will become the best deterrent for the abuse. At least for some time.

Vasya peeps out of his new hiding-place, the bathroom: his eyes dry, his mouth twitching even more now, hiding a smile – nobody has ever defended him before. Taras walks out, ignoring the screams and the swearing behind him, not bothering to close the front door. He knows that they will not call the police: their family is well-known for its drinking habits and the police won't bother. He goes back to his flat, to wash his hands again and to make himself another sandwich.

He wipes the corners of his mouth, folds a napkin and reaches to the top of the fridge. There, in a green plastic folder, are the pages he copied from the case N1247. There is not much left for him to do with the present, so he might as well escape into the past.

To Field Marshal Razumovsky, St Petersburg, June 1748.

From the agent Khristoforov Zakhar. On devitsa *Sofia Polubotko, travelling across Europe, we have the honour to report the following . . .*

Chapter 24

Palace of the Empress Yelizaveta, St Petersburg, June 1748

Power is more important than wealth. He knows it now. He is sitting on the windowsill, watching his wife in hunting costume trotting across the courtyard, thinking of the events of earlier today.

It was the morning after the Great April Ball; they had just finished a late breakfast. The stale smell of burned candles and hair powder still lingered in the air. Yelizaveta was chatting to him about the kaftan that Count Naryshkin had worn at the ball. The back was embroidered after the fashion of a tree: the broad golden band of a trunk in the middle, the silver lines of branches running down the sleeves to his wrists.

'You must look better than he does, *mon cher.*' She used a French expression, learned from that Parisian fox Lestoque last night. 'I'll order some diamond buttons and epaulettes for you.' She asked a butler to bring the post in.

'Can you read to me, Alexey?' she said gently. 'I have trouble making out the letters today. I still have a headache from all that dancing.'

Razumovsky knew perfectly well, as did the whole Court, that

267

Yelizaveta not only abhorred reading, but she considered it dangerous – and was convinced that too much reading was the cause of her beloved sister Anna's death.

The letter was from Count Saltykov, the Russian Ambassador in England.

'. . . *and I hasten to inform you, Matushka*,' read Alexey, '*that I saw the enemy of the Empire, French Count Orly (born Ukrainian Cossack Grygory Orlyk) at Child's coffee-house the other day. He brought with him a young and, dare I say, attractive lady of Little Russian background. Women are allowed into some of the coffee-houses, as you know. It was quite difficult to hear the whole conversation above all the others, as London coffee-houses tend to be on the noisy side, but they were talking about some documents and further travels. The name of the girl is . . .*' Alexey stopped.

'What's the matter, *mon cher*?' asked the Empress. 'I have never noticed that you had trouble reading before.'

Alexey continued, repeating the last phrase: '*The name of the girl is Sofia Polubotko. Her further destination is still unknown to us. Awaiting your orders,*

Nizhayshy poklon – *my deepest homage, your humble servant Poslannyk (Ambassador) Count Saltykov.*'

'How shall we reply, Alexey?' asked the Empress. 'Look, the girl has quite a notorious name. The Polubotko family has been considered an enemy of the Empire for over two decades. Or maybe this is a different Polubotko – all these Little Russian names sound the same to me. You don't happen to know this family, by any chance?

Count Razumovsky thought of the day when his friend Yakiv became a father. How upset he was, that it was a girl, not a boy. 'Never mind, I'll raise her as a real Cossack,' he said to his friend then. 'We are calling our daughter Sofia. Would you be her god-father, Olexiy? You are the most obvious choice. Your name, Rozum, means "mind", and Sofia means "wisdom". Mind and wisdom always need each other, don't they?'

They had had too much to drink then, obviously, otherwise he would never have agreed. It happened only four months before *the owner of such an angelic voice should present himself at the court* letter, four months before his life changed for ever. Not that he has forgotten his duties. He was always happy to receive news from the Polubotko family about Sofia, and once even wrote a note back doubting the necessity of Sofia's education. He was just too busy here, had a lot to face up to at the court. Constant intrigues, gossip, flirting. He even had to lose in those evening card games to show that he was not smart enough! All his life here has been a gamble.

Count Razumovsky shook his head. 'I don't believe so, Matushka. The name is not familiar to me.'

Yelizaveta looked at him intently. 'Strange. Not impossible though, she must still have been very young when you left your old world behind you. Well, *golubchik*' (she always called him 'little dove' when nobody was around), 'you are a Field Marshal now, so you can handle this yourself. You know how much I enjoyed the visit to your country and how much I love your people. I find them gentle and guileless, but one can't be too careful these days. I am fed up with these French intrigues at the Court. You have always been the one to protect me. I want to know everything about this girl's travels. Where, why, when. Please take care of it, *golubchik*.' The Empress looked at her secret husband with tender-ness. Nobody, apart from Father Pavel, knew that they had married in Perovo three years earlier.

Count Razumovsky looks out of the window, admiring his wife's horsemanship. She is such a good rider, such a clever woman! Why did she ask him to read the letter to her? Does she know about the connection? Is she testing him? He is losing power, losing it fast.

First, he became the laughing-stock of the whole Court following his mother's unfortunate visit. The poor woman, mistaking her own unfamiliarly dressed, rouged and powdered reflection in a large mirror for the approaching Empress, dropped to her knees.

And now these daily visits of Vanka Shuvalov, a handsome young bastard, to see the Empress. He would often bring one of his uncles, Peter Shuvalov, the most dangerous man in the Empire, with him. Alexey preferred religion to politics, and was well known at Court for never involving himself in gossip and intrigue, but even he could see that these liaisons were dangerous.

Olexiy Rozum has always known that one day, his humble past will catch up with him.

He looks out of the window again. His wife's horse gallops, she slips off the saddle, but manages to stay on the horse.

Count Razumovsky cannot afford to be thrown out of his saddle.

He will ask dragoons to arrest Sofia at the border and have her escorted to St Petersburg. 'At least with soldiers acting under my orders she'll be safe,' he tells himself, 'and then I'll help her to get back home.'

He turns to Yegorov, his Private Secretary: 'Please write to our Ambassador in London, directing him to keep a careful watch on the girl.'

He writes on a separate piece of paper: *Provide protection. Will need to be questioned by me personally*, asks his Private Secretary to send it with the letter to the Ambassador.

Yegorov is surprised by the note. Quite suspicious of it, in fact. He has never trusted this Field Marshal anyway. A Ukrainian Cossack as a lover of the Empress? Rumour has it that they might even be married!

He much prefers Vanka Shuvalov – young, bright, does not steal from the Empress yet. Such a rare quality at the Court! Everybody steals here, even old Count Panshyn was caught the other day by the kitchens, passing banknotes from the gambling table to his servant in his hat! No, Shuvalov is not like that. Shuvalov is the master he would really prefer. It is not wrong at all to inform him of Razumovsky's decisions. Besides, as he is acting in the interests of the Empress, this can hardly be called betrayal. Or does money put a different name to it?

Yegorov does not send Razumovsky's note with the letter to the Ambassador. Instead, he hands it in the envelope, addressed to Ivan Shuvalov, to his servant. Then he decides to have a quick check of the kitchens: as there were three hundred dishes served at the ball last night, surely there are still some pieces left of that amazing chocolate concoction of the new French chef. His cooking is very good, even though he is too French for Yegorov's liking. He even insists on the French name for his sweets – he says they should be called 'desserts'.

Taras turns over the last page of the Secret Police report. *Following the arrest of* devitsa *Sofia Polubotko, we can report the following . . . Dragoon Commander Alexandr Morozov.*

'*Good morning. It is five o'clock in Moscow. I am Irina Strelnikova . . .*' the radio talks to him, but Taras does not listen.

He looks at the last lines of the report, rereads them carefully and sees very clearly what is going to happen next. Not with Sofia, but with Kate.

'Just a fellow traveller,' he had said firmly, when Karpov showed him the airport photographs, and his boss seemed to believe him. How much do they already know about her? Flight details, her name, her telephone number?

Taras opens the kitchen drawer, not getting up from the table – one advantage of a kitchen so tiny is that everything is within reach – and takes out a piece of paper. He looks at the piece of torn newspaper, at the number, scribbled in blue ballpoint pen next to the headline: *Safe Journey to Europe* for a long, long time. It is so easy to memorise the eight-three-two double sequence. 'She did not even tell me her name,' he had said to Karpov. She did not need to. He knew it anyway.

Kate. Her name is Kate. That's what Andriy's handwriting says on the back of the photograph Taras took from his desk in Cambridge when he was searching for the documents: *Kate, March 2001.*

Taras pulls out the photograph from under the neatly folded tea cloths. It is a Polaroid, and the fading colours have a greenish tinge at the edges, but the checked oilcloth is still bright red and white, and the faces are well lit by the languid candle in the hurricane lamp.

Two people are looking at the camera, smiling. Two people, who shaped his past and his present, and robbed him of his future. Andriy and a happy, grey-eyed girl with a pony tail. Andriy's hand only touches her fingers, but it is a clear statement: 'She's mine.'

He recognised her straight away in Kiev, in the Lavra Museum, even though she was not smiling any more.

'The Will was brought to Ukraine by a British solicitor. Female,' said Karpov. Taras was one step away from guessing it himself.

He should have asked himself a question: what was a girl from the photograph in Andriy's room doing in Lavra, in Kiev, three days after Andriy's death? But he was too focused on his next task, on his date with Oksana, to think the situation through. Perfect case study, supporting Surikov's 'Ignoring coincidences is a first step to failure'!

He should have held Kate's elbow tighter in the museum, when she almost fell. A smile, asking for directions, or just walking out of the museum together would have done it. How could he act so irrationally, being just one step away 'from the rest of his life'?

'Dance with me, destiny!' It sure did. Waltzed him into his dark kitchen, turning his head, twisting his will, laughing at his lost chances. Why didn't he guess what her commitment was? Why didn't he stop her at the airport?

'Give me one day, Comrade Colonel,' he had asked Karpov. 'Give me one day to sort things out.'

An hour later, Taras praises the improved ticket-booking services, the new Aeroflot 'one call does it all' campaign and the reluctance of the passengers to believe it – which means that seats for next day's flight are available – praises the British Embassy for giving him a multi-entry visa for a month, and himself for buying the smart new briefcase. Aeroflot is providing a new service, a girl at the other end of the receiver has told him: 'We can book a hotel room for you as well.'

'Thank you. I'll try your new service, then,' replies Taras. 'There is one particular hotel I would like to stay in.'

The receiver clicks and clicks and minutes later comes back: 'The suite you requested is available, but this is a very expensive option. Maybe we can offer you something cheaper?'

'I'll take the suite,' says Taras. 'I am planning to stay for a day or two, but please book it for three nights, just in case.'

He arranges everything neatly in his leather briefcase – a couple of shirts, his old belt. He opens another kitchen drawer and takes a pack of dollars from a cigarette box. He has dreamed of staying in this hotel for a long time. And not only because it overlooks the Thames. He read about it in so many files in the Archives – apparently, it has always been *the* spies' meeting place. He requested the suite on the fifth floor – the rooms where the Russian Embassy was based during the Second World War. Just to add a touch of history to the touch of class. Yes, it is expensive, very expensive, but what has he got to lose? He has lost everything already. Well, almost everything. At least he still has his life.

Chapter 25

KATE

London, Monday 9 April 2001, 10.30 a.m.

She could pay him to stop, but he wouldn't, she is sure of it. He is at one with his saxophone; they are living this forlorn melody in unison.

This corner of the underground passageway has been his spot for three months now, maybe even four. She has heard him playing so many times, but has never really stopped, has never really listened to this nutty grey-bearded musician, who seems to live for his lament.

Kate sighs, leans over to put another coin into the open saxophone case and is jostled by a bulky red-faced man, carrying a huge box.

'Oi, what's up wiv you? Wosser ma'er? Wha'ya fink yer doin', blockin' the way like a dummy'ead? This is the fuckin' passageway, mate, not the fuckin' Barbican.'

Welcome home. Back to the office, back to Amy's chirruping and the impressionist painting.

'Oh, Kate!' Amy looks up from her screen as Kate walks through Reception. 'Miss Fletcher was looking for you.'

Kate manages to stretch her lips into a smile. It is easier than she expected. Amy's taste in make-up (raccoon-crayoned eyes, shimmering lilac eye-shadow) certainly helps.

Of course Miss Fletcher was looking for me, she thinks as she gets into the lift. I have a lot of explaining to do.

She has spent her whole weekend crossing out her 'diary failures' one by one. First she made a call to Philip who, judging by the music and laughter in the background, was in a club somewhere, in a state close to heavy alcoholic intoxication. ('It is four in the morning here, Kate!' he shouted.) Next, a call to Fiona, who was enjoying her third day of Spanish sun by now and who had fortunately managed to find another, *responsible* cat-feeder.

Kate left a mumbling message for Marina about the dress fitting, relieved that Marina was out and that her answering machine did not leave much time for lengthy explanations.

Now she hovers outside Carol's door, but instead of knocking on it, she turns left and goes along the corridor, to her own office. She is not ready to be confronted by Carol yet. Her face muscles are not strong enough.

She slides into the slot between the chair and the desk, adjusting herself to the familiar noises and a view of the sandwich shop across the road. Mission accomplished. How is she supposed to live now?

Looking out of the window, she notices it all as if for the first time: the red and green *Tonino's* sign across the road; Tonino's German girlfriend serving coffee, with her usual sour expression; Jamie, their office intern, queuing for sandwiches and wincing at the wind, his spiky hedgehog hair sticking up defiantly – he'll have forgotten the order list again, and will bring back the wrong things. Her eyes wander to the tree outside her window. The

branches are stark and black, but the April leaves are already confident, almost fully grown; only the colour gives away their freshness.

Kate discovers that simple, everyday actions can be fascinating.
She shifts the coffee cup to the centre of the desk and watches a
brown splash on the coaster changing shape; builds an obstacle
course to stop a pencil from rolling off the edge; arranges the
envelopes from the in-tray in a stack. A bulky brown package does
not fit on top of the tower, so she puts it aside. Bold letters in the
left corner catch her attention: *Service historique de l'armée de
terre. Château de . . .*

French Military Archives . . . Why? She tries to tear the envelope open, but does not have enough strength and reaches for the
scissors. The envelope contains a typed letter on headed paper,
several photocopies and a newspaper clipping.

Ah, now she remembers. She sent a letter to the Archives in
France more out of curiosity than necessity. When she was reading
Andriy's notes, there was one thing she found odd. According to
the Polubotko family legend, the Will was kept in France by the
French Count Orly, then by his descendants, before being passed
to Grygor Polubotko's grandfather at the end of the nineteenth
century, when he stopped in France before emigrating to Latin
America.

'Why was a French Count, of all people, chosen to safeguard
the Will?' she wondered, then dropped a three-liner to the *Service
historique*. In the whirl of the last weeks she has completely
forgotten about the request, but somebody else obviously hasn't.
In fact, her request was taken very seriously. Some meticulous,
balding, retiring archivist has spent a day of his life on her story
– dug the documents out, has written a letter: *Thank you for your*

request. Count Orly was a remarkable figure in French history. During the Thirty Years War he was a Commander of the Cavalerie Royale Allemande. *We enclose two copies of the articles that describe his military exploits. Count Orly often acted as a political agent of the French King and in this capacity he frequently travelled around Europe, building up support for the French Monarch. As his reports were often signed by different names, such as Bartel, Gare, Lamont, etc., it would be impossible to trace all his correspondence.*

You have asked whether we have any documents confirming the connection of Count Orly with Pavlo Polubotko. Unfortunately, an extensive search through our documents did not bring any positive results. However, we are in possession of a letter dated 18 July 1748, from Count Orly to Yakiv Polubotko. Considering the dates, this could be a letter to a son of Pavlo Polubotko or another relative of that generation. If you find this information relevant to your research, you are welcome to visit us and examine the letter and other documents. Our archives date between 1630 and 2001. We hold manuscripts, private papers, maps and photographs. Our working hours are between 10.00 and 17.30, Monday to Saturday. We are closed on Sundays. Please bring a form of identification with you when visiting the library.

'Thank you, Monsieur . . .' Kate checks the name below. 'Thank you, Monsieur Brisson. I'll visit your archives one day. When I retire, maybe.' She slides the letter back into the brown envelope and throws the envelope into the paper bin. This story is over; she does not want any more reminders.

She is totally absorbed in aligning the sheets into a seamless, perfect pile, when the phone rings. It's Amy, the receptionist. 'Kate? Marina is on her way to you. She said that there was some urgent business you needed to discuss.'

Kate replaces the receiver, carries on with her aligning exercise, and then the words sink in. *Marina* is here?

Kate has always wondered what it would be like to be caught in a tide, and now she knows: panic seeping through her toes, reaching her knees, quickly rising to her shoulders and totally engulfing her. Not Marina, of all people!

Kate considers barricading the office; measures herself against the gap between the desk and the wall – not entirely crazy choices, if you weigh them against speaking to Marina now. But she is too late.

Marina fills the room, her maternal bosom appearing first, then her waving hands, as if she were trying to break a swimming record, the jangling of countless bangles and finally the cooing voice of a contented dove, interrupted by the occasional gasp for air. She has obviously been running up the stairs, which is no easy task for someone of her large frame. But knowing Marina, waiting an extra minute for a lift to arrive would have been even harder. She needs action, and she needs it now.

'Katerynko!' She corners Kate, who tries to retreat to a defensive position behind the chair. 'I know, I know – I could have sent the dress by courier, could have waited for our jaunt tomorrow, but there will be other girls around, and I am dying to hear about your trip! I only discovered you were in Kiev from Sandra the other day, when you did not turn up for the fitting. How could you *not* tell me? I would have sent a parcel with you!'

Kate is trying to make sense of Marina's words: 'Our jaunt tomorrow ...' The tide rushes in again, as she remembers. Tomorrow is Marina's hen night in a smart 'girls only' spa, booked months ago; she's getting married next Sunday and she, Kate, is a bridesmaid.

Kate met Marina three years ago, when the agency recommended her as a Ukrainian translator. At first she was overwhelmed by Marina's personality: she was big and noisy, talking too much about too little, but Kate soon realised that Marina had a rare gift – she was a people magnet. Her soothing low voice, the grace of her movements and the warmth she radiated made her a centre of attention at parties. Especially for men. Kate knew that venturing to have a drink with Marina never meant 'having a friendly chat' – she inevitably ended up fending off men of various ages, professions and even sexual orientation.

Marina told Kate her life story within minutes of their first meeting. As a former Intourist guide, at the beginning of the *perestroika* years she was asked to accompany an aging British rock star on a tour of post-Soviet Russia. The hunger for everything Western meant that he was received with surprising hype, attracting full stadiums. During his adrenalin-fuelled trip he asked Marina to marry him. By the time she discovered that his spontaneity – and later regrets – extended from her to drugs, alcohol and the occasional blonde, it was too late. She was pregnant. Her next shock came nine months later, when the aging rock star, backed by his solicitors and his drug habit, decided to serve Marina divorce papers, claiming that the baby boy, now three months old, wasn't his son. Marina's mother in Kiev made it clear that she would welcome her new grandson with open arms, but for short periods only, since Marina's old bedroom was now being occupied by her paralysed grandmother.

Anybody would have broken down, given the circumstances. But Marina wasn't anybody. She rolled up her sleeves – literally – to wash the dishes in an Italian café in Clapham, running upstairs every half-hour to check on her Sashenka, who was sleeping in a tiny studio she rented above the café. She was doing translations during the day, rocking Sashenka's cot at the same time. And here she is, seven years on, contented and cheerful, getting married to Mario, the owner of that very Italian café, on Sunday.

'The spa is amazing, you are going to love it, I promise. Oh, come on, you must tell me about the Kiev trip, you absolutely must.' The bride-to-be stops cooing, pulls Kate's chair away from her and sits on it like a diligent pupil, hands on her knees, bangles resting against her wide wrists, prepared to listen.

Kate steps back, confused, and decides to lean on her desk: she will certainly need some extra support for this meeting. To clear the decks, she removes the pencil obstacle course she has built, then the papers she has arranged so neatly on the table – and discovers an unexpected escape route. Well, at least something that will give her a temporary respite. She picks up a document with the text, printed in Cyrillic.

'Great to see you, Marina,' she manages. 'Thanks for bringing the dress . . . Look, I was given something in Kiev, something very important, but it is all in Ukrainian. Could you scan it for me, please? Just to get the gist?' She places the sheets into Marina's hands, not giving her any chance to contest the flow of events.

Marina sighs, looks at the sheet and starts the thing that she is so good at – transferring the meaning from one language to another, keeping the style and the accents of the original: '"*Ukrainians in the Service of the French Crown*". Sorry, Kate, *French Monarchy* probably sounds better. "*Ukrainians in the Service of the French Monarchy – an article by Vera Maxymovych.*" Who is this Vera Maxymovych?' Marina stops. 'Her name seems familiar . . .'

Kate remembers Andriy's words. 'There is one more person we have to go and see about this. If anybody knows all the details of this gold story, then it's her.'

'She's a historian, a friend of a friend,' she says to Marina. 'I went to see her in Kiev at my friend's request. When she gave me an article, I was supposed to come back the next day for another talk, but other meetings prevented me from doing so. I should write to her with an apology, actually.'

Kate is surprised by the lightness of her own words. How guilt-free she sounds, about missing an important meeting with the Professor. How neatly she manages to squeeze a trip to Lviv, the horror of the return train journey and the audience with the Metropolitan and the President into the curt 'other meetings'.

'"*Ukrainians in the service of the French Monarchy*"'. This time Marina recites the title as if she is announcing the next concert performer. She sighs again, a little too loudly, and looks at Kate. 'Honestly, I never knew you had such an interest in French history. Can't we do it later? I was hoping you could try the dress on since you missed the final fitting. Here, I have brought Sashenka's school photo with me to show you. You won't recognise him on Sunday, he has grown so much!' She is about to hand the article back to Kate.

'Marina, dear, can we finish this first, please?' Kate pushes the papers back. She hopes to find an excuse for her sudden interest in this Ukrainian article and another excuse for sending Marina away by the time she finishes reading. She is so engrossed in this task that Marina's words become a distant echo.

'*Ask any Ukrainian about the title of this article, and he would guess straight away that it is about Anna Yaroslavna. Indeed, the eldest daughter of Yaroslav, the Grand Prince of Kyiv, became Queen of France in the eleventh century, when she married the French King Henry I at Rheims Cathedral in May 1051 (or in 1049, according to some researchers). She was described as "one of the most educated women in Europe" by a chronicler in a French monastery, and justifiably so: she could read and write (while the King couldn't) and spoke several languages. Anna carried her family Gospel to France with her and she took the oath during the coronation ceremony, placing her hand on her own Gospel, written in Cyrillic script. This sacred Gospel was used in the coronation ceremonies of all the French kings from 1059 to 1793. "Évangéliaire of Rheims", as the Gospel became known, is kept in the Manuscript Department at the Rheims Municipal Library . . .'*

'I certainly did not know about the Gospel.' Marina lifts her head from the article. 'We all learned about Anna, the Queen of France, at school, but not in such detail.'

Kate is about to ask Marina to continue as she has not come up with any exit plan yet, but there is no need. Her friend, genuinely interested in the article, carries on.

". . . We would not want to retell the story of Anna here, since much has already been written about her.

"Instead, we would like to turn our attention to a topic that rarely appears in publications – the connection of the Ukrainian Cossack families with the French Court in the eighteenth century. If you have ever got stuck at the notorious Paris 'Periphérique' on your way to Orly airport, it would hardly have occurred to you that the name of this airport is directly linked to one of the world's first democratic constitutions. You might be wondering what the connection is. It is less complicated than you think.

"Orly airport was built on land that in the eighteenth century had belonged to the French Count Orly. He was, in fact, a Ukrainian Cossack, Grygory Orlyk, the son of the great Cossack Hetman Pylyp Orlyk, author of the first Constitution of Ukrainian Cossacks (*in*

Latin, 'Pacta et Constitutiones Legum Libertatumque Exercitus Zaporoviensis') . . .'

'Wow, Kate, did you hear that?' exclaims Marina. 'I haven't forgotten my Latin yet!'

'Yes, I heard you. A Ukrainian Cossack!' gasps Kate. 'Could you repeat it, please?'

'"*Count Orly was a Ukrainian Cossack, Grygory Orlyk, the son of the great Cossack Hetman Pylyp Orlyk . . .*"' repeats Marina and carries on: '"*So, how did Grygory Orlyk end up at the French Royal Court? Three top personalities of the Age of Enlightenment were directly responsible for this: Karl XII, the King of Sweden, Pylyp Orlyk, Ukrainian Hetman in exile, and . . . Voltaire! Yes, the greatest writer and the greatest plotter of the eighteenth century was involved in this plot as well.*

'"*In the first half of the eighteenth century, with new trade routes developed by England, and the continuous rise of Russia, the Swedish-French alliance was in desperate need of strengthening. And who could provide better assistance than the Cossack Hetman in exile in Sweden, the Commander of the bravest European troops of the time?*

'"*Voltaire visited Sweden under the pretext of writing a book about the great Karl XII. (Which he did, by the way, and in very masterly fashion indeed.) The Swedish King introduced Voltaire to Hetman Orlyk and to his remarkable son. What happened next was, excuse the pun, history. Grygory Orlyk married the daughter of an influential French banker and courtier, and demonstrated such courage in battle and such devotion to Louis XVI that he was made a General of the French army.*

'"*There is an interesting link between two noble Cossack families of that time: Polubotko and Orlyk . . .*"'

'What did you say?' interrupts Kate.

'Honestly, Kate, why are you interrupting all the time? If you do it again I'll stop reading! These are Ukrainian family names. "Orlyk" you know already, and "Polubotko" is another.'

Oh boy, don't I know *that* name! thinks Kate, and bites her tongue.

Marina carries on: "*Pylyp Orlyk, who was forced to spend many years in exile after his attempt to organise the Cossack uprising against the Russian Tsar Peter, was in active correspondence with another Hetman, Pavlo Polubotko. In fact, one of the accusations, presented to Polubotko during his arrest in St Petersburg in 1723, was his contact with Orlyk, who was by then declared an enemy of the Empire. Their correspondence is well documented and researched. Far more intriguing, however, is the theory about the joint plans and mutual assistance of the sons of the great Hetmans, Count Orly (Grygory Orlyk) and Yakiv Polubotko. Their corres-pondence was discovered by the Ukrainian historian Mykola Marchuk in the 1930s, during his work in the Military Archives in France, at the . . .*" Kate, I don't know the translation, so I'll read it in French as it is: "'Service historique de l'armée de terre'. *Marchuk suggested that together, following the legacy of their fathers, they might have been developing a plot for the independence of Ukraine.*

"*Unfortunately, his research could not be taken further due to the arrest of Professor Marchuk as an enemy of the nation in 1935. He was called back to Moscow from Paris and later died in the Karlag, one of Stalin's camps in Northern Kazakhstan. The constraints of my age would not allow me to travel to France to research this matter further. I hope this publication will help to reignite an interest in this subject. We are actively seeking sponsors to provide funding for a research trip by one of my assistants to continue this important work in support of our national heritage.'''*

Kate has a sinking feeling that something is terribly, irreversibly wrong. *Marchuk suggested that together, following the legacy of their fathers, they might have been developing a plot for the independence of Ukraine.*

A ball of anguish rises from her solar plexus to her collarbones. Is this what they call intuition?

Marina tears herself away from the article. 'This is fascinating – it reads like a novel! Kate, what's wrong? Why are you rummaging through the bin? You've thrown away something important, no doubt. Kate, can you hear me?'

Kate looks above her friend, at the office clock: 11.00, Monday. Three days before the visit of the Ukrainian President.

'Marina,' says Kate, firmly clutching the brown envelope she has just found, 'I cannot go to the spa with you tomorrow. Nor can I try the dress on now. I have to go to France.'

Chapter 26

It is just past midday when Kate finally turns off the autoroute. At least she did not have to drive through Paris. Last year's experience was more than enough. Philip negotiated the streets in the Latin Quarter for hours, as he wasn't prepared to squeeze into tight parking spaces. 'Like a squashed frog,' he said.

The conversation with Marina yesterday was easy. Mainly because Marina, who usually talks non-stop, mixing together words from various languages in some exotic linguistic cocktail, was absolutely speechless. Kate had neither the strength nor the inclination to explain the reasons. 'Not now,' was all she said, and her friend huffed off. Kate will have to deal with it on her return somehow. As well as with the other usual suspects – with Miss Fletcher, hovering by her door, asking for a meeting – again; with Philip – calling New York at some civilised hour; with Fiona's cat – calling Spain and finding the name of that *responsible* feeder in London. And God, she has not called *Babusya* for a week, so she has a lot of explaining to do there! At least, being a suspect herself, she hasn't heard from a stammering policeman yet. He seems to be the only person for whom 'she hasn't left the country'.

. . . She swerves sharply – my God, she was on the wrong side of the road. *Concentrate, girl.* She drives past a small sandstone church. The spike of the lead dome looks like the beak of a thirsty bird, desperate for a drop of rain. The shop signs read like a page from her GCSE textbook: *Pâtisserie, boulangerie, épicerie.* She's already had a chance to practise her French, yesterday. Without much success, though.

When she dialled the number typed under the archivist's name, the voice on the other end of the line was trilling and rumbling, like pebbles rolled by the waves: '*Service historique de l'armée de terre, bonjour.*'

So far, so good, thought Kate. My French can cope with this.

'*Je voudrais parler avec Monsieur Pierre Brisson, s'il vous plait. C'est* Mademoiselle . . .' At least her name sounds the same in all languages.

She was surprised by how much French had been drummed into her by Madame Gamin. Obviously not enough, because the tidal voice answers in accurate English: 'Pierre Brisson speaking. Good morning, *mademoiselle.* I recognise your name – I wrote a letter to you two weeks ago. How can I help you?'

You can help me by saying that the letter from Yakiv Polubotko does not exist, thinks Kate. Tell me in any language that you have misread that name. Or at least tell me that the letter is not accessible to the general public, and I'll need to wait for six months to get a pass. I cannot possibly face another trip now, not another train journey, not another airport.

'. . . So you reckon driving is the easiest way to get to you?' she finds herself saying. 'Round Paris on the Périphérique, then route N10? I will be with you tomorrow.'

Kate slows down at the T-junction in the middle of the village.

There is no road sign for a château, and no sign of a château anywhere either. Her 'go-getter' spring is loosening, and in a minute will be replaced by a spiral of panic. Where is this place? Whom can she ask?

She crosses a bridge with carved, sad-faced sea monsters, parks the car and walks over to the fast-moving shallow stream, where she washes her face, letting the water run through her fingers.

There is a gate at the end of the bridge, with crisscrossed swords on the shield there, and a poplar alley leading to a building that looks like a château. As she gets closer, she sees that the building is a mini-version of a real château, with a moat and massive turrets. Two black swans are floating on the dark water of the moat, like giant question marks. The provider of the answers is expecting her, and he's not the finicky Frenchman she imagined at all. He is tall, broad-shouldered, farmer stock. He knows she is driving back today, he tells her, and arranges everything very quickly.

Too quickly for her to realise that the letter is in French. That she has forgotten her dictionary. That it is a wasted trip, as they will not allow her to photocopy it or take the letter out. Too many thoughts for a minute, because this is exactly how much time he takes to return. Was my French on the phone really so bad that I did not even need to ask him for the text in English? wonders Kate.

'I have done the translation for you, *mademoiselle* – in case you want it. I must apologise for the spelling; my English is not good enough.'

If he had followed the plough with the same efficiency, thinks Kate, they would have had three *boulangeries* in this village. She turns to offer her *merci*, but Pierre Brisson is gone. He respects her time and her privacy. Her curiosity of the researcher.

If only he knew what was at stake! thinks Kate, and she turns to the first page.

Champagne, France
18 July 1748

To Yakiv Polubotko, his humble servant Grygory Orlyk (Count Orly) presents his respect. I am totally indebted to you, Yakiv, for sending your bright and courageous daughter to support our great cause ... It is a long and hard journey for Sofia, but I know that her faith and our prayers will help her to get to you safely.

Sofia did not miss this familiar creak of the worn-out wheel springs at all, this pattern of tones over and over again. She has forgotten how uncomfortable her father's festive carriage is! He will be so proud of her. It will take her days, maybe weeks to tell him everything about this journey. God, where to start?

Maybe with her visit to the Titular Bishop's library in Warsaw, the world's second-largest book collection after Biblioteca Vaticana – 300, 000 volumes! 'I could camp in those rooms for days, *Tato*, I really could!' And she met her first real Englishman there. Mr Williams, a poet and a traveller, spoke much better Latin than she did. When Sofia asked him about England, he exclaimed: 'It is a wonderful country, almost quite as free as Poland!'

Or she could start with London, the world's largest city. With its colours and sounds, with Ranelagh Pleasure Gardens and the coffee-houses. Such a dangerous place, London. She will tell *Tato* about the pickpockets in the crowded streets, especially around the Bank and—

No, she will start with her happiest memory. With the day when, after coming back to France from London to stay with the Orlys, she was taken by the Count and the Countess to see their neighbours.

The 'neighbours' lived a two-hour carriage drive away. Sofia was taken aback by the geometrical splendour of the gardens – green squares and circles and triangles, divided by the gravel lines of the paths. The hostess herself looked like a complex mathematical instrument, similar to the one Sofia saw at 'Cabinet de Lecture', their Academy bookshop. She was a tall, thin woman with a straight, almost stiff bearing. She has a mind to match, thought Sofia, when the Count explained to her that La Marquise du Chatelet was a scientist, who worked eight hours a day writing books on physics and algebra.

The Marquise touched Sofia's wrist with her long bony fingers, leading her into the hall, to the ringing laughter of a pretty girl, who was running towards them through the enfilade of rooms, white waves of taffeta following her smiling face. She resembled a weightless, carefree cloud on a clear summer sky, followed by the rolling r-s of a faraway thunder of an elderly servant, trying to catch up with her: '*Arrêtez, Eloise! Arrêtez!*'

That feeling of warm, fresh summer rain stayed with Sofia all evening. The guests resembled a cast of great comedy, directed by one man with sunken cheekbones. His sparkling eyes were emitting such a contagious energy, that it made all the household move, talk, laugh every minute of the day. He was the only one making comments through dinner, he had written the play for the marionette performance, and when it came to poetry reading, nobody could recite better. While the guests were moving in a minuet, the energetic man invited Sofia, together with her hosts, the Count and Countess, into his study. He pulled a small volume from the shelf in one quick, jerky movement and handed it to Sofia.

'He wants you to have the book,' smiled the Count. 'He was the first in Europe to write about Ukraine, Sofia.'

Sofia looked at the cover: *Histoire de Charles XII, Rouen, 1731*. Author: *François Voltaire*. Sofia remembered the whispered rumours at the Academy about the powerful Frenchman whose writings dared to attack the Church. The Frenchman, who was destroying kings and governments with ridicule. '*Merci.*' She finally managed the single French word she had learned.

When she was bidding farewell to the Count and Countess, Hélène tried to persuade Sofia to take an enormous muff with her. 'It is the latest fashion in Paris, *ma chère*. Some ladies even carry their dogs in their muffs! Oh, and don't forget to—'

The Count sighed and turned to Sofia. '*Dytynko*, if you don't go now, you never will!'

Sofia smiled. Her new dress adjusted, Voltaire's book hidden safely in her luggage, she was now ready for her trip back. Or so she thought.

Only five hours into the journey, and she is already reminded how uncomfortable her father's carriage really is. Oh, she has to ask Vasil to stop, she cannot bear this torture any longer! As if reading her thoughts, he shouts: 'Hold tight, Sofia!' She can hear his raucous laughter as he takes the carriage at a gallop down the steep hill.

A polite cough brings Kate back to reality. Pierre Brisson is standing by her desk, trying to get her attention. Kate feels that by now, she could write an expert paper on the 'patterns of behaviour of

European archivists' – first a document that can change the researcher's world, then a polite cough in your left ear, then another offering of documents. Pierre Brisson and Jolly Roger should talk, perhaps.

'Mademoiselle, I don't know if you are interested, but we are also in possession of a draft letter from Maréchal Lecoq to the Lithuanian Prince, resident in Warsaw. This is another document we have, where the names "Orly" and "Polubotko" are mentioned together. I did not bring it on . . . sorry, bring it *up* in my letter to you as it was only a draft, a beginning – *pas beaucoup*. But, as you are here today, I have decided to show it to you, just in case you might be interested.'

He places a letter in front of her. There are only four lines on the faded paper, but with such calligraphic turns and twists, with so much crossed out, that she cannot even recognise the language it is written in. She does not need to. Pierre Brisson has done a handwritten English translation.

. . . and as I had my most stimulating meeting with the wittiest Elizabeth Montagu at Child's Coffee-house near the Bank of England yesterday, I had another most pleasant encounter there. My old friend Count Orly introduced me to a young lady of Little Russian origin, called Sofia Polubotko . . .

'Monsieur Brisson,' starts Kate. Her voice is so low that he needs to lean over to her to hear the question. 'Monsieur Brisson, do you know what Sofia Polubotko was doing in London?'

'Ah, we don't have any more records of her, mademoiselle, I am afraid,' apologises Brisson.

Kate is afraid too. Afraid to look again at the lines in the two letters in front of her . . . *indebted to you for sending your bright and courageous daughter to support our great cause . . .*

*Count Orly introduced me to a young lady of Little Russian origin
. . . Coffee-house near the Bank of England.*

Afraid to do a simple analysis – any first-year History student
would have been able to draw the right conclusions. All she has
to do is add to those lines the fact that the Will got to Argentinian
Polubotkos from France, from the descendants of Count Orly,
and . . .

Macpherson, her tutor of Medieval History, would have loved
this, absolutely gloried in it. 'Hi-story indeed,' he would have said.
'Maybe, Kate, you could think of an essay about this, calling it
"High-story"? You could present and discuss a perfect example of
an ordinary girl, a granddaughter of a Cossack, influencing major
political decisions.' And Philip would have said, leaning over her
shoulder: 'But she wasn't *that* ordinary, Kate, was she? Her courage
and determination look pretty *extra*ordinary to me!'

There is a familiar polite cough into her left ear. 'I would also
allow myself to mention to you,' Brisson murmurs, 'that the Château
de Cirey is only ten minutes' drive from here. The owner, Émilie,
Marquise du Châtelet, was Voltaire's lover, you know. The great
philosopher spent many of his summers at the Château; the Orlys
spent many happy evenings there too. It was Voltaire, in fact, who
introduced Count Orly to his future wife. I have printed out the
directions for you, if you are interested. Would you like to go?'

She would. What has she got to lose? She has lost everything
already . . . Then she thinks of the long list of people who died
for the Will. Well, almost everything. At least she still has her
life.

Chapter 27

London, Wednesday 11 April 2001, 9.00 a.m.

'Good morning. It is nine o'clock. I am Belinda Carson'. The radio is talking to Kate, but she does not listen. She has reread her notes three times, but cannot find any answers. The familiar train is gaining speed again: *do-it-for-him, do-it, do-it* . . . Just when she thought that it could not get any worse, this story catches up with her again. It is running close, too close, breathing down her neck, ready to knock her down.

She has been in the office since eight. Last night, shattered by the long drive, she just scribbled some reminders for today and is now deciphering them one by one.

1. Start boardroom

What on earth does that mean? Ah, yes. There is a full set of *The History of the World* in the boardroom.

Kate marches decisively over to the shelves, squeezing past the tea lady who is setting out the coffee cups for the morning meeting. She has probably never seen anybody using these books before.

Kate pulls out a red-bound volume, *Europe in the Eighteenth Century*, and scans the chapter headings: 'War between France and Britain', 'Russia and Sweden', 'Influence of the Prussian King'.

She cannot grasp the full picture: court intrigues and marriages, secret pacts and alliances are constantly changing the map of the continent, shifting the power, creating a patchwork of borders.

To concentrate, back in her office, she reads aloud: "'In the middle of the century, the rise of Russia and Prussia coincided with the diminishing strength of France. England and France continued to compete for the new trade routes to America and India. With its large population and great natural resources, France did not have the best harbours, and needed to strengthen its insecure borders in the East. Moreover, all attempts of France to counteract Russia were becoming increasingly difficult. As a result, by the middle of the eighteenth century, Europe was more or less divided into two groups: England, Austria, Russia and Portugal versus France, Spain, Prussia, Denmark, Poland, Turkey and Sweden. Ukrainian independence would have strengthened the second camp significantly. So, it is hardly surprising that the 'Ukrainian card' became an important factor in European politics in the first half of the eighteenth century, actively played by France, Sweden and Poland'."

Kate looks at her second scribbled reminder. *2. Airport travel.* What is it – Sofia's travels? A flight to Kiev? No – Orly. Orly airport . . . Count Orly. He was travelling around Europe as the King's political agent, building up support for Louis XVI. What if he was secretly masterminding the support for the independence of Ukraine?

The third reminder: *3. PROJECT FINANCE!!!*

Money. Sofia Polubotko was travelling across Europe on her own to meet Count Orly and possibly go to London with him, to 'support a great cause'. It was not just dangerous, it was lethal, almost from the outset. Yakiv Polubotko would have decided to send his beloved daughter on such a journey only if it was really worth it. If it was worth a lot. What if the suggestion about the 'sons of great Hetmans preparing a plot for the independence of Ukraine' was right? Sofia and Count Orly were seen in a coffee-house not far from the Bank of England. What if the funding for the 'great cause' came from . . .

The train gives a loud whistle and grinds to a halt, as if some-body powerful and controlling has pulled an alarm cord decisively inside her head.

'These are only assumptions, Kate,' this cold voice is telling her. 'Stop. Think. You are a lawyer. You need proof.'

There is only one place where she could try to get proof this morning.

She calls the Bank of England. Tyre Woman picks up the phone.

'Please, please, can I have a look at the bank ledger of 1748?' Kate does not offer any explanation.

Tyre Woman remembers her, because her voice rustles, like dry leaves in autumn. 'Well, you should know the procedure by now. You have to fill in the form and the ledger will be available in three days. You have to make an appointment.'

'No, no!' If Kate ever bends her own principles and grovels, today is the day. 'I really, really, *really* need it now! Please!'

'I am sorry.' Tyre Woman is not convinced. 'It is not possible. The archives from that period are in another building; it takes time to present the requisition form, and—'

Ahoy, Jolly Roger, remembers Kate.

'Can I speak to Roger, please?' She tries to sound calm.

The phone dies on her for a second before she hears a familiar friendly voice.

'Roger, please help me!' shouts Kate, as if loudness can explain everything. 'I am in trouble, I really am, if I don't see the ledger, dated 1748, and the 1720-1734 ledger with Will abstracts today!'

Roger is either too impressed or too embarrassed by her shouting and his colleague listening. All he says is: 'Come and see us in three hours, Kate.' He hasn't forgotten her name.

This time, Kate is genuinely pleased to see Roger. She is in dire need of his encyclopaedic knowledge right now.

She comes straight to the point. 'Are there any records of money transfers between Britain and France in the middle of the eighteenth century?'

Roger shakes his head. 'Not much was happening at this time, I am afraid. France and Britain were at war from 1744 to 1748, so the moneys could hardly be transferred.'

'If a foreigner had deposited his gold in the Bank, could he take it out easily at that time?'

Roger looks above Kate, as if he is reading an autocue on the wall, and showers her with all his knowledge on the subject.

'The historic period you are asking about encompasses the notorious "Black Friday" – the sixth of December 1745 – the bank crisis caused by fears of French invasion.

'Strictly private trade in bullion yielded very little profit, and this business was at an unusually low level during the mid-1740s. Reserves were severely depleted and the Bank was using all possible tools to replenish its store of gold.

'It was quite common at that time to give out loans against the deposits of foreign gold on very favourable terms. But not many private loans were taken out. All of them are recorded in the Minutes of the meetings of the Court of Directors.' He places a heavy volume on the desk in front of Kate. 'These records might shed some light on the subject of dealing with foreign gold deposits at that time.'

She reads the familiar extract from the Will again. As she touches the page, she feels the cold creeping through her fingertips, up to her arm, her shoulders, seeping into her chest. Because now the words at the bottom of the page, which she overlooked the first time, stand out very clearly:

Also my Will is that then it shall be in the power of my executors Pylyp Orlyk or his survivors or survivor of them to receive in all such sum if any of my legatees shall be under the age of twenty-one years for a man or married at twenty-one years for a woman. But for more surety's sake it is the best to have the opinion of the Banks Council thereon for the executors disposal of the principal funds.

Kate opens the Records of the Court of Directors, brought by the helpful Roger. She is seeking their opinion, just as Count Orly probably did in 1748, when he travelled to see them with Sofia. She is not at all surprised to see the Minutes, dated 17 July 1748. She expected and dreaded this, like a public announcement of a verdict, like a doctor's confirmation of imminent death that you suspected, you guessed, you knew about all along. But on page seventeen of the Records of the Court of Directors, somebody diligent took the trouble to spell it out, and all the courtesy and flowery curls cannot hide, cannot embellish the glaring truth:

The Court of Directors at the Bank on Thursday, 17 July 1748
Present – William Fawkener, Esquire – Governor
Charles Savage, Esquire – Deputy Governor

Foreign gold examined.
Mr Deputy Governor reported that having examined the Bank

Stock in the name of deceased Colonel Polubotko, by the request of the Executor of the Will of the abovementioned, Count Orly, born Cossack Grygory Orlyk, the stock to be transferred to his survivor Sofia Polubotko, not married under the age of twenty-one. The Council are under the unanimous opinion that a loan is to be issued upon the Polubotko stock security for the same. The Council requested punctual compliance in repayment upon account of the loan secured by gold, deposited at the bank.

Kate does not need to open the ledger dated 1748-1763, since she knows only too well what she will find there. One line, crossing everything out: Andriy's death, her trip to Kiev, months of research. She swallows hard and turns the first page with stiff, cold fingers.

. . . permit to withdraw . . . deposit . . . delivered to the cashiers . . .

She moves to the next page; then to the next. Three pages later, she finds what she has been looking for.

To the Cashier of the Bank of England.

Permit Mister Grygory Orlyk to write off or draw from my account any sum or sums of money he shall demand, and this shall be your warrant.

Signed – Sofia Polubotko

Kate leaves the bank, her eyes fixed firmly on the floor. Past the

Tyre Woman, past Jolly Roger, past the security – out, to get some air, to run away. As if they all know what she knows now. She has made the classic mistake of the first-year student, drawing the conclusions before checking *all* the facts. Simple and unforgivable.

The money had been taken out two hundred and fifty years ago, to fund a great political mission. Was this loan ever repaid? Count Orly died in battle in 1752, and she does not know what happened to Sofia.

To try to claim the inheritance now, at the highest possible level, would be like repeating Guy Fawkes's attempt to blow up the Houses of Parliament. Only this time openly, carrying the gunpowder barrel across the city, under the flashes of the press cameras, past the security guard at the entrance, and still hoping to succeed.

She can see the scenario unrolling: the President's announcement, the British reply, something detached and non-belligerent, with a hidden meaning that might be something along the lines of: 'What a load of cobblers! The money went centuries ago! And by the way, sir, what was the name of that British solicitor who sold this whole story to you? *How much* did she say it was worth?' Just like that. A diplomatic scandal of vast proportions. The press would love the details, especially the sums involved, and the President would hate losing face. No doubt her name would be mentioned, more questions asked.

She remembers the chessboard she saw in the Kiev Museum, smaller than a pinhead. That's what she is – a pawn on a pinhead, with the hostile world of history around her. The giant machine is munching its way through the centuries, looking for new victims . . . She has to do something to stop the trouble she has started.

She walks into the office. The embossed card greets her from her desk. *The President of the Republic of Ukraine requests the pleasure of your company.* She has been invited to the banquet with the British business community that the President is attending tomorrow night. She will be introduced to him after standing in the long line of Ambassadors and Ministers, and then she will be seconds away from her disgrace. She will have only seconds to say: 'Don't present the documents tomorrow. It is all wrong, even dangerous. I have no time to explain now. Just don't do it.'

Chapter 28

Power is more important than wealth. He knows it now. He is sitting on the windowsill of the Presidential Suite, looking at the green oasis of Hyde Park, thinking about the bizarre developments of the last month.

Only a fortnight ago, the Metropolitan had persuaded him to give an audience to that weird English girl with a Ukrainian name. 'I don't often ask you to meet people, but this meeting could be important *for you* and for the country. Spare her five minutes.' The President did not like the way the Metropolitan has stressed 'for you'. Fearing provocation, he asked two of his security people to attend the meeting.

The girl could have been pretty, had it not been for the haunted look in her eyes and the two sorrowful lines running from her nose to the corners of her mouth. She did not talk much, just handed him the documents. They seemed to be genuine, but she refused to say how she had acquired them.

He did not like the fact that she neither smiled nor looked at him. When he asked her why she was doing it, she went silent for a long time, before she replied, 'I am following the instructions of my client.' The answer was professional and neutral, just as it should have been. Was that *really* her reason?

When she left, he turned to his Head of Security. 'I want to know everything about this girl. Where she comes from, her address, her interests, her movements for the next two weeks. People don't bring such documents to the Head of State purely because of the "client's" instructions. And another thing: for the matter of such state importance, the legal firm should have sent a senior partner. Why have they sent her, unaccompanied?'

The discovery of the documents was a timely surprise, just before his official visit to Britain. Just three months ago, he had given yet another interview, dismissing the gold story as a legend. But deep in his heart he always knew it was true. He spoke to experts, saw reports . . . but never really had time to take the matter seriously. And then, fate smiled at him, sent this unsmiling girl.

He is going to present the documents officially to the Prime Minister tomorrow. If this amount of money were returned, his country could finally stop teetering on the verge of a crisis; at least the pensions and the salaries of the miners, teachers and doctors would be paid. Dependence on Russian gas would become less of a worry, too. The costly Black Sea shipping route might be the alternative way to go . . . He would turn from a National Scapegoat into a National Hero, which would certainly help in the coming elections.

Today has been a hard day. He has shaken hands, nodded, smiled all day, and was looking forward to a well-deserved half-hour break in the hotel before the beginning of the evening's programme. But no such luck. Five minutes later, the Head of the Protocol Department rushed into the room, saying, 'We have the PM's

Private Secretary outside, Mr President, requesting a seven-minute informal meeting with you. This unscheduled meeting was not agreed between the Protocol Departments. Since it is not in the official programme, you have the right of refusal on the grounds of a breach of protocol. On the other hand, it might be something important, and if we refused, it might affect an official meeting with the PM tomorrow.'

The President waved his hand, parting the air. The gesture, as the Head of the Protocol had already learned, could mean several things:

'For God's sake, can't I have some rest like any normal person?'

'You are talking too much. Just do what you think is right in such circumstances.'

'You may as well ask him in, if he is already here.'

The Head of Protocol, pale and tense, strained by the first day of the official visit, read the gesture as a joint second and third option, and two minutes later came back with a gaunt, grey-haired man in a navy pin-striped suit.

How do they do it? They always look so effortlessly gentlemanly, thought the President, while I have a whole staff of designers and image-makers, and our newspapers never stop criticising me for not looking like a President!

After a meaningless, necessary exchange of polite formalities, the Private Secretary looked straight into the President's non-presidential eyes and said, 'The PM is looking forward to seeing you tomorrow, Mr President. However, there is one item on the agenda that he has found slightly disturbing – indeed, he asked me to discuss it with you before it is raised officially. I am talking about the presentation of the documents for claiming back *the* inheritance.' The President's interpreter noticed the accent on 'the', but could not translate the nuance. He did not need to: the President knew exactly what the Private Secretary was referring to.

God, he thought again. How *do* they do it?

There was no mention of the inheritance in the agenda presented to the British side for the discussions tomorrow. It was planned that the President would deliver the message unexpectedly, when they reached the seventh item on the agenda, entitled *Other Business*.

Was it the girl? flashed through his mind – but she seemed too timid for this! Could it have been his Head of Protocol? The President was only waiting for the right opportunity to get rid of him: the fellow was too knowledgeable, too smart, too diplomatic – in other words, too dangerous.

'The PM understands the desire of your country to claim the funds now, at this historical and, unfortunately, not the easiest of times in the development of your state,' continued the Private Secretary. 'Provided that all the documents are in place and the inheritance does exist' (the interpreter was struggling with the nuance again), 'Her Majesty's Government would do everything possible to help you to recover the funds. I also feel that it is my duty to include a note of caution, Mr President. Claiming an inheritance could be a lengthy and expensive process, perhaps taking years and costing millions in legal fees. Bearing in mind the sums involved here, I am inclined to believe that this inheritance case might fit that scenario. As far as I am aware, the Presidential election in Ukraine is next year, and in this situation, spending the funds on the legal fees in Britain might not appear to be entirely justified.'

The President nodded, acknowledging the PM's concern. He did not volunteer any comments.

'I would also like to emphasise, Mr President, that we see your country as an important emerging European player and would be delighted to support your country's applications to various international institutions.'

The President expressed muted gratitude and nodded again. He knew exactly what the Private Secretary was saying, even though he was not saying much.

The other man rose. 'Well, I am glad we have reached an understanding. I will see you tomorrow, Mr President.'

When he left, the Head of Protocol hurried after him, looking at his watch. The meeting had lasted exactly seven minutes.

Honestly, how *do* they do it? he thought in admiration.

Alone at last, the President knows he is facing a difficult choice.

If he does not make a claim tomorrow, he can play on this for a long time. He will hope that his British friends would support the country's European aspirations. He will not say 'in return': there is no need – they will understand this perfectly. If his country, with the support of their British friends, joined NATO, he could focus his efforts on 'securing a peaceful future for the nation' in his pre-election speeches. And then the pensioners, who still remember the Second World War, would shout less about their rights; they would put up with poverty just to live in peace. And pensioners are an influential lot; he cannot afford to underestimate them. They are the ones who will go to the polls and tip the balance. Not the disappointed lost generation of forty year olds, who grew up on socialist ideas and still cannot accept all this free market palaver. Nor the Westernised youth, interested in everything but politics.

But his country desperately needs this money. Needs hope that

there is a lottery ticket, an unexpected win, to get it out of inflation and poverty. Yes, the legal process might indeed take years,
but what great publicity this story will attract! He will be called
the Saviour of the Nation. Of course, if the money got into the
budget quickly, he would have to spend his days mediating squabbles between Social Services and nuclear power stations, the army
and the miners. Everybody would want their cut immediately.
This situation might create more enemies than friends.

So, he has to choose – either a cash injection and pre-election
publicity, or the support of their British friends and the money
squabbles at home.

The President looks out of the window. A group of young riders
is trotting in Hyde Park. Suddenly, one of the horses gallops. A
little boy slips off the saddle, but manages to stay on the horse.

The President cannot afford to be thrown out of his saddle.

He has a lot to think about.

He turns to his Private Secretary. 'That girl – the English solicitor who brought the inheritance papers. Have we sent her an
invitation for tonight? I want to thank her personally when I see
her.'

'Everything is under control, President,' nods the Private
Secretary as he disappears out of the door, giving the President
the chance to relax for the remaining twenty-two minutes of his
break.

Actually, thinks the Private Secretary, I need to relax as well.
It has been quite a day, and this girl has been hard work, too.

He was really surprised when the President spent so much time
in Kiev in the unplanned one-to-one meeting with an unknown
British solicitor. She wasn't particularly beautiful either. Worse
still, he was not allowed to be present at the meeting, while the

Head of Security was called in. So the Private Secretary decided to conduct his own little investigation: accompany the girl to the airport, watch her, take some photos, and send the findings by a special courier to Moscow. One cannot classify his actions as betrayal, surely! And the word 'treason' is completely out of context here. Vice versa, in fact. His actions show the loyalty to the organisation he signed up with twenty years ago. Or does the money put a completely different name to it?

He looks at his watch – he has got just enough time for a cup of tea and a piece of cake. He'll ask for the Black Forest gâteau. He loved it when he tried it two years ago in this hotel. He deserves it today, he certainly does, with all the preparations. Even though his wife keeps nagging him to lose weight. She says that being bald and round, he reminds her of a dough ball.

Chapter 29

TARAS

London, Thursday 12 April 2001, 4.55 p.m.

It is five to five when he finally wins today's battle. He has spent all day trying to persuade Amy the receptionist to let him see Kate. The familiar dotty painting is now too familiar, in fact. When he called a scribbled number this morning, the voice and the accent of the receptionist sounded familiar as well.

Do they have a certain standard for legal receptionists? wonders Taras. The girl informed him that Kate would be out all day, but gave him the address of the office. When he checked the map, he wasn't surprised at first. He had read that London lawyers congregate in the same area. But as he got closer to the entrance, noticed the familiar cream chair and the dotty painting, he had to swerve sharply and march away, pacing the Embankment for half an hour, rethinking his plans.

Amy was pleased to see him – or rather, she was pleased to see the good-looking Polish Baron, who had had a meeting with Miss Fletcher in March. She opened her heavily made-up eyes wider than necessary, as the Baron still remembered her name.

'Good morning. I came to see the lawyer you recommended

me last time, Amy. Your expert on Eastern Europe, you said. Kate, wasn't it?'

And so it began. The battle for Kate's whereabouts, her plans, her home address.

Amy offered him an appointment for tomorrow, but refused point blank to give Taras any personal information. She held the fort with her head high and steely determination. All day. Taras wondered whether she had received any military training.

He tried the silent waiting game with an element of surprise at the end. Tried to walk away 'and come back after lunch'. Tried asking generic questions about the firm first, followed by details. All in vain.

He was even reduced to intercepting the postman on his way inside the building; the man was only too glad to offload a bag of papers to a new solicitor, but there was nothing for Kate in the mail. Eventually, at ten to five, he surrendered. Amy was close to calling the police. She told him that in her usual, amiable tone.

As he turned his back on her, making his final move to the door, he overheard her on the phone: 'You are sending a wedding present? Here – for Kate? No, she must have ordered it for her friend's wedding. Must have given the office address by mistake. She has been quite absent-minded recently for some reason. No, no need to call her, I know her home address. Please deliver it to . . .'

Taras breathes a deep sigh of relief as he leaves the office. He checks the map and decides that to hail a cab would be the fastest way.

KATE

It is five to five when she finally finds the car keys. She checks herself in the mirror; she needs to look the part. The bridesmaid's green dress for Sunday's wedding works well. It is fluid, low-cut, but so tight at the waist that she had to hold her breath to do up the zip. She hopes it won't burst at the seams in front of the President and the press! Then she rushes out of the flat.

The security in the City is horrendous, the parking even worse. She must look ridiculous tottering in high heels and a long narrow dress past the cheering pubbers towards the Guildhall. By the time she gets to the entrance, the long line of guests has thinned down to a trickle of latecomers.

'Your invitation, madam?' A man in a blazer with a Guildhall emblem smiles at Kate.

'The invitation?' The only time in her life she has felt more embarrassed was when she spilled a glass of red wine on the white silk blouse of a senior partner's wife. 'I haven't got it with me, sorry. But I have my . . . Law Society library card with me, it has my photograph and my name – oh, and my driving licence, of course.'

'I am sorry, madam, but we are on high security alert tonight. We need your invitation.' The smile of the security guard is not for her, it is now for the person behind her. She does not exist as an invitee any more, as far as he is concerned.

She considers her options: A, B and C.

Option A. She can wait outside the Guildhall until the President comes out. Shout across the courtyard, with all the press and security around. It'll make good headlines for the morning newspapers: *A New Generation of Eco-Warriors*.

'Just don't do it, President!' shouted the crowd outside the Guildhall last night. They were protesting against the decision of the Ukrainian President to reopen two nuclear power reactors in Chernobyl.

Accompanied by a photo of a girl in a long green strapless dress, half-frozen from waiting outside for a good three hours, with the inevitable red nose and tousled wet hair.

Option B. Beg the security guard to find the President's Private Secretary, the dough-ball man who looked after her in Kiev. Ask him to come to the entrance and pass him the message. She looks at the Guildhall entrance, swallowing the last of the guests. He probably can't be torn away from the President for a moment now. And where is the guarantee that this haughty security guard would actually agree to do it?

She has to surrender to Option C, then. Stalk the President in the hotel lobby tomorrow, try to ambush him as he walks out to his morning meetings and get her seven seconds of shame then, with his retinue around. Hopefully, he may even recognise her, remember their meeting. He certainly will remember her if she *does not* tell him.

It is six-thirty. Kate's Golf is driving through the Friday rush-hour traffic. She is lucky so far; at least the traffic on the Marylebone Road towards Paddington is moving. Slowly though, bumper to bumper.

This car behind her is too close for comfort. Both for his comfort and for mine, thinks Kate, glancing in her rear mirror. The driver's face is a mask of concentration, his hands are gripping the wheel tightly – obviously not a Londoner, he doesn't know the road well. He is dark-haired, suntanned, middle-aged. Bulgarian? Romanian? The traffic eases up after the flyover, and Kate accelerates. She is fed up with half an hour of sitting behind the truck with the huge red lettering *Eastern European Logistics* on the back.

I didn't know they allowed such massive trucks to wander round the centre of town, she thinks. Got lost maybe, trying to get to the North Circular. Blocking my vision completely. Plus this idiot on my tail! She spots the gap to her right in the middle lane and is just about to move into it when it happens. The truck brakes hard, just as the small car behind her nudges the rear bumper of the Golf. She stamps on the brakes, but the distance to the rear of the truck is too short, and her speed is too high. At first it is just an external crunch, somebody else's fear, then a heavy thump, and her car is twisted into the surrealistic shapes of Dali's nightmares.

There is a burning, tingling sensation in her arm. Blood rushes to her ears and an avalanche crushes her. She is in a dark lift, plunging down at an unbearable speed. Neon lights around her flash faster and faster, fusing into a blazing kaleidoscope. She falls into a soundless, indifferent darkness. There is no pain. Is this what death is like? is her last thought.

Chapter 30

London, Friday 13 April 2001, 9.55 a.m.

At five to ten Taras is walking along the Embankment against the heavy flow of traffic. A car with a blue and yellow Ukrainian flag pushes ahead, squeezed between the motorcycle escort. As it goes past, Taras can see the Ukrainian President, absorbed in his briefing papers.

Fifteen minutes later, Taras is standing under the dotty painting. Amy barely acknowledges his presence, her smile getting more and more tense.

Taras, who has spent the sleepless night of a watchman, is reduced to pleading.

'Amy, I really need to see Kate!' He hands her the scribbled number. 'She wanted me to come and see her – look, she gave me the number herself. I met her in Kiev, I promised her!'

Amy does not react.

'You don't understand,' continues Taras. His accent makes him sound harsh and impatient. 'You just don't understand – I absolutely must see her. Her life is in danger.'

Taras has never seen such a quick transformation in anyone.

317

Amy purses her lips tightly, trying to contain a sob, and surreptitiously wipes the outer corners of her eyes. One gesture – and she is magically transformed from a pretty raccoon into a sad, tired Samurai.

'I know,' she says. 'I know that her life is in danger. Carol has just called from the hospital. Her condition is still critical. She is not allowed any visitors. The car crash was absolutely massive.'

Taras walks out very straight, without saying goodbye to the stoic Samurai at Reception. Does not need to ask *how* it happened. He can guess.

Back in the hotel room, he orders the most expensive dish they have on the room service menu. 'How long does it take to prepare? Thirty minutes? No, please, make it fifty-five.'

He aligns three pieces of paper and studies them carefully. It is amazing how repetitive they are in their methods. Three different girls, three centuries – and still the same old approach. What did Surikov call it? 'The Ride of Death'?

Taras pushes the pieces of paper up with his finger, one by one.

A copy of the Dragoon Commander's report on the arrest of the enemy of the empire, Sofia Polubotko. A chase and a carriage crash.

A copy of the interrogation report of Oksana Polubotko with Karpov's verdict: *Provide survival . . . Identity might be needed in the future.* A roller-coaster drug ride.

A crumpled piece of torn newspaper with the eight three two double sequence. A simple car crash, so easy to organise. They probably used the 'slow truck in front, car behind' operation.

His finger stops on the first piece of paper.

Bequest

To Field Marshal Alexey Razumovsky

Following your orders to arrest the enemy of the Empire Sofia Polubotko, our Dragoon Squad was waiting for her coach at the border with Poland. After a short chase the coach overturned. The coachman was killed instantly, the girl was losing colour, but still breathing when we found her. She died at dawn, without having spoken or opened her eyes.

Found in the coach:
Brocade pillows – five
Wooden skrynya *with female clothes of Little Russian character*
Silver spoons of small size – two
Pigskin purse with twenty-five golden talers – one
A book by French author François Voltaire, 'L'histoire de Charles XII, Rouen, 1731, *with one page dog-eared and two phrases under-lined:* Ukrania is the country of the Cossacks between lesser Tartary, Poland and Muscovy. It has always aspired to freedom.

With this I remain your humble servant,
Dragoon Commander Sveshnikov

Taras carefully folds the copy of the report. He will never find out why they did it. For him, the case N1247 is closed.

Ah, Sofia . . . thinks Taras. You nearly made it. But they don't do 'nearly', do they? I knew, after reading what they did to you, that Kate would be next. The photos Karpov showed me were taken by an insider. They knew who she was, of course. One day was all I needed – to warn her, to protect her.

How does that old Russian saying go? 'There is only one step from love to hatred.'

Nobody warned him that there is also one step from hatred to love, one simple step towards a microscope with a rose inside the human hair, towards a mole on her long, elegant neck. He remembers the way she was biting the corner of her lip, looking at him from under her fringe. The way her skin felt when he touched her hand: tight, heat coming from within. He knew he was tough enough to survive burning pain, loneliness, humiliation, twenty-four hour questioning with white noise, but no training at the Academy had prepared him for this.

He'd had 'lust at first sight' before, but then Carmen had this magic effect on most males. This feeling was different. The light headiness, the warm wave of tenderness washing over him, the incredible yearning to put his arms around her, shielding her from the world.

Was it her vulnerability that attracted him in the first place? Or was this feeling rooted in his own possessiveness, his desire to have something that Andriy had had before – the same emotions, the same girl?

Taras looks at Kate's smiling face in the photograph, tracing her contours with his finger. The hair he never stroked, the lips he never kissed.

He sees the sparkle in Kate's smiling eyes, the way she leans her head to her shoulder, her Slavic cheekbones. How she bears a nebulous resemblance to another woman. The woman who stays with him always.

Taras gets up and closes the heavy curtains, turns away from the unusually sunny day, from the sirens and tyre screeching. He sits in the dark, his back to the window. Cuts himself off from those who remain. He allows himself one last weakness, one last memory.

'*Nie-e-se Ha-a-a-lya . . . vo-o-odu . . .*' He hears his mother's voice. She is singing to him, laughing, wiping his hair with a linen towel. She would never have left him, he knows that. He still misses her every day – her touch, her smell, the way she talked to him, not from above, but squatting down so that her eyes would be on the same level as his. Taras remembers how she tried not to scream when his father hit her in his bouts of drunken jealous rage. She did not want to wake her little boy, unaware that he was watching, hiding behind the flowery curtain.

He is a coward, he finally admits to himself. He is so relieved that finally, today, he can admit that. He should have run for help, should have jumped at his father, biting and kicking him, when he started strangling her – but he was so, so, so frightened! When his father dragged her out, the world became too quiet – as if nothing had happened. Ever since then, Taras has hated silence. Radio, dripping tap, white noise – whatever, but no silence, please.

Two days after his mother's disappearance, Taras saw his father in the wood, under the *smereka* tree. He was sitting on a heap of mouldy leaves, sobbing drunkenly, wiping the tears from his cheeks. Taras went to that tree the next day. He sat on the same heap of leaves, but it did not cushion him. He started digging into the mushroomy dampness, then into the soil, terrified of what he might find. He scratched with his nails and poked around with a broken branch, dreading any discoveries, but found nothing. Scared that his father would guess what he had been doing, seeing his soiled palms, Taras ran to the stream and sank his hands into the icy water. He washed and scrubbed them again and again, scraping the black earth from under his nails with a sharp stone.

When his father died, Taras did not cry. It was an accident

waiting to happen. Especially if somebody drank half a bottle of moonshine in the morning – no wonder he tripped on a rocky path. His head was smashed, almost as if somebody had hit him repeatedly, the militiaman said. Probably, after the impact, he rolled down the hill and crashed again and again on the sharp stones. Probably.

Taras had waited three years for this, hoping, planning – but the revenge did not help, the pain did not disappear: *he did not protect his mother.* That is irreversible, however he would try to justify it now. *He did not protect Kate.* Did not help her when she was looking at him across the table at the airport, biting her lip, her eyes filled with tears. '*Do you know how hard it is, when you are alone and the world is against you?*' He does.

'*Do you think it is possible to carry on living like this?*' He fights his memories every day. There is only one way to stop them.

Taras looks at his watch. It's time. He gets up slowly and goes to the bathroom. He has thought the whole operation through – threats, resources, logistics, communication – so now all his movements are precise and methodical. He puts all the pieces of paper, his return ticket and Kate's photograph in the bathroom sink. Strikes a match and watches the headline 'Safe journey to Europe' disappear slowly, one letter at a time: S . . . A . . . F . . . E . . . The fire swallows Andriy's hand, Kate's smile. Soon a twisted black line of burned paper and a yellow stain in the sink is all that is left. He washes the remains down the drain and meticulously scrubs the stain away.

He lathers his hands for longer than usual. Covers his upper lip with shaving foam and carefully shaves off his moustache. He rinses his hands, wipes each finger and hangs the towel on the edge of the bath to dry. He checks his face in the mirror. His landlady was right – indeed, he looks younger without his moustache.

Back in the room he opens the briefcase and gets out his old Army belt. '*You know the ropes, young man, you know the ropes. Just be very careful with them.*' He suddenly remembers the Cambridge fortune-teller. So that's what she meant.

He knows the belt will take his weight – the one that was used for this purpose in the barracks lasted for five hours. He remembers the day when one of the new recruits in his regiment hanged himself in the barracks, unable to tolerate the Chechen Kings' tortures any more. The soldiers were not allowed to touch him before the arrival of the official investigation commission, and just stood there, in a silent circle, watching the corpse. Taras had been surprised to see the dead soldier's lips twisted in a smile. A knowledgeable Muscovite explained to everybody calmly that sometimes suffocation could create a sensation similar to an orgasm.

He puts on a neatly pressed white shirt and carefully buttons it from the bottom, leaving the top button undone. Then he walks to the front door of the suite and leaves it ajar. That is the way he wants them to find him: fresh shirt, clean hands, a victorious smile, not hidden by a moustache. All in all, a winner.

He will not hear Monica, the Polish waitress, screaming and crossing herself forty minutes later, will not see the concerned face of the Duty Manager watching him, listening to Monica's story. The thing that scared her most of all, she kept repeating, weeping, was the strange grimace on the face of the young man. It looked like a smile.

At ten o'clock the Presidential procession arrives at the doors of

Downing Street. After the photocall and the inspection of the Guard of Honour, the two leaders and their Private Secretaries go upstairs to the Green Room for one-to-one discussions, which last for fifty-seven minutes instead of the planned forty-five.

The big hand of the clock on the mantelpiece in the Green Room is moving towards eleven. The official agenda has been covered, and the protocol has left five minutes for official farewells. Item number seven, however, is still outstanding. *Other Business* has yet to be discussed.

The Prime Minister looks at the President. 'I think we have covered everything.'

'Mostly,' says the President, turning to his Private Secretary. 'Where is the gift? I'll present it myself.'

Two Private Secretaries eye each other nervously. Neither are fond of surprises.

'Forgive me for the breach of protocol,' starts the President, 'but I feel I should give you this gift personally, from my heart!' He unwraps a carved wooden box.

'This year, the Protestant Easter and Ukrainian Orthodox Easter coincide – they are both celebrated this Sunday,' continues the President, as he hands the box to the Prime Minister.

With an expression of polite expectation, the Prime Minister forces himself to open the box. He holds back a sigh of relief, studying a brightly painted wooden Easter egg.

'It is a *pysanka* – a traditional Ukrainian Easter egg,' explains the President. 'The children decorate them with their parents before Easter, not with paint, but with beeswax. All the patterns and colours are symbolic. Green, for example, is the colour of health, gold is the colour of wisdom. This one was decorated in an orphanage not far from the village I come from. We are giving much help to our under-privileged children, but the budget does not allow us to . . .'

. . . What a way to lead into the subject, thinks the Prime Minister. It's not that difficult to guess what is coming next. He has given me a gift. Now he is going to deliver a bombshell.

'. . . but we persevere,' continues the President. 'As for the legendary Cossack treasures . . .'

The two Private Secretaries try to read each other's facial expressions. One starts tapping his pencil on the thick green tablecloth. The other looks out of the window and takes a long, deep breath.

The President smiles thinly. 'Shame that the twelfth of April – our Astronaut's Day – was yesterday. We could have aimed for the stars!'

The Prime Minister studies the President's face. Is it too early to be relieved?

'But I am not going to be the bearer of bad news on Friday the thirteenth,' continues the President. 'As for the legendary Cossack treasures, which are supposedly waiting for their time in the vaults of the Bank of England,' he pauses, 'it's such a shame that they are only a legend!'

One Private Secretary throws his pencil on the table and leans back with a polite professional smile. The other Private Secretary loosens the knot of his shiny red tie just a little. This part of the visit, the toughest meeting, is over.

The clock chimes.

EPILOGUE

Edmonton, Canada, July 2009

Hot and cold weather do not mix in Edmonton, just like water in the taps of chintzy English country hotels.

The first snow usually falls in late October; in January it can get down to minus 40 Celsius, but the parks of the river valley would still be full of people tobogganing, skating and cross-country skiing along the trails of the city's extensive park system.

In July the town bursts into a festive mood with the heated atmosphere of Capital EX, when hundreds try their luck at gold-panning, dipping into the crazy atmosphere of the 1890s Gold Rush. Then Edmontonians settle down on the grass for their corn dogs and mini-donuts.

Crowds gather to watch the spectacular waterworks of the Great Divide Waterfall and Sourdough River Festival, where competing rafts race down the North Saskatchewan River.

If you want to escape the crowds, walk past the glass pyramid – the City Hall, past the 'Château on the River' – the elegant, century-old sixteen-storey Hotel Macdonald – towards the North Saskatchewan River. If you continue along River Valley Road, you will see the University of Alberta campus on the south bank. The facilities are impressive – the redbrick Faculties share the grounds with the futuristic white buildings of the research centres and libraries.

The Faculty of Law is one of the oldest in the university. Its reputation is built on the research facilities, unrivalled in Canada, and the highest teaching standards: members of the Faculty have written the textbooks on the core Law courses that are now used across the country.

Three years ago, a new lecturer joined the Faculty staff and immediately became the topic of debates during the breaks between case studies and statutes analyses.

She teaches the course on Wills and Administration – everything about drafting Wills, probate practice, the appointment of executors and their duties. Her lectures are interesting, as she obviously knows the practical side of things, but some students find her British accent and her reluctance to give examples from her own experience irritating. Some say that she is pretty, but others call her 'Zombie' because of her lacklustre eyes and the way she turns her whole body, not just her head, when somebody asks her a question. Her strained movements and the noticeable limp create another source of speculation. Is it a birth defect or did she have an accident? She lives on her own with a dog as enigmatic as herself: they often see her walking Proby, her Weimaraner, down the paths of Emily Murphy Park, near the campus.

I know what they say about me. I have overheard them more than once. They don't realise that I can still hear well, even though I cannot turn my head. But I don't mind. I am who I am. And I love it here. I feel almost at home in Alberta. With every tenth Albertan being of Ukrainian origin, nobody finds my name unpronounceable any more.

I love the lingering sun of June, when the skin of my dog shimmers silver. I love walking for miles, moving from one park to another along the Ribbon of Green, watching Proby disappear, blending with the silvery-grey bark of aspen. Summers are fun here. There is always something happening in this City of Festivals: Heritage Days, the Folk Music Festival, the Fringe, the Labatt Blues Festival – plenty to watch and to listen to.

I like Edmonton winters, too. Sometimes, on a dark winter Saturday afternoon I escape to West Edmonton Mall. It is the largest mall in North America apparently, so you can wander for miles. They even have the recommended walker's route, 'in the safe and climate-controlled environment'. I watch a fashion show at the Centre Fountain or listen to Andean music by the Ice Palace, look at the laughing faces of the passers-by, sitting at a cafe on the Europa Boulevard.

Sometimes I take the LRT (just like the London one) from the university to Rexall Place, to watch the Edmonton Oilers play, and then go to Uncle Ed's. The restaurant has pretty good Ukrainian food and it's only twenty minutes' walk from the stadium, on 118 Avenue. There are other great spots there, where Ukrainian *pyrohy* lovers order their favourite food. Sometimes you can hear the older Ukranians ordering in *his* language. With strong Canadian inflexions, in voices that age has reduced to husky whispers.

But as you leave Edmonton and take Highway 16 – the Yellowhead – driving east through the towns and villages of Central Alberta, Ukrainian does not whisper. It screams out loud: with the world's largest Ukrainian Easter Egg (*pysanka*) at Vegreville; the Giant Ukrainian Sausage (*kovbasa*) at Mundare; the 20,000 square kilometre Kalyna Country Ecomuseum, the Ukrainian Cultural Heritage Village.

Driving is the only thing I don't like here, actually. And not only because I can feel the steel plate in my left leg every time I push the pedal. I still have to negotiate with myself every time I open the car door. I know that my grip on the steering wheel is firmer than necessary. And my excessive concentration on the road brings inevitable headaches. I don't mind them though. Physical pain, I have discovered, can be quite distracting in itself.

It was a classic accident, they told me. The only surprise was the lack of witnesses. Police found a small car smashed into the wall in a dead-end street in Tooting. They checked the number-plate – it was stolen from the sheltered accommodation car park that morning; belonged to some old geezer who reported the theft about an hour before the accident. They never found that Eastern European truck though – which is surprising, given its size.

The sickly-sweet smell is the first thing I remember when I came round. And flowers, lots of them. Flowers and cards – from my university friends, whose birthdays I have forgotten, from class-mates who were struck from my Christmas list a long time ago. There was even a fruit basket from Carol with a curt note: *Do get better, Kate.* I remember faces, too. Intermittently – my father's concerned frown, my brother's stubble scratching my cheek, my mother's suntanned cheekbones, Marina, leaning over, and, somehow permanently, my grandmother's presence. Strange, but I don't remember Philip being there, though I was told that he used to pop in every day. Well, almost every day for the first month I was in hospital – when he did not have to prepare a presen-tation or attend a meeting with clients or have a round of golf with partners.

There were so many things to fix that the Consultant asked me if he could quote my case to his students. My notes read like a page from a clinical medicine manual:

1) *An unstable C-spine fracture of the second vertebral bone in the neck, following the blunt trauma. Requires stabilisation with neck collars and external fixation devices.* (This is when I hit my head on the windscreen.)

2) *A comminuted fractured femur, a metal rod required to support the bones.* (That's my thighbone, left in bits, when the bonnet crumpled in and my legs took the impact.)

3) *Ruptured spleen.*

4) *Broken tibia.*

I would get exhausted just repeating the whole list.

Staying in hospital was not the hardest bit though. I was drifting in and out of consciousness most of the time. God knows what painkillers they were giving me.

Coming out was hard. Walking with the frame to the kitchen, learning to turn my whole body towards the speaker to listen. Feeling the familiar metallic taste in my mouth months later, when I was venturing into the world, crossing the road, hiding behind the backs and the bags. Avoiding Philip's questions, for which I could not provide the answers. Philip was wise enough to leave first.

I came here for a conference five years ago. Something about 'Alternative Conflict Resolution'. I could not offer any alternatives really, but it was a great way to get out of the office and away from Carol.

I saw the notice outside the Dean's office. They were expanding the Faculty and, as the notice said, *in the view of growing globalisation of businesses and internationalisation of the legal profession*, were planning to add new, international staff. I applied on the spot. The work permit came through quickly, I was sent the list of reputable removal companies and estate agents – and here I am, in a rented two-bedroom apartment in Edmonton.

My apartment is on Whyte Avenue – not the quietest area, but quite convenient: close to the river valley and the bus to the university. Great walks for Proby, too.

You know the first rule when you walk along a dark street and see a group of drunken teenagers: cross the road, keep your head down and walk fast. You keep a safe distance and nobody gets hurt. So that's what I have been doing here, head down, living in my memories, observing the laughter and the anger from a distance, limping my pain off down the river paths with Proby.

Until last year.

There is this boy, you see. It is impossible to explain what I love most about him. Maybe the way he holds my hand: tapping my wrist with his fingertips first, then quickly slotting his palm into mine. It fits like a lid on a Victorian pencil case. Or the way he erupts in sharp, husky bursts of laughter, when Proby licks his cheek in the morning with his sandpapery tongue.

I never planned to take him on. It just happened – last summer, when I volunteered at the Ukrainian Cultural Heritage Village. It's a big, open-air museum, thirty buildings or so, and everybody working here takes their roles extremely seriously. You have to walk, talk, behave like Ukrainian pioneer settlers to Alberta at the end of the nineteenth and beginning of the twentieth centuries. I don't mind acting. Living here, I am playing a role every day anyway. In August the village has summer camps for children. They live the life at the turn of the century and love it. They cook, spend a day in a one-room school, play historic games.

When the camp co-ordinator asked me, 'Do you love children?' I nearly said, 'I don't know,' but she got there before me. 'You need all the love you can find, honey, as we have a group of Ukrainian orphans, sponsored by a private foundation, arriving this year.'

And so they came, ten quiet, scared, obedient kids from the same flock, with guarded looks, subdued moves. They never asked for anything, ate everything put in front of them, ran when they had to, clung to grown-ups, the same questions written all over their faces: 'Are we doing the right thing? You are not going to punish us or send us back early?'

And then there was an eleventh child – the boy called Vovchyk – which is very, very appropriate. The name is a diminutive for 'Vladymyr', but it also means 'a wolf-cub'. And that is exactly who he is: piercing eyes, sharp features, always ready for a fight, ready to bite. Neither a follower, nor a destroyer – mostly an observer.

God knows why he took to me. Maybe because I was the first adult who was not trying to change him or control him. Or maybe his intuitive little soul felt that we were both very alike in the way we have built our defences. Vovchyk – with latent aggression in his every move, me with polite aloofness.

As I walked across the camp after dinner, he used to appear from nowhere in the dusk. He would plant a kiss on the back of my hand, squeezing it with his dry hot palms; he would give me a quick tight hug and then he would run off, not looking back, not expecting any reaction – or maybe he was too scared he would not see a reaction. I have never been confronted with such an open demonstration of love, never had a stranger friendship. I missed him when the group left, but that was it. Until December.

Tanya, the Foundation co-ordinator, sent me a Christmas card with his drawing: two creatures – different sizes, but otherwise identical – holding hands. Bodies like sticks, circles for faces, with accurate lines for eyes and hair and disproportionate mouths with curves of smiles, from ear to ear. *Vovchyk wants you to smile more* was Tanya's explanation underneath, in neat rounded handwriting.

He is staying with me for a month this year – Tanya has arranged everything. I have planned our days with military precision: we tried most of the rides at Capital EX; I am taking him to the World Waterpark tomorrow, and we are driving with Proby to Elk Island National Park on Thursday where hopefully, we'll see bison and moose.

I tried to explain to Vovchyk yesterday that we might even see a porcupine there: I drew him a piglet, a plus sign and a hedgehog. Vovchyk laughed so much, that Proby thought that he needed to rush to the rescue. I'll try to buy Vovchyk a postcard at the park on Thursday, just to show that such an animal really exists!

From where I am sitting on the sofa, I can hear and see Vovchyk through the open door of the small bedroom, making rumbling noises of distant thunder, kicking off the blanket, still fighting in his sleep. A little Mowgli, who lived in a pack much more cruel than Kipling's wolves. I have bought him a bed, but he still prefers the floor – that's where he has slept for the majority of the long seven years of his life. They think he is seven, Tanya told me, but he might be eight or even nine, just too small for his age.

He leaves a trail of clothes behind him as he jumps on his mattress and switches off after his busy days – his jeans on the rug in the hall, his socks by the door, his T-shirt crumpled on the armchair, covering the red and black flowers of *Babusya*'s embroidered cushion.

I have several of *Babusya*'s things in the apartment: two embroidered cushions, a tea-towel under Andriy's photograph; five Meissen tea cups with blue lines running through the dainty porcelain like veins. I brought all these treasures here two years ago, when I flew back from her funeral.

As I wandered through her empty terraced house, picking them up, inhaling the smell of *Babusya*'s medicine mixed with dry flowers, I so wanted to stay there, wrapped in my world of make-believe, sit in her sunken armchair in the conservatory, tucking my legs underneath me, watching blackbirds in the garden until dusk, until my legs became numb, until I got thirsty and hungry – as long as she came back from her 'somewhere'. Returned to sit next to me, occasionally touching my hand, patiently answering all those questions I still had to ask her.

There was only one thing I wish I had never discussed with *Babusya*. But I did, and I have to live with it now. I cannot erase it, or throw it away.

I don't remember how that conversation started. We were sitting in her garden a couple of months after I left the hospital. That afternoon was all about the last warmth of late-September sun, the smell of drying mint, hung in her conservatory, the silver threads of Indian summer, binding us together. For the first time in months the world did not look a hostile place.

So I told *Babusya* about Andriy. About Polubotko's treasures and about the new free country she was forced to leave all those years ago. About the glow of tapers at the Lavra and the skateboarders at the main square. Bits, carefully selected by memory – lighter, brighter pieces of a jigsaw.

My grandmother listened the way she always did – her right hand supporting her jaw, head slightly tilted. I was talking about the musical fountains in the main square when she got up, took my hand and led me into the kitchen. She opened the kitchen drawer, picked up a wad of papers and spread them on the kitchen table. Pension payments' stubs, repeat prescription requests, an expired coupon for a cereal brand – all those important documents which get you an entry pass into the eighty-plus world. She found a yellow piece of paper and handed it to me, without any explanation.

As I unfolded it, the unfamiliar Cyrillic words jumped at me in different colours and shapes – tiny, hardly legible, in lilac ink – on the stamp, cold black letters of the official standard form, and next to them a personal name, written in blue, in calligraphic professional handwriting.

'It is my birth certificate,' said *Babusya*. 'The only thing that remained with me from the moment I was pushed into that train for Germany until today. The only memory of my country, the only real me, with my maiden name on it. I knew that if this piece of paper survived, I would survive too. It is yours now, Kate.'

There was something in the way she said it . . . I guessed before I looked at the Cyrillic letters: П, Л, Б, Т, К. I knew before I transliterated them into P, L, B, T, K, before I added the perfect circles of the Os, the same Os I wanted to add to a screeching: '*Nooo!*' that was stopping the world inside me from crashing down. So that's what she always meant when she said I had a Cossack spirit.

'I don't want it, *Babusya*,' I nearly said then. 'I honestly don't want to know. How can you do this to me? I have left this story in another country, which was once yours. I gave the plastic tangerine-smelling folder away, lifted the curse, fulfilled the promise and now – look, this name is smirking back at me from the yellow page of your birth certificate, the imprecation of a perfectly written Cossack Hetman's name, Sofia's name and yours, *Babusya*. How can the Polubotko story be *your* story? And *mine*?'

I nearly said all this. Nearly . . . But the day was too perfect, the world was too mellow, so I just took the certificate and thanked her. I planned, hoped, was gathering strength to talk to her about it soon, very soon – when the pain subsides a little, when the fear loosens its grip, when the memories become black and white.

'*Shovay* – hide it, Kate,' she said to me in Ukrainian then. 'What a suitable word, *hovaty*,' she sighed. 'The whole history of my country is about hiding. Just think about it: even such crucial words as "bring up" and "bury" – *vy-hovaty* and *po-hovaty* in Ukrainian both have the same heart, the same trepidation in them. To hide, to conceal, to protect yourself from your enemies. It is your turn now, Kate. Hide it well.'

Babusya's birth certificate is here with me, tucked behind the Ukrainian icon I brought back from her flat. Another country's future protected by the almond-eyed Madonna, who scrutinises me from the wall as I talk. There is no compassion in her look – she has heard it many times before. But she still listens, so I tell her everything.

'It's a shame,' I tell her, 'that I cannot use my story as a case study for my students. They are such a smart lot, they would have spotted the discrepancy straight away. "Hang on a minute," they would have shouted. "The lawyer in your story did not follow it through: she should have conducted further checks with the Bank of England! What if the loan was never repaid, let alone taken out? She should have checked other records, should have sent a request to France. If the loan was never given, or if at least some of the loan was repaid, then the inheritance is still there, waiting to be claimed, isn't it?'"

'Yeah, it sure is,' I would have answered them. They would have laughed at my English accent not working with the Canadian turn of phrase. 'It sure is. And by the way, *The Guinness Book of Records* this year lists Polubotko's gold as the second largest unclaimed inheritance again.'

Only yesterday I watched the Ukrainian Ambassador to Canada being interviewed by the CBN Channel.

'I am a professional diplomat,' he said firmly, 'and I don't like sensations. But what I am about to say might be considered sensational. The Embassy has got hold of unique evidence,' he continued, 'which will allow Ukraine to claim the Cossack Treasures back for the benefit of the nation.'

Nearly a kilo of gold per Ukrainian citizen apparently. He is such a smooth talker, this Ambassador. He spoke of the role this great discovery would play in changing the destiny of Ukraine and shifting political balance in Europe, about the need to build a strong, united, democratic country.

He paused only once actually, when the presenter asked him: 'And how did the Embassy come into possession of these documents?'

He winked at the camera (not at the presenter) and said, hiding a smile, 'Well, this whole story had a mystic feel for centuries, and the way the new evidence was discovered just adds to the mysticism.

'It is quite expensive for those who live in the Canadian Western provinces to come to the Consulates in Ottawa or Toronto. So our Consul visits Edmonton every month for a couple of days to issue passports and deal with visas. Last month, a package was posted through the letter box of the Consulate Department in Edmonton during such a visit. It contained a covering note, with a brief outline of the search for Cossack treasures in the twentieth century, a letter claiming possession of a descendant's birth certificate and instructions on where to find the rest of the documents. Though the package was left at night, the security cameras caught a silhouette of a hooded teenager hurrying away. We could not see the face, but he had a strongly pronounced limp.'

The Ambassador looked straight into the camera again and said, addressing the viewers, talking to me: 'We would strongly urge the person who provided this information to come forward. It would help with our investigation enormously.'

'What do you think?' I ask my Madonna. 'Should I? I have given them the detailed instructions of where to look and where to go, but should I actually get involved? Should I do it for the grey-haired woman with tired eyes and high cheekbones, who smiles at me from the photograph on the sideboard? For the man who was touching my hand with his long fingertips in a restaurant in Argentina? For the country that is hiding in the centre of Europe, the country pulled out of the politicians' pack like a trump card again, the same way it has been pulled out for centuries, in the eternal game of power and greed?'

I am not afraid of humiliation, if the money is not there, nor of all the legal 'conditions' and 'preconditions' if the inheritance can be claimed. After all, the world has the right to know, and I do, too. *The Guinness Book of Records* might have an updated line next year, if nothing else.

I'll tell you what I *am* afraid of. I know that to go ahead with this, I'll need to take my hood off. And not just in front of the Embassy security cameras.

I'll have to tell the whole story. Starting from the chill room in Cambridge with the fluorescent tiles, from the hangover after Philip's party and the conference that day. Or maybe beginning with my first childhood memory, of *Babusya*'s Christmas fare . . .

'So,' I ask the Madonna, looking straight into her almond eyes. 'Should I?'

I watch for a minuscule nod, for a sign, for patches of moon-light on her face. But she does not look at me any more. Her glance slides above my head into the warm, cosy depths of the small bedroom, from where soft, grumbling noises are coming.

Proby hears me talking and comes to check on me. He stands in the middle of the room, watching my face, and in the moon-light his skin is glowing silver. I look at him and think: What a trio. A Zombie woman, a ghost dog and a wolf-cub! He pads back to the kitchen, still wondering why I am sitting so straight, so motionless.

It is almost midnight when I say *Babusya*'s prayer.

The words roll out of my mouth like glistening marbles, clinking with clear, long sound.

It is pure and simple, like a C-major scale. Where every note is new. Where every note is familiar. Perhaps, in some ancient, extinct language it was one magic, immortal word, that meant 'harmony', 'the beginning and the end', 'the flow of life'.

I repeat it slowly, carefully, as if I have always known the melody, but have never dared to sing it aloud.

I have this courage now.

HISTORICAL NOTE

The story of the Cossack gold is more than just a legend in Ukraine. It has become the national dream. There are numerous discussions, interviews, publications and even an Act of Parliament. Everybody knows where the gold is and how to get it; everybody has his or her version of events.

This book is my own version, very much inspired by my grandfather's Cossack stories.

The Cossack Polubotko family indeed existed, and the speech that the dying Cossack Pavlo Polubotko delivered to Peter the Great is quoted in many books and textbooks. Both Count Razumovsky (1702–1759) and Count Orly (Grygory Orlyk (1709–1771)) were real people.

Pavlo Polubotko had a son called Yakiv and a granddaughter called Sofia – but as far as we know, she never travelled to England with a mission.

Ostap Polubotko went to see the Ukranian Ambassador in Vienna in 1922, but he came from Brazil, not Argentina.

The Congress of Polubotko's descendants was indeed organised, and held in the town of Starodub, not Kiev, in 1909.

Though there are numerous claims from descendants not only

in South America but also in the United States and Canada, all modern characters have been invented.

Finally, all the Bank of England documents quoted in the book are fictional.

ACKNOWLEDGEMENTS

This book would never have been written without the support and help given to me by so many people.

First and foremost, I owe an enormous debt of gratitude to my grandfather, Fedir, a great historian and a great man. He taught me that history never remains in the past. His war diaries were the inspiration for the diaries in Chapter Two and the *raison d'être* for the whole book.

I am totally indebted to my grandmother, Rosa, for giving those diaries to me and encouraging me to tell the story.

I would like to thank my agent, Robert Kirby, for his bottomless patience as well as for believing before I did, and my editor, Flora Rees, for holding my hand and guiding me all the way along the labyrinth.

Sarah Ballard and Charlotte Knee from the United Agents – thank you for being there for me from the start.

I am grateful to the people who let me into their fascinating worlds during the research: Chrystyne Kaye – the world of Ukrainians in Edmonton; Olga Kerziouk – the enormity of the British Library; and Carolyn Eardley – the secret world of English grammar.

A.K. Shevchenko

I would like to express my sincere gratitude to Sarah Millard for all the support given to me by her and her efficient staff during my research at the Archives of the Bank of England.

I would like to thank my mother, Olga Shevchenko, for all her stories of living through the thaw of the sixties.

A very special 'thank you' goes to those voices of the lost generation that survived the break-up of the USSR, who wished to remain anonymous, but whose stories of army bullying and working at a mental hospital will stay with me forever.

And finally, a huge 'thank you' to my long-suffering family for giving me space and strength.